PETOSKEY STONES

Lois Santelo

Books by Lois Santalo

The Wind Dies at Sunrise
Oops, I Lost my Sense of Humor (memoir)
The House of Music
The Women of Stormland
Petoskey Stones

PETOSKEY STONES

Lois Wells Santalo

iUniverse, Inc.
New York Lincoln Shanghai

PETOSKEY STONES

iUniverse books may be ordered through booksellers or by contacting:

iUniverse
2021 Pine Lake Road, Suite 100
Lincoln, NE 68512
www.iuniverse.com
1-800-Authors (1-800-288-4677)

This is a work of fiction, and any similarity to persons living or dead is purely coincidental.

ISBN-13: 978-0-595-34858-9 (pbk)
ISBN-13: 978-0-595-79580-2 (ebk)
ISBN-10: 0-595-34858-0 (pbk)
ISBN-10: 0-595-79580-3 (ebk)

Printed in the United States of America

For Jessica and Vic

Contents

❀

Author's Note. . . . .*xi*

Part I   Boston and Grand Rapids

Chapter 1   Weezy 3
Chapter 2   Grace 10
Chapter 3   Weezy 16
Chapter 4   Del 22
Chapter 5   Del 31
Chapter 6   Del 38
Chapter 7   Weezy 45
Chapter 8   Del 52
Chapter 9   Del 60
Chapter 10   Weezy 68

Part II   New York

Chapter 11   Weezy 77
Chapter 12   Weezy 85
Chapter 13   Weezy 92
Chapter 14   Weezy 101
Chapter 15   Weezy 109
Chapter 16   Del 119
Chapter 17   Del 128
Chapter 18   Weezy 136

Chapter 19   Weezy..144
Chapter 20   Weezy..151
Chapter 21   Del 157
Chapter 22   Grace 165
Chapter 23   Del 172
Chapter 24   Del 180
Chapter 25   Del 186
Chapter 26   Del 194
Chapter 27   Weezy..203
Chapter 28   Grace 210
Chapter 29   Weezy..218

Part III   Saugatuck and Petoskey

Chapter 30   Weezy..229
Chapter 31   Weezy..238
Chapter 32   Weezy..246
Chapter 33   Weezy..252
Chapter 34   Grace 259
Chapter 35   Del 269

Acknowledgements

My thanks and eternal gratitude to the Thursday group, Howard Fisher, Evelyn Dahms, Marlie Moses, Ellie Fellers, Izetta Siegel, and Prudy Tallman Wood, for their input and suggestions. Thanks also to the Tuesday Group, Bob Moore, Mary Blue, Ellen Perkins, Virginia Natwick, Eleanor Simmons, and Dale and Suzanne Gega.

Author's Note

1948 was the worst of years for recent women graduates. With veterans leaving school to hit the job market, not only were women not hired, those already working were fired without cause to make room for men. Not since the Great Depression had there been so few jobs open to women. Except for those in traditional fields, teaching, nursing, social work, women were pretty well out of luck. For the rare few who did find employment, salaries were far lower than men received, sometimes as little as half. Also, they were open to ridicule, said to wear the pants in the family, even labeled neurotic—and their husbands were scorned as Milquetoasts.

Sent back to the kitchen, Rosie the Riveter was sternly reminded that her role was that of backup and support for a man. To compete with a man would be unnatural, unthinkable, a denial of woman's rightful place in life.

Some women adjusted to the post-war order of things, and abandoned their jobs to throw themselves with enthusiasm into buying and decorating their all-alike houses in the new projects, preparing a room for baby. Yet those dedicated to a career never ceased to seek alternatives.

This is the story of two women who in that year coped with their world, one who struggled to embrace the media-endorsed role of women, another who sought to escape it.

The Langston Family

Douglas Langston m Rebecca Tiehl

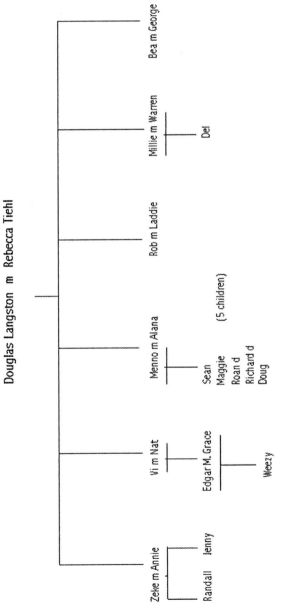

Zeke m Annie

Randall   Jenny

Vi m Nat

Edgar M. Grace

Weezy

Menno m Alana

Sean
Maggie
Roan d
Richard d
Doug

(5 children)

Rob m Laddie

Millie m Warren

Del

Bea m George

PART I

❀

BOSTON AND GRAND RAPIDS

CHAPTER 1

Weezy

On a lovely spring morning in Boston in 1948, Della Eloise Ward, known as Weezy, gravely discarded every part of the life she'd led. Her writings, notebooks, papers, even her diary went into the trashcan. Couturier clothing was put out for Goodwill. She kept only two new blouses and a skirt, along with a plain black dress suitable for the upcoming funeral of her putative father, Jonathan Ward.

A tall, slender young woman with brown hair in a smooth page-boy, Weezy stood by the pile of trash at the curb and dumped things in the container. Summoned home from college just three days before her graduation ceremony due to the sudden death of the man she'd always believed to be her father, she'd never dreamed she might arrive to learn that Jonathan Ward was no blood kin to her.

True, in grade school she'd been teased by a bully kid who claimed she was adopted, but she'd assumed he was making it up. Never once had she imagined his words might reflect facts, especially since he was the only one ever to mention the idea.

Her mother hurried from the house, paused on the sidewalk, and surveyed the mountain of discards overflowing five trashcans. She stood finger-combing her brown hair, so like her daughter's, rumpling the smooth perfection. Grace Hannaford Ward had retained through the years the slim elegance, the sorority-girl look, Weezy envied but could never achieve. Though the two had the same chocolate-brown hair, the big-boned younger woman had always been forced to select clothing carefully to conceal broad hips such as no one else in the family coped with. Weezy had started exercising young to fight lumps of fat. That should have been a clue, she now realized, that her heritage differed from that of her slim parents. Why hadn't she seen it?

"Do you mean to throw me away, too?" her mother demanded. "Shall I climb into the trashcan? Save you the trouble of tossing me?"

"Not if you tell me the truth for a change." Hands on hips, Weezy frowned. She knew her expression was mutinous but she didn't soften it. "I'm ridding myself of a lifetime of polite lies. Now I need to know who I really am. Where's the other side of my family?"

The obituary notice about Weezy's purported father, published that morning in the *Boston Globe,* had stated: "A lifelong resident of Boston, Mr. Ward is survived by his wife, Grace, his mother, Sarah Lington Ward, sister Adelaide, and adopted daughter, Della Eloise."

Weezy had rushed through the house, paper in hand, screaming, "Adopted? Adopted?" She climbed the stairs two at a time, seeking her mother in her studio. "Mother, is this true?" She felt sure it was a misprint. She knew that, except for those broader hips, she resembled Grace; people often commented about their similarities.

She found her artist mother at work cleaning paint brushes under the studio skylight. Grace looked up with a shocked expression, eyebrows vanishing under bangs as her eyes widened. Her face went paper-white. She opened her mouth, croaked, "I—I—" and seemed to lose her ability to speak. She kept shaking her head while her hands went on of their own accord stroking a brush with a cloth. After a long silence, she asked, "How in the world did that get in the paper?"

"Well, is it true or isn't it?" At her mother's pallor, panic tightened Weezy's midriff. Grace Ward had never been prone to loss of control.

When her mother remained silent, Weezy demanded, "Tell me!"

"Yes—I mean, no. You're my flesh and blood daughter. Surely you can see the resemblance?"

"But—?"

"But Jonathan adopted you when I married him."

A cold wave washed over Weezy. "I'm illegitimate?" She choked out the words.

"Weezy! Of course not, what an idea! When you were born, I was happily married—to someone else."

Weezy stared in shock. "Someone else?" She sputtered the words over again. "Someone else? Who, Mom?" At her mother's hesitation, she demanded, "How come I never heard about this?"

"I couldn't talk about it." Her mother's eyes teared. "The breakup was terrible for me. You wouldn't want to know." Her fingers seemed to work of their own accord putting brushes away. When she turned her back, Weezy heard a stifled sob. In a shaky voice, Grace said, "Jonathan was a good father to you, all the father you needed." She dabbed at her eyes with a tissue.

Looking down at her own hands, Weezy thought: Not such long fingers as Mother's or Jonathan's. Sturdy, working hands. Whose? Who bequeathed them to me, along with these broad hips? Why the mystery? She asked, "Was the man a jailbird? A wife-beater?" By now she felt cold all over, and shivered at the dastardly thoughts forming in her mind.

Visibly bringing herself under control, Grace managed a frown and headshake. "Don't be silly, he just wasn't—our kind."

"Oh, Mother! Our kind! That's humankind, or so you've always claimed. Don't go snobbish like Granny Hannaford. Just explain. Talk to me."

"Unfortunately, there are many specimens of humankind with which other specimens can't manage a successful marriage." Grace put both hands on the chair-back and pushed out words with obvious effort. "Your grandmother warned me, but I didn't listen. I was young, naïve and…foolish. I came home to Boston, learned I was pregnant and wanted to rush back to Michigan to marry. My head was full of flowery dreams. Gran tried to save me from my folly, but at the last minute she gave in and took me to be married just before your birth."

"And later you divorced and married Jonathan. So why not say so? What's the problem?"

"I had the marriage annulled. You were Jon's daughter from the time you were a few weeks old."

"Mother, stop stalling. Who's my birth father?"

Grace slumped into a weary pose, leaned against the wall, and rubbed her forehead with a paint-daubed wrist. "I can't talk about it, Weezy."

Shock gave way to anger. Weezy snapped, "Forget the swooning maiden act. It's not *you*. We have to discuss this."

Giving a determined shake to her head, Grace clammed up. Weezy clenched her fists, stalked out, paced the floor of her bedroom, and steamed over her mother's silence. Finally, she made the decision to discard her past. If she didn't know who she was, at least she knew who she wasn't. She wasn't the young woman who'd grown up as the only child of Jonathan Ward, descendant of an old-line New England family. She'd been living a lie. Jonathan's ancestors were not hers.

So, into the trashcan went meaningless accomplishments, her high school yearbook, her photographs of the non-existent Weezy Ward. She grabbed armloads without even sorting. These weren't her things. She was Weezy Someone Else. She needed to find and assert a new identity.

Much became clear. The fact her Ward 'grandmother' had never acted grandmotherly, never invited her over for home-made cookies nor regaled her with lengthy stories of the family's two centuries in Boston. The fact her father and her aunt seemed to take little interest in her, and asked about her only as an afterthought.

"I'll tell you this," Hands still toying nervously with her hair, her mother stood by the pile of discards. "Your birth father named you after his young cousin, Delia Eloise. Her nickname was Del so he chose Weezy for you."

"Delia Eloise what? Give me a last name so I can check."

Grace closed her eyes and again touched the back of her hand to her forehead, feigning weakness. "I don't recall. I've blotted it out."

Ruthless, Weezy persisted. "Shit, you can't forget a thing like that. Aunt Addie must know. I'll call her." She hurried into the house and headed for the phone.

Following, her mother took a deep breath and spoke pleadingly. "Don't call Addie. I'll tell you. You were born in Grand Rapids."

"Michigan?"

"Yes. The name on the original birth certificate is—is McCurdle. That's all I'll say."

Skipping lunch, Weezy went to the library to check the Grand Rapids directory. She found no McCurdle listed. From a pay phone where her mother couldn't interfere, she called Addie and demanded, "Did you provide the information for that obit?"

Addie admitted it.

Weezy persisted. "You knew something I didn't know. You knew your brother adopted me."

"You mean he never told you?" Addie sounded incredulous.

"First I heard of it was when I read this morning's paper."

"Oh, Weezy! I had no idea. I'm so sorry you had to learn it that way. Of course, it was a closed chapter in your parents' lives, but I never thought it might be a secret."

"Mother wouldn't tell me anything, so you'll have to, Addie." Weezy deleted the word *aunt*. Miss Adelaide Ward was no blood kin to the Hannafords, certainly not to anyone named McCurdle.

"Wouldn't care to cause trouble," Addie protested.

You've already done that, Weezy thought. Aloud, she said, "You'd save me time. I'll just trace the records."

Addie sighed. "Come on over. I'll tell you what I know, which isn't much."

After a short bus ride, Weezy arrived at the Victorian house Addie had inherited. She seated herself in an overstuffed chair in the dark front room, beside the old reed organ she'd always loved, with those buttons for beautiful sounds like *celeste* and *vox humana*. She quashed nostalgic memories of childhood days playing that organ, and focused her attention on the sturdy woman on the couch opposite. Jonathan's silver-haired older sister, a one-time suffragette, had yet to show a hint of frailty. To Weezy, she was Miss Birdseye in Henry James' *Bostonians,* always volunteering for good works in support of women.

It seemed Addie had had second thoughts. She poured coffee from a silver pot, creamed and sugared it, and handed the cup over. Taking her own cup in hand, she crooked her little finger in proper Boston fashion, pressed thin lips together, and explained her reticence. "If neither of your parents wanted you to know, it's not my place to break the silence. It wouldn't be right."

"The silence is already broken," Weezy argued. "I know I was born McCurdle in Grand Rapids, twenty one years ago. I have only to go there, find newspaper accounts of the wedding—if it's true Mother married—and track down people who attended. Someone will know what happened."

With a sigh and a droop of her shoulders, Addie gave in. "Try the name Langston. I understand Langstons raised your father, Edgar, after his father died. Don't tell Grace I told you," she added.

"Edgar," Weezy mused. "Edgar McCurdle. Weezy McCurdle." She explored the sounds. "What was wrong with him? Why couldn't I have been told about him?"

"I've no idea. As I say, it's news to me you weren't told. Believe me, when I sent in that obit, I never dreamed I'd drag a skeleton from the closet."

After a few sips of coffee, Weezy set her cup aside. "May I use your phone? I'll pay for the long-distance calls." She knew she had to act quickly before she lost her courage. If she stopped to think, she'd convince herself this idea was crazy.

From the operator, Weezy obtained a list of Langstons in Grand Rapids. There were several. She got no answer from the first number. The second was an old lady with a quavery voice. Weezy said, "I'm trying to locate a man named Edgar McCurdle. I understand he lived with the Langston family. Do you know him?"

"Sorry, never heard of an Edgar McCurdle. You must want the other Langstons, the construction outfit, uh—Menno, I believe it is, and his brother, what's-his-name."

Weezy thanked her and hung up. She asked Addie, who still sat sipping coffee, "Do you know the first name of this Langston person? Could it be Menno?"

With a frown, Addie gazed off into the distance and seemed to struggle with her memory. "They were Mennonites so—probably."

Weezy dialed again. A youthful voice said, "Junior Langston speaking."

Weezy repeated her prepared statement, but lest the Langstons, like her mother, should be angry with the mysterious, unacceptable Edgar, she tried a different name. "I'm looking for Delia Eloise Langston. Do you know her?"

"I have a cousin Delia Eloise, but the name's not Langston." She heard him shout into the distance. "Ma, what's cousin Del's married name?"

Cousin Del! Weezy felt her throat tighten, her mouth become dry, her hands grow shaky. The person she was named for! She was getting close to the truth now.

She heard a woman's voice in the background. The young man spoke into the phone. "It's Kingsley. I thought she'd married but mom says not. Del lives in New York," he added.

"The rest of the family is in Grand Rapids?" Weezy wondered if she dared mention the name Edgar McCurdle.

"Rob and Millie moved to California. Aunt Bea's in Chicago. Here's mom, I'll let you talk to her."

"Alana Langston," a woman's voice said. "Who is this?"

Weezy gathered her courage and gave her birth name. "Della Eloise McCurdle." Just speaking it brought tears to her eyes. She'd stepped into a new personality about whom she as yet knew nothing. She felt frightened, excited and newborn.

The woman gasped. "Della Eloise! I can't believe it! You're not kidding, are you? We thought we'd never—is it really you? Lord, I wish your father—I wish Edgar were here!"

"Tell me about my father. Is he still living?"

"Yes, but he's—not well. He's in a sanatorium. Oh, Della, it would be so great if you could come out here. It might make all the difference to Edgar. Do you suppose you could?"

"Why? What's wrong with him?"

"It's hard to explain over the phone. We'd so love to meet you; we only knew you as a brand new baby. We waved at you in the hospital nursery."

"Of course, I'll come. But please tell me about my father. Did he marry again? Does he have other children?" She realized she could have siblings she knew nothing about.

Alana didn't answer directly. She said, "This would be the perfect time for you to re-connect."

Weezy made a quick decision. "I'll leave after the funeral tomorrow."

"Funeral?"

"My adopted father. It was through the obituaries that I learned I was some-one else's child. No one ever told me."

"So that's it! We wondered why you didn't get in touch. It'll be so good to see you! I'll tell your grandmother, Vi Dexter. She lives up the street. I'm your great-aunt—by marriage, that is. My husband, Menno, is your great-uncle."

"I look forward to getting to know you, Aunt Alana."

When Weezy hung up, she wiped away a tear. "Thanks, Addie, I appreciate your help."

Shoulders drooping, Addie shook her head. "You may not thank me in the end, my dear."

CHAPTER 2

Grace

Hands to her head, Grace Ward stood alone at the curb surveying mountains of discards. She forced her reluctant fingers to paw through and retrieve yearbooks, diaries, photos, a teddy bear beloved by the young Weezy, and old notebooks containing original stories. Weezy had begun writing stories at age seven, and Grace kept several in her own desk drawer, safe from her daughter's predations. Weezy tended to tear up her work.

Grace's hands shook as she carried the armload of salvage into the house. She hid it at the back of the hall closet and covered it with her own things. She believed—or hoped—Weezy would one day regret the impulse that led to this wanton severance of her past, and would long to have these things back.

Items concealed, Grace went to the bathroom for aspirin, and then wandered to the kitchen, pills in hand, for a glass of water. Gulping both, she returned to the living room, lowered the shades, flopped into a chair, and with her hand over her eyes struggled to bring her tempestuous thoughts in order.

Of course, this moment had to come. She should have been ready for it. She knew her proper friends avoided all semblance of gossip, and would not have discussed in front of their children her mysterious return from Michigan with a baby, nor questioned the baby's parentage. That meant she'd been free to come home and get on with her life as if nothing had happened. As far as she knew, there'd been no childhood banter and cruel teasing at Weezy's school. Though Grace had braced for the tearful question: "Why do the children say Daddy's not my real father?" the query never came. Postponed from year to year, her planned talk with Weezy about her origins never took place.

Now she doubted it had been a good thing. By their silence, her friends had colluded in changing history. Events seemed not to have happened.

So, long after she'd ceased to ready herself, after she'd forgotten her rehearsed explanations, she had to deal with this explosion. Clearly it would have been better if Weezy had been told early on. Now events were out of control. Unless Grace found a way of fixing things, the girl might come to hate her, not without justification.

Worst of all, Grace lacked time to sit here brooding. There was much to be done before the funeral.

The front door burst open. Blinking against the light, Grace saw a commanding, white-haired figure dressed in black. Her mother, Persis Hannaford was still, at seventy, an imposing woman. The child of an old-line Unitarian couple who'd known Emerson and Bronson Alcott, she carried the torch as if she felt a personal responsibility to keep alive her forebears' Transcendentalism. Author Van Wyk Brooks had interviewed her for his books about New England literature.

"What's going on?" she demanded. "All that trash out there—a strange moment for housecleaning!"

Grace tried to make light of it. "It's just Weezy, getting rid of kid stuff she should have discarded long ago—old school notebooks, that sort of thing. She got carried away. No harm done. No trash collection until morning."

"Where is Weezy?" Mrs. Hannaford looked around. "I expected her to come and help prepare food for the mourners."

"Weezy is—" How in the world to explain? "I wouldn't count too much on Weezy's help right now, Mother. She's going through a bad patch."

"Of course she is; she lost her father. Though I never noticed they were all that close."

"It's not the death." Grace realized she couldn't shield her mother. She would have to tell the truth. "Fact is, Weezy read the obit on Jonathan this morning and learned he adopted her. She's so upset she threw away all her belongings. Claims she isn't Weezy Ward and those aren't her things."

"Holy Moses! Where is she now?"

"She rushed off to interrogate Addie."

"Addie? Why Addie? Surely you or I could better answer her questions."

"I found I couldn't talk about it. I know you won't understand, Mother, but I just—the words wouldn't come. Anyway, it's all so long ago. I'd begun to forget it ever happened." That was a white lie. Had there ever been a time in all those years when she hadn't dreamed of herself still married to Edgar? And awakened to feel a twinge of disappointment at finding Jonathan beside her? Edgar had been such a charmer, promising the kind of happiness life couldn't deliver. Even now, thinking of him, she found herself sinking back into reveries of a non-existent paradise.

"The child should have been told long ago," Persis insisted. "I urged it but you wanted to wait until she was 'ready,' whatever that means."

"I thought the question would come up naturally, and I could explain that some children are semi-adopted, like herself, with a birth mother. She never asked, and when she went off to college it seemed too late."

"A child should always be given the facts of her background," Mrs. Hannaford asserted. "I don't know how many times I've told you that."

Her mother also didn't know, Grace reflected, how often she herself had worried and wrestled with the question of how to introduce her daughter to this potentially upsetting information. Persis never seemed at a loss to deal with anything; her rights and wrongs had been established long ago. Grace winced at her own predicament.

"It won't be easy at this point—" Here Mrs. Hannaford stepped to the window to peer out. "—to tell her what a rogue her birth father was."

To her own surprise, Grace felt an urge to defend Edgar. She stifled it. "I believe she's about to find out for herself. She seemed determined to investigate."

"How can she do that if no one enlightens her about where to go for information?"

Grace admitted she'd told her daughter she was born McCurdle in Grand Rapids. "It won't take her long to fill in the details."

"Grace, you fool! What did you do that for?" Persis Hannaford straightened, effortlessly, as if finding it a struggle to revert to her commanding posture. Grace, who'd never imagined old age would dare attack her mother, waved her to a chair. Her mother scorned the offer.

"You just said she should have been told the facts long ago," Grace reminded.

"I meant the fact Jonathan adopted her. Not the facts about dreadful Edgar and his uncouth family. No need for her to know about that."

"Uncouth?" Grace frowned and bit her tongue. "What do you mean? Granted, Edgar wasn't a prince, but that doesn't make him a rogue. And his folks were good people."

"That depends on your definition of 'good.'"

"Mother, your snobbery is showing," Grace snapped.

Her mother had managed once again to draw herself up to her commanding stance. "Grace, for heaven's sake, face reality. I had nothing against Douglas Langston; he came from an old Maine family. It was the overall circumstances. He married a country girl—a Mennonite—who had no idea how to cope with big-city problems. The situation was a mess, teen-age pregnancies, shotgun marriages, children raising children. Not a clue among them how to rear a child properly. With no father, Edgar grew up as he pleased, no guidance, no self-discipline or any other discipline. Why you chose to involve yourself—"

Grace felt her old defensiveness reasserting itself. "That's harsh, Mother. Mennonites are good people. The Langstons may not have been Harvard educated, but they were kind-hearted and generous." She'd felt at home with them, felt a sense of belonging in their big, comfortable house called Stormland.

"Well, look who's talking! You rushed away from there fast enough."

"I was willful when young; I should have given the matter more thought."

"Yes, you were willful, and Edgar was spoiled rotten—practically a juvenile delinquent." Ignoring Grace's protests, she added, "I worry that Weezy inherited Edgar's bad genes."

"Mother, you live in a museum. People don't believe in 'evil genes" any more."

"How you do romanticize!" Mrs. Hannaford seated herself, leaned back in her chair and stretched out her legs. "I should have left you in Grand Rapids until you learned what 'life' in your definition is all about." Restlessly, she stood up again. "Right now, with a death in the family, we have no time for this discussion. The mortuary wants us to select a casket."

"I thought Jonathan's mother was doing that."

"Sarah went to pieces and couldn't decide. No mother should be asked to do such a terrible thing. The hand that rocked the cradle shouldn't select the coffin."

Grace sighed and headed for the stairs. "Give me a few minutes to change my clothes. There's coffee in the pot if you want some."

Weezy came in just as her mother and grandmother were leaving. Though curious what her daughter had learned, Grace didn't ask. She said, "We're off to the mortuary. Your grandmother will need you later to help prepare for the funeral."

"You can go over now and put the roast in the oven," Persis Hannaford said. "You know where I keep the key."

Ignoring them both, Weezy moved toward the stairs in silence. Trying to seem casual, Grace asked, "Off speaking terms?"

"I'm not interested in flapping my gums," Weezy said. "Where there's no communication, talking is flap."

"Weezy, where do you pick up those vulgar phrases?" Persis demanded.

"What am I supposed to do, act nice and polite?" Weezy grasped the newel post and swung back from the foot of the stairs. "I've just learned that my father wasn't my father. Try to understand, Gran. I spent my whole life struggling to please that man; for him I majored in a field I didn't care a hoot about. I thought I was a failure in life because I couldn't be the Ward he wanted. Now I learn I'm not a Ward at all. One grandmother and my only aunt are no blood kin of mine. Furthermore, I have a whole family, father, aunts, uncles, cousins, that my mother and my real granny never thought to tell me about." She straightened and demanded, "Is that supposed to be just a minor event in a girl's day?"

"Impertinence is particularly unbecoming in a house of death," Persis said.

"I happen to agree that your mother shouldn't have withheld that information, but all the same—"

"And you shouldn't have helped her do it. Conspiracies of silence are not nice."

"Will it help if I say I'm sorry?" Torn between tears for Weezy and anger at Persis, Grace tried to think how to stop the older woman from putting her oar in. This should have been a moment of true communication between mother and daughter, without judgmental interferences. Grace longed to take Weezy in her arms and sooth away her mother's ugly accusations. She knew Weezy had suffered a shock. She couldn't imagine how her daughter must be feeling.

"Late for apologies." Weezy again started up the stairs. "Excuse me, I need to make travel arrangements. I'll be heading for Michigan right after the funeral tomorrow."

Grace spoke quickly so that her mother couldn't intervene to forbid the trip and create a confrontation. "You're not returning to college for your graduation ceremony?"

"I'll be just as graduated if they mail me the diploma instead of handing it over."

Uncertain what to say, hoping somehow to shatter this brittle anger, Grace pleaded. "Weezy, you worked four years for that diploma."

"Weezy Ward worked for it. Weezy McCurdle has to find her own life." She ran up the stairs and added, leaning over the banister at the top, "I'll go put on the roast, Grandmother. Just so you understand I'm not mourning a father. My father's in a sanatorium in Michigan."

Grace swallowed hard to regain self-control. "Mother, you shouldn't have—lord, I never thought it would be this bad." She gave way to an impulse to wring her hands. "She's of age; I can't stop her from—. Dear God, I don't know what to do."

Persis Hannaford raised a hand. "Let her go. She'll learn about Edgar, just as you did, and her good sense will assert itself."

"I don't want to see her hurt. More than she has been, that is."

Her mother made a dismissive gesture. "You can't protect your child from life's hurts. I discovered that fact twenty-two years ago."

Though it was warm outside, Persis, as always, drew on her gloves. She adjusted her hat and gave her daughter an impatient glance. Grace knew she was being silently commanded to find her own hat and gloves and put them on, with no complaints about the heat. She sighed and went to the hall closet.

CHAPTER 3

Weezy

"Why Grand Rapids?" Weezy demanded of her mother next day.

Dressed in black, the two women waited in their living room to be picked up for the funeral. "What were you doing there?" After fuming through a restless night and a moody morning, recalling her long years of struggle to live up to what she supposed was her father's wish that she be more of a Ward, Weezy finally felt calm enough to talk to her family again.

"Studying art." Her mother bit her lip as if she feared that anything she said would be the wrong thing.

"It's news to me that Grand Rapids has an art colony."

"The nearby town of Saugatuck has." She took a deep breath and explained. "During high school, I studied at the Boston Art Museum. After graduation I wanted to get away—Paris or at least New York—but Mother wouldn't hear of it."

Weezy nodded. She could well believe that the child of Persis Hannaford would have an urge to move out and go her own way—and as surely would be forbidden to do so.

"I spent the summer in Saugatuck," her mother continued. "In the fall, my instructor went to the bigger city to work on a mural, and I followed to continue my private lessons."

Weezy'd heard about Saugatuck. Grace had told her how she'd been offered a college scholarship but had elected instead to study at the Chicago Art Institute, summering in the town on the Michigan dunes where the Art Institute held its warm-weather program. "As I said, I'd hoped to go to New York and live in Greenwich Village, but your grandmother nixed the idea. Chicago did have a Bohemian community, you understand, but Mother insisted I stay in a 'proper' home for women. The place was worse than a prison; one girl almost killed herself trying to have an evening out. She slid down from a third-floor window on sheets tied together, and when the knots didn't hold, she fell. Broke both legs and a hip and was on crutches for months."

"Lucky she didn't become a paraplegic." Weezy tried to focus on getting the information she wanted. "All right, we have you in Grand Rapids. There you met—uh—Edgar?" She couldn't bring herself to say, "My true father." She felt she might choke up over the words.

"I met him on the dunes," Grace admitted.

"He's an artist, too?"

"He was a wild kid with a motorcycle. He crashed thirty feet from where I'd set up my easel. He took his eyes off the road to look at me and hit a tree. I dragged him, bloody head and all, off the fallen machine. Yet through it all, lying in the sand, he had the *panache* to claim he staged the accident on purpose so he could meet me." Grace narrowed her eyes and smiled vaguely as if seeing the event again in her mind.

"Then you nursed him back to health, he raped you, and you were forced to marry him." Weezy spoke bluntly, hoping to move the story forward.

"Weezy! What awful thoughts you have! My goodness, Edgar wasn't—he never—Oh, I don't want you to think that he—I mean, we were in *love*. You can't rape a woman who's—who's—"

"All right, so why refuse to talk about it? Nothing you've told me so far sounds so terrible. A wild kid with a motorcycle—the world is full of them. You fell in love and married. That qualifies as a skeleton in the closet? A life-long family secret?"

"No, no, it wasn't like that. You're creating mysteries where none exist. I loved him, I married him, I found he wasn't the kind of man I could make a life with." She managed a wispy smile and misquoted Poe. "He was young and I was young in our kingdom by the sea, and we loved with a love that was more than love, I and my handsome Edgar." Prosaically, she added, "I grew up, he didn't. I came home with you to Jonathan, who'd waited. There now, I've told you—it's over—we can mourn in peace. Jonathan was a good soul even though not your birth father. He earned your caring; he did a lot for you."

"Did he do it for me? Or for you?"

"For both of us. Please, let's forget Edgar, dear. I've explained everything."

Weezy doubted that. She sensed that the real story lay between the lines, in what Grace wasn't saying. It had to be bad to make her mother cut herself off forever from the procreator of her child, denying him parental contact, denying Weezy the right to know him. How come he lacked visitation rights? Had he abandoned his family? Walked out?

Judging by the warm welcome she'd had from Alana, it seemed unlikely. From such trauma there would be scars, making her aunt dubious about meeting her again.

Grace peered out the window and stood to reach for her coat and gloves. "The limousine is here."

Weezy survived the funeral with head bent in a show of mourning. While the minister spoke, she recalled her adoptive father, the repeated hurts, his lack of response to her struggles to attract his attention. She remembered how her mother had always come alone to school functions. When the disappointed child asked where Daddy was, Grace would explain that he worked hard to support the two of them and couldn't spare time for children's affairs.

Well, he did support me, Weezy admitted to herself. I owe him for that.

While the minister extolled the deceased's community work and charitable efforts, Weezy thought about his remoteness and inaccessibility. He'd always seemed merely to put up with her rather than to participate in her upbringing. Looking back, she felt sure he'd merely accepted her as the price of getting her mother. She could have saved herself those years of hungering for his affection and seeking to please him.

Had Jonathan not adopted her, she reflected, her birth father might have been granted visiting rights. She could have exchanged letters, kept in touch with him.

When the mourners gathered at Persis' beautiful old Back Bay home, Weezy felt tempted to remark on this, but with her mother distraught, she couldn't bring herself to speak. All would be known anyway when she went to Michigan.

Later, at North Station where Grace had come to see her off, Weezy contrived to fight her anger and give her mother a hug. She even managed condolences. "I'm sorry to leave you at a time like this, Mother. I know you've lost your life companion." The words sounded hollow. She realized as she spoke that Jonathan hadn't been all that much of a companion to her mother. He'd never entered her studio, never praised her art work nor given it more than a glance and a nod. No, Jonathan was not her mother's true love. He was merely her rescuer in a crisis. Her life with him must have been a desert. Weezy studied her mother's face as if to find a hint that Edgar still invaded her thoughts.

"I hope you enjoy your trip, Weezy." Her mother kissed her cheek. "I'll be at home for the next few days; you can call me if anything comes up."

Weezy pecked her mother's cheek; it was the only farewell she felt able to handle right now. She hopped aboard, located her compartment and removed hat, jacket and gloves. She still felt restless and, watching out the window as her mother walked back to the car, promised herself she'd soon go sit in the observation lounge and find passengers to talk to. She leaned back and tried to calm the butterflies in her midriff.

The New York train pulled in on the opposite track. Carrying luggage, holding onto hats against the early-evening breeze, several people ran from it to the Lakeshore Limited. Weezy noticed a blonde young woman in a large-brimmed brown and white hat race across the tracks and pause to confer with a porter, showing her ticket. When the porter pointed to Weezy's car, the young woman hurried toward the entrance. Weezy eyed her. A New Yorker, for sure. There was no mistaking New York women in Boston. Bostonians preferred understated elegance, like her own unadorned oatmeal-colored shirtwaist, pleated brown skirt, single strand of pearls and tiny pearl earrings, small hat and medium heels. New York women opted for flair: wide-brimmed hats, full skirts, dangle earrings, gloves to the elbow, spiked heels. All that was lacking for this blonde woman to spell New York sophistication was a long-handled cigarette holder.

Weezy wondered why, when New York had its own train west, the woman had come up here to travel out of Boston.

The train pulled out of the station. When Weezy went down the corridor to the restroom, she passed the blonde, whose compartment door was open. She leaned her head in and offered a smile. "I saw you board. Going far?"

The young woman, who appeared to be a few years older than Weezy, had removed her large hat and laid it on the seat beside her. Weezy could see her face and hair, the latter, really more copper than blonde, tucked into a chignon in which she was now adjusting the pins. She wore dangle earrings, the handcrafted cloisonné sold in Greenwich Village boutiques.

When she looked up, something about her registered as—familiar? Hardly that, but raising echoes. The eyes, Weezy decided. Not their color; they were greenish-blue where Weezy's were brown. It was the shape, like the almond eyes Weezy saw in the mirror. The pixie look, her mother called it.

"Michigan." The young woman tossed the word off casually.

Weezy felt she'd known the answer ahead of time. She asked, "Grand Rapids?"

A flicker of interest, a faint smile. "How on earth did you guess?"

Weezy took a deep breath, steeled herself, and ventured, "You wouldn't by chance be Delia Kingsley?"

The almond eyes widened in astonishment. "Do I know you?"

"No—that is, you did once long ago. I'm Della McCurdle."

"Of course! Edgar's daughter! I should have known!" Delia stood, reached out to draw Weezy into the compartment, and offered a quick hug. "Well, Cousin, it's been a while." The flicker turned into a real smile. "I'm on my way to the family reunion. It didn't occur to me we might travel together; I assumed you were in Michigan already." She gestured toward the opposite seat in the compartment. "Come join me. This is amazing!"

Weezy stepped in and slid onto the facing seat. "It's unbelievable. I heard you lived in New York, and I figured you'd go directly from there."

"I came early this morning and stopped en route to visit a former roommate. Anyway, I love the Lakeshore Limited. It's so scenic, skimming through the wetlands on the Erie shore. Ever traveled on it before?"

Weezy shook her head. "This is my first trip west—at least since infancy. We vacation in Nantucket." She straightened her skirt. "I kind of guessed who you were. We look alike."

"You're my namesake," Delia told her. "You were born when I was seven, and named after me. I was heartbroken when Grace took you away; I'd always wanted a baby sister and I considered you my special gift."

Weezy started in surprise. "You know what happened back then?"

"I know the facts. What does a seven-year-old know of the whys and wherefores? I've wondered about them." Delia leaned back and closed her eyes. "I can still see your mother driving away in Edgar's truck with the baby—you—in the seat beside her. She was in a fury, nose in the air. She abandoned the truck at her hotel and none of us ever saw her again." She opened blue eyes and studied Weezy. "Your hair is like hers. I should have recognized you. How is Grace?"

"You just missed her; she came to see me off. She's grieving over the death of my adopted father. Funeral was earlier today."

"I'm sorry." Delia gazed out the window, eyes narrowed in thought. "Still, I'd be surprised it she loved him madly. She and Edgar were crazy about each other; she'd battled her mother for the right to marry the guy. I was flower girl—a lovely wedding." She returned her gaze to Weezy and offered a quick smile. "I even recall their song, *O Perfect Love*. It inspired me to want a similar romance for myself—so much so that later I couldn't come to terms with marrying my steady, reliable boyfriend."

Weezy nodded. "I learned from your cousin that you'd broken off the engagement." She studied Del curiously but when Del seemed unwilling to explain, she reverted to discussing her parents' breakup, and added, "Soon after the wedding my mother and Edgar must have had a battle royal."

"Yes—and Edgar seemed devastated. I always thought Grace was the one woman he'd have remained faithful to."

"Is that his great sin? Womanizing? Mother would hate that."

Del bit her lip ruefully. Weezy urged, "Please, I don't need any more conspiracies of silence. Do tell me the truth!" She stood up. "I was on my way to the rest room, but when I come back I want to hear everything."

Del shrugged. "I was a child; I didn't understand everything."

"Maybe we can put our heads together and figure it all out. No one ever told me a thing, not even that Jonathan Ward wasn't my birth father. I learned of that yesterday from the obits."

"How courageous of you to set out at once to locate your birth family! It would've taken me ages to get used to the idea. Different father—I can't imagine it." Del closed her eyes. "Dad's so much a part of my life. Being a Kingsley is part of my life. To lose those roots—" She shook her head. "I wouldn't be me."

Weezy struggled against choking up. She confessed that she'd never really felt like a Ward. Worse, she'd seen herself as an unwanted intruder. It was as if somewhere in her she'd known of this situation all along. "My dad and I weren't close. I suspect Jonathan wanted my mother, and I was part of the package." Brusquely, batting her eyelids to fight tears, she stepped into the hall. "Be right back. I want to hear the unexpurgated version."

"Fine with me." Delia waved her away. "I love to tattle."

CHAPTER 4

Del

Alone in the compartment, Del kicked off her high heels, let her seat back, propped her pillow, and made herself comfortable. She tried to relax, no easy matter at this moment of learning the outcome of a family mystery. She felt an impulse to rush through the train shouting, "Listen up, everyone! I've discovered a long-lost cousin!"

A happy coincidence, this meeting had cheered Del. Until now, facing problems with both her job and her love life, she'd been in a gloomy mood. The job, which she'd loved, had been pre-empted by a newly-graduated returning veteran, and her glamorous Catalan boyfriend, Hilario Soler, had proved not to be the marrying kind. She felt in limbo, her world crashing around her.

She threw her mind back to the long-ago summer of '27. It seemed everything important in her childhood had happened then. Cousin Maggie had died leaving five small children. Aunt Bea'd disappointed everyone by marrying the stick-in-the-mud who hung around while she dated the charmer she'd seemed crazy about. Del's father moved their small family from Del's beloved Michigan town of Petoskey to the dreary tenements of Chicago, where the el train clattered past their rear window and the child was left with only a collection of Petoskey stones for remembrance. At her grandmother's house, Stormland, Edgar and Grace swept her into dreams of perfect love with a fairytale wedding, and then contrived to ruin it with their angry separation.

Through it all, Del had received lessons in birth, death and lost love such as she'd never wanted or asked for. In that one summer, her happy childhood had been forever compromised by her discovery of the limits Nature placed on human life, particularly women's lives.

How in the world was she to tell her new cousin about all that? She'd never clarified the drama in her own mind.

Weezy came back commenting that she understood Del's life had taken dramatic recent turns of its own. "Doug said you'd planned to marry but canceled."

"Oh, you don't want to hear about all that." Del sighed. "It's a dreary tale."

"We've a long train trip ahead." Weezy also shed her shoes and snapped her seat back. "Let's start with Edgar and work up."

Del closed her eyes. "Edgardo and Grazia of Stormland. It was sheer grand opera, an American *Lucia di Lammermoor*." She sighed. "I can tell you only the barest facts. I wasn't privy to the beginning; I've no idea how Grace and Edgar met and fell in love. I do know they *were* in love—wildly. Even a child could see that."

"Mother said they met in Saugatuck. She's an artist, and Edgar crashed his motorcycle near where she'd set up her easel."

"That's Edgar: crashing, hurting himself, breaking things—the family daredevil." Del hesitated. Should she admit to Edgar's daughter that the man had been the black sheep of the family? Would any young woman want to learn that about her father?

No doubt owing to the fact she'd grown up hearing Edgar referred to as the wild kid, Del tended to focus on his bad side. *I mustn't present him that way to his daughter*, she reminded herself.

"How much do you know about the family?" she asked.

"Until yesterday, I believed I was a Ward. When I learned I had a birth father named Edgar McCurdle, I looked him up in the phone book. No listing. I tried the name Langston and got through to Alana. I still don't know how Langstons are related to McCurdles."

"Edgar's a Langston on his mother's side, so Alana is your great-aunt. Violet, your grandmother, married a man named Nat McCurdle, who died eight years later leaving her widowed with five-year-old Edgar." Del again tried to force her mind to back-track. "You need to keep in mind that Edgar had no father; he grew up with no discipline except that of a grandfather who was not a disciplinarian. Gramps—dear Gramps, I adored him—was the Henry David Thoreau of our family. He'd have been happy in a hand-built cabin on Walden Pond. I'm sure Edgar inherited his impractical ways from Gramps."

She shuffled her feet restlessly as she continued. "If what I have to tell you seems bad, remember it's the badness of a kid desperately searching for direction in his life. To the best of my knowledge, Edgar never got in trouble with the law or anything—"

Weezy withdrew her gaze from passing suburbs to give Del a probing look. "Why do I get the feeling there's something here you want to hide?"

Del twitched her shoulders restlessly. "I just—I wouldn't want to say the wrong thing and set you against Edgar. People set *me* against him—a mistake I now regret."

"Don't worry; I'm past the age to let anyone influence me, especially about my father."

Del struggled to send herself into that summer. At first her mind resisted. Then, as if hypnotized, she drifted back. Suddenly she was a child again in the big, old fashioned kitchen at Stormland. While Gram combed her hair, she sat on a high stool, feeling cool fingers sort out the knots from what her mother referred to as her long golden curls, actually auburn.

Del's mother had gone downtown to shop with Aunt Bea, who had a day off from work. Del's older cousin, Jenny, played outdoors with friends and could be heard shouting and laughing. Edgar was away at his job in the family construction business.

Aunt Alana arrived from her home up the street bringing her two youngest grandchildren, her daughter Maggie's babies. She left their net-covered buggy on the porch so they could sleep in the open air while she sat in the kitchen. Gram reheated the coffee, and on hearing the postman at the front door, sent Del to get the mail. Del returned with a letter, handed it over, and watched Gram, now seated at the table, study it in bafflement.

"Boston? I don't know a soul in Boston."

"Sure you do," Alana reminded. "That girl Edgar was going with. Haverford, wasn't it? Grace Haverford."

"Hannaford." Gram brought the envelope close to her nose to read the return address. "You're right. Hannaford, Mrs. S.H. The battleaxe mother." She reached for her glasses, settled them on her nose, and slit the envelope. She read: "I'll be bringing my daughter to visit you on June twenty-fifth." She looked up. "Why, that's today!"

"Land sakes, they could come any minute!" Alana looked around frantically as if it were her job to neaten the house.

"Without an invitation?" Gram frowned. "Is that considered good manners in Boston?" She read on. "Please be at home as we have something important to discuss. *Important* underlined twice."

"Do you suppose the kid got herself in the family way?"

"If so, Edgar can't be responsible. It's nearly seven months since Old Lady Hannaford dragged Grace home. And I do mean dragged. You'd have thought Edgar was Typhoid Mary."

"As I recall, the woman had someone else in mind for her precious child, a good marriage all fixed. She feared Edgar might throw a monkey wrench in her plans."

Gram sighed. "I suppose I'd better straighten the living room." She started to push herself out of her chair.

"Why?" Alana waved a hand. "You didn't invite the warhorse. Let her take you as you are."

"I'd hate to give her an excuse to look down her long Bostonian nose at me."

Alana tossed her head dismissively. "Snooty Bostonian nose, you mean. I heard she charged in here during dinner and literally grabbed Grace by the collar to haul her away. Not even a thank-you for the kid's meals."

Gram studied the letter. "Doesn't say what time they'll arrive."

Alana stood and leaned to peer over Gram's shoulder. She reminded Gram that she and Gramps were Edgar's guardians. Gram shook her head. "Edgar's too old to have a guardian. He's what?—nineteen, isn't it?" She reached out to steady the coffee cup Alana threatened to spill. "*Will* you sit down and stop making me nervous?"

Alana settled down again, fastened loose locks of hair into her bun, and looked thoughtful. "Let's see, he was eleven when baby Richard died. That'd make him going on twenty now."

"Old enough to handle his own affairs. Why didn't Witch Hannaford write to *him*? What does she want of me?"

Alana shrugged and said she couldn't imagine. "I'll stay and offer moral support if you wish. The other kids are lunching with neighbors."

"I'll make sandwiches for us. There's leftover ham."

Seeing the ice man pass the window, Del crossed the kitchen to open the screen door so he wouldn't bang it and wake the babies. He came in carrying a block of ice on his back, and with giant tongs slung it into the top section of the ice box. Del continued to hold the screen door until, with a farewell wave, he left, mouthing a brief, "Thank you."

A fly had flown in, and Gram told Del to get the swatter. "Put the leftover chunk of ice in the cherry cider," she added. "It's melted to where it'll fit into the pitcher."

Lunch was over when Mrs. Hannaford, accompanied by a young companion swathed from head to toe in a hooded brown cape, climbed the front steps. When the two were standing in the living room, the swathed figure threw back its hood, unbuttoned the cape, and revealed itself to be a young woman with a protruding stomach. Del wondered how the lovely Grace, whom she recognized from snapshots, had grown so fat so quickly. Edgar's photos showed her as slim and agile. Now, with hair rumpled by the hood, skin blotchy, expression wary, she seemed far from the beauty Edgar had loved.

"We have a problem," Mrs. Hannaford said.

Gram pursed her lips. "Seems you've had it for a good while. Why didn't you tell us sooner?"

"Because I thought—at least I hoped—Grace would give up the child for adoption. Since she refuses to sign the papers, she leaves us no choice but a quick wedding. I just hope Edgar won't be difficult about it."

"Edgar won't be difficult; I'll see to it," Gram snapped. "No child of the Tiehl family has ever been given up for adoption, nor will if I have anything to say about it. Even in our most desperate moments, we've kept our flesh and blood with us."

"Are you certain the child is Edgar's?" Alana asked Grace.

Grace gave her a disdainful look. "What kind of question is that? No other man touched me."

"Edgar forced her," Mrs. Hannaford said.

"He didn't *force* me, Mother." Grace argued. "I've told you before, he—I had no idea when to stop him." She hesitated and glanced uneasily at seven-year-old Del, who was indeed wondering what Edgar had forced her to do. Grace took a deep breath, lifted her chin higher, and faced her mother. "I didn't know any of this stuff about babies being planted, my body becoming a growing ground. You told me some nonsense about a stork."

"I repeatedly cautioned you not to let a man get too close to you."

"Mother! I was in love. People in love are *supposed* to spoon and bundle."

Del tugged at her grandmother's skirt. "Gram, what's she talking about? How did Edgar plant a baby?"

Gram frowned and shook her head. "I'll explain later."

"Oh, tell the child," Alana urged. "Grace is right, it's foolish not to talk of it."

Gram tossed her daughter-in-law a protesting look, but Alana ignored it and turned to Del. "When a man plants baby seed, it grows in the woman's tummy."

"In her *tummy*?" Del gazed in shock at that distended abdomen. "How will it get out?"

"When the time comes, it'll find the way."

"See what you started?" Gram frowned. To Mrs. Hannaford she added, "Let's see what Edgar has to say. He's working at the construction site up the street."

"I'll send young Jenny to get him." Alana turned toward the foyer. "She's outside."

She departed. Del still studied Grace's bulging abdomen. Gram offered chairs and asked if the guests had had lunch.

"We went to a restaurant near the station," Mrs. Hannaford said. "Grace is hungry all the time. She'll be fatter than a pig."

Grace stood erect, refusing the chair, seeming to let her mother's insults roll off without penetrating. Gram managed no such calm. Del could sense her worry so strongly her own stomach knotted. She knew that Gram, for the sake of peace in the family, avoided confrontations with Edgar, who had a temper.

"Edgar never talks of marrying," Gram said. "Faced with a wedding and a baby in one package, I don't know how he'll react."

"I'm sure it won't come as a surprise," Mrs. Hannaford said. "He knows what he did to Grace."

"Too bad you rushed Grace away. If they'd been together, the young people could have worked this out, come to terms with it."

"I had no idea Grace was in the family way. I sent an eighteen-year-old innocent to study art in the company of a chaperone. Seems neither her teacher nor her chaperone had time for her. Too busy pursuing their own interests on my money."

"Grace boarded with us," Gram reminded.

"When I found out about her condition, I took her to a home and arranged for an adoption. But she—"

"I told you I wouldn't sign the papers," Grace said. "You knew I planned to keep the baby."

"I thought, when you grew big and the baby kicked, you'd come to your senses."

Del again studied the bulge, hoping to see a small foot kick through the clothing. Grace asserted, "I *did* come to my senses. I realized Edgar and I belong together. We have a child."

"Call that sense? When you have a wonderful fiancé who loves you and is willing to forgive?"

"Arranged marriages are out of style." Grace contemplated her fingernails as if trying to distance herself from the conversation.

"You promised Jonathan Ward."

"No, you promised him. I didn't know how to get out of your promise."

Del teased, "I want to see the baby kick."

"You can feel it." Grace took her hand. "Touch right here."

"Grace, for heaven's sake!" her mother protested. Gram looked horrified. But Del slid her hand onto the spot, and sure enough, felt movement. She marveled. "There really is a live baby in there! Where did Edgar get that wonderful seed to plant?"

Gram tried hard to ignore all this. She remarked to Mrs. Hannaford, "I must admit Grand Rapids seemed a strange place for a Bostonian to come for art lessons."

Mrs. Hannaford explained that the instructor was doing murals here. "Grace wanted to continue her studies—or so she claimed, though I doubt she showed up for them."

"Lessons were an hour twice a week," Grace pointed out

"I supposed a painter painted. I assumed you'd be hard at work in the studio I rented for you. All that concern about proper lighting so you could entertain Edgar!"

Alana entered the room from the kitchen, bringing Gramps, who'd been working in his watch repair shop in the made-over carriage house out back. She announced that Jenny was on her way. She explained to Mrs. Hannaford, "Vi is Edgar's mother." She introduced Gramps. "This is Mr. Langston, Edgar's grandfather."

Everyone looked at Gramps, a dapper white-haired man with a goatee. His moustache wiggling nervously, he nodded to Mrs. Hannaford and greeted Grace. "You say Edgar is responsible for this baby?" he asked the younger woman.

"My mother says that. I say Edgar and I made the baby together. I didn't know it would happen and I doubt if Edgar did."

"Probably not," Gramps agreed. "Boys have these myths, how it's safe if the moon isn't horned or some such nonsense. Boys like to swagger as if they know everything when really they know nothing."

"Where do they get the seed to plant?" Del persisted.

"It comes out of their bodies," Alana said.

Awed, Del couldn't wait to study Edgar and see what part of his body produced this miracle.

Mrs. Hannaford questioned why Edgar lived at Stormland instead of with his parents. Gramps explained that Edgar didn't get along with his stepfather. Del glanced out the window and saw Edgar hurry toward the house, a breathless and puffing Aunt Vi in tow, long-haired Jenny skipping beside her. The room grew quiet with tension. When Del went to the foyer to open the door, she eyed Edgar closely. She felt disappointed in what she saw. He was the same old muscular Edgar, in clothes cement-stained and sweaty, his straight brown hair falling across his forehead. No hint of how he managed this baby-making. He smoothed his hair and stepped into the house behind his mother. When Jenny followed, Gram told her to go back to her playmates.

"This doesn't concern you," Gram said. "Take Del with you."

Both girls protested loudly. Del obsessed with curiosity. What punishment would Edgar receive for having engineered all this? He was too big for Gramps to spank.

Gram gave in. "Oh, well, the damage is done, though what your mother will say, Del, I can't think." She turned to Edgar, took a deep breath, and admitted, "Grace and Mrs. Hannaford are here. Grace is far along in the family way, and claims you helped."

Breaths were held, and then let out in sighs of relief when Edgar's face lighted. He flung himself forward, stood over Grace in his smudged overalls, and grinned broadly. "Grace! It *is* you! Swell to see you again!"

Everyone seemed surprised at his joy. Grace beamed. Gram's eyes widened in astonishment. Mrs. Hannaford muttered, "Holy Moses!" Vi smiled.

Edgar embraced Grace, hugging her hard despite her girth. Gram breathed, "The only predictable thing about Edgar is that he's unpredictable."

"This is perfect!" Edgar said. "Now no one can stop us from getting married."

"Oh, Edgar!" Tears sprang to Grace's eyes. She snuggled against him and let her head rest on his shoulder. "I worried that you might hate me for letting it happen."

"Hate you? Never. We must be married right away—like tonight." He hugged her. "I feared I'd never see you again."

Vi too wiped her eyes. "Edgar, I wouldn't have—you're being very good."

Gram commented, "I guess there's nothing of Nat about you after all."

"Oh, yes, there is," Vi said. "His looks. He's every bit as handsome as Nat."

Del bit her lip in bafflement. She'd understood that Edgar had done a terrible thing, planting a baby. Now it seemed that by acting happy, he'd made it all right. He wasn't even going to be punished. She gazed around at smiling faces and puzzled.

CHAPTER 5

Del

The train lurched, the dinner gong sounded. Del stirred and blinked; she felt she'd wakened from sleep. Her legs tingled from long immobility and she uncrossed them. She broke off her narrative so the pair might go to dinner. While they ate, she explained "We had three weddings that year, none truly happy. Two were shotgun, and Aunt Bea's was a disappointment to all of us because of her choice of—well, I'll tell you about that later. Besides, we had two funerals that summer."

"Who died?" Weezy asked.

"My cousin Maggie, for one. Meg, as she preferred to be called. Alana's only daughter. With five babies in a row—I guess she wore herself out. At twenty-one, she developed pneumonia after number five. Alana had to take over and raise the tots, with the help of their father. I learned young what child-bearing can do to women."

"I would love to hear about your broken engagement," Weezy confessed.

Del hesitated, rubbed her hands together, and with reluctance described how, after a seven year engagement to Bradley Boynton, she'd panicked when the wedding date was set. She bit her lip. "I hate talking about this; I can't explain it and I feel guilty. My mother was devastated at the cancellation and still doesn't understand it."

Faltering, dragging out memories stored in the attic of her mind, Del went on to remark that, except for the pregnancy, she'd been in the same situation as Grace with her faithful, waiting-at-home fiancé. Her mother, Millie, was crazy about Bradley, hot for her to marry him. "For myself, I doubt I ever loved him.

Yet he was tall; I liked that. Perhaps you've noticed that I tend to tower over people." Tears flooded her eyes and she batted them away. "Walking out on your own wedding—it's awful. I was the villain. Everyone took Bradley's side; no one understood my reasons, least of all my—" She choked up, took a deep breath. "—my mother, who was a musician and adored Brad."

Weezy squeezed her shoulder and left off questioning. They finished eating and returned to the compartment, where Del settled in her seat, leaned back, and swung again into the past. She put herself in the Stormland living room, seeing in her mind's eye the view of passing cars on the street, hearing Gram at the window exclaim: "Look at all the rigs go by! Land sakes, where do they come from? Where are they going?"

Del described the living room, fragrant with lilacs for the wedding, the dining room festive with streamers and the three-tiered cake Aunt Bea had created. "I can still see Bea working over it, putting rosettes of white frosting around the edges while mother stood holding the bowl."

Del's mother and her Aunt Bea had been flappers back then, slim, modish, with brown bobbed hair and skirts which appeared short due to the low waistlines of the day, though actually they covered the knees. Gram had given up trying for high style and settled down to wearing gray hoover dresses reminiscent of the Mennonite clothing of her youth. Wrapped in a large white apron, she scurried about setting out dessert plates.

Dressed in a suit borrowed from a friend—he'd never owned one of his own—Edgar looked neat and handsome but seemed restless. He wandered from room to room, checking on everything. Gram complained he was underfoot. "I wish I could send you out to play with the other kids," she told him.

Clearly, Edgar was fearful something might yet go wrong. Even Del felt relieved when the best man arrived and lured her cousin to the porch to talk. Mrs. Hannaford had gone upstairs to help dress the bride. Uncle Rob's younger children, aged one and three, napped in Gram's bedroom.

With armloads of gifts, Alana and Menno entered by the back door. They brought their son, Doug, who skipped off to join the other children. When Del teased to follow, her mother reminded her she might dirty her dress. Del pouted; she longed to go out and play with her cousins.

Uncle Menno carried the gifts into the dining room. In response to Mother's question about the rest of the family, Alana explained that Sean was minding the little ones, and Maggie was coming in the truck. "She didn't feel up to walking."

Gram frowned. "Maggie's not bouncing back the way she usually does after childbirth."

"I worry about her," Alana confessed.

Gram gazed around reflectively. "Seems hardly any time since we had Maggie's wedding here."

"And Millie's, shortly before." Alana put out a hand to touch Millie's arm. "Remember, Millie? You said you planned to postpone having children for several years. In May we got the news: you were preg—uh, in the family way."

Mother gave her a protesting look, then glanced at Del. That meant they wanted to talk baby-in-the-stomach stuff again, all hush-hush. Del realized she too must once have been in her mother's stomach. Like Grace, she'd been told the stork story. When she'd asked her father where the stork had got her, he'd said, with a teasing look, "I asked the stork that question but he didn't answer. You can't talk to a stork."

"Little pitchers have big ears," Gram said now.

Alana expostulated, "Oh, for heaven's sake!" She sounded disgusted. Del promised herself she'd get Alana alone sometime and ask the questions Mother and Gram wouldn't answer, like how the baby got out of the stomach.

"Ah, well, those were the days." Alana winked at Del. "Eight years ago! Can you believe it?" She eyed the salad platter. "Let me help here."

"You can finish cutting these radishes." Mother laid the knife down. "I need to powder my nose." She yanked the apron from her waist and handed it to Alana, who whipped it around herself, tied the strings, and picked up the knife.

Mother hurried upstairs with Del in tow. They found Grace in tears, complaining that her store-bought wedding gown fitted awkwardly over her big stomach.

Mrs. Hannaford frowned. "You'll have to make the best of it. There's no time now to hire a seamstress."

A tall girl, Grace must have been willowy and stunning-looking when Edgar met her. Too bad, Del thought, she couldn't look that way for her wedding.

Returning downstairs, Del saw that Maggie, pale and bloodless, had finally arrived. Uncle Menno was helping her to a seat in the only overstuffed chair remaining in the parlor. When the rest of the furniture had been moved out to make room for rows of folding chairs facing the improvised altar, this one had been left for Meg, who held the new baby while her mother, Alana, hovered over her.

The house seemed crowded. Relatives came from other rooms and found chairs. Gram called the children in from under the chestnut tree, where a pile of crates served alternately as playhouse or fort, depending on whether boys or girls were using it. Uncle Rob began strumming his mandolin.

The crowd, men standing, women seated, silenced. The children sat on the floor in a circle near the altar, leaving space for the wedding party. The minister took his place at the altar. Edgar and the best man stood off to the side, Edgar looking solemn but dashing.

Del scurried back upstairs, where a bouquet was thrust into her arms. From downstairs she heard Aunt Laddie singing *O Perfect Love.* She waited until the song ended, then, nudged by Aunt Bea, went down again carrying the flowers, and stepped slowly past the seated guests to the altar as she'd been told to do. Behind her came Bea as bridesmaid. Uncle Rob played *Here Comes the Bride*, and Grace walked in on Gramps' arm. Awash in dreams of romance, Del pictured herself as a bride.

Smiling, the bridegroom stepped over to join Grace. The vows were exchanged under a bower of lilacs. Women dabbed at their eyes. Del wondered where she'd meet *her* perfect love.

The bride and groom kissed, the music grew light-hearted. Smiling, hand in hand, the young couple made their way, almost skipping, to the dining room, where everyone kissed the bride and shook hands with Edgar. The children eyed the stacks of presents and whispered to one another, guessing what might be inside gift-wrapped boxes. On being introduced to Maggie, Grace held out her arms for the baby and cradled her. "Isn't she a love?"

"You two will be neighbors when my daughter grows strong enough to go back to her own place," Alana said. "She lives just two doors from the apartment Edgar rented for you."

Grace smiled warmly at her new cousin. "We'll raise our kids together. I'm so glad to know you, Meg."

The photographer arrived and addressed Grace as Mrs. McCurdle, causing her to beam with happiness. The wedding party went to the front porch for a photograph session, with Del told to stand in front of Grace so her delicate condition wouldn't show. Afterward Alana brought out the platters of food, along with sandwiches for the children, who were sent outside to have a picnic. Del still wasn't allowed to join them.

Del and her mother filled their plates from the platters and took their food to the living room, where they joined Gramps with his plate. Mrs. Hannaford followed them, and, perched on a folding chair, managed to look like an aging queen on a throne. She asked Gramps what part of Maine he came from. Bangor, he told her.

When Gramps tried to smooth his hair, it bounced right back into snowy curls. He wiggled his moustache and explained, "My father was a lawyer."

"I'm a Coffin on my mother's side—once a Quaker family. You must have heard of us."

Gramps shook his head. "I left New England at age seven."

"I know nothing of the McCurdles," Mrs. Hannaford said. "What's their background?"

"I can tell you little, I'm afraid." Gramps stroked his pointed goatee. "Edgar's father, Nat, died young and I had little chance to discuss family matters with him."

"They were pioneers in Michigan," Millie said. "Edgar's grandfather was wealthy in his day. His two sisters, Nat's aunts, were lovely women—dead now, unfortunately. You'd have enjoyed meeting them, Mrs. Hannaford."

"From New England originally," Gramps added.

"I never heard the name McCurdle. Scottish, I suppose?"

"Oh, definitely. I've seen the plaid of the clan; I'll look it up for you." His brown eyes snapped with a secret humor, making Del wonder what could be funny about a clan plaid.

Mrs. Hannaford seemed unaware of the undercurrent of laughter. She said, "I'd love to see it. Now that my daughter is a McCurdle, I'll want to know—"

She was interrupted by shouts and commotion from the dining room. Gram hurried in.

"Mrs. Hannaford, you'd better come. I think it's your daughter's time."

Mrs. Hannaford put aside her half-eaten plate of food and rushed to the dining room. Del followed, and heard Grace admit she'd been suffering cramps and pains since early morning. "Didn't want to spoil the wedding by complaining, but they're—" She bent over and grimaced. "—they're hard now. I think they're the real thing."

Mrs. Hannaford grasped her arm. "We'll rush you to the hospital."

"Edgar's getting his truck," Gram said. "I sent Bea to the grocery store to call Doc Lapham on the telephone."

"So much for their honeymoon at the summer resort." Millie sighed.

Mrs. Hannaford hurried Grace upstairs to change out of her wedding gown. The others stood around ready to help if needed. Gram expressed the hope that all would go well. Alana consoled: "Don't worry, she's young, she'll have an easy time."

Alana and Gram began talking of their own childbirth adventures. Del and her mother followed Gramps back to the living room. As they sat down by their abandoned plates of food, Millie told Gramps, "You were outrageous, Dad. The plaid of Clan McCurdle! Really!"

Gramps theorized that the name appeared to be a misspelling of McCardle, so there probably was a plaid. He told Millie she was outrageous, too, calling Old Man McCurdle wealthy.

"But he *was* wealthy—from gambling."

"Cheating, you mean—skinning others alive. I hear the saloon keepers along the old Boardwalk used to dump him in the Grand River. Somehow, drunk as he was, he managed to swim back."

"I didn't know that."

"I was tempted to tell Hannaford that Rebecca's family came here shortly after the Pilgrims. It would have been hilarious to see her struggle with the name *Tiehl*. I wonder what she'd make of the Pennsylvania Dutch? Do they count as old American families?" He tilted up his nose and imitated a falsetto voice. "I'm sure I don't know any Tiehls. Pennsylvania, you say?"

Millie wondered how Edgar and Grace had found anything in common. Gramps told her they both attended the Unitarian young people's society.

"The Hannafords are Unitarian? I thought she said Quaker."

"That's Coffins. Hannafords are true blue Transcendentalists. You notice she hired the Unitarian minister."

The bride came downstairs wrapped again in her brown cape, and at Doug's urging, paused for a quick swipe at the wedding cake so it could be officially cut. Then she hurried to curbside to join Edgar, who was driving the truck. With no time for either the rice or the tin cans, everyone rushed outside to wave the couple away and wish Grace good luck.

There was a letdown after they'd departed. Slices of cake were eaten in silence. Mrs. Hannaford took a taxi to the hospital with a small suitcase filled with Grace's nightclothes and a few baby things hastily donated by Alana.

"I just hope everything goes well," Gram said. "Edgar's a different person since Grace arrived. I can hardly believe the change in him. He seems to have grown up overnight."

"I always said my son was a good kid," Aunt Vi told her. "A bit wild, perhaps—but who wants a namby-pamby boy?"

Del's mother remarked what a tease Edgar had been as a child. "He used to drive me crazy. But a good woman can change a man, or so they say."

The wedding notice appeared in the evening paper. At about eight o'clock, with the last guest gone, the family sat in the living room while Bea read the announcement aloud. When the doorbell rang, Del went to answer. With the western sun shining in her eyes, she barely managed to make out on the porch the small, pale, frightened-looking creature with protruding abdomen.

"I'm Patience Patterson." The woman spoke in a shy, barely audible voice. "I'm here to see Edgar."

"Edgar's gone," Del told her.

"Then could I talk to his mother, please?"

"His mother went home."

The woman seemed disconcerted. Though young, she appeared deformed. She asked, "His grandmother?"

Patience wore a loose, voluminous black dress which failed to hide the mound beneath. Del held the door open. "Come in, then."

For no apparent reason, she had a bad feeling about this visit. There was something about the visitor, a no-nonsense kind of persistence underlying her seeming diffidence. Del sensed trouble.

A waif in comparison to tall and stately Grace, the woman, seen in better light in the foyer, appeared to have a twisted spine which caused one shoulder to be lower than the other, her chest to heave out. With a crablike gait, she stepped into the living room, revealing an odd mixture of boldness and timidity. Del pointed to Gram, who came forward wiping her hands on her apron. The woman inched to the center of the room, not seeming intimidated by the other people: Gramps, Aunt Bea, Jenny, and Del's mother, all sitting on the folding chairs now arranged in a circle.

"My name is Patience Patterson." Struggling to do the impossible, straighten her spine and stand erect, the woman added in a firm voice, "I'm here to see Edgar."

She drew herself to her full four-foot-nine and lifted her chin. "I'm his fiancée, and we're to be married in two weeks. That wedding announcement in the paper was wrong. It's me, Patience—*I'm* the bride."

CHAPTER 6

Del

"The paper said, 'Edgar McCurdle and Grace Something,'" Patience explained to the astonished group in the living room. "I knew it had to be a mistake." She looked around, took in her surroundings, widened her eyes. "Except—flowers, gifts, altar." Suddenly her face crumpled toward tears. "It was no mistake, was it? You had a wedding here. But he can't—he promised me!" Her face became a mask of sorrow. She touched the stomach-bulge while a tear rolled down her cheek. "My Edgar, married to someone else?"

Gram looked nonplussed. "Edgar and Grace were married at noon, Miss—uh—Patterson. I'm sorry; we didn't know about you."

Patience swiped at her eyes with a finger. "He wouldn't let me meet his family. He claimed he wanted to surprise you all." She frowned, batted her eyes and clenched her fists. "He can't do this!" She held out a small but calloused hand to show off a ring with a tiny diamond. "I'm his fiancée; I'm carrying his baby."

Gram seemed speechless. Del marveled that Edgar had managed to scatter so much baby seed. Gramps put his arm around Gram, and together they confronted the visitor.

"You'll need to talk to Edgar, Miss Patterson," Gramps said. "We know nothing of his affairs. He doesn't confide in us."

More tears trickled down the blotchy face. The commanding stance collapsed. Looking small and shrunken, Patience searched her pockets, brought out a handkerchief, and wiped her eyes. "Where is he, then? Where is he?"

"He's at the hospital. His new wife's baby is on its way into the world right now."

"Oh, that can't be! Edgar wouldn't—my Edgar—she's lying. I'll find him!" She thrust out her chin and turned back toward the door.

"Hold on, they won't let you into the maternity ward. Best you wait until morning. Edgar will be here then."

Patience leaned against the wall, blew her nose with a loud honk, and switched from angry woman to heartbroken child. "How could he? How could he do this to me? The promises, the ring, my delicate condition—"

Gram repeated, "I'm so sorry, Miss Patterson."

"I'll sue!" Angry again, Patience clenched her fists and lumbered back to the foyer. "I'll get that woman for alienation of affection!"

She stomped out and slammed the door so hard the glass rattled. Del checked to make sure it hadn't broken. Gram and Gramps looked at one another in stunned silence.

"What do you know about that!" Gramps finally said.

"I know Edgar's in trouble. How could he have done that? He must have been seeing Patience right while he was seeing Grace."

Gramps sighed. "I truly believed Edgar had turned over a new leaf. He seemed a different person after Grace came."

Del's mother spoke up. "Shades of Nat McCurdle! If this is the new Edgar, he's not so new after all. A chip off the old block."

"However will we explain this to Grace?" Gram asked. "The poor child—at a time like this!"

"And that dreadful Hannaford woman," Mother added. "She'll think we're trash."

Gramps slumped into a chair. "I'm fed up. Eddie will have to work this one out for himself. No more Gramps to the rescue. I've felt sorry for Edgar because I know what it's like to grow up without a father—but this is too much."

Gram nodded. "Getting two women in the family way at once! Really!"

Edgar came home at two a.m. and aroused the household. When Del heard his voice from the front hall, she woke Jenny in the other bed and hurried downstairs followed by her cousin.

"It's a girl!" Edgar shouted, triumphant. "I have a daughter!"

Mother and Aunt Bea also came downstairs, tying their bathrobes, rubbing their eyes. Gram and Gramps came from their bedroom in nightclothes. Edgar stood in the dining room, where his unopened wedding presents still filled the corner.

"It's a girl," he repeated. "Six pounds eight ounces. Not a preemie at all, they must have miscalculated. She's beautiful. Gorgeous. Perfect. I can't believe she's mine!"

"Congratulations." Gramps straightened and squared his shoulders.

Though his voice had sounded dubious, Edgar, failing to notice, turned to Del. "We named her after you. Della Eloise."

Del reminded him, "My name is *Delia* Eloise. I'm named for my great-grandmother, Bedelia Kingsley, and for Mother's friend Eloise in the Woman Suffering movement."

"Suffrage," Mother corrected.

Edgar's face fell. "I got it wrong. Now it's on the birth certificate."

"Oh, well, let the kid have some individuality," Gramps said. "You can still call her Del."

"To save confusion we chose Weezy. Della Eloise—Weezy. Get it?"

Gram said, "Eddie, what have you done?" She wrung her hands. "We had a surprise visitor."

"Sit down, Ed, we have something to talk about." Gramps seated himself at the table and gestured for Edgar to join him.

Looking puzzled, Edgar slid into his usual chair. "What's up?"

"As your grandmother said, we had a visitor, a young woman named Patience Patterson."

"Ye gods!" Edgar paled.

"She seemed under the impression *she* was to be the bride. She's pregnant and claims to be carrying your child."

Edgar gulped, grimaced, and sighed. Mother told the two girls to go back to bed. Determined to hear Edgar's side of the affair, they went only as far as the stairway where they sat listening.

"Lord," Edgar said. "I didn't think she'd find out about it."

"It's hardly a secret. It's in the paper."

"I hoped she wouldn't read the notice."

"Women expecting to marry read wedding announcements. Come on, Eddie, what happened here? Patience claims she's your fiancée."

Edgar put his head in his hands. "Truth is, I felt sorry for her. She cried on my shoulder; she claimed her deformity made her ugly and no man would ever want her. Besides, I never dreamed I'd see Grace again. She's wealthy, she's beautiful, and she had a rich store owner for a fiancé. When Old Lady Hannaford dragged her off, it was exactly what I'd expected."

"You might have waited to find out if she'd come back to you."

"From a store owner to a construction worker? Come on, Gramps!"

"So this Patience is telling the truth? You consoled yourself with the woman and promised to marry her?"

"You could put it like that." Head in hands, Edgar spoke so softly Del had to strain to hear. "I bought her a ring."

"She threatens to sue for alienation of affection."

Edgar looked up in alarm. "Can she do that?"

"Of course she can do that. I don't know if she'd win, but I can tell you one thing for sure: you'll have to support that baby. Since your income won't cover two households, you need to search out another husband for Patience. Let's hope you have a noble friend who'll marry her to salvage her reputation."

"Are you kidding?" Edgar sounded despairing. "Patience is no raving beauty as you may have noticed."

When Del and Jenny headed for bed, Edgar was again sitting with head in hands. Gramps remarked to Mother, "Someone should write a book about this situation."

"Someone already has," Mother said. "Don't you read Theodore Dreiser?"

Patience arrived early next morning while Del stood in the kitchen waiting for Gram to brush her hair. Edgar stumbled downstairs, yawned, looked half awake but rebellious. Though glowering, he agreed to take Patience out for breakfast.

He returned later, long-faced, frowning, chewing his lip. Gramps asked if he'd straightened things out.

He shook his head and admitted that Patience claimed she'd sue. "It's just a threat. I don't think she'll go through with it. Costs money."

"Lawyers often take cases on a contingency basis."

This news caused Edgar to wince. "She better not sue. She'll spoil every-thing. Grace isn't the type to suffer through a lawsuit." He'd dressed in suit and tie, ready to go to the hospital to visit his new wife and daughter.

"I doubt Patience cares if she spoils everything. You'd better pray she finds another man real soon."

"Hell and damnation!" Edgar flung out of the house.

Grace remained in the hospital for the then standard period for new moth-ers, ten days. During all that time, nothing more was heard from Patience. Gram admitted to the family that she'd prayed the woman might find another husband, and fancied perhaps her fervent prayers had been answered. Edgar cheered up and visited the hospital every day after work. He seemed confident that something would happen to solve his problems. When asked, he admitted he hadn't found the courage to speak to Grace of Patience. "I won't unless I have to," he said.

The day came when he was to bring his little family home. It was planned that they would stay at Stormland for a few days until Grace was strong enough to climb the two flights of stairs to their new apartment. Meanwhile, Jenny and Del were to camp out in the tent and give the newlyweds their room.

While Edgar was gone, a black sedan pulled up at the curb. The two men within failed to step out. From the front window, Gram and Mother eyed the occupied car uneasily, asking one another who the strangers might be. Mother speculated that perhaps they should get Gramps from his shop out back and have him inquire. "They make me nervous just sitting there."

The men stayed. In time Edgar's truck drove up and parked behind them. Holding the baby, Edgar got out and helped Grace climb down from the high seat. Mother hurried outside and down the steps, followed by Del.

Mother had only just taken the blanket-wrapped baby from Edgar and settled it in her arms when the two men emerged from the car. They walked over to Grace, the taller one holding a paper which he thrust at her.

"Grace McCurdle?" he asked.

Grace nodded and looked at the paper. She gasped. "What do you mean, summons for a court appearance? And who on earth is Patience Patterson?" She thrust the paper toward the already-retreating strangers. "Hold on here, you've made a mistake. I know no one by the name of Patience Patterson."

The men ignored her and hastened to their car. She followed and demanded an explanation. The shorter one, from the seat beside the driver, rolled down his window to talk to her. "I understand Patience Patterson is Edgar McCurdle's fiancée."

The driver slammed his door and gunned the motor. The car rolled away. Grace stood by the curb, looking stunned, repeating, "His *fiancée*?"

Edgar flushed and clenched his fists. Mother opened her mouth and closed it again, seeming unable to think of anything to say. Everyone stood frozen. Mother held the baby. Grace clutched the summons. Edgar eyed his new wife nervously.

Grace broke the silence. "Edgar, what is this all about?"

Edgar straightened and squared his shoulders. "Ignore it, Grace. It's my former girlfriend trying to break us up. We can't let her do it."

"The man said she was your fiancée."

"She was, but…" His shoulders slumped. He ran his hands through his hair. "Honey, you must understand. I had no idea you'd come back. I thought you planned to marry that store-owner. You talked about him like—like it was all settled."

Grace read the summons more carefully and went white. "It says here she's six months pregnant."

"Yes, but—"

"Your child?"

He hung his head and didn't answer. She persisted. "Eight months ago I left for Boston, fancying you were my beau. All the time you had another girl-friend!"

"I didn't. It was afterward."

"Instantly afterward, like the very next day." She thrust the summons into his hand. "Oh, I must have been out of my mind to think I could rush back here and we'd live happily ever after. I've been naïve; I see it now." She took a deep breath. "Tell your Patience to call off her lawyers. I give you to her. I won't be a party to an alienation of affection suit."

She reached over Del's head to take the baby. "Give me the baby, Millie; I'm going to my mother at the Pantlind Hotel."

"First, come in and let's talk this over," Edgar pleaded.

"There's nothing to discuss. I'll have no part of a scandal and lawsuit. You're no better than a bigamist. I don't need a man who can't be faithful to me."

"Grace, will you just *listen*?"

"So you can talk me into ignoring your treat on the side? When all the time I worried that you were agonizing over our separation?" She opened the door of the truck. "I've been foolish but I woke up. You go back to your fiancée and I'll go back to mine."

"Grace, we're married."

"That can be remedied."

"You can't do this! Take away my child? My Weezy?"

"Can't I, though?" Grace reclaimed the crying baby, gently patted her to silence, and climbed up to place her again in the basket on the truck-seat. She hurried around to the driver's side, pulled herself up, and started the motor. She rolled down the window to call out, "I'll park the truck near the hotel. You can pick it up any time."

"Wait, let me drive you."

But Grace was already gunning the motor and pulling away from the curb. She drove to the corner, turned around, and headed in the opposite direction, toward Michigan Street. She flew past without even waving to the group gathered on the sidewalk.

"She has to come back, she's my wife," Edgar wailed. "I'll walk down to the Pantlind and talk to her, try to calm her down."

"What can you do, Eddie?" Millie asked him. "You can't change the facts."

"I'll remind her I love *her*, not Patience."

"You already communicated that. It didn't seem to move her."

"She can't do this," Edgar repeated. "She can't take my baby from me. Weezy is my child."

"You can sue for custody," Millie told him, "but I doubt you'd win. The court won't look favorably on a man who got two women in the family way at once."

He contrived a wavering smile. "Aw, this is a lovers' spat. I can fix it."

"I doubt that." Millie spoke emphatically. "Grace was shocked. I'm sure things like that don't happen in her world."

"But we're married. She's a McCurdle now. Everything was fine."

"Looks like it just got unfine," Millie said. "Edgar, you have a genius for getting your life wrong."

Despite Edgar's frantic pleas, Grace stuck to her decision and went home to Boston vowing that Edgar would never see her or the child again. When the notice of her suit for annulment was served, Gram and Vi tried without success to console the distraught young man. Del, who'd seen in Weezy the baby sister she'd always wanted, also mourned the loss.

Patience and Edgar were married. Patience's son was born dead. Everyone agreed it was for the best, since he proved to be badly deformed and would have faced many health problems. Yet Edgar was inconsolable, complaining he now had no child at all.

The train jolted Del back to the present, to Weezy opposite her. She blinked. The departure scene had been real and immediate. She struggled to bring herself back to the train with its clacking wheels. "Edgar was the spitting image of Marlon Brando," she said. "Are you familiar with Brando? He's in that famous Broadway play, *A Streetcar Named Desire*."

"I've heard so much about it," Weezy said. "My father must be handsome."

"Handsome is hardly the word for it," Del said. "He and Brando are both—well, smashing looking. Grace must have fallen hard."

"I can't wait to meet him," Weezy said.

CHAPTER 7

Weezy

Under the covers in her narrow bunk, Weezy wiggled her toes in rhythm with the clacking wheels of the train. In her mind she relived Del's story of her parents' brief shared life, from their bizarre meeting after Edgar crashed his motorcycle near Grace's easel to the dramatic denouement that changed her own life and deprived her of her Michigan family.

In time she drifted off to sleep, to be awakened around nine when the porter shouted out a last call for breakfast. She put on the blouse and skirt she'd worn the day before and, hair uncombed, staggered out to the hall, heading for the rest-room. Returning, she encountered Del in the corridor in a similar state of disarray. She remarked that they'd have to hurry to eat. "I just heard the last call."

"I was coming to get you," Del said. The train had slowed to a crawl and she peered out the window. "We're pulling into Toledo, and I had a brilliant idea. We'll transfer here to a Michigan train and stop off in Battle Creek. You can meet your father."

Weezy panicked. "Ooh—I'm not ready for that! Not right now! I've had no chance to—I mean, I'm still learning about—" Her mouth went dry; her stomach churned. She couldn't imagine herself walking up to Edgar as if he were just an ordinary person. What would she say?

Del looked alarmed. "Hey, don't judge Edgar by what happened twenty years ago. I'd feel awful if I thought I'd influenced you against him."

"It's not you, it's—I lack facts." Actually, she was plain scared. "I don't yet know enough about him. Did he stay with Patience?"

"Yes, and Patience was hard as nails. Wouldn't let Edgar get close—I mean, the doctor warned her not to have more children, so she refused to—well, you know."

Preoccupied and inattentive Jonathan may have been, but he'd remained, to all appearances, devoted to his wife. His standard of behavior had become Weezy's guide. Having trouble coming to terms with this very different father named Edgar McCurdle, she hadn't anticipated an imminent encounter. She was struggling not to be shocked by his double life with double girlfriends.

"Must I meet Patience?" she asked.

Del shook her head. "She died years ago. A frail woman."

"Edgar married again, I suppose?"

"No, you're still an only child. Edgar's back to being a foreman at the family construction business—after years of war work at Willow Run. He's wildly popular with women but—it seems he's given up on marriage. Claims he lacks the knack for it."

The train lurched. Both young women grabbed the hand-rail. As the cars slowed to a halt, Weezy peered out at the roofed waiting area. Her stomach roiled. She insisted, "I don't want to rush this meeting. I need to prepare."

Del warned that the Langstons might influence her judgment. "They certainly influenced mine. I think it best you meet Edgar first, and judge him for yourself." After a final lurch to a stop, she too peered out, and then turned back to ask, "Well? Stay or go?"

Passengers with luggage emerged from compartments. Weezy gathered her courage and made a quick decision. She would have to meet Edgar sometime; might as well get it over with. "What the hell, let's go. I haven't even combed my hair—"

"We can do our hair and makeup on the other train." Del grasped her arm. "Our luggage will be held for us in Grand Rapids."

Weezy ran to her compartment and with trembling fingers stuffed her night-clothes into her carryall case. She met Del at the exit and they climbed off together. The conductor informed them that the Michigan train had just come in on the other track. They had barely enough time to rush into the station and change their tickets. Holding their hats against a strong wind, they raced down the platform and into the building. Weezy's hand shook as she slid her ticket across the counter; she wondered if she were making the right decision. Too late to change her mind, however. Their cross-country train pulled out of the station. It was time to board the other and select a seat.

The new train, a local with no diner, did have a club car where they were told they might buy sandwiches at lunchtime. Meanwhile, the coach attendant offered coffee. They went into the restroom to comb their hair and put on makeup. Del consulted the schedule posted on the wall.

"We go through Ann Arbor, my old college town," she said. "You may have to hold me down to prevent me from getting off."

Weezy wished she could look back so fondly on her college years. Brushing her hair before the small mirror, she tried, through choking anxiety, to act calm and collected. What if she didn't like Edgar? And worse, what if he didn't like her or didn't want to see her again?

Del asked if she'd been unhappy at Smith. Weezy forced herself to focus on the question. "I majored in a field not my choice. I hoped to please my fa—uh—Jonathan."

"What field?"

"Social work. Not a job I really wanted." She smiled ruefully. "After four years slaving at a major I cared little about, I came home to learn that the man I tried to please wasn't my real father. I may never get over the shock of it."

Del smiled. "I'm tempted to spout a platitude about pleasing yourself rather than others." The train swayed; her lipstick smeared. She wiped it off and started over. She asked, "Why was Jonathan so enamored of social work?"

"It was an appropriate field for a woman, and besides, he was known in town for community service. I fancied that if I followed in his footsteps, he'd notice me. Now I know why I failed. Putting up with me was the price he paid to get my mother."

"Oh, Weezy, I'm sorry." Del snapped her lipstick-tube shut and reached out to squeeze the arm Weezy'd raised for hair brushing. "I wondered how that situation played out."

Weezy didn't choose to recall the pain of those years. She realized it must have been difficult for Jonathan, too, having to accept and raise an unwanted child not his own. She'd think about him eventually. But right now she had her hands full with events in the present. After a few strokes, she replaced her hairbrush and snapped her case shut. "Are you ready? Shall we go back?"

Del nodded and followed her out to the corridor. At their seats, the car-attendant handed them cups of coffee, "With cream and sugar, as ordered." Del thanked him and added a tip to the payment.

Holding the steaming cup, Weezy tried without success to relax and enjoy the scenery, the spring green of the fields. She confided that she was terrified. "What if we don't like each other?"

Del urged her to give it time. "People don't instantly fall into a close relationship after so many years. You'll need to spend days together, develop shared memories."

"No doubt you're right." Though Weezy had sometimes fantasized that she'd been adopted, in her mind she'd provided herself with wealthy birth parents, usually famous actors for whom a baby would interfere with their careers. She'd speculated that her love of drama and playwriting had been inherited from them.

"I hope I didn't make a mistake in telling you all that garbage about Edgar," Del said.

"I'm glad you told me," Weezy asserted. "From now on I want only the truth, even if it's shocking. I'll come to terms with it."

"This train arrives in Battle Creek about noon," Del remarked. "Perhaps we can lunch with Edgar."

Weezy nodded and fought her fears.

At Ann Arbor, Del sent a telegram to Alana to notify her of their late arrival. Weezy climbed off with her, "Just to make sure you get back on," she explained.

Laughing, Del admitted that she could stay in Ann Arbor forever. Weezy told her she had no such fond memories of college. When they were back aboard the train, moving on, she added, "I only managed to sneak in two classes I cared about—Shakespeare and Contemporary Drama. I'd hoped to study creative writing with Mary Ellen Chase, but Jonathan scoffed."

"Why? What's wrong with being a writer?"

"He considered it self-indulgent—though he put up with Mother's art work. I never understood that. Why is it all right to capture life in paint but not in words?" Weezy closed her eyes and thought back to the days when she wrote in her room with the door closed and hid her manuscripts under the bed. "I threw away all my stories and plays the moment I decided to be a McCurdle instead of a Ward."

Del frowned. "You should never discard your past."

Weezy wondered if she'd been too hasty. Perhaps she should have waited to meet her new family. At the time, she'd been making a statement, expressing her determination to embrace her authentic background whatever it might prove to be. Now she suspected it might have been wiser to pick and choose, selecting the best from each, and not to assume that what Grace left had been better than what she rushed home to.

She sighed. "I jumped in with both feet and now I have to take the consequences."

Del leaned her seat back and announced that since the night had been short, she wanted to have a nap before arriving. Weezy would have loved to do likewise, but her emotions denied sleep. While the train jiggled onward, she eyed passing fields and woodlands and recalled her dreams of being a writer, how she'd deliberately turned her back on them in hopes of winning Jonathan's approval. A futile sacrifice. She could have studied any field she chose. She wondered if Edgar would be more sympathetic to her writing dreams. Though it was tempting to picture him as supportive, she cautioned herself not to build up unrealistic hopes.

She occupied herself with trying to visualize the meeting with Edgar, how he'd react to the discovery that his lost daughter was found. Would he be happy or would he feel he should have been notified in advance and given time to prepare? Or might he hold against her what Grace did, walking out on him? She worried that perhaps she'd made the wrong decision. When the train went through the city of Jackson, she looked out the window and tried to place her thoughts elsewhere, to imagine what life was like here.

When, after what seemed an interminable time but was probably only an hour, Del awoke and stirred, shifting her position, Weezy said, "Let me get everyone straight now." She raised her hand to count on her fingers. "Your mother is Millie, right? Edgar's mother, my grandmother, is Violet. His step-dad—"

"Don Dexter."

"And my grandfather was—?"

"Nat McCurdle. He died in his thirties. Liver trouble."

"And Aunt Alana is sister-in-law to Millie and Violet?"

"Yes, she married their brother, Menno. I know it's a lot of people to keep track of."

When the conductor announced lunch, Weezy confessed she was glad they'd postponed eating until they met Edgar. "I couldn't swallow anything, I'm so jumpy."

Del studied her curiously. "Edgar won't blame you for what Grace did."

"The man's a stranger, Del. How do you talk to a stranger who's your father?"

The conductor called out, "Battle Creek." The train pulled into the station. Weezy stood on shaky legs, grabbed her carryall case from overhead, and followed her cousin down the aisle. The conductor helped them off, and a cool breeze toyed with their hair. No escape now. Del slung her purse over her shoulder and tucked her overnight case under the arm that held her hatbox, leaving her hand free to grasp Weezy's arm. While Weezy fought the urge to jump back aboard and travel on, Del guided her cousin across the platform.

Sensing her reluctance, Del consoled. "Don't worry. Whatever Edgar may think, he'll be nice to you."

They hailed one of the waiting taxis and climbed in. Del asked for the sanatorium.

"It ain't the San no more," the driver told her. "It's just a hospital these days."

"Is that a fact?" Del settled her bag beside her on the seat while Weezy, with shaking fingers, stowed hers on the floor.

The cab moved through town. The driver reminisced about the "San," saying it had been big in Doc Kellogg's day. "Celebrities came here, movie stars and the like. It's mainly a place now for drunks to dry out." He pulled up before a once-elegant building now looking merely old fashioned. Del paid him, and again took Weezy's arm to guide her. At the front desk, the attendant rang Edgar's room but received no answer.

"He may be on the veranda," she said. "It's a lovely day."

Weezy realized she'd been too nervous to notice either the weather or the town. They followed directions and went to a shady veranda overlooking a pond with ducks.

"There he is!" Del led her shivering, reluctant companion past people in deck chairs.

Weezy could hardly breathe. She saw everything as a blur. She could focus only on the patient in blue bathrobe Del had pointed out.

"Cousin Edgar!" Del called. When he turned his head, she said, "Remember me? I'm your cousin Del."

Thin and drawn, the man wore the robe over tan-striped pajamas. With his thick brown hair, he looked younger than Weezy had imagined him. As Del promised, he was handsome. Weezy thought of fathers as balding, middle-aged gentlemen with a paunch and an overlarge nose like Jonathan's. This man, who had to be her mother's age, forty or so, could easily have passed for early thirties.

Though Del said, "Don't get up," Edgar extracted himself from the chaise and stood. Weezy wasn't sure he recognized his cousin; he smiled timidly, first at Del, then Weezy. Weezy recalled Del's comment about his charm. He certainly had it, and more, a kind of vulnerable quality. She saw at once why her mother had been smitten.

"Del Kingsley, is it really you? What a surprise! Last I heard, you were in New York—or was it California?" He reached out both hands to her.

"New York. My folks are in California." She set down her bag and they hugged. Edgar asked, "What lured you to the middle of the country?"

"I've brought someone to meet you, Edgar." She stepped back to let him see Weezy. "This will be a *real* surprise. I hope you have a strong heart."

"It's only my liver that gives me trouble." He studied Weezy curiously. She felt pierced by his blue-eyed gaze. She thought her quaking knees might let her down.

"Edgar, may I present your daughter, Della Eloise McCurdle," Del said.

Edgar blinked, frowned, turned from Weezy to Del. "Come on, you're kidding. Don't do this to me."

"Hey, I'm no practical joker, Eddie. Take a good look. She's the spit and image of Gram when young. She has the Tiehl eyes, pixie-slanted."

"You're really not kidding?" He studied Weezy again.

Weezy told him, "It's true, I'm Weezy." Tears flooded her eyes; her voice choked. "Grace—Grace Ward's daughter. From Boston. I'm told that—that you named me."

Edgar's eyes misted. He passed his hands over them, smoothed his wind-blown hair, and stepped toward her. He started to thrust out a hand, changed his mind, and reached for her with both hands. "Come closer, then, and give your old man a hug."

Tears threatened as Weezy moved into the arms of the man who, she now felt, should have been her father all along. She smelled his after-shave. He drew her tight against him. She returned the hug and batted her eyes, fighting emotion.

"I can't believe this. I thought I'd never see you again." Edgar's voice broke.

"I didn't even know about you," she confessed. "They didn't tell me." Her own voice grew unsteady. She hugged him tighter and let the tears fall. "I'd have come sooner if I'd known." Her voice, too, broke as she added, "Oh, Dad, can this be real? I just can't take it in. I have a father!"

"And I have a daughter!" he said.

CHAPTER 8

Del

Though Del hadn't admitted the fact to Weezy, she'd been apprehensive about this meeting. She knew no one could second-guess Edgar. Charming when he chose to be, he could as easily simmer with hidden anger. Again, he displayed a silly streak and loved to clown. At those moments there was no sobering him; everything tickled his funny bone; he could laugh at burning buildings.

Del's mother often remarked, of her days at Stormland where she grew up, "I never cared what Edgar did, but always wished he'd do it elsewhere, away from me."

Seeing Edgar teary, Weezy fumbling for a handkerchief and dabbing at her eyes, Del suppressed a sigh of relief and wiped her own eyes. Edgar's questions tumbled out faster than Weezy could answer them. "What's been happening all these years? Do you still live in Boston? Is Grace okay? Does she still paint? Didn't she ever mention me at all? No, you said you didn't know about me—so I guess not."

Through her tears Weezy managed a smile. "Yes to those first questions, we live and Boston and she paints, and no—she never mentioned you. I was furious with her when I found out. I'm still furious. Family secrets are—unforgiveable. Not to know half your family—it's terrible. I mean, I'd have come here long ago if I'd known."

Edgar spoke sadly. "She blamed me for our breakup. I kept hoping she'd forgive me eventually and get in touch." He pulled himself together and tried to be a good host. He asked if his guests had eaten, and when they shook their heads, he offered to send down to the hospital kitchen for extra lunches. Anticipating exorbitant charges for such services, Del suggested they all go out to lunch instead. "We should go somewhere fancy and celebrate. They *do* allow you to leave here, don't they?"

"Sure. I'd love to go out with you. I'll need to dress. Where are you girls off to?"

When they mentioned the family reunion in Grand Rapids, he at once announced he'd go along. "You can't leave me out of such a grand occasion!"

"Is it all right?" Weezy was still wiping her eyes with a hanky. "Healthwise, I mean?"

With a shrug, he declared he'd checked himself in and could check himself out. "It's not prison." He grasped her arm and Del's to move them along. "If I should be tempted to sneak a drink, I'll have two beautiful young women to break the glass and hide the booze. Two is all I need."

"I've heard that once you start, an army can't stop you," Del reminded him while they walked.

"That was then, this is now. I'm on the wagon, permanently. Haven't forgotten what happened to my dad, dead at thirty-seven, four years younger than yours truly. Believe me, I have no wish to follow in his footsteps. We're dead a long time; no use hurrying the process."

"It'll be great to have you with us," Weezy said. "It'll be perfect. We're staying two nights, and could bring you back on our way home Sunday afternoon."

Edgar looked at his watch. "We can catch the 2:10. We'll walk in on Ma and Alana and surprise them." When Del reminded him about lunch, he suggested they get sandwiches in the club car. He stopped to notify the clerk at the desk that he'd be away.

While he went to his room, the two women waited in the lobby, Weezy collapsing into a chair and holding the handkerchief to her eyes. Del kept quiet and let her process her thoughts.

Edgar returned nattily dressed in brown jacket, tan trousers, tan-and-brown striped tie. Del saw that the years had been kind; he'd grown, if anything, more handsome. Though pale and thin, he sported his old debonair manner. Illness hadn't really changed him. When Weezy rallied and even failed to suppress a smile, Del realized with joy that her cousin felt proud of this newfound father. Apparently she'd forgiven him for his unfaithfulness to her mother.

A doctor came to talk to Edgar. Weezy waited with Del by the door and in a whisper confessed her excitement at finding herself with such a handsome dad.

"You were so right about his good looks." She drew back with a sudden look of alarm. "You don't suppose this trip might be too much for him?"

Del reassured her that more likely it would be good. He had something to live for.

Del had put on her large-brimmed hat, which, on rejoining the women, Edgar noticed and admired. "You've turned sophisticated, Del. I wouldn't have known you if you hadn't identified yourself."

Edgar opened the door and, with a flourish, held it for them. When Weezy asked what the doctor had said, Edgar shrugged. "The usual medic talk: 'Don't eat, don't drink, don't overindulge.' Doctors feel compelled to say those things."

On the steps, he hailed a taxi and again held the door for the women. While they drove to the station, Weezy asked about his illness. He admitted he'd gone on a drinking binge and precipitated a liver attack. "I'll never do that again; I'm not suicidal."

"If ever you need help to resist drinking, call me and I'll come," Weezy said.

Seated between the two young women, Edgar squeezed Weezy's hand. "It's great to have a daughter. I feel so lucky. You're—um—nineteen now?"

"Twenty one. I just graduated from Smith College."

"Smith! Sounds Bostonian and impressive. I'll want to hear all about your life, the years I missed out on. You, too, Del. How's everything with you?"

It was not the moment to discuss her problems. Del sensed Edgar really wanted to know about Weezy and Grace, and had asked about her only to be polite. She lied, "Things are okay. I have a job in a museum."

He persisted. "I heard you were getting married. What happened?"

"Heavens, Edgar, that was ages ago. Four or five years at least."

"That long? I guess I lost track of time. Any new heartthrob?"

Del couldn't talk about Hilario. Even the thought of her glamorous Catalan folk dancer sent a wave of depression sweeping over her. Such an attractive, desirable man, but for some undefined reason, not available for marriage, or so his many admirers claimed—and apparently it was true. Things had seemed so promising at first, but drifted into incomprehensible immobility. She'd lain awake nights pondering why they didn't move forward.

She spoke instead of Bradley. "That awful second guessing: Do I really want to spend a lifetime with this man? When I couldn't decide if I did or didn't, I opted for saying no. It seemed the safest."

Edgar admitted he'd felt sorry for her mother. "Millie so looked forward to you coming home to marry that guy. She used to rave about him."

"Well, Mom's a musician and she hoped to have another musician in the family. But that's old news now. Bradley married someone else."

"Wow, I *am* behind the times." He shook his head. "Your folks like California?"

"They love it—too much. I doubt we'll ever get them back here."

"Now that Gram and Gramps are gone, they have little reason to come back. Stormland without Gram and Gramps is a house without a soul. Of course, Alana and Menno are there—but it's not the same." Edgar turned to Weezy. "Someday, my dear, Del and I must tell you about Stormland."

Weezy admitted that Del already had. Edgar flushed and eyed Del uneasily, as if he feared the story hadn't been complimentary to him. She reassured him. "Just the facts, Edgar. I was too young to understand the intricacies."

They'd reached the station. Edgar went to buy a ticket. While they all sat on a bench in the shade, awaiting the train, Edgar quizzed Weezy about Grace. Weezy urged him to go to Boston to visit. "Mom's a widow now."

"That bossy mother's still living?" Waving his hands as if to brush away flies, he said he'd do no more bumping against that brick wall. "The old lady's too intimidating. She ripped us apart. But I wish Grace well. You did say she still paints?" He added, as Weezy nodded, "When I first met your mother in Saugatuck, Old Baldy dune was sitting for its portrait, holding so still it didn't even let the sand blow on its bare head." He sounded wistful. "I was impressed with her talent."

Weezy gazed at him with a startled expression. "That painting hangs over our mantel. I wondered why she valued it so highly. She's done better work."

Clicking his tongue, Edgar marveled, "So it really did mean something to her!"

"Are you kidding? No woman forgets her first love." Weezy made the assertion with such vehemence that Del turned to study her. The comment had sounded too heartfelt to be casual. Did Weezy, too, have an unforgettable first love?

Thinking back to their night on the train, Del realized that she'd done most of the talking and had learned little about her companion. She eyed her new-found cousin, hoping for a hint of what might be hidden behind the poised exterior. She saw only the excitement of the moment, face flushed, expression eager, hair not as smoothly brushed as usual.

The train pulled in. They boarded, bought sandwiches and drinks from the club car, and took facing seats. Del rode backward in order to allow Weezy and Edgar to sit side by side. Weezy talked to her father about her college years, describing for Edgar her frustration at missing out on longed-for studies because of her stepdad's wishes—or demands. She made no mention of social life or boyfriends. Del wondered how to broach the subject without seeming to pry. She suspected that Grace and Mrs. Hannaford must have caused Weezy's reticence. No doubt they were tartars around their sole chick.

Edgar echoed Del's thought. "I'll be surprised if your Grandma Hannaford doesn't rush out here and snatch you from us."

"Unlike my mother, I'm not easy to snatch," Weezy assured him.

"I hope not; I can't go through that again." Edgar sighed and shook his head grimly.

Del looked out the window at the familiar scenery of her home state, the farmlands, the oak and maple trees and white pines, a pond gleaming blue against the greenery. An occasional sand dune reminded her of the proximity of Lake Michigan. She'd passed through this countryside many times during Sunday outings in her childhood, and remembered every detail. She remembered, too, her adolescent visits here with Bradley. She forced those out of her mind and thought of Stormland, where she hadn't been since Gramps' funeral six years before. She worried that indeed the place would seem to lack soul. All her memories included Gram and Gramps.

On arrival in Grand Rapids, the trio took a cab which stopped at the curb below the house. Stormland! Del stood below the embankment looking up at it. It seemed unchanged, looming behind the great chestnut tree Del and Jenny had played under as children. It would always be home to her. She led the way up the steps and past the maple tree near the dining room window, the rhubarb patch, the bald spot in the grass where the swing had been. She instinctively bypassed the front porch with its trumpet vine and headed to the kitchen entrance always used by the family.

The trio went single file along the narrow walkway, Del first, followed by Weezy, then Edgar. For a brief moment, Del felt choked with memories. It seemed she could, if she listened closely, hear familiar voices calling across the years, Gram urging Edgar to take off his heavy shoes so as not to scratch her polished floors, Gramps scolding Del for painting a sign on the door of his watch-repair shop out back proclaiming: This Is a Home-Owned Shoppe.

The familiar fragrance of simmering strawberries came from the kitchen, along with a companionable sound of women's voices. Stepping onto the porch, Del almost forgot to knock. It seemed natural to open the screen door and rush in. She had to remind herself the house was Alana's now.

She called out. "Hello! Aunt Alana, we're here!"

"Del!" The screen door flew open. Alana stood there with Vi behind her, both women with gray hair tucked into buns, wiping hands on aprons just as Gram used to do. Del hugged her two aunts. Alana gave her a peck on the cheek and told her she'd have met her at the station if she'd known what time she'd come. Then she looked past her niece and shouted. "Edgar! What a surprise!"

Vi, suddenly teary, rushed to embrace her son, saying it was great to see him, yet at the same time protesting. "Edgar, you shouldn't have—. It's too soon for you to—. We planned to call you."

"I'm okay, Ma," Edgar insisted. "Long as I watch my diet—and no drinks." He hugged Vi, then reached out to Alana and embraced both women.

Vi had grown chubbier since Del had last seen her. She'd once been a local beauty, invited to the homes of wealthy socialites in the company of the up-and-coming bank clerk she'd dated before she married Natty Nat McCurdle. She still retained the Gibson Girl face and shapely legs. Only her middle had become roly-poly.

Vi now eyed, somewhat shyly but with curiosity, the young woman hovering behind her son. Edgar stepped aside and drew his companion forward. "Ma, here's our Weezy. Isn't it great? We have her back!"

Vi moved forward and enfolded her granddaughter in an all-encompassing hug. "Weezy! We last saw you as a newborn at the hospital. I can hardly believe this! It's so wonderful! I'm your grandmother, by the way." She stepped aside. "This is your Aunt Alana."

Unlike Vi of the shapely arms and legs, Alana was uniformly portly and solid.

She too clasped Weezy tightly. "We feared we'd never see you again, dear." As Edgar had done, Weezy hugged both women. "Hello, Grandmother. Hello, Aunt Alana. This is so wonderful! Del's been telling me about you both."

"I can't believe your mother never told you," Vi said. "Grace seemed so—well, smitten with Edgar. I can't think how she managed to eliminate him and all of us from her memory."

"I don't think she eliminated you from memory—just from her conversation. I got the feeling she remembered everything but didn't know how to talk about it."

"It shouldn't have been that hard," Alana said. "She and Edgar were properly married. It's not like she had to speak of illegitimacy—unless of course she mentioned Patience."

"Well, Patience was a part of the story," Vi said. "Unfortunately—for all of us. Oh, if only she hadn't been! She deprived me of a grandchild."

When they entered the house, Weezy exclaimed over the fruit odors. "The kitchen smells so good! I do wish I could have spent summers here! Del says this was my great-grandmother's home for many years."

"I'm sure she still sits in her rocking chair," Alana said. "They say it rocked with no one in it the night she died. Since her spirit laid claim to it, we've left it in the living room for her."

Edgar brought in the overnight cases, banging the screen door behind him as he'd done all the years Del had known him. He asked if the chair had ever rocked since then.

Alana shook her head. "I can't say the house is haunted, though I'm sure Rebecca would be a benign ghost." When Del mentioned that their bags were still at the station, Alana promised that Uncle Menno would drive down for them later. "Del, you and Weezy are to share the room at the top of the stairs. Edgar can have the back bedroom."

True to her Boston upbringing, Weezy made the polite offer. "If we're crowding you here, Del and I can go to a hotel."

Alana's eyes widened in horrified protest. "Weezy, dear, we never send relatives to a hotel. Not even if we have to bring out rollaways and sleeping bags."

"Especially not long-lost relatives," Vi added. "Not in a million years."

"I feel lucky to be made so welcome." Weezy squeezed her aunt's arm. "Del told me about the way my mother stormed off without a farewell to any of you. I'm surprised you even want to hear the name Ward."

"You're not to blame for what your mother did. We're just happy you're here."

Vi echoed, "My house is just up the street and it's your home, too, dear. You can come any time." Weezy promptly offered another hug and murmured her appreciation.

As they moved on into the living room, where indeed Gram's rocker still sat, Del noticed subtle changes. A new print over the couch sported a still-life of flowers. In Gram's day a somber painting of a house dark at dusk had hung there, prompting young Del to ask Gram why the residents didn't come home and put on a light. Gram had studied the painting and speculated. "Perhaps their child died, and they can't bear to return to the place where it played so happily." Trust Gram to come up with a sad story.

While behind her Vi and Alana both talked at once, asking questions about Grace and about how Weezy had learned of her birth family, Del looked around. Gram's ferns still graced the front window, and her old wind-up Victrola sat beside her rocking chair, sharing space with a modern Crosley radio. Some of Millie's opera records still occupied the cabinet shelves—old time recordings of Caruso and Galli-Curci, the music of Del's infancy. A wave of nostalgia washed over her.

Though the two aunts seemed insatiable in their questioning, the young women did finally manage to make their getaway and carry their overnight bags upstairs. Del led the way to the room under the eaves and waved an arm at slanting ceiling, gable windows, morning-glory wallpaper, and dust-ruffled twin beds. She pointed. "Jenny slept in that bed, and this one was mine. Oh, look—here are the Petoskey stones I left behind when I went to New York!" She grabbed from a shelf two small spotted stones, highly polished. "They're fossil coral. I collected them when I lived in northern Michigan in my childhood. They're my centering and grounding pieces; they remind me who I am."

Weezy studied the stone and remarked that she wished she might have been in Michigan to collect stones like that. "Stormland sounds such fun. All those cousins. I never had playmates. I used to practice hopscotch all by myself to get good so the older kids up the street would let me play with them." Summer vacations, she recalled, had seemed endless and lonely.

Del held out the stones. "Here, these will be yours—to remind you of your roots. I polished them myself with steel wool. They're found only in Michigan—Little Traverse Bay—and they're the Michigan state stone."

"Thanks, Cousin. They're beautiful; I'll cherish them." Weezy studied the two small stones in her hand, then secreted them in her purse. "I can't forgive Mother for robbing me of a childhood here. I'd have joined you every summer."

Del commented that poor Grace was under her mother's thumb. "I sympathize; I have one of those powerful mothers."

For Del, coming home reminded her of Bradley. Aware he lived only a few blocks away, she tried to forget about him.

That wasn't to be. When she went downstairs, Alana said, "Come to the kitchen, Del. I need to talk to you about Bradley."

CHAPTER 9

Del

Del felt not at all eager to talk about Bradley, but she assumed Alana was merely trying to give Weezy time alone with her new-found father and grandmother. Though she'd never canned anything, she offered to help with canning. She thanked Alana for saving her Petoskey stones, and followed her aunt to the fruit-fragrant kitchen, where bubbling preserves and sterilized jars waited in readiness. "Mother always chose to do things herself rather than take the time to teach me," she explained.

"That's Millie." Alana pressed her lips together and shook her head. "She moves at the speed of light. Always did. No patience." She gestured toward the table. "Sit, have coffee. I don't need help. I've done canning since I was eight years old."

Del poured and creamed a cup of coffee. She slid into a chair at the oilcloth-covered table, and glancing around, missed the bowl of cucumbers in vinegar which had always graced it. A part of the seven sweets and seven sours Mennonites kept available, they were obviously no tradition in Alana's Irish family. She scooped out sugar, reached for a spoon, turned to watch her aunt at the stove, and awaited enlightenment.

Alana glanced back at her, hesitated, and finally blurted, "A week ago I had another phone call from Bradley."

Del's eyes widened in surprise. Her hand paused on her cup. "Why is Bradley calling here now he's married?"

"Not married any longer. His wife went to Reno. It caused questions and scandal so he's leaving his church job." She glanced at Del apologetically. "I should have written you but I'm so bad about letter-writing. Gossip has it his wife felt she was living all these years with a ghost. Bradley never forgot you."

The words made Del squirm. Bradley divorced! A can of worms reopened, hard decisions to be made over again! She voiced a protest. "Come on, Alana, we parted four years ago. Nearly five. Bradley can't still be carrying the torch."

"I only know he phoned twice wanting your address. I refused to give it without your permission, but I got his phone number so you can contact him if you choose. When I learned you were coming, I called him. He claims he can't wait to see you again."

A stifling tightness constricted Del's chest. She wailed, "Alana, I don't need to open old wounds. I have a life in New York; I'm dating a handsome folk dancer named Hilario Soler." *At least I hope I am. I pray I haven't become another of his ex-girlfriends.*

Blinking at her niece's distress, Alana calmly explained that New York was where Bradley would be going. "He's to be Minister of Music at some big church there."

Elbows on the table, a gesture she knew Emily Post wouldn't approve, Del slumped and put head in hands. She closed her eyes, forced herself to relax, sipped her coffee, and recalled the tall young man with the straight brown hair who'd been her choirmaster. He'd provided a thrill by singling her out as the girl he wanted to date. Yet even then, and even when he'd proposed and given her a diamond ring, she'd sensed that her choirmaster-crush was adolescent. Slick, proper, free of tears of either joy or sorrow, the affair was a movie role and she an actress. She'd felt flattered by his regard but without passion.

The women of the family were split in their opinions of that situation. Aunt Vi and Alana believed a woman should feel passionate about a man. Aunt Bea and Del's mother claimed that passion came with time, and women had to learn the feeling.

"He meant to drop in and surprise you," Alana said. "I urged him to call first. You'll need to plan what to say."

Remembering her vow to herself, Del asserted, "That requires no planning. I'll say you can't revive a dead relationship."

Alana, her wooden spoon held aloft and dripping fruit-juice onto the stove, gazed at her niece with widened eyes. "It's that dead, then? No left-over regrets after such a long engagement?"

"None at all." A lie, of course. The subject was still painful. She'd spent years wondering, *did I do the right thing or was I foolish?* Her mother accused her of imitating Cousin Jenny, who always considered herself too good for the men she met. This man was too skinny or had warts, that one sported a gross nose or prominent Adam's apple. Insisting that her perfect knight would come if she but waited, Jenny made fun of them all. Now, at thirty-six, the woman was stuck in a tedious job plugging in phone lines on one of Ma Bell's exchanges, her dreams grown ridiculous. Del shuddered at the thought she might be following in her cousin's footsteps, with a job leading nowhere, a folkdance partner who lacked interest in marriage, and a future as a spinster.

Just before dinner, the call came. On the other end of the wire, Bradley sounded excited at hearing her voice. She didn't remember him that way; she remembered his importuning, his perpetual urging that she should abandon her career dreams and marry him.

The timbre of his voice had deepened, suggesting greater maturity. "Del, I've thought of you so often. I hope to see you and catch up on all the years."

She tried to speak her rehearsed response: Come on, Bradley, you know the dead can't be raised. We both need to forget the past and move on. Instead, she heard her own voice say, "Drop by if you wish."

Insane. Why did she offer that invitation? Well, she'd be formal, ask about his new job, tell him about her newfound cousin. They'd share reminiscences, not renewal.

"We'll drive to the lake," he said. "I recall you loved the dunes."

Bad scene. Summer evenings were beautiful at the dunes and lakeshore. Too romantic; she'd be sucked in. She cautioned herself to say no, but the word stuck in her throat.

"Be ready at seven-thirty so we'll be there in time to watch the sunset." His obvious excitement added to her alarm. She hung up furious with herself for failing to object to such a seductive plan. Her mouth went dry thinking of the forthcoming evening.

Keep things impersonal, she scolded herself. Talk about his ex-wife, the breakup, his current girlfriend. Be a chum, not a sweetheart. You don't need this involvement.

With the family gathered at Gram's familiar oak table for dinner, Del maintained an uneasy silence, letting her brown-haired cousin carry the conversation. When Alana effortlessly, without embarrassment, quizzed Weezy about boyfriends, Del tried to focus on the response. Weezy explained, "There's no one special at the moment. That was another issue my father and I locked horns about. The men he selected didn't interest me. Those I liked, I was forbidden to date. There was an Irish boy, Catholic of course—"

"This Jonathan sounds like Old Lady Hannaford," Edgar commented.

Weezy remarked that the end of Jonathan's life meant the beginning of hers. She was free now, free for a new family, new vocation, new men. "I can have the career I want and the man I fall in love with." Her face flushed with excitement again. "The Petoskey stones Del gave me will be a reminder of that; they'll prod me to have the courage to assert myself."

Del managed a smile. A life unencumbered by parental pressures sounded wonderful. Even a continent away from her own parents, she'd never felt free of those pressures. She spoke up. "You could come to New York and be my roommate."

"Thank you, Cousin, I may do that." Weezy returned the smile. "I love the sound of those words, cousin, aunt, uncle. I never got to use them before, except for Aunt Addie who was never—oh, and grandmother. To me that word always suggested good behavior and proper deportment. I'm learning that it can also say warmth and love."

Menno and Alana beamed. Vi wiped away a tear. Weezy squeezed her grandmother's hand, then touched Edgar's hand on her other side and added, "And Dad, of course. I called Jonathan *father,* and *sir*. We were never close enough for *dad*."

"I'll try to be a good—dad." To Del's surprise, Edgar choked up. She'd never seen him emotional; now she'd seen it twice in one day. "I have no experience and I'm getting a late start but—I'll learn."

Del recalled what pals she and her own dad had been, the days of camping on the dunes, hiking on woodland trails. Unable to imagine how it would feel to be limited to formal relations with a father, she confessed sympathy with Weezy.

Del had started to help gather up the dinner dishes when the doorbell rang. For the first time since high school she felt shy. She longed to flee to her room and let someone else deal with Bradley.

Alana eyed her expectantly. "That'll be for you, Del."

Knees shaking, palms sweaty, Del went to the door. She reminded herself Bradley meant nothing to her any more.

The man who stood on the porch hardly looked familiar. He must have been working out; he appeared sturdier than she remembered. He opened his arms and seemed huggable. On stepping into his embrace, she was intensely aware of his arms enfolding her. It was as if they'd parted only days ago. His hands slid down her back in a sensuous gesture she couldn't remember the old Bradley ever indulging in. He whispered her name. "Del, Del. You haven't changed. It's great to see you again." He released her with obvious reluctance.

At the moment, Del couldn't recall why she'd broken up with this man. When she thought of their stormy parting, the canceled wedding, she could recall her mother's disappointment—no, devastation—her own weeks of mourning—nothing about Bradley except the droop of his shoulders as he left the house. She must have been preoccupied with self-justification; guilt feelings had overwhelmed her. Her life had seemed ended.

"Won't you come in?" She smoothed her hair and tried to recapture formality.

He urged, "We need to get started if we're to watch the sunset over Lake Michigan." He pointed to the car at the curb, a sporty neon-blue roadster unlike his former black sedan. "If you're ready, that is."

"I'll get my hat and purse." She felt a stab of relief that he would not at once meet her attractive cousin, Weezy. She chided herself while she hurried to put on the broad-brimmed hat which matched her spectator pumps. Jabbing the hatpin into a swirl of hair, she reminded herself she wasn't to renew this thing with Bradley. Lest she forget, she felt she ought to write a note to that effect and paste it on her mirror to keep it perpetually before her.

When she stepped out again wearing the hat, Bradley's eyes widened in astonishment. "Oh, my ears and whiskers! Is this really Del Kingsley?"

She laughed. He never used to say clever things like that. She flipped her hand and tried for a light tone. "It's just a hat, Bradley." In fact, she loved wearing the hat, which almost hid one eye and made her feel like Bette Davis in *Now, Voyager*, stepping onto the ship deck, to the awe of Paul Henried, in her glamorous cousin's outfit.

Holding the brim against the evening breeze, she recalled how Paul Henried had been safely attached to an ill wife he couldn't divorce. Bette was free to love without facing decisions about the future of the relationship. Not so in her case; Bradley's wife was out of the picture and this situation was wide open to complications. She needed to keep her guard up.

After a low wolf-whistle, Bradley stood back to let her go down the steps. Hurrying to open the car door for her, he asked, "What on earth went wrong between us, Del? I look back on our separation as a time of madness."

She paused, sought words. "It wasn't your fault, Bradley. It was me—I wasn't ready to be a housewife and mother." *Am I now?* she wondered.

She slid onto the car seat. He jogged around to the driver's side, climbed in behind the wheel, and in deference to her hat, put the top up. He admitted he understood her feelings. "I went to New York recently and the city radiates excitement. It's so vibrant. You must have felt a let-down, coming home to my petty affairs."

The statement seemed to beg for a denial, but she gave him an honest answer. "I felt imprisoned. The moment I stepped off the train, Mother started talking about the house you guys had picked out for us, the wedding gown she'd selected. I wanted to turn around and rush back." While he started the car and engaged the gear, she remarked, "I hear you plan to move to the big city."

Heading north, he glanced at her and smiled. "I used to wonder what you saw in the place. I found it noisy, dirty, trafficky. But after being there a while, I got caught up in the rush. So much to do, so much to see. Everyone on the go, excited, in a hurry. Now I look forward to living there."

Del reminisced. "Mother couldn't believe I liked having a bedroom window that looked out onto a brick wall. But who bothers to look out the window in New York?"

"Dear Millie—how is she?"

"You'd hardly know her; she's become a Californian. Yard full of desert rocks, petrified wood, quartz, chalcedony. She scorns my beloved Petoskey stone collection which means home and roots to me."

Turning west, Bradley started out Leonard Street toward the old County Poor Farm where once Del's grandfather had been Keeper. Del wondered if the grave of her baby aunt, Blanche Kingsley, might still be found in the nearby cemetery. In her childhood, her Kingsley grandparents had taken her every summer to visit the grave of their middle child, dead of diphtheria. She remembered how they used to point out the other victims of the epidemic. "Over there, in that fenced area, lies our dear friend Katherine with her husband and three children. An entire family wiped out! And beyond it there's another family of five children." The young Del had gazed in horror at the group-graves and asked why God allowed whole families to die. Gran Kingsley shook her head in bafflement and offered no theories.

Del turned to Bradley. In profile he had a Roman nose that gave him a classical face. "Aunt Alana tells me you were married and divorced." She kept her tone light.

"More madness. I shouldn't have married; I wasn't over you—us." He glanced at her with a rueful smile. "I found that out the hard way. So did Betty Jane, poor soul."

Del squirmed at his implications. She tried to sound formal. "Betty Jane?"

"Betty Jane Dormeyer. You didn't know her; she's an interior decorator. Went to Reno, liked it, and decided to stay."

"No children, I gather?"

"No, luckily—under the circumstances."

"You don't speak as if the divorce were painful."

He hesitated, chewed his lip, and remarked that to suffer pain, one must experience a wrenching, and that happened only where there'd been bonding. "No such thing occurred with us. I never felt married. Betty took little interest in my music."

"You and Betty parted friends, though?"

"Disappointed friends, with expectations unrealized. She made my work seem just another job. I felt naïve and foolish for being so committed." He tossed Del a wry smile. "Perhaps you saw things the same way but were too polite to say so."

Still with that vulnerable quality that had once kept her intrigued, he awaited her answer. The appeal was so open that Del felt compelled to respond. She chose her words carefully. "No, I liked your enthusiasm." A stay-at-home career, it had been incompatible with archeology and her dreams of travel to digs, but she decided not to add that.

"Then there was your mother," he added. "Such a strong personality, so much on my side it was frightening. I fear she tore us apart." Bradley groped for Del's hand on the seat, squeezed it, and declared they'd get along better now Millie was far away. Del sought words to protest his assumption that they'd have occasion to get along at all.

As if he realized he'd gone too far, he changed the subject. He asked, "What's new in your life?"

She told him about spending two winters in the desert southwest, and two months on a dig in Greece. "Now I'm reconstructing an Egyptian tomb." And folk dancing with a handsome Catalan whose intentions remain an enigma, but she didn't mention that. She tried to erase from her mind the awful moment when she'd lunched with several women from the folkdance club and been warned Hilario was a confirmed bachelor. Though she'd tried to console herself the women were jealous, she'd later admitted that Hilario probably was indeed not the marrying kind. Pushing thirty and still living with his mother, studying television camera work, he served as the instructor's assistant and was eyed adoringly by all the women as he led the Greek and Yugoslav line dances, twirling his red bandanna above his head. Del had wondered why he'd zeroed in on her, a newcomer, when there were so many top-notch dance-partners available to him. At that luncheon, she'd learned the other women had given up on him. "Don't get too attached to him," they'd warned. "We've all suffered heartbreak over that man." It seemed that each in turn had believed herself to be the one who could lure him from his mother, and each had been destined for disappointment.

Including, now, Del herself, who'd shed tears when she finally confronted the fact Hilario had never spoken about the future, that the dreams had been in her own mind.

Another Jenny-trait, she accused herself. Longing for the man who isn't available.

"Do you still have your Village flat?" Bradley asked.

"Yes—though Jan's married and gone." The moment she spoke, she knew she shouldn't have. Bradley would be living in New York, and the expectation of a roommate's arrival was always a useful excuse for resisting men's unwanted advances.

They stopped off at a county park to admire the scenic Grand River flowing between its tree-lined banks. When they drove on, Del offered an expurgated version of Weezy's situation, describing Grace and Edgar's separation which had consigned her cousin to an adopted father. He shook his head and commented again that he was thankful he'd had no children. "That situation would throw any man into a depression."

"Weezy and Edgar are together now," Del said. "We came here for the reunion."

When they passed the County Poor Farm, Del commented that her grandparents used to run the place. "Granddad was Keeper. My baby aunt died there and her grave must be sadly neglected. I should come and spruce it up."

He offered to drive her out next day. "We'll bring a picnic supper to eat in the park—since you refuse to let me throw a party for you."

Del told him she was not a party person. "That was one problem between you and me. I felt destined to become your social secretary." It all came back to her, his everlasting reminders that she must impress and please church members who were collectively his bosses, the stifling sense of life closing in around her.

The air freshened as they neared the lake. Del removed her hat and opened her window, letting the breeze toy with her hair. She pondered, "What would it have been like for us if there'd been no pressures from you job? Just you and I together?" Hearing Bradley's casual comment, "We now have a chance to find out," Del realized she'd ignored her own warning to herself. She'd hinted at a future for them. She'd set a trap and fallen into it.

Yet when he squeezed her hand, she squeezed back.

CHAPTER 10

Weezy

After having too few people in her life, Weezy now had more than she could keep track of.

There'd been her morning meal with Grandmother Vi, who'd breakfasted alone when Weezy came downstairs. Grandmother had pulled out a chair for her, poured her a cup of coffee, served up a helping of cheese omelet from the fry-pan, made toast, opened a jar of delicious home-made strawberry preserves, and assured Weezy she'd brought a ray of sunshine to the family. Feeling wrapped in love and acceptance, Weezy settled down to enjoy her moment alone with this new relative.

"I'm the type of person," Vi said, resuming her seat, "who should have a flock of grandchildren. But you're my only one. You can't imagine how devastating it was to lose you." She set down the coffee cup she'd just lifted and reached out to cover Weezy's hand with her own warm one. "Truth is, I've always harbored a secret guilt for bringing all these problems on my family. I married a man they all considered no good. Pa violently opposed my wedding."

"But *you* didn't consider my grandfather no good," Weezy defended.

"I loved him. I understood his need to break rules, try forbidden things. Actually, Pa was like him in many ways. I always suspected Pa saw his own worst faults in Nat." She remarked that both of them did what she wanted to do and, as a woman in Victorian times, couldn't: break out of conventions. "There have to be rebels like Pa and Nat—and Edgar. Without them there'd be no change, no growth. I—I loved them for it."

"I hope I'll have your courage when I meet the right man, and can stand up to Mother and Gran." She told Grandmother Vi she'd decided to kick over the traces, to join Del in Greenwich Village and pursue her lifelong dream of becoming a writer.

"You'll visit me, though?" Vi spoke longingly.

Weezy was quick to reassure her. "I'll probably pester you to death. I've been deprived of relatives, too, you know." She couldn't imagine Granny Hannaford sitting down with her for a conversation like this, admitting she might have been wrong about her marriage. When Granny Hannaford spoke to her grand-daughter, it was in a tone of disapproval, and the subject was always Weezy, her bad grammar, her unfortunate choices and actions, her deportment—or it was to warn her of evil consequences of her behavior. In response, Weezy tended to clam up and hide the truth—or alter it. She'd never have dreamed of confess-ing her love affairs to her mother or other grandmother. It was wonderful to feel she could share them with this newfound relative.

While eating, she talked of her childhood in stern and rockbound New England with her stern and rockbound family, adding that she never could talk freely like this.

"I hope you'll tell me everything." Vi squeezed her hand. "Today I'll take you to Wurzburg's and show you where I used to work. I loved working there; the place seemed so glamorous to me. Now they have a nice new store, a real department store."

Spearing a chunk of omelet with her fork, Weezy declared. "It sounds like fun, Grandmother. I love shopping."

"Why not call me Gram?" She added, as Weezy repeated the word, "Tomor-row we'll all go to Reeds Lake for a picnic. There's an amusement park there; you can ride the roller coaster with Edgar. Not me, though. You won't get me on one of those things."

Back upstairs, Weezy found Del sitting on the bed, coppery hair in disarray, top button of her pajamas open. When Weezy flopped onto her own bed, Del began talking about Bradley as if she and Weezy were college dorm-mates. She confessed she hadn't slept all night for thinking about him. She rubbed her hands together nervously. "Did I do the right thing, breaking up with Bradley? I'm wondering if I made a terrible mistake."

"Has he changed so much, to cause this re-thinking?" Weezy leaned back on her elbows and studied her cousin curiously. Del's hair, covering her shoulders, was longer than Weezy had realized, and without makeup, she looked young and unsure of herself. Her New York sophistication, Weezy perceived, wasn't even skin deep.

"I used to find him stuffy and rigid about rules. Things must be done this way and no other. Everything just so. Now he seems more—he actually kidded with me."

"Maybe you've changed, too," Weezy ventured. "They say we mature when we near the three-decade milestone."

"I admit I enjoyed his company last night. I can't remember ever before having fun with Bradley. He never laughed and joked." She ran her hands through her hair. "We have this cousin named Jenny who scorns every man who dates her. I don't want to be like that, and I'm wondering if I—"

Weezy assured her she didn't come across frosty like that.

Abruptly, Del slid off the bed. "I'd better shower and dress and go help the aunts. With a crowd coming, they'll be in a dither." She delved in her suitcase and brought out fresh underwear. "It's good to talk to you, Weezy. I do hope you'll come live with me in Greenwich Village."

Weezy eyed her fingernails, considering. "I certainly can't go back to Boston and pick up where I left off, so if you really mean that, I guess I'll go with you tomorrow night if that's okay. I'll phone my mother to tell her."

Del smiled. "Of course I mean it. I'm delighted! We'll be roommates!"

A while later, Weezy joined Edgar in the living room. Earlier, hearing from the kitchen a clatter of pans as the women prepared to feed a crowd of relatives, she'd offered assistance, only to have Alana shoo her out saying the guest of honor shouldn't have to work. She'd decided to seek out her father.

"So how come you grew up at Stormland?" she asked, sitting opposite him.

He laid his newspaper aside and considered the question. "I didn't get along with my stepfather. He was a steady, hard-working man who scorned the memory of Nat McCurdle, your grandpa—called him a black sheep, a gambler, a good-for-nothing. When he married my mother, he vowed to make sure I didn't take after my dad. I didn't appreciate his attitude and wasn't in the market for reformation. We fought. Thank God, Gram and Gramps came to my rescue and let me live with them. Otherwise, I'd have run away. In those days I wanted to be a hobo."

Weezy laughed. Now that she'd got over her initial shock, she found Edgar's and Nat's past titillating, even glamorous. It was so different from her strait-laced girlhood. "You and Butch Cassidy," she said.

With a chuckle, Edgar admitted he'd never thought of robbing a train. "I might have given it a try if the idea'd occurred to me."

"Del says you used to speed on a motorcycle with a girl on the seat behind you."

"I was just showing off for my cousins." With a wry grin, Edgar added. "Del should talk, she wasn't exactly Miss Priss herself. I remember wild escapades that were her suggestion. She was the youngest of the cousins but she could think up stuff."

"Ooh, I'd like to hear about those. Was Nat McCurdle really a rogue?"

Edgar relaxed and stretched out his legs. "Who sees himself as a rogue? Aren't we all the good guy in our own eyes? Dad was an adventurer who knew how to win at gambling. My granddad, too. They were wealthy until they had to retire and shell out for medical bills. Ma says Dad owned the most elegant carriage in Grand Rapids. Everyone turned to stare as he passed."

When Weezy asked about Grandmother's elopement, Edgar repeated the story more briefly than Del had told it. He asserted, "It was a scandal at the time. Written up in the newspaper, all that. How Gramps fought to save his daughter from a fate worse than death. The whole town had a good laugh; Gram and Gramps were embarrassed to death."

Weezy realized that Grace had definitely been out of her depth in this family. Yet, as an artist, she must have been intrigued. Though this wasn't a Paris-left-bank kind of ambience, at least it was well outside the parameters of what she was used to in proper Boston. Weezy asked what Grace had said when she learned of the scandal. Edgar didn't recall that they'd ever discussed it. "*Scandal* is another word like *rogue*; it defines the society as much as it defines the person. One society's scandal is another's everyday happening. Take Grace and me—scandalous by Boston standards but reasonable to a child of the Wild West like myself."

Weezy convulsed with laughter. "Wild West! Oh, Dad, you're fun to talk to. I'm so glad I found you. I was never cut out to be Jonathan's daughter."

He grinned again. "Of course you weren't. You inherited my genes, and I'm not your white-shirt-and-tie type." He leaned back, crossed his stretched-out legs, and placed intertwined fingers behind his head. "I'm glad you found me, too. I hate to wish anyone dead, but I can't help being happy that Jonathan's gone and I have you back. I faced a childless old age, and now the world has brightened. I may even have grandchildren someday."

"I do wish we could have known each other all along," Weezy said. "If Granny hadn't put her oar in, Mother wouldn't have rushed off to Jonathan like that. She'd have stayed here and worked through the Patience situation."

"You think so?" Edgar asked. "I've always tended to blame Witch Hannaford, but I have to admit my own faults were glaring. I felt lost when the witch tore us apart and took Grace away—but I didn't handle the situation well. I turned to Patience for consolation. That was folly—and I paid dearly for it."

"Well, you were only nineteen. Too young to know how to cope."

"Also, I never did know how to get along with older ladies. Not like Del's fiancé, Bradley Boynton. Talk about natty! He was the slickest 'gentleman' I ever encountered; he could wrap older women around his little finger. I'm sure even Old Lady Hannaford would adore him." He sighed and settled back in his chair, crossing his legs. "Personally, I hope Del doesn't take up with Brad again. Though Millie Kingsley is my favorite aunt, she's wrong to push Del into the choir director's arms."

"Del claims Bradley's changed. They must have had a romantic evening."

Edgar shrugged. "The man's not Del's type. Too smooth, his life all laid out."

Weezy admitted she hoped Del wouldn't be seeing too much of the famous, or infamous, Bradley. Edgar consoled that, since Del was engaged to him for seven years and never made the decision to marry, they needn't worry.

Weezy suspected that whatever had happened on the dunes the previous night had been fairly passionate. She didn't mention her suspicions or concerns. She remarked, "They'd meet again in any case. I hear they're going tomorrow to tend some grave—"

She was interrupted by an exclamation from Edgar, who'd glanced out the window. "Here's Bea! She must have flown over."

Weezy got up to peer out. A slim, smartly dressed woman in a gray traveling suit with red scarf and a black hat with red flowers climbed from the taxi at the curb. Weezy gasped. "She's beautiful!" She followed Edgar out to the front porch to await the newcomer.

"A Thin-Jane, on a perpetual diet," Edgar said. "Terrified of losing her wealthy husband, who wouldn't leave her if you paid him."

To Weezy's question why, if they were so in love, her husband hadn't come with her, Edgar explained. "George has his own business and works on Saturday. They live in one of those expensive beach communities north of Chicago."

Moving sedately toward the porch, Bea raised eyes startlingly dark in her white face and gazed at her nephew. "Edgar! I didn't expect to see you here! Heard you were in the sanatorium."

"I snuck away." Edgar hurried down the porch steps to embrace the chic woman. "How are you, Aunt Bea?" He gave her a peck on the cheek. Weezy saw that they were almost of a generation. Though they were aunt and nephew, they must have grown up together, this youngest child and older grandchild of the Langstons. Bea's face was youthful, almost doll-like, her dark eyes large and soulful. After hugging Edgar, she mounted the porch steps and eyed Weezy. "So—here's my long-lost grand-niece, Della Eloise. We finally found you again—or you found us."

The voice was formal, lacking the gushing enthusiasm Alana and Vi had shown. Bea held out her hand rather than offer a hug. Weezy squeezed fingers in her best Bostonian manner and reminded herself this situation was awkward for Bea who must recall that embarrassing long-ago parting. "Hello, Aunt Bea. So nice of you to come all this way for our reunion." She added, "I did some heavy-duty detective work to locate my other family."

"And weren't we lucky that she did?" Edgar said. "Mother and Alana are waiting for you, Bea. You'll be sharing a room with my ma, who's staying here while her living room's painted."

"Good. It'll give us a chance to visit."

"Del and Weezy have the east bedroom."

"Del's here?" Bea seemed surprised. "Wonderful! I'll just say hello to everyone." She removed her hat, set it on the hall table, and fluffed out masses of curls which, but for color, were reminiscent of Shirley Temple's. It was the only thing about her that didn't seem high fashion. Weezy remembered what Edgar had said about the woman's fears of losing her husband, and wondered if she were trying to look younger than her years.

The taxi driver had brought up her bags. Weezy helped her father carry them upstairs, and remarked that Bea hadn't seemed as friendly as the others. Edgar shrugged this off, explaining that the younger kids in the family had always been stand-offish. "They tried too hard to meet the town's social standards. Don't let Bea intimidate you; she'll thaw in time."

Weezy then asked for a genealogy so she'd know people coming to the reunion. In the front bedroom, Edgar set the bag down and began counting on his fingers. "Start with Gram and Gramps, who built this house and moved in when it was new. They had six children. Two, Rob and Millie, are in California, so you have only four to remember. There's Zeke, the oldest, father of Jenny.

Menno—married to Alana. Then there's Vi, your grandmother, and Bea, the baby."

"Wait, let me write them down." She ran to her room for pen and notebook. Returning, she scribbled, "Gram and Gramps," then drew a line down.

Edgar peered over her shoulder and chuckled. "That's Douglas and Rebecca. Douglas came to Michigan as a child on an orphan train. He was born in Maine; his dad died in the Civil War and his mother married a man who didn't want kids and sent him away. He suffered from the effects of that rejection." He sat on the bed. "Oh, I have so much to tell you, Weezy—and so little time. There's the party tonight, and tomorrow your grandmother wants us to go picnicking at Reeds Lake."

"Yes, I'm looking forward to all of it," Weezy said. "It's a whole new life, and I'm loving it." She admitted it could have been intimidating, meeting so many new people she was related to. "But not with you here, Dad. As long as we're together, I can handle them, even the cool ones like Bea." She turned and gave her father an impulsive hug.

He hugged back. "Weezy, you're wonderful. I feel so lucky. It's like a miracle, finding you again."

Overcome with emotion, Weezy could only squeeze his hand as a rush of love for her new family and new father overwhelmed her.

PART II

NEW YORK

CHAPTER 11

Weezy

Grand Central, at nine a.m. on Monday morning, was a cross between dream and nightmare, exciting yet unreal, a vast confusion of rushing people. Arriving there half-awake, Weezy stumbled after her cousin. She kept bumping her suitcase against the legs of passersby and apologizing.

Long train trips always created in Weezy this sense of unreality. Added to that, today she'd slept until almost arrival time. She and Del had talked far into the night—or mostly, Del had talked, reviewing her years with Bradley, pondering again the question: Had she been wrong to break up with him? Should she date him now he was moving to New York, and give love a chance to grow? Or were they finished with each other?

Half asleep, Weezy had listened to the voice from the lower bunk while her cousin confessed to the emptiness in her life since she'd parted with her former fiancé. "I haven't made use of the extra years. I've been marking time, waiting for life to happen." Those archaeological digs, intended to be the beginning of her career, now appeared to be all of it. She wailed, "My future is behind me. I lost my place to a returning vet and now I'm limited to museum work."

Weezy roused herself enough to assure her cousin this current anti-woman hiring policy couldn't last forever. She felt confident that eventually all the vets would find jobs, and women would again be summoned to the work force.

"That could be twenty years away." Del argued. "Meanwhile, I'm not getting on with my life—and the man I'm dating is the darling of every female folk dancer in New York, making me just one of the crowd."

Having run out of consoling words, Weezy settled down to listening. When, late at night, Del's voice silenced, Weezy, exhausted by the emotional experiences of the last few days, drifted off to sleep.

Awakened by a porter twenty minutes before arrival, she'd struggled into her clothes, brushed her hair, and when the train stopped, had staggered, bleary-eyed, out to the mass confusion of Grand Central, to follow her cousin into the esoteric underground world of the initial subway trains, IRT and BMT.

They boarded a crowded shuttle where they had to stand, their luggage beside them. When Del remarked, "At least we missed rush hour," Weezy asserted that she hoped never to see rush hour if it was worse than this.

Del consoled. "Only a couple of minutes to the IRT."

Indeed, they soon left the shuttle, ran for a less crowded local, and were able to find seats, though not together, for the short ride to Del's stop. When they stepped off and, still clutching their suitcases, emerged from underground, Weezy blinked in the sunshine while Del led the way to her apartment building. Hurrying to keep up, Weezy was only peripherally aware of the charms of the shoulder-to-shoulder red-brick houses of MacDougal Street, each with shutters and with stone steps leading up to elaborate front doors. A group of dancers in long skirts and ballerina slippers hurried past.

They went on to the next street, where the buildings were bigger and less intimate-looking. Del indicated one of the largest. Weezy noticed and remarked on an Italian restaurant on the ground floor.

"It's good, and best of all, it's handy," Del said of it. "No need to go outside when the weather's foul." Shoving open the door to her lobby, she held it for Weezy, then stepped to a wall of mailboxes and inserted her key. Stuffing a handful of mail into her purse, she unlocked an inner door, grabbed her suitcase, and led the way upstairs. "Fourth floor walkup," she warned. "I hope you're in shape for exercise."

"My shape's okay, but I'm not quite awake," Weezy confessed.

"How could you be? We haven't had coffee. I'll get the percolator going right away."

With their bags, they trudged upward. On the lower floors, the halls smelled of garlic. On the third floor, the odor of frying onions predominated. As they approached the fourth, cooking odors vanished. Del explained, "We're working people up here; we eat out."

A man sat on the top step, back-lit by the hall window behind so that he showed only in silhouette and could not be identified. Reminded of Bradley,

Weezy thought: *It can't be.* Yet when he stood and turned toward the light, she saw that, improbable though it might be, he was indeed Bradley, wearing a sporty brown sweater and tan slacks. Somehow he blended with this weird dreamscape she'd been moving in.

"Brad?" Del too seemed astonished. "How in the world did you get here?"

He produced a quick smile and held out his arms to her. Reaching the top of the stairs, she set down her suitcase and, after hesitating, batting her eyes as if she couldn't quite take this in, stepped into his embrace. Behind them, Weezy waited, feeling vaguely annoyed that the man had upstaged her on her first morning in New York.

"A friend drove me out," he said. "He was headed here and offered to come a couple days early just for me. We'd hoped to meet you at Grand Central but were delayed by heavy traffic. Your neighbor let me in after I identified myself as your former fiancé." He hugged her once more, and added, with feeling, "I had to come; I couldn't let you get away again. I feared I was making the same mistake twice."

Oddly, that was exactly what Del had said. Weezy remembered hearing the remark as she drifted off to sleep. "I wonder if I'm making the same mistake twice."

Over Del's shoulder, Bradley winked at Weezy and offered a brief, "Hi there." As Del started to move away from him, he caught her hand to hold her back. He declared, "I've come up with the perfect plan, dear. We'll elope. We'll drive to Maryland—there's no waiting period there—we can be married in time for a wedding dinner tonight. Tomorrow we catch the Hudson Day Line for a honeymoon at Niagara Falls."

Del flung hand to chest. "Oh, Bradley, no. It's too soon. I need time—I need to think about this."

"Dearest, that's precisely what you *don't* need to do. That's been the trouble all along—too much thinking. We thought for nearly seven years, and endured a mistake for four more. It's high time we begin to live our lives, to face our fears and go forward."

"But—I'm due at work this minute. In fact, I'm late, I must—"

His smile broadened to a grin. "Tell them you didn't show up because you were getting married. Best excuse anyone ever offered."

Del sighed and fumbled for her apartment key. "God, Bradley—you may be right. There does come a time when a person has to stop pondering and take action. Maybe we shouldn't flub this second chance." While Weezy worried over this too-sudden capitulation, wondering how to protest it, Del unlocked the door and reached for her suitcase, which Bradley grabbed from her. She added, "Come in, I'll make coffee. Then I can think. Weezy and I slept through breakfast on the train. Where's your friend's car?"

"We parked down the street." Bradley explained, "Ron did most of the driving last night, and now he's snoozing in the back seat, waiting for us to join him and head for Jersey."

"You can't sleep in your car in New York City. It isn't safe."

"He'll be okay for a little while. There was no one around. Start that coffee."

Del flung the door open, and then dropped into a chair and put her hand to her forehead, seeming exhausted by the mere effort of decision-making. Weezy stepped in behind her and debated whether she ought to put in her two cents' worth and urge caution. Uncomfortable about placing herself in the middle, she chose to appear neutral.

On looking around, she was diverted by the charm. The place was everything she'd always imagined a Village flat should be—small, cozy, artistically decorated with milk-chocolate walls and white woodwork. A large crate covered in monk's cloth stood against one wall. Storage, she supposed.

Del noticed and winced at Weezy's pondering glance. She bit her lip and confessed, "That's the bathtub."

Weezy laughed. "Perfect! It's just what a Village flat ought to have—a bathtub in the living room!"

Bradley chuckled. "Our Weezy has a sense of humor." He claimed he'd always felt his true love shouldn't have to put up with such inconveniences; he admitted he hadn't been enamored of this place. "The bedrooms are miniscule, the bathroom is a made-over closet with no room for anything but a commode and a tiny washbowl, and the view—except from the front windows—is of a brick wall."

"I like it," Weezy declared. "It's—Villagey." She stepped to the bookcase for a closer view of the Petoskey stones on display there, a cluster of them, all larger than the two Del had given her in Michigan. She picked one up and commented on its beauty.

There was an open door into a room with desk and a bed with pillows propped against the wall to resemble a couch. Del pointed toward a second, closed door. "That's the spare bedroom. Weezy, you can put your bag in there." She roused herself out of the chair and took her jacket to the couch-bed in the study, which apparently also served as her own bedroom. Returning, she looked around in confusion. "I can't think what to do first."

"Make coffee." Bradley set the bag inside her room and folded his long form into an overstuffed chair. "Then find a larger suitcase and start planning what you'll need for a week-long honeymoon."

"Week-long? What about work? What'll I tell them?"

He shrugged. "Save yourself trouble. Have Weezy call and say you're still in Michigan."

Del not only brewed coffee but managed to create a brunch out of food from her refrigerator, with bacon-and-tomato sandwiches and minestrone. After eating, Bradley left to check on his friend and make travel arrangements. Del locked the door behind him. Consulting with Weezy about clothes, she unpacked and repacked. She removed the monk's cloth to reveal an old-fashioned bathtub with claw feet and a wooden cover attached to the wall. She showed Weezy how to hook the cover to the wall above the tub. Then she ran water which, to Weezy's surprise in this cold water flat, came out steamy hot.

Del stood back. "You can bathe first. I need to pack another bag." She closed the curtains and dimmed the room.

Weezy felt uncomfortable about removing her clothes in this large space. Looking around uneasily, she asked if Bradley mightn't return.

"If he does, we'll make him wait in the hall," Del said.

Reluctantly, Weezy shed her clothes. The out-of-place tub worked fine. Half an hour later both women had bathed and dressed, Weezy borrowing from Del an outfit in yellow and brown, full-skirted, unlike her usual garb. Del wore an off-white suit with pleated skirt. While they dressed, she talked about Bradley. "He's right, I've spent too many years undecided. I'm timid about decision-making; I need to be more forceful." Though Weezy felt her cousin was talking herself into something, she again resisted the urge to comment. This was not her business. She hadn't known her cousin long enough to have any real sense of what her relationship to Bradley had been. Perhaps Del felt more for him than she was admitting.

When Bradley returned, he brought a braided gold wedding band. Del tried it on and seemed pleased. Bradley explained that he hadn't included the diamond ring as he wanted Del to help pick it out. "You'll wear it for a lifetime, I hope, so I want you to like it."

"That's thoughtful of you," she said.

Bradley displayed his travel reservations. "Hudson Day Line to Albany tomorrow morning." Weezy allowed herself to caution that in her opinion this was awfully quick. Brad responded that after all these years, even quick was too slow. He went on, to Del, "Evening train to the Falls, where we'll have three days, returning Saturday. Saturday night I'll fly home; I'm doing the music for Sunday services."

Seeing Del nod, Weezy vowed to protest no more.

By mid-afternoon, they were on their way to the wedding chapel. To avoid disturbing Bradley's sleeping friend, a thin, red-haired man, Weezy squeezed into a corner of the back seat. The man drew his legs up and snored lightly. When Bradley said, "That's Ron," the sleeper managed to open one eye briefly.

Though the distance to Maryland was not great, the roads at this hour were clogged with heavy traffic and trucks. The wedding party proved unable to make much time. When Bradley's friend awoke and rubbed his eyes, Bradley formally introduced him. "Ronald Bancroft. We've known each other since we were boys, so I asked him to be my best man. Ron, this is my fiancée, Del Kingsley."

"Whom I met years ago." Ron reached a hand across the seat-back to Del.

"That's right, you did," Bradley acknowledged. "And beside you, her cousin, Weezy McCurdle." The hand shifted and Weezy placed hers in it.

Ronald's bright red hair stood up in a crew-cut, and he blinked his pale gray-blue eyes. Apologizing for being bleary, he shook hands with Weezy and offered Del good wishes. He seemed to have no qualms about this sudden wedding journey, but to take it very much for granted. Weezy couldn't help wondering if this whole caper had been set up in advance by these two with the intention of rushing Del into it. Long trips required planning.

Ron remarked that he was hungry. Bradley told him they'd brought along a sandwich for him, but he urged instead stopping for hot food and coffee.

"We could have an early dinner and wait for this rush-hour traffic to clear," Bradley said.

Since they all agreed to the plan, Bradley pulled into the parking lot of a café. They piled out of the car and went inside to locate a booth. Conversation, while they waited to be served, was desultory; no one seemed to know what to talk about on this surprise trip. Bradley spoke of the need to brief his successor on the work he'd done with the choirs, and reminded Del she would be alone during the summer while he completed this chore. "I feel awful about turning you into a grass widow so soon, but I do want to make the job-transition as smooth as possible."

Del smiled. "I have a job, too; I'll keep busy."

Weezy had longed to get Del alone, to comment on her suspicions that the woman was being railroaded into something, but when they went together to the ladies' room, she found she couldn't speak. Seeing Del admire the diamond flashing on her finger, Weezy cautioned herself to mind her own business.

An hour later they were on the road again, while dwindling traffic enabled them to make more headway. Well before sunset they crossed into Maryland and came upon a wedding chapel, white with green shutters, a rose-garden before the entryway.

"Does this look okay?" Bradley asked.

Del warned that the first one would be expensive. "Near Baltimore, there'll be competition and—"

"After eleven years, I'm not bargain-hunting." Bradley parked the car. With a grim feeling that what was happening was inevitable—and wrong—Weezy, while Ron held the door, trooped in behind Del and Bradley. The tiny chapel's interior was garlanded with fake roses. At the front stood a bower with rows of benches facing it.

The Justice of the Peace came out and shook hands with the bridal couple. Weezy and Ron sat on a bench to wait while Del and Bradley were taken into the office to be issued a marriage license. Then the foursome gathered before the bower and the vows were spoken. Bradley slipped the ring onto Del's finger and kissed her passionately. The Justice's wife came out bringing a tiny wedding cake to be cut by the bride and groom together. Canned music played in the background. While the pair clutched the knife over the cake, the Justice grabbed a camera and took pictures to be forwarded to Del's apartment. They cut the cake into small wedges and passed it around. More shots were taken.

It was over—far too quickly in Weezy's opinion. This was not the wedding she'd have designed for her sophisticated New York cousin. To the sound of canned music, they left the chapel. On the steps, Bradley paused to kiss Del again and promise her they would live "happily ever after." They all piled into the car and started back to New York. The sun still hung in the sky.

Traffic was lighter now, and they made it back to the Village before full darkness set in. Bradley held reservations for himself and Del at a hotel, Ronald planned to visit friends, so Weezy was dropped off alone at the apartment. Del gave her the key and provided directions to the Day Line dock, where she was to see the newlyweds off next morning.

Thoroughly weary now, Weezy memorized the route while she climbed the many stairs to the fourth floor. Alone in the apartment, she felt let down and depressed, convinced that what they had done was not right. She went into her bedroom and collapsed onto the bed. Too tired to undress or even lift the covers, she kicked off her high-heeled shoes.

In the middle of the night she awoke, stared into the darkness, and wondered: Did that really happen? Did Del get married or did I dream it? Could I have stopped it?

She got up, pulled off her dress, and went back to bed in her slip. She recalled a thought she'd had the previous night, listening while Del debated about Bradley: If you can't make the decision to marry, perhaps Fate is saying you don't belong with that man.

She'd been too sleepy to speak up, and now the deed was done. She could only hope for the best for her new-found cousin.

CHAPTER 12

Weezy

Next morning, after waving the newlyweds away from the Day Line dock, Weezy rushed back to the Village flat, where she dialed the first of two numbers Del had provided of friends to be notified. She tried to relax on the couch, and while awaiting a response, looked around the room. So, here I am, she thought, alone in a strange apartment, trying, with no idea how to go about it, to be a different person.

To the female voice on the phone, she identified herself. "I'm Weezy, Del's cousin. Del asked me to call and tell you her news about Bradley."

"Bradley?" Low voice, midwestern accent, note of surprise, disbelief.

"They eloped," Weezy said. "She wanted me to let you know."

"*Eloped*?" Del's former roommate, Jan, shouted so loudly that Weezy had to hold the phone away from her ear. "With Bradley? Are you kidding?" Then, in a yet more skeptical tone, "Who did you say you are?"

"Weezy, from Boston. Del's cousin. Del was en route to meet me when she visited you four days ago."

"Oh, the family reunion."

"I'm the lost relative. I'm to notify you of Del's wedding last night in Maryland. This morning she and Bradley boarded the Day Line for Niagara Falls."

"Elope? Why would she do that? Her family *wants* her to marry Bradley. Her mom was in tears when they broke up." Jan still sounded skeptical.

Acknowledging cause for doubt, Weezy explained. "I hear Aunt Millie makes a big production of weddings. She scared Del off. Not to mention the question of where they'd live. That problem is now solved as Bradley is moving to New York."

Dragging the long phone cord behind her, Weezy crossed the room in her slip and stocking-feet to perch on the high seat of the covered bathtub. She found this a more interesting sit-spot than the couch; she could look down into the street from here, and besides, as Del had remarked, it seemed movie-ish. She was Bette Davis in one of her Bohemian, artist's-life films; it only needed the glamorous male protagonist to come and light her cigarette.

Shafting between the buildings, the morning sun slanted in through the front windows. From the phone, Jan said, "Del always dragged her feet about Bradley."

"She claims she's matured, no longer looks for glamour but for a solid, dependable man."

"How did those two happen to get together again? I heard Bradley was married."

"Divorced. He asked her out. She says he's changed, too."

"God, I hope so. I thought he was a pill; I rejoiced when they broke up." Jan sighed. "Well, have her call me when she comes back. And thanks for letting me know."

Feeling uneasy, Weezy hung up. She admitted to herself that she too felt Del had been precipitous. She'd hesitated to protest the rush to elope—especially after Del confessed to fearing that at age twenty-eight, she'd already postponed the decision too long—but she still wondered if that had been a mistake. Maybe Del had needed someone to apply the brakes. She seemed to be suffering from a classic case of talking herself into something.

Too late now. Weezy hopped off her high perch and went to finish unpacking in the small second bedroom where, with shades drawn against a brick wall, she needed lamplight even in the daytime. She eyed the books in the bookcase and found mostly archeology and anthropology. Her scientist cousin didn't seem to go in for Weezy's favorite reading matter, novels. She studied again the Petoskey stones with their hexagonal starbursts of ancient coral.

In time she went to the tiny but functional kitchen, peered in the refrigerator, but saw nothing promising for dinner. Earlier, before she rushed off, she'd had cereal, milk and bananas, and planned to lunch on peanut butter and jelly sandwiches. That was the limit of the kitchen's offerings.

She wondered where the nearest grocery store might be. She would need to canvas the neighborhood. Though Greenwich Village was full of boutiques, she couldn't recall seeing, on previous visits to the area, a place selling groceries.

The other name on her phone list, a young man Del had recommended as a good person to show Weezy around the town, was Danny Benikoff, a poet Del had known since her college days. On urging Weezy to call him, Del had cautioned, "A friend is all he can ever be. He's not otherwise interested in women."

Weezy had never, as far as she was aware, known a homosexual. Embarrassed, she'd dragged her feet about calling. Now she decided perhaps she should. Danny lived just two blocks away and could tell her where to shop for groceries, perhaps explain the subway system. She'd always been baffled by the IRT and BMT. When you sought directions, people spouted those letters, leaving you confused and sorry you asked.

The phone was answered promptly. Hearing a male voice, Weezy explained, "I'm Del's cousin. She asked me to notify her friends she was married last night."

"*Married*?" Danny shouted as loudly as Jan had done. "She's only known Hilario for a few months!"

"It wasn't Hilario. It was Bradley Boynton."

"Oh, my God! Oh, please say you're kidding. She never loved Bradley."

"I guess she does now. She went out with him a couple of times in Michigan, and he attended a family gathering."

Danny expostulated, "Bullshit," then quickly apologized. "Sorry, bad language. But really, she let herself be spooked by her twenty-eighth birthday—or maybe it was her failure to get chosen for the dig. The man she was training as her assistant was given the post instead. It drove her crazy."

"No doubt that explains a lot. By the way, I'm Weezy McCurdle."

Again there was silence on the other end of the wire. Danny, she supposed, struggled to recall if he'd ever heard of Weezy McCurdle. She added, "I'm a writer, and I'm told you're a poet. I hope we can get together. Del loaned me her apartment while she honeymoons, and I'm new to the city; I need to learn about shopping and the subway system."

"There's a good Italian restaurant in your building," Danny said. "Let's meet there for dinner tonight. You can tell me about Del's wedding and I'll tell you about the subway."

"Fine. How will I know you?"

"I'm tall and blond, and I'll be wearing a Mexican shirt with a blue Mayan design. Five thirty? If we beat the rush, we'll find a quiet corner where we can talk."

"Good. See you there."

Danny indeed proved to be tall, blond, with eyes of intense blue to match the pattern in his open-collar shirt. He waved to Weezy from a booth in the restaurant.

"Knew you by your resemblance to Del," he said as she approached. He stood and warmly reached out a hand, which she clasped. He studied her intently. "You have the same almond eyes. I'm Danny."

While she seated herself, he smiled. "Lose one cousin, gain another. Boston, huh? Welcome to New York, Weezy."

"Thanks. I'm glad I only had to come downstairs to dinner. I get so lost here."

"I'll draw you a diagram. BMT covers the east side, IRT the west side." His eyes narrowed as he studied her further. "So you're a writer?"

"Shouldn't call myself that yet. Only been published in school magazines. However, I have hopes—or anyway, dreams. I plan to take classes at Columbia. That would require the IRT, right?"

"You're catching on." He grinned. He was good-looking, with blue eyes which turned to half-moons when he smiled. If she hadn't been known better, she could have fallen for him. It seemed a waste that he would never marry or have children.

The waiter approached. Weezy consulted the menu. Danny recommended the eggplant parmigiana. "They do an outstanding parmigiana here. Veal, too, I hear—but I don't eat veal. The growers torture the baby animals to prevent them from developing muscle. Keep them crowded together in a tiny area, no room to move. What the poor creatures must endure, I hate to think. Young animals love to run and cavort."

Weezy nodded. "I never eat veal either." She was surprised to find that she and Danny had so much in common. The man seemed remarkably easy to talk to. "Nor lobster. They boil the creatures alive."

He nodded. "Barbaric, isn't it? But—I do love lobster. It's a struggle to say no. I'm trying to be vegetarian."

They both ordered eggplant parmigiana. She complimented him on his shirt, even though, since no hetero man would have worn anything so bright, it proclaimed his sexual preference. He confessed he loved the shirt but was careful where he wore it. "Not outside Greenwich Village. I teach in a boys' school and wouldn't want to arouse suspicions. I guess you know what I mean; I expect Del has explained." He flushed. "I usually dress conservatively, and I try to have a girlfriend. Del and I got along great until I lost her to Hilario. To think, I introduced them. Stupid, huh?" Seemingly free of bitterness, he spoke cheerfully.

"And now Hilario has lost her to Bradley." Weezy laughed. Danny's gaze was affectionate and he seemed interested in her; she could see why he had to be open about his non-availability to women. He must, she thought, have suffered much embarrassment before developing this frank approach—not to mention inflicting painful disappointment.

"Don't let's talk about Bradley," he said. "I met him once when he visited Ann Arbor. A stuffed shirt, not Del's type. I hope in time Del will realize she made a mistake. Let's talk about us."

"All right. What about us?" She dug into the small casserole of eggplant which had been placed before her along with a plate of salad and basket of garlic bread. "Ooh, this *is* good!"

"Glad you like it." He sampled his own eggplant, considered it, nodded, and then eyed her again. "Since you're new in town, I guess you don't have a boyfriend here?"

She shook her head and tried not to look disapproving. In any other man, this question would constitute a "line." A fast one.

"Then we need each other. I'll squire you around and teach you the subway system. Can we begin tonight? Someone gave me tickets to the Tennessee Williams play."

"The famous torn-shirt thing?" She melted; she really wanted to see that play. She'd heard so much about it. "Del claims the guy who plays the lead looks like my father when young."

"Well, then—triple fascination. Tennessee Williams, torn shirt, and your father's look-alike. What more can a woman ask for?"

"Sounds good, but—are you sure you want to take me? Isn't there someone special that you—?"

"Hey, don't get me wrong. I love women, I enjoy their company. I had a serious girlfriend in college; we even went to bed together. I mean—" He flushed again in embarrassment. "—we slept side by side. On trips we used to save money by sharing a room."

Weezy felt her own face flame, but reminded herself writers needed to know these things. She'd chosen not to be the over-protected Weezy Ward any longer. It was time to acquire sophistication, to become a woman of the world.

"Don't spread the news around, though. I don't want the whole world to know this stuff." While Weezy shook her head, Danny added that he felt he had a better relationship with women than hetero men did. "I'm relaxed with them; I have no agenda."

Weezy congratulated herself that on her first day alone in New York, she was having an adventure. She wondered if it could be as easy as Danny made it sound, this dating in a pseudo-normal way. Danny remarked that Del had never mentioned having a Boston cousin. "I thought all her relatives lived in Michigan or California."

Weezy decided to tell him the story of her exit and re-entry into the McCurdle family. While they ate, she described the wonder of her discovery about her birth father, the pursuit of her true roots. Danny said, "I envy you. I have no family either." Seemed his father was an orthodox Jew, opposed to intermarriage. When the man's schiksa, Danny's mother, got pregnant and urged marriage, he walked out and disappeared. "I've never looked for him. He's a bastard, excuse my French."

"You shouldn't cut yourself off from your Jewish background, though."

"I could hardly do that in New York City." His ready laughter crinkled his face and half-mooned his eyes. "Not that the Jews accept me, since my mother isn't Jewish. I'm a man without a country. Would you like dessert, or shall we wait until after the play?"

"After the play sounds like a great idea."

Weezy'd had cause before now to regret that she's saved out so few clothes from her Great Giveaway. After a child had spilled cider on her skirt, she'd had to borrow a dress from Del for the family reunion. Now she searched Del's closet for something for the theater. Since Del owned a variety of outfits, Weezy brought out and tried on several, finally selecting a black shantung blouse and black and white striped skirt which she carried to the living room. Removing the spread and lifting the cover of the "sarcophagus", she turned on the faucet.

Even in this, her second experience with the bathtub, she felt exposed in this large room. She giggled as she settled into the warm water.

Though she feared Danny might recognize the full skirt she'd chosen, had probably seen it on Del, she dressed carefully and worked on her makeup. She resolved to job-hunt next day and use her first paycheck to buy clothes of her own. The alternative was to ask her mother for money, and that she had vowed never to do. Her mother's money was Jonathan Ward's money, the filthy lucre of a marriage made for the wrong reason, a marriage that should never have happened and probably, if her mother hadn't had a child, wouldn't have happened. Unencumbered, her mother might have been more insistent about returning to Edgar, and the Patience situation would not have arisen.

She headed downstairs and out to the lobby, where Danny, looking like any handsome young man on a date, awaited her, dressed now in a dark blue suit and blue-striped tie. He offered her his arm.

He could have fooled me, she thought again.

CHAPTER 13

Weezy

After the play, Weezy went to the Automat with Danny and his friend, Moe Rifkin, who'd joined them as they left the theater. Moe, a short, middle-aged, balding man, had been introduced as a music agent. When, during the stroll down the street to the restaurant, Weezy had asked what music agents did, Moe had explained that he sought gigs for musicians. "The big bucks are in jazz, of course, but I handle classical, too."

Having each obtained a sweet roll and coffee from the coin-operated windows, the trio had settled down at a table to discuss the play. Upset by the drama yet unwilling to admit the fact to the person who took her, Weezy tried to articulate her thoughts without letting her disappointment come through. "Granted, the play is powerful." She chose her words. "It's just—I wasn't *rooting* for anyone. Most of the time I didn't even *like* the characters." Shaken on seeing her literary assumptions turned upside down, she wondered if she sounded naïve. Was one supposed to like characters in plays? Or did only Hollywood provide nice guys as protagonists? Had she succumbed to movie-slick values? "I mean," she added, fumbling to clarify, "I couldn't identify with anyone." Not wimpy Stella. Not crude, torn-shirt Stanley, even though he belatedly tried to salvage the marriage by sending Blanche away. Not Blanche, the intruder into the home of the formerly happy young couple. From the moment of her arrival, Blanche had set out to break the couple up. Scornfully criticizing both the young husband and the home he provided, she'd damaged the marriage unalterably. Weezy had grown annoyed, then disgusted, with the wife, Stella, for not fighting back. Stella, she decided, was wishy-washy like

Grace, who'd let Patience take Edgar from her. Weezy'd felt she was seeing her own family up there on the stage, and she didn't like the experience.

"I guess it's Stanley's play," she ventured.

Moe argued, "Our sympathies are all with Blanche. She's so fragile and—well—breakable."

Weezy burst out, "Not my sympathy, I don't like home-wreckers." At once she felt her face redden as she realized how Boston-puritan she sounded. She scolded herself. It seemed Weezy Ward was still firmly ensconced within. "I mean—" What did she mean? She meant that to her Blanche was Patience the home-wrecker, who'd deprived her of her father. And Stella was wimpy Grace, who hadn't fought to keep her man.

"Tennessee is trying to show people as they really are," Moe said

Weezy settled for conceding that the play was gripping. At least the young actor who so much resembled her father was handsome. She knew she'd always think of Brando as Stanley Kowalski; he'd so deeply lived the part.

"Personally, I felt sorry for Stanley," Danny said. "When Blanche called him a Polack, I knew how much it hurt."

"I wanted to feel sorry for him but you have to admit he was a slob." When the words popped out, Weezy instantly longed to recall them. So Bostonian-snobbish.

She squirmed in discomfort until she recalled her vow to focus on the play like a critic and discard her personal views. Face it, it's Mother you're angry at, she reminded herself. Nothing to do with the play, really.

"I believe in marriages like that," Danny said. "The Stanley Kowalskis of the world are the salvation of effete families, offering an infusion of new blood. We're lucky we're a country of immigrants. Without Stanley to help produce a half-Polish baby, we'd have been watching *The Fall of the House of DuBois.*"

This being exactly what she'd been thinking about Hannafords and McCurdles, Weezy could only nod.

Eyeing Weezy, Moe seemed to sense her discomfort and changed the subject. "Danny tells me you're a writer."

By using first names, Tennessee and Marlon, Moe had established himself in Weezy's mind as a name-dropper. She wondered if this meeting had been arranged beforehand. It had happened so casually she hardly knew how Moe came to be included in the party. Still, she decided to answer truthfully. "I'm a wannabe. I haven't published much."

"Sorry—can't help. I'm in music. Don't know book publishers."

"I'm told I need to paper my walls with rejection slips before I can hope to succeed."

"Have you tried the writers' colonies? I hear Yaddo is great."

"Can't afford those. I'll need work. Waitressing, maybe."

"Not waitressing!" Danny slammed his hand on the table. "In New York, that's a killer job. Rush, rush, rush. Not to mention that the patrons often—um—have—um—*expectations*."

"Expectations?"

"You know—um—of more than just being served their meal."

Moe echoed the thought. "You said it!"

Startled by their vehemence, Weezy frowned. "I thought it'd be a way to meet people, gather story material."

"Not on your life. Hey, maybe I can help out, after all." Looking thoughtful, Moe drew his chair closer to Weezy. "I seek out people interested in becoming patrons of young artists. Mostly the guys are looking for ballet dancers, actresses or opera divas, but I might find one who'd take on a writer."

"Patron?" Weezy frowned. "Are there such things these days? It sounds so eighteenth century." She squirmed and asserted, "I wouldn't want a patron. I'd feel forever indebted."

Moe threw back his head with a gutsy laugh. "Believe me, there's no question of 'indebted.' Men who sponsor young artists get their pay-back as they go along."

"Oh." Weezy blushed, feeling naïve. The casting couch—she should have known. "As in mistress." She fought the urge to straighten her back and act disdainful. Get thee behind me, Della Ward; I *chose* to explore other aspects of life. I need to be more open.

"Mistress, schmistress. Call it protégé. Sounds better. Overcomes parental objections, looks good on your bio when you become famous." In response to the horrified expression Weezy knew she'd failed to conquer, he patted her shoulder. "Look at it this way. The man gains an intelligent—maybe brilliant—companion for plays and concerts while his wife stays at home in Connecticut with the kiddies. You gain an education plus exposure to people you wouldn't otherwise meet. Of course, life becomes limited. No cheating, no outside men friends—except Danny." He laughed again. "Danny's acceptable."

"You make me feel like the eunuch in the harem." Danny didn't seem to mind; he grinned.

Weezy instinctively drew away from Moe. Her impulse was to shout, "Forget it!" Though her toes curled inside her shoes, she swallowed the words. As

Edgar's daughter, she shouldn't be afraid to toy with the idea of tossing aside social conventions.

"As I say, I can't promise," Moe added, "but I know someone I can introduce you to, and see what you and he can work out."

His gaze swiveling, Danny watched the pair of them with interest. "Can't hurt to look into it," he said. "Without something like that, you're just one of the crowd in New York City."

Fighting her urge to rise and walk away, Weezy sat still and forced out words. "I'll talk to him." It would be an adventure; that's what she came here for. She knew she'd end by finding a waitress job. This patron business was too unsavory even for her new McCurdle persona.

"I'll try to set up a meeting for tomorrow night. This literary gent may be happy with a writer." Moe patted her arm again as if he suspected she needed consoling.

Aware she'd seemed unsophisticated throughout this conversation, she struggled to avoid blushing.

Next morning, Weezy went job-hunting. She needed a secure income, not a compromising situation.

Waitress jobs were not hard to come by. At the first place she applied, The Cast-Iron Fry Pan, she was given a uniform and put to work. As Danny had warned, the male customers flirted and swatted her rump. By noon, rushing madly from table to table, her legs ached so badly she wanted to scream. By mid-afternoon, shaky with weariness and tearful with customer demands and innuendoes, she found herself giving Moe's suggestion some thought. Carrying heavy trays, running to the kitchen, keeping track of various orders, getting the right food to the right people, she found no time for chatting, not even with the help, let alone the customers. Danny was right; this was not a job to promote anyone's literary bent. She labeled people only as "table four" or "table seven." No chance to gather story-material. And those winks, swats on the rump, and fumbles toward her breasts soon stopped being funny and begun to seem menacing.

When she hurried home in late afternoon to soak her aching feet and restore her aching spirits, she actually hoped for Moe's call. It would be a diversion, at least. The four flights seemed interminable. She dragged herself up, hating the food-odors of garlicky sauces wafting from the apartments along the way. No food for her; after smelling it all day, she'd lost her appetite. She fumbled for the key and let herself in.

The phone was silent. She drew the shades, shed her clothes, lifted the tub-top, turned on the water, and still marveled to see it run so steamy hot. Why, she wondered, did they call this a cold water flat?

Relaxing in the tub, she began making bets with herself: Moe would call. No, Moe would forget. The patron would prove bossy, cranky and demanding. The whole thing would be distasteful. It couldn't work out. She'd feel repulsed, unable to imagine going to bed with the person. How do women do it, she wondered; how do they sleep with men who are not their choice of mate? Though there'd been only one man in her life, at least he'd been one she chose and was attracted to.

She rationalized. If it's only one man, how bad can it be? It's not exactly prostitution. Besides, she argued to herself, he'll be busy, he'll have his work, his family. He can't bother me all the time.

Then came the thought: Me, Weezy? Become some man's plaything on the side? Unthinkable. Out of the question. Forget it.

"I can't believe I'm really considering this," she announced aloud to the shaded windows. She sank deeper into the warm water, stretched her legs, and sighed in relief as the aching eased.

When the phone finally rang, she climbed out of the tub and, though there was no one to see, instinctively wrapped herself in a large towel. She hurried to pick up the receiver.

"Moe here," the voice on the wire said. "Is that Weezy? I called the publishing firm where Yuri works."

All her instincts warned her to say, "Forget it." The returning ache in her legs forced from her a cool, "Yes?"

"Yuri's out of town for a couple days. I'll have to get back to you."

"No problem." Relief flooded through her. The tension in her midriff relaxed. She hung up, climbed back in the tub, and settled down for a lengthy soak in warm water.

With her legs still sore, the next day at the restaurant was worse. She dropped a tray, confused orders, was yelled at. The boss reached out to feel her up, and five patrons tried to date her after work. By late afternoon, her legs again ached intolerably, her head pounded, and she'd taken so many aspirin her ears were ringing. She went home to collapse and wonder if she could face another day of this.

On the third morning, her boss called her into his tiny office for a confer-ence and told her straight out that he wouldn't put up with her haughty manners and her scorning dates with customers. He'd had complaints, he said. She'd have to loosen up, unbutton herself, or else. Near tears, she asked one of the other waitresses how she managed. The woman shrugged. "You learn to kid the guys along and postpone the inevitable—and often they lose interest. If not, you go out with them, kid them along some more, then plead a headache. Often, you can get off. After a few headaches, they get tired of spending their money on dates."

"There must be better situations than this," she said.

The woman shrugged. "There are ladies' tea rooms but I warn you, pay is low and tips nonexistent. This place is one of the best, moneywise."

That night when Moe called, she didn't allow herself to sound snooty. She forced out a pleasant, "Good evening."

"I've set things up," he said. "Dinner tomorrow night at Sardi's. The man's name is David Yurovsky, called Yuri. He's thirty-eight and never had a protégé before. As I warned, there are no guarantees, he's not sure about this, but—can't hurt to give it a try. It might turn out great for both of you."

"All right, thank you." At least Yuri wasn't decrepit. To Weezy, at twenty-one, thirty-eight seemed only moderately old.

"He'll send you a red rose to fasten on your hat. He'll be wearing a red carnation. Know where Sardi's is? I'll give you directions."

After jotting these and managing a somewhat cool goodbye, Weezy hung up and almost yielded to an urge to bite her fingernails. She wished the meeting might take place this very evening so she could cope and have it over with.

She thrashed all night with aching legs. In the morning she debated calling the restaurant to say she'd decided to quit her job. She resolved to see it through. The tips were good, and she'd been promised a pay-check at the end of the week. She could buy clothes and also claim experience in seeking a better job.

She'd planned without her boss, who now warned her that if she continued to refuse to meet the men patrons after work, this would be her last day. She responded that in that case, he shouldn't expect her to return. He shrugged and said, "Fine."

So that was that. At the end of her shift, clutching her check, she faced the long stair-climb again. She promised herself a lengthy soaking session. But even in the warm water, she was unable to relax. She kept thinking about the miserable day just past, and about the scary night to come. What should she wear? Something not sexy? Something business-like and impersonal? No, she didn't want to turn the potential patron off; that would be self-defeating. She wanted to retain her options. Maybe a suit a bit less muted than her Boston outfit.

The florist's delivery man called on the intercom to say he was leaving red roses in the lobby for her. She went down to get them, dragged herself back up the four flights, and after reading the card, dutifully affixed a rose to the side of her hat. She looked in the mirror and wondered: Is this really me, Weezy, doing this crazy thing?

When it was time to go, her weariness fled and nerves took over. Terrified, she debated changing her mind—but recalled the alternatives, her dreadful waitress job and the worse prospect of going home to her mother and Gran Hannaford with her tail between her legs. Neither option was acceptable.

She'd settled on the black and white striped skirt because it provided the right background for a red rose. Inspecting her outfit, she decided she looked the best she could, and although her neat Bostonian hat didn't go with this flamboyant garb, she checked her hose-seams, grabbed her purse with shaky fingers, and went out, locking the door. She ran downstairs clutching the directions.

Following Moe's suggestion to stick to the local trains, she found her way on the subway. When she arrived at Sardi's, her knees felt rubbery. What would this Yuri be like? Would he be super-sophisticated, sardonic? Someone she could never really know, let alone like?

I can always say no, she reminded herself.

She spotted him the moment she entered the restaurant. Rather, she spotted a red carnation on the lapel of a dark blue suit, and eyed the man wearing it. Youthful, almost boyish looking, muscular, well built, he had curly brown hair receding only slightly at the temples. At least he isn't portly and balding, she consoled herself.

He gave her a brief wave. She told the maitre d' she was meeting someone, and moved along to the carnation man's table. "You must be Mr. Yurovski." She knew she sounded stiff and formal. She felt frozen.

"Miss McCurdle? Please sit down." He half stood and offered his hand, which she clasped. "Call me Yuri." A waiter came to hold her chair while she sat.

About her height, the man had a rugged face, strong chin, and penetrating brown eyes. While she studied him, he remarked, "Bet you're thinking I don't look Jewish. People always think that; I hear it all the time."

She hoped she wasn't blushing. "I'm not a New Yorker, Mr. Yurov—Yuri. I have no idea if you look Jewish or not."

"No Jews where you come from, eh? Boston's Beacon Hill?"

"How did you know that? I don't remember telling Mr. Rifkin where I'm from."

"He must have guessed from your manner and accent. 'Pure Beacon Hill,' he said. I felt intimidated, wasn't sure I wanted to meet you. Me, a Russian Jew, a patron of a Boston Blueblood? Unthinkable."

Weezy laughed lightly. "It's Grandmother who's the Blueblood. I'm only half Beacon Hill."

"The other half is Western Michigan, right?"

"My, you're well informed!" She gazed at him in surprise.

"Moe was well informed and passed along what he knew. I hear you saw *Streetcar* and weren't too thrilled with it."

"Oh, it's a great play." This was no time to confess her personal reaction. "You see, I'm hoping to become a writer, and my stories are the old fashioned kind where you're meant to *like* the characters—except the villain, of course. I find the new literary trends, with obnoxious protagonists, disturbing. I have to learn to write all over again."

Yuri nodded. "My thought exactly. I believe you and I have a similar perspective, Miss McCurdle."

"Weezy. Short for Eloise, my middle name."

"Oh I love Eloise. May I call you that?" When she nodded, he added, "I find you charmingly forthright, Eloise. I'd better tell you about me. We must get to know one another, to make sure Moe hasn't pushed us into something we'll both be uncomfortable with."

Weezy relaxed. The evening wasn't threatening to be horrible, as she'd anticipated. The waiter came to take their orders, and they paused to make their selections. This done, Yuri went on. "About me. I've been married for eighteen years, since I was twenty-one—I'm thirty-eight now—and until tonight I never dined alone with another woman. I want you to know I'm not now doing it out of dissatisfaction with my marriage, but for other reasons I'll explain. I need to make it clear I don't suffer from a roving eye."

"You've got me curious." Yuri seemed a walking paradox.

"My reasons are not mysterious." He leaned forward, folding both arms onto the table. His brown-eyed gaze penetrated hers. "I'm going to level with you and tell you something we Jews don't usually discuss with non-Jews. Fact is, I've been accepted into a business club formerly closed to us. They opened their door to me under great pressure from Jewish organizations—I'm the token Jew. I don't like it but I recognize the need to break the barrier. Business deals are done over lunches in that place, and when you're out, you're very out. Yet obviously, I can't go there as a prude. The guys all have protégés, and the girls are a favorite topic of conversation."

Weezy conceded the difficulties. Yuri went on to remark that he'd been told she wanted to do graduate work and needed financial help. "Moe didn't say why your family wasn't providing it. I mean—to look at you—well, you look expensive. Cared for, you know." He quirked an eyebrow questioningly.

Weezy couldn't think how to explain the complicated tale, how she'd learned that accepting parental help meant also accepting attached strings, including control over her life. Surely Yuri, who seemed totally in charge of his life, wouldn't understand if she said she longed to own herself and choose her own direction. She contented herself with a simplified version. "My step-dad died recently. Now that Mother's a widow, I'd hate to be a burden to her. And my birth father is having health problems, hospital expenses, all that."

"So you're abandoned twice over, eh?" He still eyed her curiously.

"Oh, I'm not abandoned. My birth dad is supportive and would help if he could." Weezy chose not to mention that her mother had just inherited a bundle. No way would she accept Grace's money. Grace was the puppet of both Gran and Jonathan.

"I'm willing to pay for your apartment and tuition, but I want it clear this is just an arrangement, no great emotional involvement. I don't want to see you hurt. I'm the type to agonize with guilt if I thought I'd set you longing for—"

"Don't worry, I'm no home-wrecker. What will your wife think?"

"Deborah's a sophisticated woman; I believe—I hope—she'll understand."

Weezy burst out laughing. "We *are* a pair! I'm tempted to rush back to Boston, and you're longing to return to your wife."

He laughed with her. "Doesn't sound promising, does it?" Touching her hand with his fingers, he added, "Now we know where we stand; we can talk." His face broadened in a smile that spread his cheeks wide. Though not exactly handsome, he was interesting looking. He had the kind of face, she thought, that an artist would choose to paint. Her mother would zero in on him—at least until she learned of the subject under discussion. Then she'd be horrified, not that Weezy planned to worry about that. This was her new life. She felt like an actress taking on a role.

CHAPTER 14

Weezy

During dinner Yuri talked of his work as publisher of manuals for business machines. Not very literary, he said, certainly not what he'd aimed for when he set out to enter the publishing field, but it did pay the bills. Weezy listened and wondered if she could bring herself to become his "protégé." She wasn't clear what he meant about this being just an arrangement. Did he mean no sex, or sex without emotional involvement? Embarrassed to ask, she doubted that for her there could be such a thing. He was an attractive man but she couldn't see herself being compelled to go to bed with him. Though the idea was not unthinkable, she wanted to reserve the right to say if, and when. She could imagine no way, so long as he was shelling out for this venture, to negotiate such a setup. While he talked, she invented a dozen such proposals but left each unspoken.

"I have a captive audience," he said. "Students and workers need my manuals. The new machines are no longer simple to use and repair." His smile flashed briefly; she sensed he was nervous and hoped to charm her. His fingers probed his pockets for something he failed to find. He flushed. "No cigarettes. I forgot—I quit." He confessed to dreams of branching out into the creative realm. "I had literary aspirations in college, that's why I wanted to meet you. I know how it feels to long to do something you can't afford to do. It's tragic to see talented, artistic people forced into the world of business. I'd be happy if I could save you from that."

He pressed for details about her writing. She told him she wasn't sure yet. She'd had so little time to read current books. "My stepfather agreed to pay my way in college only on condition I study social work," she said. "We're Unitarian."

"Unitarians disapprove of creative writing? First I heard of it. In the nineteenth century they were famous for their writers. Emerson, Thoreau, uh—Hawthorne, I think. And of course, Louisa May Alcott."

"It's self-indulgent, you see. Okay for free time. A career in public service should be one's primary goal."

"A bit puritanical, was he?" Yuri produced that fleeting smile again.

"Jonathan was a descendant of puritans. Have you read Hawthorne?"

"Everyone reads Hawthorne. We did *House of Seven Gables* in junior high."

"Then you know what my stepfather was like. His last name should have been Pyncheon."

The smile again rounded Yuri's cheeks and narrowed his brown eyes. "I do hope you don't have a curse on the family ala Matthew Maule's curse on the Pyncheons."

"There's no guarantee we don't." She smiled, too. She was beginning to like this man. Maybe the "arrangement" was conceivable after all.

Serious again, she spoke of her plans to take literature and writing classes. "I'd like to write something sociological along the lines of Sinclair Lewis's *Main Street.*"

"Do you have a novel in mind?"

"Yes, I even have a title: *Call Me Cassandra.* It's to be about a woman seer who foretells the Holocaust in Europe but is not believed."

He nodded. "A good theme—painfully realistic."

When they finished eating, Yuri suggested visiting the Belle Turrets Residence Hotel. "It's the only place in town—the only nice place—willing to let women stay while men show up only occasionally."

Weezy hesitated. "Well, I—"

Yuri eyed her speculatively. "I'm not trying to push you into anything, Eloise. It's just—Moe tells me they have a vacancy right now, and as there's usually a wait list, I thought we might look."

Weezy bit her lip. "So long as we're only looking."

"If you're not willing to commit to this deal, please do be honest with me."

Weezy realized her fingers were picking at each other in what her mother would term an unladylike manner. She forced herself to still them. "At this point I'm not sure what to think. This is so new to me."

"I wouldn't want to feel I talked you into something."

Weezy admitted, "*I'm* talking me into something."

"Suppose I show you the quarters and then leave you to think it over. No need to make a decision immediately."

"I appreciate that."

When she rose from the table, Yuri hastened to hold her chair. He did seem to treat her with respect. Out in the warm summer twilight, he signaled a taxi. While Weezy held her breath to fight off the quivering in her body, the cab zigged and zagged around other cars, weaving through traffic. In a short time they flew up to the glittering entryway of an elegant-looking hotel, and she was helped out by a doorman who handed her on to Yuri as he approached.

Though it sported rather ridiculous turrets, the place proved to be a plush high-rise with a huge chandelier in the lobby and carpets thick enough to sink into. It was the epitome of everything Jonathan Ward scorned, luxury far beyond human needs. The concierge gave Yuri the key, and they rode in a satin-lined elevator to the ninth floor. When they stepped into the main room of the suite, they saw, from a picture window, a panoramic view of lights sliced by the dark pathway of the East River.

The unit seemed all too obviously a pleasure palace. Besides thick carpeting, there were plush couches and chairs, no desk or bookcase. The few wall shelves held only a radio and ceramic pieces. In the bedroom, one entire wall sported a mirrored dressing table with lights above it. Beyond was a walk-in closet. Peering into this, Weezy stifled a chuckle, thinking of the two dresses salvaged from her giveaway and how lonesome they would look in such a vast space.

"The women here must spend a great deal of time on their makeup and hairdo," she said doubtfully.

Hands in pockets, Yuri watched her in concern. "Not your kind of ambience, is it? Perhaps the management could put in a desk and bookcase."

Before leaving Del's apartment, Weezy had powdered her nose, reddened her lips and lined her eyebrows. This was pretty much the extent of her usual makeup. She wondered if she'd ever find a use for the long dressing table.

Yuri seemed to sense her hesitance. He remarked apologetically, "I admit the place is small."

"Small? It's palatial." She confessed that she'd expected to live in a loft or a crazy flat with orange crates for furniture. She'd never imagined this kind of luxury. She'd dreamed rather of burning a candle in a wine bottle, talking literature with friends while sitting on cushions on the floor. With a chuckle, Yuri said they could burn candles and discuss literature right here. "Who's your favorite character? Mine's Alyosha Karamazov, with Stephen Dedalus a close second."

"Oh, I love Stephen Dedalus." She confessed she had yet to read *The Brothers Karamazov*. Her days in college had been spent reading sociology books like *Middletown*.

"Suppose I put down just enough deposit to hold this place for a few days? You can come over tomorrow and think about it. I see you need time to make up your mind."

The best she could say right now was that it wasn't as unthinkable as she'd supposed. She admitted, "It is pretty sudden. Until I met Moe, I hadn't ever—"

He squeezed her hand. "Take your time. I want you to be sure."

"I appreciate it." He was really a nice person, she decided. Too nice to fit into the male-snobbery world he hoped to join. She couldn't picture him as part of the clubby set. Even so, he was a stranger and she couldn't picture herself entering this bedroom with him, removing her clothes, allowing him to touch her, and—. Her mind balked at finishing the thought.

Downstairs, she waited in the lobby while Yuri spoke to the manager. On joining her, he handed her the key. "I rented a suite for one week. That gives you time to decide if it's what you really want. I'll meet you here tomorrow, sixish, and we'll discuss it further. If you say no, I'll leave."

He paid for her taxi and waved farewell. At Del's, she climbed the stairs and sank onto the couch, pondering what her mother would say. "That plush décor is one step away from a bordello." And what demands might she face? What *did* Yuri mean by "just an arrangement?" Why hadn't she asked? She couldn't keep saying no to the man who was paying her way, nor even plead perpetual headaches as did that waitress at the Cast-Iron Fry Pan.

My mother lives in a bordello, she argued with herself. Any house where a woman lives with a man for money, propriety, or appearances rather than for love is a bordello, even if the couple has taken marriage vows. At least I'd be doing this to realize my dream of becoming a writer. Yet again her mind balked at the thought of shedding her clothes, of touching and being touched by this stranger.

She wished Del were here to talk to. She knew no one in New York except Danny, and this was a problem not to be discussed with a male of any stripe.

What were her alternatives, after all? New York wasn't holding out its arms to her. Waitress work was back-breaking and would take up much of the time she'd hoped to spend in studies and writing—and it didn't pay well unless one worked at those male hangouts where she'd encountered harassment. Quality restaurants hired waiters. The only other option she could think of was a job in publishing. Enter her chosen profession by the back door, so to speak.

But would publishers hire her with her lack of literary background? Only one way to find out: try. She could go around to their offices in the morning.

Up early next day, she arrived at the first office, Random House, when they opened. They told her they weren't hiring. She went on to Harper's which wouldn't even accept her application. Knopf needed an expert typist, and she didn't qualify. Bobbs Merrill had an opening for someone to write blurbs for book covers. "The pay is thirty a week," the personnel woman told her.

"Thirty a week?" As a waitress, she'd earned that plus liberal tips. She bit her lip and asked hesitantly, "Can anyone live in New York on thirty dollars a week?"

"Our younger employees mostly live with their parents," the woman told her. "Their salary goes for clothing and lunches. We expect our staff to be well dressed." She eyed with distaste Weezy's basic black.

"I'm from Boston." Weezy tried to sound snobbish. "I'll need enough salary to pay my rent."

Refusing to be intimidated, the woman shook her head. "It takes time to work up to a good salary in publishing. I don't advise trying it. There are few openings in the field; people wait years for good jobs."

Weezy clutched her purse and rose. As she started out the door, the woman stopped her by adding, "With your social work degree, you could earn a fair wage as a welfare worker. Forget publishing; it's a labor of love, no way to get rich."

Tempted to offer a sarcastic, "So I see," Weezy restrained herself and said only, "Thanks for your time."

On the way out, she passed a room full of typists all clacking loudly. She wished she'd taken typing in school. These women probably made twice what the blurb-writers earned.

Her next stop was the office of a literary agent, where she applied as assistant. She'd found the job listed in the want-ads. She learned the pay here was twenty-six a week. Worse and worse. "Afraid I can't live on that. Sorry." No need to rise, she hadn't yet sat down.

"No parents or husband to help support you?" the slight, balding man asked.

"I'm from Boston and I'm not married." She felt both surprised and angered over the way people seemed to assume that young women would be subsidized. Young men, expected to be on their own, were paid accordingly. No one would dream of asking an adult male to let his parents support him.

By ten-fifteen, she'd applied at five places and been turned down five times. Discouraged, she stopped at an English Tea Room, was hired at once, and on legs already weary with pavement-pounding, she dragged herself through lunch and dinner, trying to act cheerful to those she served. She learned the truth of what she'd been told: Women patrons tipped little or not at all. The other waitresses admitted they were here only to gain experience for a better job. She finished her shift at eight and departed with relief.

She decided to stop by the Belle Turrets and see if the place looked more acceptable, more thinkable, in daylight.

At least, as she entered, the thick carpet felt restful on her feet. In the lobby, she passed a group of young women heading outdoors to walk their poodles. Clipped and be-jeweled, the dogs resembled their owners, who sported beauty-parlor hairdos, full skirts, hats perched at rakish angles. Glittering jewelry adorned ears, necks and wrists. Tottering on heels so high as to suggest stilts, the women held cigarettes in long holders. They spared not a glance for this working girl in her basic black. Had they done so, they would presumably have supposed she was here to do typing or filing for the management. Weezy passed them and went to the marble-and-mirror-lined coffee shop, where she ordered coffee and Danish. She stretched out her legs to rest them while she tried to imagine herself living in this place, becoming one of the poodle-walkers. Not even her writer's imagination could cope with the thought.

A slender young woman in a green dress, with wide-apart brown eyes and a mass of blonde curls held back by a blue ribbon, stopped to speak to her. "Moving in? I haven't seen you around before." When Weezy admitted she was still deciding, the woman added, "It's a great place, Sugar. You seen the swimming pool? Bigger'n the one at the Y, and that's for the public. Exercise room, too. The restaurant ain't—isn't—super-duper, but there's a good Eyetalian place down the block."

Weezy knew that if Gran Hannaford were here, she wouldn't allow Weezy even to speak to this "common" sounding person with the heavy Brooklyn accent. But, seeking a new life with new people, Weezy fought her distaste and managed a friendly nod. The Beacon Hill girl, the Smith College graduate, was gone. "I'll try it."

"Mind if I jern you? I came by for a cherry coke. Gotta watch the waistline and stay away from them—those—Danish."

"Lots of calories, huh?" Weezy gestured toward the opposite chair.

"Name's Flora." Dropping into the indicated seat, the young woman returned Weezy's smile. No flamboyance here.

"Weezy, from Boston."

Flora nodded. "I could tell. You talk Boston." She eyed Weezy's undecorated neckline. "Your guy don't buy you much jewelry, huh?" She herself sported a pearl necklace and gold bracelet. "My guy bought my poils—I mean pulls—a year ago."

"I don't have a guy," Weezy told her.

"You don't have a guy? And you're in this place? Whadja do, kill him off and inherit his dough?" Flora bent over in a fit of laughter. Her gaze fell on the room key Weezy had laid beside her coffee cup. Straightening, she added, "Ain't many that have the moola to support theirselves in the Belle Turrets. Even the Broadway actress and our two opera divas don't do that, not without a little help, anyways."

"Well, I—I just wanted to try it out for a week." Weezy couldn't think how to explain her scruples to this woman who seemed to have none. She asked, "How do you keep busy when your—uh—guy isn't around?"

"I have a television. I take elocution lessons and a charm course. I figure my guy will divorce his wife one of these days, and when that happens, I gotta be ready; I gotta know how to talk right. He's a big society doctor, he needs a wife that talks good and knows where the forks go on the table, know what I mean?"

Weezy was intrigued by Flora's speech patterns, alternating as they did between good English and street talk. "You don't expect to live here permanently, then?"

"Shee-yit, no one expects to live here permanently. All the guys want young ass. The pernt—punt—is to make hay while the sun shines. Get the guy to divorce his wife and marry you before you lose S.A." At Weezy's look of puzzlement, she explained, "Sex appeal, Sugar. Without it, a gal's up shit creek without a paddle." She fingered her beads. "My guy don't love his wife, so I figure I have a good chance of becoming a Mrs. Of course, I can't dress gaudy like them gangsters' molls I saw you looking at when you came in. Their guys load them down with fur and jewels. I gotta be—uh—subdued."

At the back of her mind, Bostonian Weezy Ward still scolded: This milieu is not for you. Weezy ignored the nagging voice and reminded herself a writer needed to know the world.

A tall, dark-haired young woman in diaphanous peach chiffon floated up to the table, greeted Flora, and announced she expected to be married soon. Ignoring Flora's dubious look, she asserted that her guy finally broke down and agreed to divorce his wife. "We had it out last night. I told him I'm not waiting any longer. He promised to head for Reno soon as he can arrange the days off."

"Don't buy your gown just yet, Sugar," Flora cautioned. "I hear that stuff daily. It's the standard line of talk around here."

"Not from me you didn't hear it. This is a first for my guy."

Flora introduced her friend. "Betty Ann, this is Weezy, from Boston."

"A new girl?" Betty Ann gave Weezy's dress the now-familiar assess-and-reject look.

"She don't have a guy so she can only afford the place for a week," Flora explained.

"You don't have a guy?" Betty studied Weezy in concern. "I might could fix you up. My guy has friends. If you—uh—could wear something a little—uh—" Her hands formed an hour glass. "I mean, you got a good figure and all. Me and Flora could make you over."

Embarrassed, Weezy swallowed the last of her coffee, wrapped her Danish in a paper napkin, and picked up her check, purse and key. "Don't worry about me, I'm okay. Guess I'll go take a shower. Nice to have met you, Flora, Betty Ann."

"Maybe we'll see you at the pool," Flora said. "We take a wake-up dip around ten."

Weezy nodded, hurried to the cashier to pay for her food, then returned to the lobby and crossed to the elevator. Yuri was to stop by later, after a business meeting, and she wanted to shower and freshen up before then. Her legs ached unbearably from pavement-pounding and waitress work.

Entering the suite, she admired the early-evening view and watched barges on the river, still touched by patches of late sunlight forking between tall buildings. Observing only the rush and hurry of the city below her, ignoring the loud and flamboyant décor of the place, she felt like a princess in a tower. She kicked off her high heels, sank onto the sofa, stretched out her legs, and thought about the two women she'd just encountered, living on hopes their guys might one day marry them.

That life isn't for me, she repeated to herself. Tell Yuri tonight the answer is no. Then back to pavement-pounding and table-waiting tomorrow. If these feet survive this first week, they'll get used to the punishment. Or so I hope.

CHAPTER 15

Weezy

Yuri called to say he couldn't make it that night. "My wife has plans; I'll need to rush home and change. I'm so sorry; I hope this won't inconvenience you."

Weezy felt deflated. She'd had her speech prepared: how she appreciated his interest in her, his willingness to let her decide without pressure. How her decision wasn't personal, implied no dislike of him, but was based entirely on her conviction she couldn't share this life among these women. How he must never think it reflected on him in any way.

Though the words were on her tongue, she couldn't offer them over the telephone. Lacking her accompanying smile, the light touch of her fingers on his arm, they would sound blunt. She needed to set the scene.

As if he sensed disappointment and hoped to cheer her, he spoke consolingly. "I'll come tomorrow at five and bring my swim trunks. We'll try out the pool. How about that?"

She started to say, "Make it seven." She stifled the words when she recalled that another waitress at the Tea Room had wanted to change shifts with her. By postponing her pavement-pounding, she could go in early. "Five is okay," she said. "I'll be here."

One more day couldn't hurt, and since Yuri had paid for the pool, he should have the use of it. After their swim, she resolved to explain: *This lifestyle won't work for me but my decision has nothing to do with you. You've been considerate and I appreciate it.*

His voice grew warm, almost caressing. "I'm really sorry about tonight. I'd looked forward to seeing you, Eloise."

She hung up feeling uneasy. That was not the way she wanted him to feel. Her rejection speech had been designed for a specific audience, the nervous man of the first encounter, not the warm and affectionate voice on the phone. Awash in guilt, she wondered what she'd said or done to cause this change in him. After all, she'd agreed to his contract—this would be a business arrangement, no friendship involved—though admittedly he seemed an interesting person with whom she could have been friends under other circumstances.

A bouquet of roses arrived, increasing her guilt-feelings. She phoned the other waitress to arrange a trade of shifts next day, and then wandered around the room wondering if she'd unconsciously done something to set Yuri afire. From the clothing she wore to the cool mannerisms she affected, she'd tried to keep their meeting muted and low-key. Why, oh why, hadn't she asked him to be more specific about his wishes and expectations?

Weary from her long day of pavement-pounding and waitress work, she drifted off to sleep on the soft couch. She awoke, hungry, around nine and decided to have soup and salad in the coffee shop. She checked her hose-seams, combed her hair, and powdered her nose.

On stepping into the hall, she paused, hearing music. Radio? No, live. The singer stopped, repeated a phrase. Familiar with opera, to which she'd often been dragged by her parents, Weezy recognized an aria from *Carmen*. Was this one of those singer protégés Moe had spoken of? If so, she was good. Weezy moved on while the trained and lyrical voice began again.

In the lobby she noticed two well-dressed young women in black sheaths, one with a single strand of pearls and pearl earrings, the other with a hand-made cloisonné pin and earrings from a Village boutique. So then, not everyone here dripped with gaudy ornaments. Like herself, these women wore only moderately high heels, and their hairdos were simple, one in a pageboy, the other in a chignon. Smiling, they joined two dignified, white-haired men in evening dress who waited by the door. Each man bent to offer an arm to a woman, and all four went out together.

These young women appeared neither common nor flamboyant; in fact, they seemed to be people she would like to know. It was a relief to see that diamonds, furs, and elegantly-groomed poodles were not the norm.

As she entered the coffee shop, Betty Ann, swathed now in lemon voile, waved to her from a booth. When Weezy joined her, Betty handed over the menu she'd been studying. She explained that Flora was out for the evening with her guy. Weezy nodded, sat, and surveyed the salad list.

"All unpacked and settled in?" Betty asked.

Weezy admitted she hadn't brought her stuff yet. "It's at my cousin's place, where I've been staying."

"Need hay-elp? I know a guy owns a truck."

"I have nothing big enough to fill a truck, but thanks anyway." Weezy changed the subject. "There must be an opera star living next door to me. I heard singing."

"I often think every woman in the world lives here," Betty Ann said. "Half the Yankees ball team has girlfriends here. Out of season, we see the team every weekend. There are also ballet dancers, musicians, actresses." She winked. "They say a famous orchestra conductor has a girlfriend here, and visits her whenever his wife is off with her cronies. Don't quote me on that. We try not to gossip."

So perhaps the vast dressing tables weren't designed for high class call girls as Weezy had supposed, but for women in the performing arts who needed to make a good impression on the public.

"A Broadway actress lives next door to me," Betty added. "She don't have just one guy, she has about ten. She forgets and invites two or three the same night, and then the fur flies. Whenever I stay-ep into the hall, I hear yelling." She chuckled.

Weezy commented, "Good place for a murder."

Betty Ann shrugged. "Don't know of none, but we've had suicides. One singer jumped from the top floor. She'd blanked out in the middle of her first musical, couldn't recall the words. The critics panned her and her guy walked out. Then there was the old dame, late fifties; her guy had lost interest and she was stuck to go on the street. She trudged out there for three weeks, then yanked her radio into the bathtub with her and electrocuted herself."

"How sad." But what a wealth of stories here, Weezy thought. The place is a writer's mecca; I can't walk away without investigating further. She gave herself orders: meet Yuri again; give his arrangement a chance. This residence hall could prove more valuable than a graduate-school education to a wannabe writer.

"Me, I'd go home to Texas rather than end it all." Betty Ann waved to a waitress and asked if Weezy had decided on eats. When they'd both ordered, she went on. "I got a cousin there owns a bar. He promised to give me a job any time I need one."

Weezy inquired where her guy was now. Betty explained that on Friday nights he showed up late. "He's gotta take his wife somewhere first. When they go out, she always wants to head home early. She worries about the baby-sitter not looking after the kids good enough. Bill fibs to her he's going back to the party, but he comes here instead. His friends won't tay-ell."

Stifling an urge to flee, Weezy forced herself to stay with this conversation. It seemed Betty Ann was a bridge player. "Not to boast, we're world-class in this building; one gal even writes bridge moves for a newspaper. Do you play?" She scrutinized Weezy's face as if seeking the answer there.

"Not on your level."

"I might could help you improve your game. Me and Flora want to spend time with you. You talk educated, and we need to practice that. How about lunch tomorrow?"

Since Weezy couldn't bring herself to admit that this "educated" woman would be slinging hash, she said only, "I'm busy tomorrow." She was glad of the excuse; she didn't appreciate being sought out as a source of free elocution lessons.

Later she went back to Del's to get her things, and tucked in a borrowed beach towel. Returning, she sprawled on the couch and called Danny. "Guess what? I'm in a luxury suite. It's temporary, until I figure out what to do. I lost my waitress job, found another at ludicrous wages. I applied for a job in publishing, and you wouldn't believe the salaries. Thirty a week. Who can live on that in New York?"

Danny clearly knew all about the problem. He told her, "Those jobs are grabbed by college grads still supported by daddy—one or other kind of daddy, biological, step, or sugar. It's a start for them, gets them into the field."

"Sugar? Oh." Like Yuri, for instance. My sugar-daddy. Weezy shuddered.

"I'd be in publishing myself if I could afford it," Danny added. "I didn't set out to be a teacher. I landed in the profession when all else failed."

Weezy sympathized. Danny asked, "How'd you like Yuri?"

"I like him fine. He's nice—and interesting. What I haven't decided is whether I'd like being a kept woman. This place is full of them, and most don't seem like tarts, but I—"

"Tarts? Weezy, what kind of world do you live in? Dividing women into nice girls and tarts! Come on, grow up. Life isn't like that. In the real world, even good people sometimes need help along the way. It isn't wrong for them to give something in return. It doesn't mean you live out your life marked with a giant A."

Weezy bit her lip; the puritan Wards had spoken through her once again. What kind of writer could she be if she kept fighting against knowing life?

"I sense your dilemma," Danny admitted. "Weezy McCurdle wants to give this a try, but Weezy Ward refuses."

"How clearly you put it! Split personality, that's me."

Taking the early shift next day, Weezy finished up at the English Tea Room at two and rushed off to Ohrbach's, where Betty had suggested she shop. She used her tips from the Cast-Iron Fry Pan to buy a swim suit and a sleeveless, slim-lined tangerine dress with white scarf. After adding elbow-length white gloves and spiked heels, she went home feeling like a real New Yorker at last.

Even though she'd rehearsed her refusal speech many times, she checked, just to be safe, the secret compartment of her purse. She found, tucked there, the rarely-used diaphragm she'd acquired in the college infirmary by showing off a fake diamond ring and claiming she was to be married. She really couldn't imagine Yuri carrying forcefulness to such lengths that she'd need such equipment; he didn't seem the type. But prudence demanded she not be caught short.

Promptly at three, she heard a tap at her door. She hurried to open. Yuri stood there in a dark blue business suit, carrying a beach bag which he set down inside. When she closed the door, he first offered a tentative smile, then moved toward her and held out his arms. He seemed shy, diffident, friendly—not a good start for her planned speech. In a voice so soft it made her quiver, he said, "Oh, Eloise." When she ventured a single step in his direction, he reached for her hand. Then suddenly, he moved closer and took her in his arms. She gasped. This was not the way things were supposed to go. Yet it seemed natural. He looked at her intently as if trying to read her mind. He kissed her, first gently, then with passion. Again he whispered. "Eloise, the girl with the rare and beautiful name."

She felt disoriented. Her planned script wasn't working out. Yuri wasn't supposed to kiss her or whisper love-words, and she certainly wasn't supposed to like it. He was a married man; this was ridiculous. Surprised, breathless, she stepped away from him.

He himself took a deep breath. "What happened to me? I didn't think I could pull this off, but it's easier than I thought. What magic did you use?"

Embarrassed, she laughed lightly. "Actually, that was supposed to be my line—'I can't pull this off.' I've been rehearsing it for two days."

He quirked an eyebrow. "So you were dubious? I suspected as much."

"I had a speech prepared, saying, 'Let's forget the whole idea.'"

He laughed. "I planned to suggest you take a job as my secretary, so we could get to know one another and work into this gradually. See if it would go."

Lacking training in secretarial work, she opted not to promote this idea. Pulling herself together, she said, "Come in; sit down. I should offer you a cocktail but the truth is I—well, I forgot to buy liquor. I just turned twenty-one; I'm not used to having it on my grocery list."

"I'm not big on alcohol," he said. "Anyway, we'll have wine with dinner." He studied her with a look of intense interest. "So tell me, how are you making out in this place? Is it thinkable? May I hope that it can work out for us?"

"Oh, it's an adventure, a writer's paradise!" She was surprised to find Yuri easy to talk to. She confessed, "I can't promise to stay, but I—I've begun a story about it."

"I want to hear. But first let's go to the pool and make like fish."

"All right." He seemed so different from the reserved businessman she'd dined with before, the man who'd warned her he loved his wife and wanted no commitment. He now acted more open, more comfortable with her. His friendly manner helped her overcome her own hesitance. She began to think it might be fun to experiment and see if the arrangement could work out. As Moe had said, Yuri's contacts would provide access to a publishing world she would otherwise have to enter from the ground floor—or rather the sub-basement—as a blurb-writer or some such lowly position.

Not to mention that Yuri was a very attractive man now that he'd thawed a bit.

Still, she felt relieved when he went into the bathroom to change. She wasn't ready for a nude scene. She hid in her room-sized closet to put on Del's suit, then stood before the mirror and wondered if, low-cut both front and back, it might be too sexy. Turquoise with a yellow dolphin plunging down the front, it showed off her slim figure, her flat stomach—and its design understated her wide hips. Well, it would have to do.

When she stepped out, Yuri eyed her appreciatively. Tempted to grab her big beach towel for cover, she reminded herself he was *supposed* to appreciate her.

He held her hand while they rode up in the elevator. The roof swimming pool was glassed in, the room sun-warmed and steamy. Two women swam laps, while a couple—young woman, older man—sat on the edge, talking, laughing and splashing their feet. Weezy dove in and found the water refreshing, not over-heated. Yuri followed, swam after her, came alongside, and grabbed her around the waist. He held her for a moment, and then let her get away. Soon he pursued her again, and when he caught her, he embraced her. To her surprise, his muscular wet flesh felt good against hers. She put her hands against his chest with its dark hairs. Together they sank down into the water. When they surfaced, he grabbed the edge of the pool to stay afloat and kissed her. She kissed back, then broke away, glanced in embarrassment at the other two people—and realized they were totally self-absorbed, their heads close to one another. People at the Belle Turrets seemed well trained not to notice others, not to intrude.

"I could learn to enjoy this," Yuri said. "How about you?"

"I'm working on it." The words came out breathlessly. While trying hard to remain cool and in control, she now feared she wouldn't manage to say no to this attractive man. She well remembered the time when she'd thrashed all night over the question of whether to meet her college-boy lover at a hotel and sample the thrills he promised, and in the end hadn't been able to resist his lures. Next day they'd gone to a cheap jewelry store to buy a fake diamond ring, and then he'd accompanied her to the infirmary to sit in the waiting room while she showed off the ring and fooled the doctor about her forthcoming marital status, her imminent need of birth control devices. When the doctor had used a blunt instrument to slash through her hymen, she'd screamed with pain and regretted—too late—her decision, thinking of the horror tales she'd heard of men who didn't want "used goods." Her boyfriend had consoled that at least, now, she didn't need to suffer pain with him. "It's better this way," he assured her.

"You make this swim sound like a class assignment." Yuri smiled. "Let's go to dinner and then have another plunge—Eloise."

"All right. I hear there's a good Italian place nearby."

They dressed and went to dinner. Weezy told Yuri the stories she'd heard of gangsters' molls at the Belle Turrets, of the patron's rejected protégé who'd killed herself. "Perhaps I'll become a pen woman like Katherine Brush," she speculated. "Didn't she write the famous story of the woman who jumped out the window of the ladies' room of a roof-garden nightclub while the attendant sat reading *True Confessions*?"

Yuri sobered. "I want to be sure I'm not pressuring you into any such tragedy. Please think carefully: Can you really handle this situation? You seem a thoroughly nice person and I'd be devastated if you were hurt."

Since Weezy's only past experience had been the sexual encounters with that college boy scarcely more knowledgeable than herself, experiences that promised much but delivered little, she was in no position even to guess about more complex relationships. She confessed she had no idea. "I don't want to get married to the first suitable man who turns up, as my college friends are doing. As my cousin seems to have done," she added. "I just attended her wedding and it didn't feel right for her—and wouldn't be right for me. The marriage-babies-suburbs route would not lead me to a career as a writer."

"We'll take this slow and easy," Yuri said. "Keep assessing as we go. Is this fun or is it hurtful? Should we go ahead or break it up?"

"I keep wondering how your wife will handle it."

"I wonder that myself," Yuri admitted. "She claims to understand my motives, but that doesn't mean she'll like the reality. I hardly like it myself. I never planned to get involved in this sort of thing."

Weezy said something she'd never expected to say. She could hardly believe the words were coming from her mouth. "I guess we'll never know the answers until we try."

"I hope you're really willing—Eloise," Yuri said.

On returning from an excellent dinner, they put on their wet bathing suits and relaxed in deck chairs by the pool until daylight dwindled. When the lights came on in the water, they plunged in again and swam laps. A strong swimmer, Yuri kept catching up with Weezy and passing her. After a while he began grasping her, frolicking with her. They were now alone in the pool. She evaded him by diving beneath his reaching arms, whereupon he went after her once again.

When they climbed out, she started toward the shower. He intercepted her and suggested they wait to shower in luxury in the suite. Dripping, they rode down, wrapped in towels.

In the suite, still in swim trunks, he drew her into the shower with him. Under the warm water spray, he slid her suit-straps down her arms, eased the suit off her breasts, and cupped them. She remembered and then discarded her prepared speech about not doing this. She closed her eyes and gave herself permission to enjoy.

Leaning against him, she lifted her arms to encircle his neck. When he lowered his head, her breasts seemed to rise of their own accord to meet his lips. An electric thrill shot through her. His hand moved between her legs, grasped her inner thigh, and slid upward along it. He peeled off the lower half of her suit. She stood there nude, the first time she'd ever done so in the presence of a man. Oddly, it didn't seem strange. She'd tried so often to imagine doing it and had been convinced she couldn't, yet here she was. Yuri's hands traveled all over her body, cupped her breasts again, moved downward again. He whispered, "Something magical happened to me when I walked into the suite this afternoon."

"Yes, I sensed it." She'd shared it; she'd experienced a sudden, wild desire. It was powerful; it was overwhelming. It was a sensation she'd wanted to feel, had started to feel, with her college-boy lover who then hadn't seemed to know how to lure her onward into further desire. Now, new vistas opened to her. Yuri drew her against him; she felt his body harden. He kissed her and his tongue explored her mouth. His hand again slid between her legs and touched exciting places. Her lower body turned to jelly; she pressed against him with a passion new to her. When he whispered, "Eloise," the name gave her goose bumps.

She stepped out of, and kicked aside, the suit he'd peeled over her thighs. She reached out to help him remove his trunks. He yanked on one side while she tugged on the other. His suit fell and was also kicked aside.

It took courage to slide her hands downward. She'd never before explored a man's body. She made her hands touch places where previously she hadn't even dared to look. She heard Yuri's groan of pleasure.

"I think we're clean." Breathless, he turned off the water. They left their suits behind and stepped out onto cold tile. Yuri wrapped them both in one huge towel and patted them dry. He carried her, hair still dripping, to the bed, dropped her onto it, and fell on top of her. His lips went to her breast, his hand moved between her legs. Hearing him breathe, "Eloise," she felt her wet thighs longing to open to his touch. She rolled closer to him.

Later, when they were lying side by side, still damp, chests heaving, Yuri admitted, "I never dreamed it could be like that."

Weezy propped herself on an elbow to look at him. "Is that good, or bad?"

He smiled and fingered her still-damp hair. "You've heard the old saying, first love is always the best? I've just discovered it's wrong. Second love is best."

"You didn't expect it to be good?"

"No, I thought I'd feel frozen with guilt. I'm the type, always guilty toward someone. I must have switched off for the evening."

Weezy admitted she'd been of two minds all along. "I seem to have buried the other mind. I've become a McCurdle all the way. Forget Hawthorne, think Jack London. Think of my pioneer ancestor who gambled his way across the wild west."

"I want to hear about him. Shall we send down for drinks and snacks?"

"You don't have to rush home?"

"My wife's away at a weekend retreat for artists."

"Your wife paints?"

"She's a collector and a patron of the arts."

"My mother paints," Weezy said. "She's quite good, actually." She got up and wrapped herself in Del's fluffy yellow gown and negligee. Yuri put on his shorts and trousers, but left his shirt off. They sat at the small table by the window and Weezy admired the dark hair curling on his chest. She knew she wouldn't send this man away. Over snacks and drinks, when they arrived, she told him about her two personalities. "The Bostonian's a nag. She keeps saying, 'This isn't for you, you weren't raised this way.'"

Yuri admitted he too felt like two people. "One of me never imagined I could be unfaithful. The other enjoys breaking out of the rut. I'm still in shock over him.'`

"Welcome to Yuri Two."

"And Eloise Two. We both—we all—have an adventure to look forward to." He grinned and reached across the table to squeeze her hand.

CHAPTER 16

Del

Standing beside Bradley at the rail of the Hudson Day Line steamer as it approached the city near sunset, Del tried, while admiring the shining, glittery-gold windows of Manhattan Island, to convince herself she was really married. She blinked as every west-facing window caught the late sun and flared like a gem-stone.

Bradley moved closer. She felt his breath against her bare neck. "No wonder immigrants think America is paved with gold," he said.

It had been a weekend out of a Hollywood movie. Bradley had put himself out to be the perfect gentleman-lover, all sources of past strife laid aside. However, there'd been a fly in the ointment, one Del blamed herself for. In her thoughts she kept replacing Bradley with Hilario. In bed with Bradley, she kept flashing on images of the curly-haired Catalan. It made her feel unfaithful to her new husband. Yet she couldn't find a way to discipline her mind. She could only console herself that Bradley would never know. She assured herself she was thinking of Hilario only because he'd been her most recent lover. In time, his image would fade.

Del looked forward to a return to the museum. These would be her final weeks; she'd promised Bradley that at summer's end she would quit her job and take the education classes he'd urged on her to qualify her for work in religious education. He'd pointed out that it was a fascinating arena where innovative techniques were being tried. She'd admitted—though without telling him of her heartbreak over her failure to be chosen for the dig—that at the moment, the under-funded field of archeology seemed to offer little opportunity for women, and that she did indeed need to seek a more promising profession.

He'd also, to her distress, urged that they find a bigger apartment. While conceding that he required space for his piano, she yet couldn't bear to think of parting with either her silly-dilly flat or the museum job. Both provided her with the kind of spiritual rewards Bradley seemed to find in churches. For years she'd been regaling her family with praises—boasts even—of life in the Village with its artists, actors, dancers, and its craft-boutiques. As to archeology, she'd felt born to the field. Even as a child, spending her Saturdays at the Field Museum, she'd wandered about awed by the artifacts of earth's history, mankind's history. From fossils and geological formations that spoke of a planet once so different, to mummies that told of long-gone cultures, she walked through halls of exhibits in a perpetual ecstasy of discovery. The Field Museum had been her cathedral where she worshiped whatever power had jump-started this incredible universe.

When the boat touched the dock, Bradley took her hand in his. Time to say goodbye; he had to return to Michigan. Though his job wouldn't officially end until Labor Day, nine weeks away, he hoped to leave early by claiming unused vacation time. "With luck, I'll make it back here in early August," he said. "Even that seems forever away."

Having waited upriver for a barge to be towed out of its path, the boat was behind schedule. Bradley had to go at once to the airport. When Del offered to accompany him, he protested. "You'd be late getting home. I don't want you running around New York at night."

She didn't tell him how often she'd done so in the past. She just smiled as he added, "I'll find you a taxi and then I'll head on out." She demurred; the subway was handy to her apartment and would do fine.

At the subway entrance, he hugged and kissed her in full sight of hurrying people. He murmured, "Darling, I'll be thinking of you every moment. You're my one and only love."

Her tongue wouldn't form the words of a response in kind. While she pondered the reason for this failure (he had, after all, worked hard to make their honeymoon a success and she should be grateful to him) he climbed on the bus, waved from the window, and was off to catch the airport shuttle. Carrying her suitcase, she went down to the subway, shoved her coin in the slot, and passed through. She reflected that while it was great to be someone's one and only love, it did place a burden on the object of the affection, demanding a responding passion she couldn't seem to muster.

In her own feelings, she was still Del Kingsley. The whirlwind elopement and honeymoon had been an out-of-time experience. With nothing remaining now but to go home, she became aware of a sense of emptiness, a let-down. She consoled herself with the thought that Weezy would be at her flat. She wondered how her cousin had fared in the big city.

She boarded the local for her stop, only a few stations away. Soon, in the twilight, she strolled past the ever-charming three-story-plus-basement houses of MacDougal Street, red brick with dark-green shutters, and moved on to the taller tenements of Thompson Street. At her building, she checked the mailbox. Up the four flights, she stepped into her apartment and found it dark and deserted. She snapped on a light. A card had been pushed under the door, and she picked it up and studied it. Signed *Danny,* it sported a picture of white roses and a formal message: *Wishing you every happiness.* Not Danny's kind of thing at all. A scribbled note at the bottom read, "Call me when you get home."

Moving on, Del noticed a sheet of paper propped conspicuously on the bathtub cover. She hurried over to snatch it. "Del, I'm at the Belle Turrets and I've met a MAN. Call me. Weezy." A phone number followed.

Del tried to remember what she'd heard about the Belle Turrets. Something unsavory. Young women were steered away from it. She felt guilty at not having mentioned this fact to her cousin.

She dialed the number given. A woman answered and offered to signal Weezy's suite. Soon Del heard her cousin's voice, sounding pleased and happy. "How was the honeymoon?"

"Fine." Del kicked off her high heels and made herself comfortable on the couch, feet up on the coffee table. "Unfortunately, we've separated now. I mean we're apart. Bradley had to go back."

"Not for long, I hope?"

"He promised to wind up his affairs as quickly as possible. Meanwhile I'm to apartment hunt. I'd planned to turn this place over to you. What's this about the Belle Turrets?"

"You're giving up your flat? I thought you loved it!"

"I do." She sighed. "Brad's right, you know. It wouldn't suit our lifestyle. We need more space." Her gaze focused on her Petoskey stone collection, and she wondered how she'd display it in a conventional uptown apartment. "What are you doing in that—place?" She'd been tempted to say, *that house of ill-repute.*

"Del, I've had adventures! I found a man who likes my writing and wants to be my patron."

"*Patron*?" Del's voice reflected her concern. As a come-on, that excuse topped even the infamous offer to show off his etchings. She saw that drastic measures were called for. "How on earth did that happen?"

"Through Danny. An agent Danny knows named Moe Rifkin."

Del decided she'd need to have a talk with Danny. She'd met his friend Moe Rifkin. He claimed to be a music agent, so how come he knew someone interested in taking on a literary person?

"Do come see my suite," Weezy said. "I have a view of the East River."

"I just got home; I'm pooped. How about if you come here?"

"Okay. See you in a while."

On hanging up, Del promptly called Danny. As luck would have it, he was out. She'd hoped to quiz him about the patron business. A suite at the Belle Turrets? There was nothing cheap about the Belle Turrets except its residents. She'd passed the place more than once and observed gaudy, bejeweled women walking their clipped and bowed poodles. You couldn't fail to recognize their type. Having heard Weezy vow not to ask her wealthy mother for help, Del doubted Grace was forking over, so there had to be something unsavory going on.

Del lifted the wooden cover, ran water in the bathtub, peeled off her clothes, and climbed in. She'd only just finished scrubbing and leaned back to relax in the warm water when she heard a knock at the door. She puzzled. Too soon for Weezy. She called out, "Who is it?"

"Danny. That you, Del? You're back?"

"Wait a sec. I'm in the tub."

"I won't look."

"Maybe not, but I'd be embarrassed." She pulled the plug, hopped out, wrapped herself in a towel, and ran to the bedroom. Her robe lay across the daybed, where Weezy must have flung it after wearing it. She grabbed it, slid her arms into the sleeves, tied the belt, and hurried to unlatch the door.

Danny entered, explaining, "I saw the light and figured one or the other cousin was here."

"I tried to phone you," Del said. "Got a weird note from Weezy saying she's at the Belle Turrets. Seems Moe found her a 'patron.' Mighty fishy. What do you know about it?"

"Fear not, it's legit." Danny slung his long body into a chair. "Moe assures me Yuri's a nice guy. 'Couldn't ask for better,' he says. Weezy wants to write, and it's impossible to find time for that when you're a waitress. With a wife he's true to, Yuri won't be demanding."

Del stared in astonishment. "Are you telling me Weezy agreed to be his *mistress*?"

In shock, she lost her grip on the belt and her robe slipped open. Danny didn't seem to notice her nudity. He removed a pillow from behind him and tossed it aside while she hastily refastened her belt.

"Protégé," he corrected. "Forget Weezy, she's in good hands. It's you I worry about. Talk about *agreed*." He imitated her tone. "What's this I hear about you agreeing to marry Bradley? You never loved Bradley; you've said so a dozen times."

"People change," she defended.

"Face it, Del, you didn't change, you panicked. You were scared silly when you didn't get chosen for the dig. I sensed it."

"Scared? Me?" Del raised an eyebrow. She sat on the couch and moved her legs restlessly, crossing one over the other.

"Damn right. You saw the grim truth: they don't choose women when they can get men."

"Of course, I was upset, but—"

"You were devastated. I worried about you."

She sighed. "It wasn't fun, yet I knew the men who fought the war had a right to come home to jobs. I've heard how in World War I, returning vets starved and had to march on Washington demanding work. My own father had trouble finding work. We don't want that again." She managed a wavering smile. "Hey, I've come to terms with it."

"I doubt you've changed that much. I think you jumped into something that appeared to be a solution but isn't."

"I didn't mean I changed, I meant Bradley changed." Even while reminding herself she didn't owe Danny an explanation, she sought the words for one. "He used to be unexciting, predictable. He's matured, widened his horizons, become more open."

"Baloney. I don't believe it. And you left behind a string of broken hearts, you know. Mine, Hilario's."

Del laughed. "Come on, Danny, you can't break hearts you never had."

Danny leaned forward; he didn't appear to be joking. He spoke with feeling. "Just because I don't sleep with my women doesn't mean I don't care about them. As for Hilario, you sent him a cold, abrupt note saying you couldn't go dancing with him on Friday because you got married. He was in the dumps over it. We met for dinner."

"Hilario?" Del had trouble believing in Hilario's distress. She again studied Danny's face for signs of kidding. "Hilario the debonair, who has his pick of women? Come on, Danny! I was just one of his dance partners, and not the primary one at that." Assistant instructor at the folkdance group, Hilario helped to demonstrate the dances as they were taught. Though flattered when he asked her out for coffee and a Danish, she hadn't thought of herself as anything more than one of many. Hilario was well known in town for his exhibition dancing with a long-time partner whom he treated with easy familiarity. True, he'd taken Del on a picnic at Far Rockaway which had stretched into an overnight after their touching and fondling on the sand had led to their seeking a hotel room. Another time, with his partner out of town, he'd taken her to a dancing exhibition where, though she watched him perform with someone else, she'd gone with him to a hotel afterward. She'd enjoyed his bedroom know-how. Among his many talents was his ability to imitate Bogart so perfectly she hardly knew if she was in bed with Hilario or Bogey. When he talked, he used Bogey lines, "Stick with me, kid," or, "We're a great team, sweetheart." He captured the tone exactly.

"Hilario never seemed all that devoted," she said. "I thought he was putting on a performance. Besides, he has a girlfriend."

"Nona Fischbein? She's married, you dodo. She and Hilario have been dancing in exhibitions for years, always with the husband as chaperone."

Del stared at him. "Why didn't Hilario tell me that?"

"Did you ask? Or just assume they were involved?"

She'd assumed more than that. She'd assumed that every woman in the group was after Hilario. She, a beginner, hoping to capture the top exhibition dancer? Ludicrous! True, she'd suffered tuggings at the heartstrings over this suave and talented man, but felt, especially when others confirmed that he'd dated—and then broken up with—most of the women in the group, that she had about as much chance with him as with the real Bogey.

"Hilario's a man-about-town," she added. "He's not ready to settle down."

"He was getting ready to—all because of you. Because of you being a Californian and—."

"A Californian? Me? Danny, you know I'm from Michigan; you went to college with me."

"Your parents own a California ranch."

"A tiny avocado ranch, newly bought. We're hardly an old Spanish land-grant family. And speaking of Spanish, how come his name's Hilario and not Elario? I've often wondered."

"It's a complicated story and I probably shouldn't be the one to tell it—Seems the Solers had planned to emigrate to Brazil but saw their chance to come here instead, on a fake passport which labeled the family as Brazilians. Because of that, they altered their son's name to the Portuguese version. But about California—I believe Hilario sees it as a place to start over with a new life—with you, or so he hoped."

"You astonish me," Del confessed. "He never hinted at any of this. Are you sure your poetic imagination hasn't run away with you?"

Danny folded his arms across his chest and gazed at her owl-eyed, like a preacher counseling a parishioner. "I'm repeating what he told me. I don't know why you rushed into marriage. No—excuse me—I do know why. It's that Doldrums Decade looming, the fourth decade. You seem to fancy that your attractiveness will switch off like an electric light the moment you pass thirty."

Del got up and paced. She paused to stare out the front window at the street below and watched the neighborhood organ-grinder with his performing monkey. "But that's the way it is. My doctor claims that after thirty a woman's chances of having a baby go way down. He told me that if I want children, I need to start now. A woman past thirty is over the hill. Read any women's magazine; you'll see."

"I wouldn't waste eyesight on them. Anyway, you still have two years. You needn't have dived in head first."

Del closed her eyes and thought about it. True, she'd feared the ominous thirties. But that hadn't been her sole motivation in marrying, had it? No—it was her discovery that Bradley had changed, outgrown the things she didn't like about him.

She eyed a group of pedestrians down below as they paused to watch the antics of the monkey. The sound of the organ came to her faintly: *Let bygones be bygones forever. We'll fall in love once again.* She didn't like to admit to Danny nor even to herself that there was also a job problem, but actually, without a Ph.D., she would never advance as an archeologist, and as a woman, probably not even then. People who funded digs rarely, if ever, put women in charge. She explained, "Bradley convinced me I need to get into a different field. I'm planning to do now what I should have done in college: take education courses."

"Well! You *have* come down to earth with a thump!" Danny again stretched out his long legs, his shoes rumpling the nap of the carpet. He reached up to run his hand over his stubby, crew-cut blonde hair. "So, you're to be the wife of a man you never loved and work in a field you never cared for. And live, I presume, in a place you never chose."

Del gave him a protesting look. "It's great to have your friends celebrate your marriage." She moved toward the bedroom. "Excuse me while I rustle up some clothes."

"Don't do it on my account." Danny smiled and his eyes sparkled.

At a tap on the door, a female voice called, "It's Weezy."

"Come in. Door's unlocked." Del again collapsed onto the couch, exposing one long, tanned leg which this time Danny did notice with a gleam of approval. That was the problem with Danny; you could never be sure. She'd charged him with this fact once or twice, and he'd explained, "I admire and celebrate the female body; I don't covet it."

Weezy entered and closed the door. Del saw that her cousin had been transformed into a sophisticate. She sported a big-brimmed oatmeal-colored hat, long-sleeved gloves, even a new dress, an almost ankle length tangerine sheath very striking with her dark hair. Danny gave a wolf-whistle. Del remarked, "You look great, Cousin." She wondered how to broach the subject of patrons and the Belle Turrets. Was it possible Weezy was too naïve to see the implications?

With a wave of greeting to Danny, Weezy sat on the other end of the couch. She asked about Del's honeymoon. "Was it dreamy?"

"Dreamy enough so I wish I were still on it." Del covered her leg and plunged into her prepared speech. "Weezy, you need to get out of the Belle Turrets. The place has an unsavory reputation. Your mom will kill us both."

"I'm hoping my mother won't know." Weezy removed her large-brimmed hat and laid it aside. "I planned to use this flat for my mailing address."

Del stared. "You intend to *stay* in that place?"

"For the present. Fact is—I don't know how to tell you this—Yuri, my patron—well, we set out to be ever so proper, but we found we're wildly attracted. We can't keep our hands off one another. He's as surprised as I am."

Del felt herself sinking in quicksand. She spoke urgently. "That's all the more reason to get out of that convenient hotel."

Weezy grinned. "I gave it serious thought and I decided a writer has to know life. There are fascinating stories there. I've filled a notebook with material from the place. By the way, what would you guys say to the name Eloise? I'm thinking of calling myself that from now on. Eloise McCurdle of the Belle Turrets—it has a nice ring."

Danny let out a laugh at Del's shocked expression. "Del, you must quit trying to prevent life from happening. It can't be done."

Del ignored him. "So you and this Yuri have already—" She choked on the words and couldn't finish the sentence. Why had she so readily turned her apartment over to a young woman in rebellion, ripe for exploitation by a sophisticated New York male? Short of money, lacking Del's assistance, Weezy would have been forced to go home—and that, it now appeared, would have been the best thing for her.

"Just call me George Sand," Weezy said. "I'm joining the *demi-monde* to learn about life and literature."

To Del it sounded more like *La Traviata*, complete with potential for Grand Opera tragedy. Her thoughts were not of George Sand and Chopin, making love while beautiful music played in the background, but of Violetta abandoned and dying alone. She wondered what horrible outcome awaited her cousin.

CHAPTER 17

Del

In the quiet halls of the museum, an anticipatory silence preceded the hour for admittance of the public. En route to her boss's office, passing cases of geodes, Del felt a familiar thrill, the sense of awe and excitement most women experience toward gems already cut and set.

Though she'd dragged her feet about giving notice, she knew Bradley was right. There was no future for her in this place. She couldn't spend the rest of her life gluing potsherds. High time she made major changes in her life. Though it was true, as Danny had pointed out, that she'd been devastated when Dr. Witherspoon broke the news about excluding her from the dig, yet at the same time she'd suffered guilt, thinking: so selfish. The men *had* fought a war, a terrible war. They deserved to come home to jobs.

But for Witherspoon to send in her stead her own assistant, Randy Ferris, the very person she'd trained! For weeks she'd felt stabbed in the back. Indeed, it seemed as if she still carried the knife in her body. A steady, dull ache had never gone away.

Definitely, she needed to get into a field with room for women. Archeology was a glamour profession, under-funded and bereft of females.

Then, too, she *was* approaching thirty. Though Danny might make light of it, facts were facts. It was time to come to terms with marriage and babies. At the moment, she couldn't imagine giving up her work to stay at home cooking and cleaning, yet even more she couldn't imagine eliminating the option of doing so at some future date. She was last off the starting line, her high school and college classmates all sporting big families, her former roommate, Jan, already five months pregnant with her second child.

Life, as Gramps had often remarked, seemed always two jumps ahead of a person. Del never felt ready for it. When the doctor told her she had a soon-or-never decision to make about child-bearing, she'd rushed off in panic to seek consolation from her old friend and former roommate. Jan had calmly pointed out that, while children were forever, childcare was not. "So you set aside a few years to guarantee a family. Then you put the child in nursery school and return to whatever you planned to do in the first place." Well, that was what she was doing, wasn't it? Maybe she'd had to hold her nose but at least she'd taken the plunge; she'd married.

On rounding the corner, she encountered, jutting from the wall, a mock-up of half the moon, complete with craters, dark areas, lighter areas. A sign beneath informed her: *We will never know what lies on the far side of the moon since the moon always turns the same face toward earth.*

She felt frustrated over that fact. A scientist, she needed to know. Danny, the poet, liked for nature to keep her secrets. He wanted his mysteries to remain mysterious. Not she. She wanted answers; she longed to learn about the far side of the moon.

Moving on, she put her hand on the cold knob of the director's office door, rotated it, then shoved. She stepped into the small outer cubicle. Dr. Witherspoon's middle-aged secretary, Mildred Johnson, sat at the desk, brown hair in an upsweep from which a few strands had worked loose.

She looked up from her typing, adjusted her hairdo, and waved. "Miss Kingsley! Welcome back! What's on your mind?"

Del doubted that Mrs. Johnson, happily boastful of her grown children's success in life, would understand what was on the mind of a younger woman trying to get a start in her chosen profession. She confined herself to the facts. "I came to report that I got married last weekend. You'll need to change the name on my records."

"Why, Del! For Heaven's sake! You never said a word!" Bubbly-happy over this news, Mrs. Johnson smiled. "What a deep one you are! I didn't even know you were seeing someone special; you never mentioned—"

"He's an old flame. I was engaged to him years ago. I broke it off, decided I'd made a mistake—and we got together again. We took a short honeymoon, that's why—"

"So true love won out in the end! How romantic!" Her smile faded and she made a grimace of disappointment. "You gave staff no chance to plan a shower or engagement party. We'd have done you proud."

"I appreciate the thought, but it was sudden. In Michigan I learned he'd divorced his wife because of me. So, I felt—well—"

"Of course, of course. You didn't want to risk losing him again, so you jumped at the chance. I can understand that." The smile was in place again.

Was that what had happened? Del wondered. Was she really so desperate as all that?

She'd hated the way Danny failed to celebrate her marriage. Now she hated the fact Mildred Johnson *did* seem celebratory. I'm getting grumpy, she reflected, and hard to please.

Dr. Witherspoon, head of the archeology division, came from his inner office. An elderly gentleman with curly white hair, he'd always reminded her of her own Gramps. She knew he'd been genuinely distressed over the task of breaking to her the news about the dig. When he'd hemmed and hawed, she'd understood that the decision had been forced on him by the museum director. Yet she could no longer feel warm toward him as she once had.

He could have warned me in advance, she thought. He could have notified me I was training my replacement. He needn't have hit me with it suddenly and devastatingly.

"What's going on? I heard the commotion." The older man's head swiveled from his secretary to Del.

"Miss Kingsley's married," Mildred Johnson told him. "It happened last weekend and she never let us know. I was just telling her we'd have—"

"Well! Best wishes, I'm sure." At his grandfatherly best, he reached for Del's hand. "What's your new name?"

"I'm Mrs. Bradley Boynton." Del spoke the name automatically; she didn't even believe in it herself.

Obviously ill-at-ease with this news so suddenly thrust upon him, Dr. Witherspoon faked a smile. "When do we get to meet Mr. Boynton?"

Del explained about Bradley having to go back to Michigan to finish his work there. She took a deep breath and pushed out her planned statement. "I'll be leaving my job at the end of summer. I'm returning to college for education courses."

"Well, well." He rubbed his hands together. "Going into teaching, are you? That should work out fine. With your background in archeology, you'll have hands-on experience to convey to students."

A dreary parade of crowded classrooms marched across Del's mind. She squelched it. Maybe she'd get to specialize, take children on field trips, show them what digs were all about.

Belatedly, Dr. Witherspoon said what he should have said earlier: "We'll be sorry to lose you." Coming so late in the conversation, it sounded perfunctory. Del suspected that in reality, he felt relieved. What do you do with a talented woman you can't send into the field? No doubt she'd proved an embarrassment to him.

With Mrs. Johnson still insisting they must have a party, she left the office.

She was to dine with Danny and Weezy and meet Yuri. She didn't look forward to the occasion. Unready to stand *in loco parentis*, she couldn't imagine how she ought to behave around Yuri. To be friendly would be to imply acceptance; to be frosty would turn Weezy off and risk the loss of a cousin. There seemed no right way. All the same, she went home and dressed carefully.

Danny arrived neatly outfitted in his blue summer suit. He smiled at her with that look of affection he was so good at, as if she were someone he particularly cherished. It had once deceived her into thinking he'd change, but as time went on, she'd learned to live with the fact he was her non-sexual escort.

"I'm almost ready," she told him. "Sit down while I finish up."

He raised an eyebrow. "All this effort just to meet a man you don't approve of?"

"But I want him to approve of me." She stepped into the bedroom to powder her nose and put on her favorite hat, arranging it so that the brim dipped seductively over one eye. "If he doesn't approve of me," she added, raising her voice, "he won't be honest with me and I can't assess him realistically."

Danny came to lean against the door jamb, watching her. "So what? Weezy's of age; she gets to decide for herself."

She couldn't seem to communicate her concerns about the relationship, her fear of seeing her cousin destroyed. It was all very well for Edgar to be a black sheep; he was a man and would be forgiven. A woman would never recover her reputation. No way could Weezy be kept by a man for a few years and then get on with her life. Her ruin would haunt her. Del couldn't imagine letting her new-found cousin get involved in that—yet neither could she think how to prevent it. She'd had some vague notion of appealing to Mr. Yurovsky's better nature but now realized it wouldn't work. Had he worried about Weezy, he'd already have pulled out of the deal.

"If Yuri were eighty instead of almost forty, you'd say it's fine for him to have a protégé," Danny remarked.

"But he isn't eighty. What a difference forty years makes!" Del shoved a hat-pin into her hat and grabbed her purse. "What is he thinking? He'll wreck his marriage."

"Weezy claims his wife approves. It seems Yuri has been admitted to an exclusive club that didn't take Jews, and his wife was all for him conforming to—"

Del didn't believe that for a minute. "There never was a wife who gave her husband *carte blanche* to have an affair with a younger woman. He's dreaming." She turned brusquely. "Let's go."

They left the apartment and clattered down the four flights of stairs and across the vestibule. Outside, while Del held onto her hat against the wind, Danny gave her his arm. "I'm always happy to squire you around, Miss Davis, in your *Now, Voyager* outfit."

"If only I *were* Bette Davis," she said, "I'd use my money to fund an archeological dig and take Weezy along as my assistant. Get her away from Yuri and the Belle Turrets, solve two problems at once. Three, if you count rescuing Yuri's marriage. I'm sure his wife would love me to death."

"You know what? You sound like a woman who gave notice at work and is having regrets about it."

"You're right on that score." Del sighed. "That was the hardest thing I've done in years. But I do need to move on. In that place they merely give you new titles that sound imposing but mean nothing."

They went down the steps to the subway and waited for their train. People eyed them approvingly. Del knew they looked great together, the perfect couple, tall, handsome, well dressed. They drew admiring glances wherever they went.

Ironic, of course.

At the restaurant, Weezy sat, drinks in front of them, in the company of a slim man who looked younger than forty, looked in fact rather boyish. As Danny and Del approached, the man stood and awaited the introductions. Weezy said, "My cousin, Delia Boynton. Aaron Yurovsky."

Yuri offered Del a hand. He showed no hint that he anticipated anything but friendliness from her. He said, "I'm so glad to meet you. A lovely name, Delia. Has an old fashioned ring to it." His voice sounded warm, interested. "You and Eloise both have such fascinating backgrounds and—"

"I understand it's really Bedelia," Weezy said.

Yuri and Danny, who seemed to know one another, shook hands. Danny held Del's chair. While they all seated themselves, Del surreptitiously studied Yuri. He was not tall; Danny towered over him. Weezy was nearly his height and wouldn't be able to wear spiked heels in his company. He had naturally curly brown hair that resisted his efforts to smooth it. He reminded Del of Jan's husband, Irv, who also had a warm, affectionate, laughing-at-himself manner. She felt disarmed. Yuri seemed not at all the type to cheat on his wife or keep a mistress. If she hadn't known of the situation, she'd not have guessed it from his boyish, enthusiastic manner. What *could* the man be thinking, she wondered, to take such a whopping great risk with his marriage?

"I hear you're just back from a honeymoon," he commented to Del.

She nodded and told him it was short and sweet. "My new husband hasn't finished his work in Michigan yet. He had to go back for a few weeks."

"But how a romantic, to elope with a former boyfriend!"

"I'm probably one of the few people who ever enjoyed parental approval of an elopement," Del said. "My mother is crazy about Bradley. She's out of her mind with joy."

"Could anything be better?" Yuri smiled and took a quick sip of his cocktail. "You missed the fuss and gained approval." His warm and open manner proved instantly appealing. Del could see why Weezy had so quickly capitulated.

When the waiter came to take their orders, he stood patiently while they all made their decisions. Danny explained that the specialty of the house, fish, was top-notch. "I especially recommend the halibut."

Once the orders had been given—halibut all around and a bottle of Chardonnay—Weezy's paramour again turned to Del. "I feel as if I've stepped into a fairy tale. Weezy had such an exciting story to tell about discovering her new family, and now there's an elopement to add to it. It's so romantic."

Weezy sat there in her orange sheath, her oatmeal hat on the seat beside her. Her brown hair had been brushed until it shone. She looked sophisticated and in control, a young woman needing no help from her cousin. Why, Del wondered, was I thinking I should take charge of her life? She knows what she's doing.

"Exciting news," Weezy said. "I've sold a story!"

"Congratulations. Tell me about it." Del leaned forward. Maybe this would be the route to a solution. Maybe Weezy would jump into a great career.

"It's about a woman at the Belle Turrets who committed suicide." She related the plot. A Norwegian, the protagonist had come to this country hoping to develop her singing career. Though she'd found a patron, he abandoned her when she failed. "In the story I made it dramatic; how she forgot the words in her first important opera role, how the audience and critics walked out, how her patron berated her and her co-stars ganged up to condemn her for ruining their great opportunity. It was the end of an American Dream. She went home and pulled her radio into the bathtub with her—plugged in."

"Ooh, grim." No help there, Del reflected.

"But realistic. *Common Ground* wrote that they're planning to find a spot for it."

Danny lifted his eyebrows in surprise. "With the sexual implications of a patron?"

"Well, of course I didn't hint at that. Not for that market!" Weezy frowned at him.

He confessed he once sold a poem to the magazine, which focused on ethnic intermingling. "It was about being Jewish but not Jewish. They paid me fifteen dollars."

Weezy bit her lip and admitted what Del had already seen: it was no way to get rich. "But it's fun to see your work in print." She added that the Belle Turrets was loaded with good stories. Yuri smiled, squeezed her hand, and wished her luck.

Seeing the warmth of the gesture, Del abandoned her attempt to steer her cousin toward a break with him. As Danny had said, Weezy had a right to play *Traviata* if she chose. What have I been thinking? Del wondered. I'm the gal who used to scream bloody murder over the fact the University confined us women to quarters after ten-thirty. I tried to organize a protest; I howled that we were adults and shouldn't be kept under lock and key. Why on earth would I want to confine Weezy in that way? Lock her in a proper hotel, deny her the right to choose her life? Perish the thought!

"Your next story should be a sad tale about your cousin," Danny told Weezy. "She's quitting a job she loves because there's no future for women archeologists."

Del squirmed, fearing he would add that second thought of his: And for the same reason married a man she didn't love. But Danny was kind to her and kept silent after his one startling announcement. Even so, she flushed when all eyes turned to her. Clearly, in Danny's perception, she faced problems greater than Weezy's.

If she couldn't even convince Danny about her own situation, she certainly lacked the power to drag Weezy out of the *demi-monde*.

CHAPTER 18

Weezy

Weezy had warned Yuri that, being the type who could never be wholly dependent on anyone, she planned to earn what she could, and she liked the idea of becoming a literary agent. Even though an income of twenty-six a week would scarcely pay more than her subway fare and dinners at the Belle Turrets, she returned to the office of literary agent Larry Lauritz and announced that she'd arranged her finances so she could manage on his pay. Though her face flamed as she spoke, he asked no questions. His casual nod suggested lack of curiosity, and she thought him a cold sort of person—until she saw his eyes gleam with approval of her new dress and hat. She realized then he didn't care where she got her money, so long as she got it.

He leaned his elbows on his manuscript-laden desk. "I've already filled the job, Miss—uh—Eloise McCurdle, but the new girl may not work out. Lit majors often have a high-hat attitude about what we do here. Despite our name, Lauritz Literary Agency is not in the literature business. We're here to sell manuscripts to publishers. That means providing what the public likes to read, usually a thumping good story with lots of action and suspense." He conceded that a story needed character development, descriptions, interesting setting. "But our real work is with plot, p-l-o-t. We don't scorn pulps, confessions, amazing tales, or *The Perils of Pauline*. Action—that's what sells."

Nodding, Weezy tried to remember if she'd ever read a pulp, and decided she hadn't. She made a note to herself to flip through a few. She wouldn't even need to purchase them; people left pulps behind in the subway trains.

"Your non-literary background may prove a blessing," he added. "No pre-conceptions. I've had no end of trouble with literature majors." He scanned her previous application. "I do have your number."

"I've moved." She mentioned the number for her floor at the Belle Turrets, where each girl had her own signal for the phone.

He jotted it and offered to be in touch. She assumed this was the rhetorical, "I'll call you," meaning, "Don't hold your breath." But two days later he called. He confessed that, as he'd feared, the literature major hadn't worked out. He added that, fed up with trying to counteract the lofty nonsense instilled by college professors, he'd decided to give a non-literary person a chance. Weezy was to report for work on Monday. "And if you took those damn college lit classes, forget everything they taught you. I don't want to hear you quote your instructor. I need a business person who understands marketing, not a cotton-picking literary lady."

Crossing her fingers in hopes she'd picked up marketing tips from Jonathan, Weezy promised and hung up. It was now late Friday afternoon. The news created a crisis regarding clothing for Monday morning. Her new sheath was not an office dress. Her gray suit and basic black were Boston-subdued. She thought of buying several scarves and wearing a different one each day. That might take care of three days each week. What about the other two?

Also, she and Yuri were to go to a piano recital the following night at which she was to meet some of Yuri's colleagues with their protégés. No doubt the men would be curious about her and, worse, critical. Yuri as the "token Jew" would be in the spotlight. She'd need to mind her dress and manners, to make sure she made a good impression.

There seemed no help for it. She would have to let Yuri take her shopping next day as he'd been asking to do since they met. The only alternative was to borrow some of Del's outfits, and since her blonde cousin's clothes, though smart, were the wrong shade for her, they wouldn't serve.

That night she dined with Betty, this time at a hole-in-the-wall place her new acquaintance recommended. Neighborhood restaurants were not crowded on Fridays. Men began arriving in mid-afternoon for a swim and cocktails with their women, followed by dinner at some well known but discreet uptown establishment.

When Weezy confessed to Betty her hesitance about letting Yuri take her shopping, her companion laughed. "Hey, doll, enjoy! This doesn't happen every day. You gotta make hay while the sun shines. Your guy could change his mind. Happens all the time."

Weezy had been too preoccupied with worries about changing her own mind to consider the possibility that Yuri might be suffering a similar indecision. She asked, "Has that happened to you?"

"Are you kidding? A half dozen times at least. They say women are fickle, but if you ask me, guys are worse. Suddenly, out of the blue, they find someone else, and your rent don't get paid."

"What do you do then?"

With a shrug, Betty told her, "You call your agent. You do have an agent, don't you, doll?"

Weezy gasped. Was Moe Rifkin officially her agent? "Gosh, I don't know. I met an agent but he didn't charge."

"'Course not. He charges the guy. I always managed to find a new guy before the rent came due, but sometimes I don't like the new one so well. It's best to hang onto the one you have."

Weezy nodded. From her table near the door of the coffee shop, she'd watched the parade of salt-and-pepper-haired gentlemen entering the Belle Turrets lobby. None looked to be under fifty.

Though she didn't say so to Betty, to herself Weezy vowed there would never be an old man for her. If Yuri bowed out, she'd find a way somehow to live on her income. She'd seek one of those East Village flats she'd learned were so reasonable. Del paid only twenty-five a month for her flat, and claimed that those on the East Side rented for as little as six or eight.

She tried to focus her attention on Betty, who went on to declare she was sticking to her guns about insisting her guy divorce his wife. At thirty, she was getting too old for this life. She wanted to settle down. "I've got him eating out of my hand and I'm determined to keep up the pressure until I pull this off."

When Yuri arrived in mid-afternoon the following day, Weezy felt ready and eager to go with him on a shopping spree. When she mentioned Klein's, Ohrbach's, and Lerner's, he shook his head and suggested Lord and Taylor.

It was the first time Weezy had ever been free to pick out her own clothes. Grace, in shopping, always remained mindful of Jonathan's and Granny Hannaford's taste in clothes and insisted on something "suitable," by which she meant something to make Weezy unnoticeable in the crowd. To avoid notice was a Ward/Hannaford goal in life.

Not trusting her judgment, Weezy made her first choices in imitation of Del's wardrobe, selecting shades more congenial to her own darker coloring. As she persisted in trying on outfits, she began to discover, partly in response to Yuri's comments, what looked good on her. Del liked full skirts that swished around her legs. Weezy found she preferred slim lines. She returned the Del-types to the racks and made different choices.

When she and Yuri emerged from the store, both carrying boxes and bags, Yuri signaled a taxi, and they rode eastward to the Belle Turrets. On arrival, Weezy took the parcels to the bedroom, and while Yuri waited by the picture window—and admired the view, commenting that there were pleasure craft on the river—she decked herself in a "new look" paisley print with long skirt for which she'd bought a scarf matching the predominant blue-green shade.

She put on her new hat and studied herself in the mirror. She looked like a model. The schoolgirl was gone without a trace, and even the Invisible Bostonian had become a thing of the past.

When she emerged from the bedroom, Yuri gazed at her approvingly. She found to her surprise that she liked knowing she'd brought a sparkle to his brown eyes.

At dinner, they were to meet one of the other couples from his club. Another taxi ride took them to a dim, candle-lit place. Never having been in one before, Weezy, as she stepped inside, reveled in feeling naughty.

From behind, Yuri steered her to a table where another couple was already seated. When the man stood, Yuri introduced Weezy. "This is my special friend, Miss Eloise McCurdle." It occurred to Weezy that her name-change had enabled her to adopt this new persona. Miss Della Ward would not be here.

When Yuri said, "Miss Linette Ainsley and Mr. Harry Owens," Weezy nodded to the young woman and extended her hand to the man, a well-preserved sixtyish person in formal evening clothes, with white hair encircling a bald spot on his head. Yuri explained, "Miss Ainsley, his protégé, is a gifted pianist."

In the dim light, Weezy recognized the young woman as the person she'd admired at the Belle Turrets in the understated black dress and the chignon. Extending her hand, she said, "I've seen you in the lobby."

"I remember you." Linette smiled and squeezed her fingers. "You're new."

Yuri seated Weezy. When the two men sat down, Yuri remarked that Miss Ainsley—Linette—was scheduled to give her Town Hall recital in the fall. He explained to the others, "Miss McCurdle is a writer who just had her first story accepted by a national magazine."

While the other couple murmured congratulations, Weezy surreptitiously studied Linette Ainsley to see how she was dressed—in black, again, with a gold choker around her throat and a bracelet of spun gold that wound up her arm. Weezy decided her own paisley outfit would measure up and she would not embarrass Yuri.

The waiter came and took their orders. Mr. Owens talked of the problems faced by musicians in getting a start. Weezy sensed that he was reliving his own youth by being involved in youthful concerns. Linette said that the young woman performing tonight, Roberta Dresden, was her closest friend. She explained that the Town Hall Recital was the big moment for musicians, the occasion which would launch or destroy their careers. "All the critics come. If you flub it and get panned, you're dead. There's no appeal, no higher court."

"I had no idea there was such pressure in the music field," Weezy said.

Linette sighed. "Town Hall is a one-time exam you can never take over. If you schedule another recital, the critics won't come. You won't get written up or receive bookings."

"What if the critics show up and don't like you?"

"Oh, generally the critics will say *something* nice. It may be backhanded. They may say, 'She's mastered the technique but her playing lacks fire.' Then you quote the first part on your resume and ignore the second part."

"Do they ever say all good things?"

"Mostly it's a few good, a few bad. At best they may talk about 'promise,' as in: 'She shows promise of becoming a world-class musician.'"

"Tonight's performance is the last of the season." Mr. Owens commented. "The recitals don't usually run this late, but this year has been unusual. Returning vets who want to launch their careers are given preference."

"Yes, Robbi had to wait, and she's been getting more and more nervous as time dragged on," Linette added.

"Robbi?" Weezy asked.

"Roberta Dresden. She lives at the Belle Turrets. You may have seen her, though for obvious reasons she hasn't been out and about much lately."

"Black hair in a page-boy?" Weezy asked. "Understated clothing? Hand-made cloisonné jewelry?"

"That's Robbi. I guess you know her."

"No, but I saw her with you once and couldn't help admiring her. She's strikingly beautiful."

"You said it."

"Beautiful but flaky," Mr. Owens said. "I wonder her patron has patience with her. Sometimes she refuses to see him for a month at a time."

"With her talent, I guess she has a right to eccentricity," Linette theorized.

"She's the best pianist I've ever known personally. We're in for a treat tonight."

"I'm looking forward to it," Yuri said.

After dinner the group went to Town Hall, where in the lobby Weezy was introduced to three other couples in evening clothes. She winced on recalling how, in the past when she'd come down from Boston to attend Carnegie Hall concerts, she'd envied well dressed young women like this in the company of older men. Assuming the men were their fathers, she'd bewailed the fact Jonathan never took *her* to concerts. Oh, she'd been naïve! She bit her lip, remembering.

The group had a row of seats together. When the hall darkened and the young pianist came onstage, Weezy recognized her even in her pink sequined gown. She realized she'd seen her more than once at the Belle Turrets—and heard distant piano music which had sounded so professional she'd assumed it was coming from someone's radio.

The young woman bowed in response to the applause, sat down, and began to play. Her first piece was a Chopin, short, crisp, serving no doubt as a kind of warm-up. Following this, she launched into the third Beethoven sonata. She started off well, but as she went on, the music began to sound more lightweight than Weezy thought it should, a tinkle rather than a grand sweep. Weezy felt uneasy; she knew Beethoven ought to be intense and passionate. Surely, the critics would carp at this rendition.

As if she'd noticed, too, Linette leaned close to her to whisper that she sensed her friend was nervous. Weezy nodded. Her mouth went dry. She identified with the young woman at the piano and felt her uncertainty.

In the second movement, something went very wrong. The audience grew restive; programs rustled; the music sounded hesitant, unnatural. People moved, whispered to one another. Weezy looked around, seeking the cause of the problem.

"She's forgotten the notes; she's improvising," Linette mouthed. "What a terrible thing! Poor Rob!"

The audience noise increased in volume until it competed with the music. All at once a row of people stood up and began to inch their way to the aisle.

"The critics!" Linette wailed, *sotto voce*. "They're leaving!"

Several audience members gasped audibly. Weezy heard Mr. Owens breathe, "My God!" The critics marched out. Seeming to sense what was happening, the pianist let her fingers falter. The music died. She started again, determinedly. She played on for about a minute, then banged the keys in noisy discord, threw up her hands, and rushed from the stage. There was a vast gasp, en masse, from the audience.

An elderly gentleman near the end of their own row rose, excused himself, inched his way past three other people, and followed the critics up the aisle. Yuri, on Weezy's left, whispered that the man was Robbi's patron. "I suspect he's walking out."

Mr. Owens leaned close to speak to Weezy and Yuri. "Did you see the scowl on his face? He's finished with her."

"But that's cruel!" Weezy protested.

Sophistication abandoned, Linette twisted her handkerchief and batted tears from her eyes. "This is awful! I can't bear it for her!"

There was more rustling as audience members stood up, gathered belongings, and prepared to join the growing parade of departures. With a sigh, Yuri said, "We may as well go, too. I doubt there'll be more music tonight."

He held Weezy's elbow as, with her purse and gloves, she rose and moved out ahead of him. She asked, "Isn't there anything we can do? Go backstage, offer consolation?"

Linette, in front of her, shook her head and declared that such a crowd would only upset her friend further. "I'll go by myself if you'll wait for me."

The group gathered in the lobby. It was not a long wait. Linette soon returned to say that Miss Dresden had locked her dressing-room door and was admitting no one, not even her mother. "We may as well leave. Robbi must be dying of humiliation. I couldn't face anyone at such a time, either."

As they walked out of the theater, Linette added with a sigh, "Now I'll be terrified of my Town Hall recital. It's all up with Robbi. She can perhaps settle in some small city and hang out a sign as a piano teacher, but she'll never make it to the big time. And after a lifetime of practice!" Out on the sidewalk, she turned back, eyes red, face-muscles working as she fought tears. "It's so ironic! Anyone can freeze and forget. And now she's lost her patron. How will she pay her rent?"

Mr. Owens slipped an arm across her shoulder. "You won't lose me, my dear. I believe in you, and I'd never walk out on you like that. If you fail here, I'll take you to Europe."

Tears overflowing, Linette reached for his hand and managed a wavering smile. "Thanks, Reggie, I appreciate your faith in me."

Behind Weezy and Yuri, someone in the group suggested going on to a nightclub. "The night is young."

They hailed two taxis and all piled in. At a nearby club, they gathered at a single large table. No one seemed to feel like dancing. Linette kept touching her handkerchief to her eyes. They ordered drinks and sat in long-faced silence.

Weezy reflected that this wasn't at all what she'd expected. Whenever she heard that wonderful drinking song from *La Traviata*, she'd fancied the world of the *demi-monde* to be one of enviable pleasure.

Yuri noticed her long face and reaching for her fingers, produced a wavering smile. "Hey, cheer up! Writers don't give Town Hall recitals."

"Same principle. If a first novel doesn't sell, you never get a second one published."

"Not true, my dear. I've seen little-read novelists zoom to fame." He clasped her hand and squeezed lightly. "You're in the right field, Miss Eloise McCurdle. There's hope for you."

Weezy thanked him for his faith in her.

CHAPTER 19

Weezy

Awakened on Sunday morning by a tap at the door, Weezy assumed, until she rolled over and peered at the clock, that it was dawn. On seeing the small hand on nine, the big hand on six, she blinked, rubbed her eyes, and tried to orient herself to the late hour and the fact she'd overslept.

When the tap was urgently repeated, she eased herself out of bed. Could Yuri have come back? He'd left at two a.m. with no mention of seeing her again later in the day.

With the chain on, she opened the door a crack. Linette stood in the hallway barefoot, in a blue terrycloth bathrobe. Her eyes were teary and bloodshot, her face streaked and blotched. Her uncombed blonde hair hung loose on her shoulders.

Concerned, Weezy unlatched and opened the door. "Linette! What happened? What's wrong?"

Linette stepped into the room, tears trickling down her face. She wept into a handkerchief. Weezy was moved to hug her new friend impulsively while the young woman sobbed. "Robbi killed herself! I heard it on the radio."

"Killed herself? Oh, no!"

"Jumped—from the twelfth floor—Lexington Hotel." She gestured toward the radio on the shelf. "Tune in the news, quick!"

Weezy snapped on the radio, waited impatiently through the static, fiddled with the knob to find a news station, and ratcheted up the voice of the announcer. "—occurred about four in the morning, with the body discovered by early-bird church-goers. Though residents of the hotel claim to have heard a scream in the night, it appears no one investigated. The deceased, who was identified by her mother, is presumed to have committed suicide following memory-failure at her piano recital at Town Hall."

He went on to explain that the woman was a resident of the Belle Turrets, where for the past weeks she'd been practicing for last night's performance. "Aged twenty-three, she is survived by her mother, Mrs. Hilda Dresden of Long Island, and her father, Jacob Dresden of Hollywood, California."

"This is too awful! I can't bear it!" Linette clutched her hair and moved toward the picture window. As other news came on, Weezy switched off the radio and went to put a hand on her guest's shoulder.

"I'm so sorry," she said. "It's such a waste. So much talent—and she was as stunning as a model: flawless complexion, perfect figure."

"Music needn't have been everything in the world for her." Linette struggled to stop her voice from shaking. "She might have made it in Hollywood—playing the piano, even acting. She had connections. Her father works for a studio."

Weezy confessed that until yesterday she'd had no idea life was so hard for musicians. Linette, when she had herself under control, told her, "For a woman, getting into the classical music field is next to impossible unless you're an opera singer—and then only if you're top-notch." She fumbled in her robe-pocket for a handkerchief, blew her nose, and wiped away tears. "For some reason, audiences prefer men pianists and violinists. And as for joining an orchestra, forget it. During the war, we were in demand. But those days are gone."

"Yet you keep trying."

"It matters to us." Linette broke down in sobs. She hid her face in her hands. "We were born to be musicians." With deep breaths she sought to control her tears. She wiped her eyes. "I'm sorry."

Weezy pressed her shoulder. Since no consoling words occurred, she offered to make coffee. She stepped into the tiny kitchen area with its small sink and two-burner gas stove, where she ran water into the pot and spooned out coffee. The rich aroma gave her spirits a lift. She commented that anyone could blank out, that it had nothing to do with Robbi's talents and abilities. "The critics shouldn't have—"

"But that's why the blank-out occurred," Linette persisted. "It's the terrible pressure women are under. We have to be twice as good as men. How can we possibly achieve at that level? If Paderewski had been a woman, no one would have listened to him—her." Clutching her handkerchief, pushing her hair from her eyes, she paced. "It shatters your self-confidence; you walk onto the stage already nervous and trembling."

"I knew right away that something was wrong," Weezy said. "The music sounded light-weight and tinkling."

Linette sighed and followed Weezy into the kitchen area. "Robbi should have stuck to Chopin. She was world-class in that. But she was determined to prove she could do something major. She hoped to impress her dad."

"I know the feeling," Weezy said.

Head in hands, Linette drew a long, shaky breath. "If only she'd let me in last night when I pounded on her dressing-room door! If only I'd had a chance to talk to her!"

"They say that doesn't help once the person has made up her mind to kill herself."

Returning to the living room to collapse on the couch, Linette added that Mr. Dresden had promised to come to New York for the recital but canceled at the last minute. "That upset her, too." When Weezy asked how long Linette had known Robbi, Linette leaned back, put a hand on her forehead and massaged. Eyes closed, she explained. "We met at Juilliard and worked as teaching assistants during the war. When the men came back and we couldn't get jobs, we agonized together over whether we should become involved with patrons who'd finance us. We couldn't see ourselves doing it but we decided it was the only way. After all, we were given a talent and presumably we were meant to use it. That's karma, isn't it?" She looked at Weezy, standing over her, as if Weezy had the answer to that question. When none was forthcoming, when Weezy only shook her head, she added, dabbing at her eyes, "I found a good patron but Rob wasn't so lucky."

Weezy could find no response. Like Robbi, Linette was a beautiful, talented, and highly educated young woman. It seemed tragic she should face such a dilemma. "Same problem for writers," Weezy said. "I can't get a job in the publishing industry that pays enough to support me." She set out cups and saucers, cream and sugar, and waited while the coffee perked. The fragrance wafted through the room and seemed to revive Linette, who straightened and sniffed back her sobs.

Finger-combing her long hair, she remarked that while the casting couch was a joke to most people, it was a tragedy to young artists. All too many so-called patrons added to the pressure by threatening to leave if things didn't go well. "Rob's the second musician to kill herself. There was a singer—"

"Yes, I wrote a story about her."

"During the war we women were needed. Now we're discards."

"That's true in every field." Weezy turned off the gas and poured the coffee. "My cousin was an archeologist, sent on digs. Now she gets to stay behind—for much less pay—and glue potsherds while the men go."

Linette nodded while accepting the steaming beverage. Her hand shook and she quickly set the cup on the coffee table. She added cream and sugar, and then lifted the cup, sipped cautiously, and winced as the hot liquid touched her tongue. She remarked, "We're all being sent back to the kitchen. The magazines lecture us, 'Give the men a chance. Don't be selfish.'"

"And worse—don't be a castrator. The possibility of that *really* scares me." After creaming her own coffee, Weezy sat down beside Linette on the couch. She theorized that perhaps Linette should go to Europe as Mr. Owens had suggested. "They lost so many men over there, they must need women musicians."

"It may come to that."

When the phone gave four short rings, Linette looked around. "That's my signal."

Weezy passed her the phone on its long cord. Linette asked the operator to switch the call to Miss McCurdle's suite. She winced again on hearing a voice so loud and teary-sounding that it was audible even to Weezy. Linette said, "Mrs. Dresden? I heard the news on the radio. I can't believe it—I don't know what to say."

The excitable voice on the other end yelled in a high-pitched tone. Linette obviously struggled to respond calmly. Weezy heard, "That's awful!" and "I'm so sorry," and "Tell me how I can help." And finally, "I'll meet you in the lobby right away."

On hanging up, Linette told Weezy, "The police will be coming here to go through Robbi's things. Mrs. Dresden wants to check the room first, and asked me to go with her. Will you come?"

Weezy protested. "I don't know the woman. I'd feel I'm invading her privacy."

"I'd really appreciate your company," Linette said. "Mrs. Dresden's awfully upset, and I'm too shook up to deal with that. I've lost my best friend."

"All right. Just let me throw on some clothes."

"I have to dress, too. I'll wait for you by the elevator." She quickly swallowed the last of her coffee.

When Linette left, Weezy went to the bedroom and put on her one plain outfit, a white shirt-waist blouse and black skirt. Black seemed appropriate for the occasion. In her mind she worked out how best to write up this tragedy. Then she scolded herself. This was no time to be planning a story.

The prim and proper Della Ward would never have learned of all these problems, she reminded herself. She couldn't possibly have been a writer. Eloise McCurdle was proving more courageous about getting out in the world.

Finished buttoning, she grabbed a hairbrush. While she worked at her hair, smoothing it into a shiny brown cap, her mind argued: This will be my best story ever; it'll be a tribute and a memorial. She continued the argument while slipping on her shoes. If not for us writers, who would remember the agonies people endure? Perhaps I can ensure that Roberta is not forgotten.

She inspected herself in the mirror, powdered her nose, drew lipstick across her lips, and went out. She met Linette at the elevator. Linette had slipped on a light green dress and stepped into gold sandals, but her hair was still down on her shoulders, her face bare of makeup. As they awaited the elevator, she dabbed at bloodshot eyes again.

"I keep thinking it could have been me. Last night I felt I was there on-stage with Robbi. I sensed everything she was going through. She *had* to succeed and so she tried too hard. I've done the same. You know you're fouling up and you feel you can't live through the failure. You want the floor to open and swallow you. You pray God to make all this be a dream and let you wake up. You fake frantically. When all else fails, you blank out. Robbi must have heard the audience muttering and realized they saw through her hasty improvising."

When the elevator came, they stepped into it. Weezy leaned against the satin-lined wall and admitted she'd sensed all that. "I felt her tension; I worried for her." She recalled how her palms had grown sweaty as the unease communicated.

"She must have seen no way to go on from there," Linette asserted. "No way to face people afterward. No way to endure the critics. So she jumped."

Weezy asserted, "We have to learn not to care so much. A career isn't worth dying for."

In the lobby, a short, portly woman awaited them. Her eyes too were red. Her black outfit, wrong for her sallow complexion, looked thrown together, the blouse partially tucked in, partially hanging out. She'd fastened her brown hair into an upsweep, hastily, missing a few strands which stuck out at angles. Linette said, "There's Mrs. Dresden," and led the way over to her. She hugged the older woman, who thanked her for coming.

Linette introduced Weezy and explained. "She was at the recital so I gave her the news."

Mrs. Dresden nodded vaguely in Weezy's direction, but Weezy sensed the woman was too distraught to truly notice her. She grabbed Linette's arm and leaned on it, announcing that the police would be coming any minute. "I wanted to get here first."

"Why are the police needed?" Linette asked.

"Well, you know, they have to be certain there was no 'foul play' as they call it. I hate to think of men going through my poor child's personal things. I want to make sure there are no—you know—diaphragms or douche bags lying around."

Linette shook her head. "I think you should leave everything as it is. If the police suspect that miserable patron, so what? I'd love to see him arrested; he was so quick to leave."

The small woman waved her hand dismissively. "He was a Johnny-come-lately. The real villain is Robbi's father. He walked out on us when Rob was a toddler, and he never did anything for her except send court-ordered child support. Money isn't the only thing a child needs. It left my baby's heart empty, and set her to looking for love in the wrong places." She fumbled in her purse and brought out a handkerchief.

The three returned to the elevator and the younger women helped Mrs. Dresden enter it. Linette asked when Mrs. Dresden had realized Robbi was missing.

"I awoke at dawn and heard screaming outside. I noticed that Robbi's bed hadn't been slept in. The window was wide open. I looked down and saw the ambulance, guys trying to move screaming onlookers away so they could scrape something off the sidewalk. It didn't occur to me it could be the remains of my daughter. I assumed Rob was downstairs having coffee."

Though she clutched her handkerchief tightly, she managed to describe this mayhem without shedding a tear. Weezy thought she must be in shock. She seemed to be reciting a prepared statement. She went on, "I put on my clothes and went down. I saw no one in the coffee shop so I stepped out to the street to learn what the fuss was about. I recognized her hair. The rest was too smashed to identify. She'd fallen on her face."

Linette mouthed under her breath, "Horrible!"

On the floor below Weezy's, the women entered a suite. The place was a mess, clothes flung over the backs of chairs and on the sofa, music piled on the grand piano, cups everywhere half full of stale coffee. The telegram from Hollywood, notifying Robbi that her father would not be at Town Hall, still lay open on the coffee table. Weezy felt a chill. It was too reminiscent of her own recent telegram notifying her of the death of the man she'd believed to be a birth parent. She was only now realizing what a shock she'd sustained on discovering that he was no blood kin.

Linette said, "I knew she was distraught—but usually that passes once you start to play. You get a surge of confidence when your fingers hit the keys."

"Not this time." Mrs. Dresden shook her head mournfully. "Poor Rob. And poor me. She was my only child."

"Should we clean all this up before the cops come?"

"No, you should not," a male voice from the doorway barked. "What are you women doing here?"

They whirled and saw a tall, thin plain clothes policeman, accompanied by a uniformed officer, step into the room. Mrs. Dresden snapped, "I'm her mother!"

"I'll talk to you later. This is a potential crime scene."

She remonstrated. "But officer, we need to—"

"I must ask you to leave. There'll be no tampering with evidence."

Mrs. Dresden moved to the door, her lower lip protruding rebelliously. The two younger women followed. All three left the room and walked down the hall.

"He didn't have to be so abrupt," Mrs. Dresden complained.

A devotee of mystery stories, Weezy told her, "They always are, I believe."

"If they're looking for a murderer, they should arrest her father and her patron. Both were guilty. Her father broke her heart by refusing to come to her recital, and her patron scared her to death warning her that if she flubbed it, he was through. Between them they drove her to suicide. Small chance the police will figure that out."

"People never blame the men," Weezy said. "They blame the woman for being too flighty."

"That's exactly what they'll do. I can hear those nasty words now: flighty, nervous, high strung."

They went to the coffee shop, where they ordered coffee and doughnuts but found they couldn't eat. They sat heads in hands, gazing at their food. It didn't seem possible that the vibrant young woman in the rose-pink dress was dead. She'd walked onto the stage looking beautiful and in control, her dark hair shining. There'd been a twitter of pleased anticipation along with applause from the audience. Everything after that was like a dream—or a nightmare.

Weezy realized she was lucky to have found a patron she was attracted to. Life must have been hell for Robbi, having to sleep with a man she didn't care for. Weezy knew she couldn't do it, not even for love of her chosen profession.

CHAPTER 20

Weezy

At work next day, her first day on the job as a literary agent, Weezy tried to force her mind from its preoccupation with Robbi to pay attention to her new boss, Mr. Lauritz, who stood beside his desk listing off what was expected of her.

He gave Weezy a six-page typed document and explained that with this outline she would have no problem writing a critique, since most of the work was already done for her. She need only select the appropriate sentences and fill in the blanks.

"Read it and familiarize yourself with it," he said.

She struggled to focus her mind and move her gaze over the first paragraph.

You have a promising story here (We always tell the client that, Mr. Lauritz had cautioned her. We never, ever say it's rotten or hopeless.) *but your main character, while well drawn, looks to others to solve his problems. A primary rule of good story-telling requires that the main character solve his problems for himself. If you send the cavalry to the rescue, help must arrive moments after Blank has already handled things. Other characters may ease Blank's predicament, even offer back-up, but they may never take on his dilemmas. It's essential that Blank find a clever solution all on his own.*

Eyeing her while she read, Mr. Lauritz explained, "The problems described there are mistakes all beginners make—but not every beginner makes every mistake. You have to pick and choose. You'll type up the appropriate passages, fill in character names, and mail off the copy along with the returned story."

Though she found it difficult to believe there could be a one-size-fits-all critique, she followed instructions. Back in her cubicle, she read the first of the stories piled on her desk, and was surprised to discover that she was indeed able to write a critique by simply choosing the right paragraphs from the six-page outline and filling in the blanks. She worked quickly and then perused her finished document.

Your main character, Ann, is well drawn. Unfortunately, the minor characters come across as mere names. You need to flesh these out, make them real people with lives and problems of their own. Janice, the antagonist, and Rex the lover are particularly important to the story and must be given distinct personalities. Provide a description. We might see Janice as a slender woman with long dark hair and buck teeth. Also mention her favorite wearing apparel. Perhaps she leans toward flaring pedal-pushers and cowboy boots. Go on to tell us how she happens to be working at ZYX ranch. Give us details of how she became enamored of Rex, how she worked to attract him while offering Ann competition. She should have something that Ann lacks. And of course, if both women are to be in love with this man, we must see him as a charmer. You'll need to describe him more fully. You will find that this can be done in a few well-chosen words.

Such a professional-sounding critique, and I hardly did a thing, Weezy thought. Of course, I did contribute the dark hair, buck teeth and flaring pedal-pushers. She added a few sentences about the plot, and then popped the typed page along with the manuscript into the return envelope, to be mailed to the author.

This is fun, she decided. It's a game. I'm going to like this job.

You should have waited around, Roberta Dresden, to find out what tomorrow had in store. The world is so full of a number of things, as some poet said.

During her lunch hour, after eating the sandwich she'd brought, she took a cab to the mortuary for the service. She arrived late and found the hall filled. Luckily, Linette had saved her a seat, and Weezy joined her. Either Robbi'd had lots of friends or there were curiosity seekers. Glancing back, she saw Yuri enter, nod to her, and slide into a seat at the back. She wished she could sit with him—but that would be too public.

The rabbi offered the same kind of fake consolation Christian funeral preachers seemed to come up with. "We who are left behind must remember the beautiful life this young woman lived, with her glowing musical performances, and try to forget the tragedy of her death. We need to recall the joy she brought to friends and relatives with her playing. From the time she was a small child, music was a guiding force in her life. She was happiest when at the piano, and if in the end the instrument seemed to let her down, this occurred only in her own flawed perception. In the heat of the moment, she forgot that we're all human; none of us is perfect. She asked too much of herself."

Weezy struggled to concentrate but her mind was still back in the office, writing critiques, filling in blanks. She applied the rules to her own planned story. *Your main character, Roberta, is well drawn but she fails to solve her problem. You will need to contrive—*

She came back to the rabbi as he began listing off the degrees the deceased had earned: Bachelor of Music, University of Michigan, Master of Piano, Julliard School. He went on to mention the concerts and recitals she'd played during her lifetime, most in Long Island where she'd grown up.

There was an organ interlude during which Weezy allowed her mind to ponder the question of how she might write her story in such a way as to have her heroine discover a solution. The rabbi put on his prayer shawl and offered prayers and chants in Hebrew. These sounded holy and awesome. Weezy found it easy to believe in the efficacy of prayers in this language so sonorous and imposing.

As she listened, she saw in her mind the telegram on Robbi's coffee table, and it seemed to become transformed into her mother's telegram notifying her of Jonathan's death. Suddenly tears stung her eyes. She felt again the disappointment of that moment, the thought that now she would never hear the words of fatherly praise she'd longed for all her life. Her mother had always told her that her father was too busy for childish affairs. When the telegram arrived, it informed her that situation would never be altered. Sharing now Robbi's desolation at the absence of a parent, she wished that just once she might have held Robbi's hand and told her how she too had hungered for approval from a father who chose to withhold it. She hastily dabbed at her eyes.

When the service ended and people stood to reach for wraps, Weezy looked around for Yuri but saw that he'd left. She knew that, as owner of his own company, he lacked the luxury of a long lunch hour.

Several women she recognized from the Belle Turrets waved to her. Linette took her arm and remarked that that patron, the turd, never showed up.

"His loss," Weezy asserted. "It was a beautiful service." She blinked hard.

"I guess Jews don't excommunicate people for suicide, like we Catholics do."

They walked out together. On the front steps, the other women from the Belle Turrets gathered around them. Not having attended the concert, they'd known nothing of the events until they read of them in the evening paper. Now they besieged Weezy and Linette with questions. "Why did she do it? She had everything to live for. We all envied her great figure and good complexion, not to mention her talent."

Weezy consulted her watch and apologized that she couldn't stop now; she was due back at work. "Meet me in the coffee shop around six and we'll talk."

While riding a taxi back to her office building and climbing to her second-floor cubicle, she shed yet more tears as memories of Jonathan, of her childish longing for his attention, flooded back to her. She wondered how writers managed to fit life into stories conforming to the literary rules. She saw no way of making her Roberta character solve her problems, which seemed to be society problems rather than individual ones, society's war against women. This was one story in which she'd have to report what happened and contrive no clever solution. She'd be the literary agent who failed to follow her own advice.

That evening, she and Linette found themselves the center of attention. Not only the mourners from the funeral, but others who'd only now heard the news, came to their table in the coffee shop to ask questions. With the ice broken, women who'd formerly ignored Weezy grew friendly. Over and over, she was asked to tell what she knew. How did it happen? What sent Robbi over the edge? In response, several women related their own tales of how they'd landed at the Belle Turrets. For most, clearly, it had been a difficult, even a harrowing, decision.

"Roberta disliked her patron," a woman named Bertha remarked. "That always makes for a bad situation. When you're doing this because you have to, the men know you're forcing yourself. You can't hide it. Her guy couldn't fail to realize that she was counting the minutes until she struck it rich and could get away from him."

Someone said, "Mistresses can't have headaches." The comment elicited snorts of sardonic laughter from the group. Weezy shuddered at their grim humor.

"Robbi didn't know how to dissemble," Yvonne, the opera singer, remarked. "She communicated her dislike of her old duffer."

Bertha commented that some men become a woman's slave when badly treated. "Too bad Robbi's patron wasn't that type."

Opera-singer Yvonne theorized that it was best to seem independent, neither slave nor slave-master. Bertha thought Robbi went too far with her independence. Weezy expressed the thought that perhaps it wasn't good to be so wholly dedicated to one thing as Robbi was to music. Yvonne insisted it was necessary if one were to become world class. "You have to put up with things like subservience to patrons." Weezy theorized that there should be subsidies for talented young artists.

"Oh—should! No use talking about should." The women around the table, some sitting, some standing, shook their heads. "You'd just better know where your bread is buttered if you're aiming for the big time," said a woman whose name Weezy hadn't heard. Linette added that Robbi'd hoped her father would provide financial aid. "I'm sure she dreamed of dazzling the man with her brilliant performance, and afterward falling into his arms in a grand reconciliation. I warned her it was unrealistic."

"We all have our fantasies." Yvonne sighed. "My father hates opera. It's the last thing in the world he'd pay for. He's furious with me for even considering it."

Clearly, everyone was upset by the suicide. Someone remarked, "There, but for the grace of God, go I." As the conversation continued, Weezy gathered that each woman had been dumped by a patron at some time in her life, left with no way to pay the rent, faced with the possibility of going on the streets. She vowed again that no such thing would ever happen to her. If Yuri wanted out, she'd find one of those six-dollar-a-week lofts in the East Village, furnish it with orange crates, and live on her twenty-six dollar salary even if it meant eating nothing but rice and beans.

When, on Tuesday, Yuri came over after work, Weezy told of going with Mrs. Dresden to Robbi's suite, the police arriving to eject them, and their later return to sort through the personal effects of one young life. She didn't mention that Robbi had been desperately trying to free herself from the need for patronage, but Yuri, who it seemed had met the pianist in the company of her patron, appeared to know that. He remarked, "She wanted independence, yet remained in a field where independence is not feasible."

Yuri suggested dinner. "We could try the Hungarian place up the street. Do you like goulash? Afterward, we might take in a movie if you're not too tired from your day's work."

Weezy assured him her work was not tiring. "I just adapt Mr. Lauritz's critiques to the stories he gives me to read. It's like a game, actually."

"I'm glad you're not tired. I don't have to go home tonight. My wife is off giving a lecture in upstate New York."

"Wonderful. I'll change."

"No need. You look fine in your office outfit. That peach blouse is becoming to you."

In the restaurant, they found a secluded booth in a dim corner. While they waited for their dinner to be served, Weezy described her job. Yuri admitted to envying her for being at least potentially exposed to literature. "You may discover the next Steinbeck."

When Weezy confessed that she'd have preferred to *be* the next Steinbeck, he laughed and admitted he shared her dream. "I always wanted to write. I never got to do much except during my last two years in the Army, when they put me in Special Services to write comedy scripts for traveling entertainers. That was fun."

Weezy urged him to talk about it. He promised to dig out some of the scripts. "I think I still have a few at home."

"Oh, good. I'd love to see them." Weezy went on to tell him, "Mr. Lauritz likes my work and promised to let me take a writer to lunch next week. Seems there are two clients coming to New York on the same day, and he'll be wining and dining the more successful one. I'm assigned to the one with 'promise.'"

"In the long run, that might be more interesting," Yuri speculated.

"Best of all, I'm to have an expense account."

Yuri gave her a wry smile. "You'll be getting independent of me."

Impulsively, she reached across the table to touch his hand. He had such nice hands, with well-manicured nails. She looked into his brown eyes and admired the way his hair fell across his forehead in tight curls. "If I chose to be independent of you, Mr. Aaron Yurovsky, I would already be so. I'd never let myself be caught in Robbi's trap, not if I had to spend my life as a waitress."

"Good, I like your spirit." Yuri turned his hand to grasp hers. "Seriously, Eloise, I want you to admit it right away if you find our relationship repellant. Don't go on the way Robbi did, hating it but denying the fact." With a quick smile he added, "Even though I'll be devastated, I want the truth."

"I'll try to walk the fine line, not falling in love, not trying to get so rich and successful I'll want to throw you out."

"Oh, go ahead and get rich." He was grinning now. "We'll stay together out of mutual attraction. I'm not the type to play the hated provider to the great diva."

"I could never hate you, Yuri. And I'm no diva, I'm a writer."

"So you are." They both laughed and clasped hands across the table.

CHAPTER 21

Del

"Aren't you worried what your mom will think?" Del asked as Weezy lounged on her couch. "In your shoes, I'd be in a dither."

Weezy frowned, bit her lip, and scanned again the letter from her mother which Del had just brought to her suite at the Belle Turrets. "I figure Mother forfeited the right to care about what I do. I'm having trouble forgiving her for snatching me from my birth father and taking me to a man who didn't really want me. It's not fun to grow up struggling to attract attention from a parent who resents your existence. You know what the psychiatrists say about that—how it makes young women too needy of male attention? That's me—I'm a classic case."

It was a Sunday afternoon. Del had discovered that Sundays were endless now that she could no longer folkdance with Hilario. The day had seemed to go on forever; she'd read a book, taken a stroll through Washington Square, and finally decided to visit Weezy at the infamous residence hall, bringing her cousin's accumulated mail. On entering, she'd suffered one shock after another, first at the poodle-walkers who never made eye-contact with any-one—so they couldn't be accused by their boyfriends of flirting, Weezy later explained—then at the plush lobby, the satin-walled elevator, the stifling lux-ury suite.

"Grace would have hysterics," she warned. "And as for Old Lady Hannaford—"

"I don't plan for them to know." Unruffled, Weezy tossed the letter aside. "As you see, I gave your address."

Del couldn't hide her distaste. "They'd call this a bordello."

"Well, so is Mom's house a bordello. Any place where a woman lives with a man not of her choosing, for money or appearances, is a bordello." She frowned at the letter and drummed her fingers on the chair arm. "You don't know, Del—you say you had a good relationship with your father. You don't know what it's like to put in a lifetime of struggle to placate a man who perceives you as the child of the enemy. I can see now that Jonathan must have been devastated when his fiancée ran off and got pregnant with another man—and of course he couldn't love the product of that union—but he never told me, never hinted. I assumed it was me, my failure, my inability to please a man. I believed I was missing some feminine attribute necessary to man-charming."

With a sympathetic expression Del agreed that the situation must have been damaging to her cousin's sense of self-worth. Weezy confessed that Yuri's strong and well-demonstrated attraction to her had helped to restore her ego. "He makes me feel so-o-o good about myself."

Del stifled disapproval and made herself nod her understanding. She got up and looked out the window, feeling surprised that classy women like Linette and Robbi stayed in this place. She marveled that Robbi's mother hadn't long ago snatched her daughter out of here. She'd listened, unbelieving, while Weezy described her attempt to help Mrs. Dresden clean out Robbi's suite. "You mean her mother *approved* of this place?" Weezy had chuckled at her shocked expression. "Face it, Del; the casting couch is preferable to dream's end. It offers a last ray of hope when all else fails. Some of us are not genius enough to start off as child prodigies, earning money for our own training. What do you do when you get no help from home, no government subsidy, yet feel no less of an artistic compulsion than did Mozart or Van Gogh?"

Del could only shake her head. She had no answers. While Weezy went to the small kitchen to make coffee, she confronted her own situation. Though her cousin had stopped short of accusing *her* of living in a bordello, she wondered if it was true. *Did I marry Bradley out of panic rather than love?* She'd asked herself the question a thousand times, and she was still asking. Was the exciting, hunger-for-closeness feeling she had for Hilario love, or was it lust? Was the going-from-day-to-day feeling she had for Bradley love, or was it the convenience of the familiar? She honestly didn't know. She knew only that since Danny had set her to thinking about Hilario, she had to battle to keep herself from picking up the telephone and offering to go dancing with him. Just visualizing him, leading the line, waving his red bandanna, she heard in her mind a song her mother used to sing: *My heart, at thy dear voice, opens wide like the shamrock which the morning breezes waken...*

Tears sprang to her eyes.

However did I get so frantic? she wondered. Pondering, she realized it was more than just the job-problem. There'd also been an awful moment, three weeks before her trip to Michigan, when the doctor had told her, "Children now or never. It's time to make a decision; time to marry if you want a family." The thought had nagged at her and put her in a mood to be receptive to Bradley. She'd been so convinced that Hilario wasn't the marrying kind.

When the doctor made his frightening pronouncement, she'd known she had to choose. Did she want children or didn't she? That night, she'd had a troubling dream in which she grasped at a string of pearls around her neck, tugged until she broke it, and tossed the pearls onto the ground where they promptly disappeared in the dust. She knew that pearls represented children. Did she mean to deprive herself?

Working her way through graduate school would leave no time for meeting or dating men. So that option had had to be closed. That left—Bradley. She'd imagined she was lucky to find him at the right moment. So much future would otherwise be lost to her. She'd met him right after her visit with Jan, who'd pumped her full of the wonders of pregnancy and begged her not to miss out on women's greatest experience: childbirth.

So why, now, did she keep thinking she'd panicked and rushed too quickly to marry?

She'd hoped to talk to Weezy about that children-now-or-never decision, but young Weezy, with her life ahead of her, wouldn't understand. Del couldn't bring herself to speak the words. Yet Weezy seemed to sense her disquiet. Returning from the tiny kitchen area, she remarked, "You're missing Bradley, I guess."

Del shrugged and confessed, "Right now, I'm thinking how much I used to love those folkdance evenings with Hilario. As a married woman, I'm supposed to have forgotten all that."

Sitting again, Weezy quirked an eyebrow and voiced her opinion that Del's marriage had been far too sudden.

Del sighed, kicked off her shoes, and stretched her long legs to put her stocking-feet on the coffee table. "Is there another way to take the plunge? You dive in, you immerse. That's what a plunge is." She closed her eyes and let her mind drift back to the days when all the girls had a crush on the new choirmaster, Bradley Boynton. She was the lucky one. She'd basked in that, she enjoyed feeling special. Then, during the war, when Bradley was rejected for Army duty because of a bad knee, she became the only girl in her dorm with a boyfriend able to visit regularly. The others had to make do with letters from the front—and several faced the tragedy of loss.

In spite of that, she and Bradley had found much to fight about. Like Weezy now, Del hadn't been ready to settle down. She'd hated the houses Bradley and her mother picked out for her; she'd seen them as pretty prisons where she was destined to be stuck doing housework. She'd argued that Bradley should move to New York. He refused to give up his job. They'd fought about her room-mate, Jan. Bradley didn't like Jan—perhaps because he sensed Jan didn't think highly of him—and urged Del not to room with her. Del accused him of being anti-Semitic. It all seemed silly now, yet it had led to a breakup and his marrying someone else.

No doubt she was lucky to have a second chance.

The smell of coffee filled the air. Weezy returned to the kitchen to turn off the gas and pour. She began telling Del about the interesting people she'd met here at the Belle Turrets, about Robbi's suicide, the funeral. Del did her best to concentrate. When Weezy handed over the steaming cup, creamed and sugared to her taste, she fought the urge to gulp and made herself sip cautiously.

"If you'd bring your suit, we could take a swim in the pool," Weezy said.

Del nodded and agreed that next Sunday she would do that. Or maybe, if the fine weather held, they might go together to the beach at Far Rockaway. There was so much of New York Weezy hadn't yet seen.

Weezy again frowned in puzzlement and Del wondered if her cousin suspected these suggestions were designed to fill in Sundays so she could avoid dreaming of Hilario and folk dancing.

After three weeks, Bradley arranged for an opportunity fly out for a visit. Del looked forward to his arrival and hurried through the airport to the gate. On seeing him walk from the plane, she reassured herself he was as tall and handsome as she remembered. There was no reason for those doubts that assailed her. His brown eyes lighted when he entered the building and spotted her. "You came to meet me!"

"Of course. I'm your wife. What did you think?" She hoped for a rush of joy; she explored her psyche, seeking it. But he was just Bradley. How long, she wondered, would it take for her to begin to feel that rush? When did love happen?

"So you are. I still can't believe it. It's too good to be true." He set down his suitcase and moved to hug and kiss her as if they'd been separated for months rather than weeks. There could be no doubt of this man's love, she thought. So, why did she always feel stifled in his company, as if she were his acquisition rather than his partner? Was it all in her mind? Something she needed to get over?

"Aren't you extravagant, flying out instead of taking the train?" she said.

He kissed her lightly on the nose and assured her that her companionship was well worth the money. "Besides, I couldn't wait to see the apartment you located. Made travel arrangements the moment I got your letter. Riverside Drive, the perfect spot!"

"Yes, it's nice," she said. "River view—all that."

"I should have moved here long ago." Bradley picked up his bag. "You were right about New York being a great place to live. I was a stick-in-the-mud not to listen—so attached to my job, so reluctant to make a change—now I can't think why. What possessed me?"

Since Bradley had only the one suitcase, they were able to bypass the checked-baggage window. He offered Del his free arm. "I can stay two nights. When the new choirmaster arrived, I knew the congregation wanted a look at him. I offered to bow out for one Sunday and let him take over. It worked out just right." He moved close to Del, slipped an arm around her, and squeezed her against him. "I missed you! And there are five more weeks to go until I'm officially free to be with you." He nuzzled his face into her hair. "You'll never know how often I've dreamed of your auburn hair and blue eyes."

He was indeed a different man. The formal, proper choirmaster she remembered would never have expressed affection in public like this. Respond, she cautioned herself—and looked up to offer him a smile.

She was aware of a sense of relief when he released her and left her free to simply walk at his side. She told him they were lucky to get the apartment. She described the dumps she'd explored—railroad flats, no sunlight, windows looking out onto light wells with brick walls opposite. "*We'll* have a kitchen window that actually looks onto a tiny garden—not to mention a bay overlooking the Hudson River."

"Sounds dreamy. Let's grab a sandwich and go right over."

"You don't want to drop off your suitcase?"

"I guess I should." At the gate, he stepped aside to let Del go ahead of him. When they reached the street, he added, "Let's get a cab."

They rode to Del's building, stopped at the deli counter of the restaurant to buy sandwiches of Italian sausage tucked into long rolls, and then climbed the four flights, Bradley carrying his suitcase while Del carried the sandwiches, one in each hand. Bradley remarked that he was glad Weezy wasn't here. "Nice girl, Weezy—but it's nicer to be alone." He winked meaningfully at Del.

"Can you get my key from my purse?" She turned to give him access to the bag hanging from her shoulder.

He set down his suitcase, fumbled in her purse for the key, and opened the door. She went inside and took the sandwiches to the kitchen, where she set out plates and glasses on a tray and poured wine. She carried everything to the table by the front window. Bradley stood looking down into the street. The organ-grinder was there again; the organ wheezed. "Let bygones be bygones forever. We'll fall in love once again."

"Ah, this is the life." he said. "Once there was a dummy named Brad Boynton who didn't appreciate all this. Luckily, he's gone now."

"You do seem like a different person," Del admitted.

"I awoke to what the world is all about." He came up behind her, put an arm around her, and swayed to the music. "I don't have to fall in love once again. I never fell out."

And I, Del admitted to herself, haven't yet fallen *in*.

While they ate, they listened to repeats of the organ-grinder's song. Bradley remarked, "I've had two lovely letters from your mother, welcoming me to the family. She told me about their home in California. It must be quite a place, a mini-ranch. She described how the wildlife shares it with them."

"The civet cat learned to unscrew jelly jars," Del said. "Mother has to keep them in locked boxes or he opens them and scoops out the jelly."

"I can't wait to go for a visit. Your mother is a queen among women. I know I'll never have mother-in-law problems with her. She's the greatest."

If Del agreed dubiously, Brad didn't seem to notice her hesitance. He went on, "I promised her we'd try to visit in the fall."

Del described her parents' ranch. Bradley told her about the farewell parties being held for him in Grand Rapids, and when he expressed a wish for her to be there with him, she said she could perhaps go out for a party at the end of the season.

After lunch, when Del had cleared away the dishes, Bradley slipped an arm around her and steered her toward the bedroom. She realized that the love-talk had been aimed at this, and wondered why she hadn't seen it coming. "I thought we were going to see the new apartment."

"Just a quick one first." As if sensing her hesitance, he said, "It's been so long since our honeymoon, and I've missed you so much."

She gave in. He guided her to the bed, unbuttoned her skirt, and let it fall to the floor. Then he slipped off her panties. It didn't feel right to her to be half undressed, the bottom half at that, so while he removed his pants and under-pants, she took off the rest of her clothes and got under covers which he threw off when he climbed on top of her.

She hadn't been ready for this. She was dry; the penetration felt painful; and the whole event seemed too hasty. Afterward, when he raised his head to gaze at her in puzzlement, she confessed, "I guess I'm not good at quick ones. It takes me time to work up to this."

"Oh, well. We'll have lots of time tonight. All evening, in fact."

Bradley raved over the Riverside Drive apartment when they reached it. He walked from room to room rhapsodizing over the afternoon sunlight, shining in full blast and not shafted between other buildings as at Del's flat. He claimed to love the big rooms, the high ceilings, the hardwood floors, the river view, even the old fashioned light fixtures. He said he'd grown up in an apartment like this and it was the way apartments ought to look, that he didn't care for modern. He remembered to ask the present tenant, who was finishing her packing, all the questions Del had forgotten: what day was garbage pickup, and how much deposit would be needed? He went downstairs to talk to the super, and returned to say that everything was settled. "I gave him your phone number, Del. He'll notify us when the place is ready."

On leaving, Bradley suggested they take a stroll. He wanted to familiarize himself with their new neighborhood. They walked along Riverside Drive as far as Grant's Tomb, then moved on to the Juilliard School where they listened, through an open window, to singers rehearsing *Tales of Hoffman*. Bradley remarked that he'd dreamed of attending Juilliard. "But I liked Westminster Choir School, too, and as a choirmaster I knew I could get a job."

Del told him about Robbi. Whistling, he confessed she was not the first musician he knew of who committed suicide after a failed performance. "What a shame. How's Weezy?"

"She's okay." Del couldn't bring herself to tell Bradley about Yuri, the Belle Turrets, or how she felt guilty, as if somehow she were responsible for Weezy being involved in all that. In fact, she was having trouble thinking what to talk about with this man so suddenly become her husband. She berated herself that she hadn't allowed enough time to get re-acquainted with him before the wedding. She reminded herself that things had always been this way with Bradley. She'd never known what interested him, what she could talk about other than his accomplishments in music. She asked now, "Are you finding it hard to leave your choirs?" He shrugged and nodded.

They rounded a corner and heard from another window a piano performance sounding professional enough for Carnegie Hall. Bradley waved. "World class, these Juilliard students." Del thought of Robbi, whose music would never again be heard in this world.

They returned to the Columbia campus, circled it, and strolled around Morningside Park, where they found several mothers with small children pushing strollers among the flowering bushes. Bradley remarked that this seemed the place to bring the kiddies. "It'll soon be your turf, Delkins. We'll want at least a boy and a girl, won't we? Anything happening in that department?"

She blushed. She couldn't get used to discussing intimate matters with Bradley. When she shook her head, he consoled, "We have two nights to try again."

"Wrong time of month, I'm afraid."

"Well, drat—as your mom would say. I'll have to fly out for overnight when the time is right." He gestured toward a small restaurant across the street. "The Dutch Kitchen. Do you suppose they serve tea or something mid-afternoon-ish? And then we'll ride that wonderful two-story bus back to the Village and resume our honeymoon."

Del forced from herself a smile and a nod.

CHAPTER 22

Grace

With Weezy gone, the summer had passed slowly in Boston. Grace struggled to occupy herself at the activity she'd once loved, her art work. She spent much of her time in her studio. Her art and her child had always been her two joys in life.

This September morning, leaving off her touch-up work on a painting for her upcoming show, she answered the ringing phone and then hastily put her brush aside. With covered receiver she mouthed an unladylike obscenity. Her mother demanded she come to lunch. On hanging up, she clenched her fists and steamed with annoyance. Seemed Persis Hannaford had elected to entertain her old friend Julia Brentwood. Grace didn't see why her mother couldn't just once manage a luncheon without her daughter at her side, especially since the cleaning lady had agreed to stay and serve. Why couldn't the two old friends chat by themselves? When she'd asked the question of her mother, she'd received no answer beyond a repeated insistence that Persis wanted her there.

Rebelliously, she cleaned her brushes and removed and flung aside her smock.

Later, she entered her mother's old fashioned Beacon Hill house to see white-haired Mrs. Brentwood in the formal parlor accompanied by her grandson, Reginald, age twenty-four. At once Grace perceived a plot unfolding. She sensed—and feared—that the young man had been selected as a suitable mate for Weezy.

Persis made the introductions. "Reggie is now a Harvard graduate with a Master's in business."

"It's nice to meet you." Grace moved closer to the obviously embarrassed young man and took his hand. He was tall, slim and bony, with straight hair that on a woman would have been scornfully dismissed as "dishwater blonde." His jaw was properly square. The teeth he showed off in a polite smile were orthodontist-perfect.

What was he doing at a women's luncheon? For Grace, the scene was too reminiscent of the way her mother had selected Jonathan for her. Though she didn't intend to allow the same thing to happen to Weezy, she hid her dismay from the guests.

The ill-matched quartet struggled for conversation, most of it revolving around young Reginald's promising career in business administration, his bright prospects for the future. When they went in to lunch, Mrs. Brentwood asked about Weezy. Though Grace refused to be drawn into a gossip session, her mother answered for her. "I understand my granddaughter works for a literary agent in New York City."

"Sounds fascinating." Reggie appeared to struggle to be polite and proper. "Imagine meeting writers, reading books not yet in print."

While they ate the fruit cups set out for them, Mrs. Hannaford scoffed. "I suspect the job pays peanuts. The child won't tell us what her salary is, but I'd guess it's not worthy of a college graduate. She's sharing an apartment with a cousin in Greenwich Village. I don't approve of the place but she hasn't asked my opinion."

After offering Grace a sympathetic glance, Mrs. Brentwood shook her head at Persis. "Young people don't, these days."

"I console myself the job will be a learning experience. I trust that by fall Weezy will be ready to chuck it and look for something more suitable."

"Majored in social work, didn't she? I remember thinking she'd need graduate work in that field." Mrs. Brentwood leaned back in her chair while the cleaning lady *cum* waitress collected the empty fruit cups and passed around plates of creamed eggs on toast.

Pouring the coffee, Mrs. Hannaford allowed herself a frown. "Right now, she seems to be going through a belated adolescent rebellion. Though I've offered to pay the tuition, she refuses to return to school…No doubt that's a phase and will pass," she hastily amended.

"I'd love to meet Weezy." Reggie lavishly sugared his coffee. "I have a friend who's looking for a literary agent."

"I doubt Weezy's experienced enough to act as an agent on her own. However, she may be getting to know people in the field." Her mother had a curious way, Grace thought, of both building Weezy up and putting her down. She tried to make her guests think well of her granddaughter, yet she couldn't hide her impatience at the girl's recalcitrance.

"I'll be in New York next week to be interviewed by prospective employers," Reggie said. "It'll be my chance to meet Weezy. If you give me her phone number, I'd like to invite her and her cousin to lunch."

Mrs. Hannaford smiled as if pleased with the idea, yet Grace grew apprehensive. Weezy would surely see this as her mother's doing. Though Grace had tried hard to keep her distance and give the girl space, Weezy seemed to perceive her mother as manipulative. It was unfair. Grace hadn't even notified Weezy of her upcoming art show. She decided she should do so at once, and also forewarn Weezy to expect a call from Reggie.

She bit her lip and silently upbraided herself for passing along to her mother the information about Weezy's job. Weezy, who'd written that she could manage on her small income thanks to low rents in the Village, appeared determined to get along on her own, without parental aid. A noble goal, certainly, and Grace hadn't interfered. She hoped her mother wouldn't, either.

"I don't know how much time Weezy has at lunch," she cautioned. "Not much, I shouldn't think." She attacked her creamed eggs without enthusiasm.

"If you claim to have written a book, perhaps she'll wine and dine you at company expense." Persis let a rare smile touch her lips.

"I'll try to get tickets to a play. Everyone's talking about *A Streetcar Named Desire*."

"Oh. That awful thing!" The smile vanished. Persis smoothed away a frown with a finger while Mrs. Brentwood commented, "Really, Reggie!"

"I don't suppose Weezy's seen it," Persis remarked. "It sounds disgusting, hardly her kind of thing."

Reggie stuck to his guns. "It's the talk of the town."

"I hear it has near nudity and a rape."

The shadow of a smile crossed Reggie's face. "No doubt the curtain falls when the rape-scene starts."

Mrs. Brentwood also refused to back down. "The things being shown on the New York stage these days, no right-thinking person would attend the theater. You must be anxious about your daughter in that town, Grace, dear."

Grace shrugged. "If you raise a child right, she'll know how to behave." She hoped and prayed she spoke the truth. If Weezy failed to behave herself, if she came home pregnant, Persis Hannaford would blame Grace and hammer at her about those "bad genes" she'd supposedly introduced into the family through Edgar. The situation would become intolerable, with Grace once again badgered by the old accusations: How could you have brought yourself to be intimate with a man of that caliber; how could you have started all this? She'd heard those words every time Weezy had done something Persis considered unsuitable for a Hannaford or Ward.

Seeing his grandmother's frown, Reggie capitulated. "I'll get tickets for some other play." He turned to Grace. "I understand you're to have a painting exhibition, Mrs. Ward?"

Grace nodded and remarked that in late September, she too would be going to New York.

"We both will." Persis spoke emphatically, and when Grace turned to her with an astonished look, raised an eyebrow.

"Why did you act so surprised when I said I was going with you to New York?" Grace's mother asked after the guests had left. "Surely you don't think I'd miss your show?"

"You've missed my shows before." Grace steeled herself to speak bluntly. "I suspect you're going along to check on Weezy."

"Someone has to. Someone should have done so already." Persis gave her a meaningful look which clearly communicated who she thought that someone should be.

Grace answered the unspoken accusation. "Mother, I can't follow a twenty-one-year-old around the country. Weezy's old enough to run her own life."

"She's a naïve twenty-one," Persis snapped. "She's never been out in the world. Now she has a job where she's meeting writers—you know what they are! And Weezy has no father to look after her."

"Not all writers are Henry Miller or even Hemingway." Grace felt frustrated and annoyed. She knew her mother wouldn't merely accompany her but would smother her. Grace had looked forward to this chance to improve relations with Weezy and didn't need Persis jumping in with rules about what Weezy could and couldn't do. That would only drive the girl farther away.

Though Persis had made a life for herself doing volunteer work during Grace's married years, since Jonathan died she'd shown a tendency to reattach herself to her daughter, wanting to accompany her everywhere. Grace was beginning to feel stifled by this ever-present overseer.

Persis remained adamant. "I've been through the experience of having a girl come home with a baby, and once was enough. I don't intend to go through it again. Furthermore, I doubt that Del Kingsley is the right companion for

Weezy. Del's a Langston on her mother's side, first cousin to the Awful McCurdles."

Grace bit her tongue to stifle the reminder that Weezy was not Persis' charge.

Her mother must have sensed what she didn't say. She responded. "When I decided to rear a child, it was not my intention to found a dynasty of nobodies like the McCurdles."

"Mother, you're a snob." Grace couldn't resist the thrust.

"Call it what you will—Weezy is my flesh and blood. I intend to make sure she doesn't ruin her life. I'm surprised you don't feel the same way."

"You're like something out of *The Fall River Legend*," Grace said. "You'll turn Weezy into another Lizzie Borden."

"Weezy is my descendant. If you won't look after her, I must. God knows someone has to. A young girl alone in Bohemian Greenwich Village—it's unthinkable."

"Mother, she's an adult. Leave her alone, let her find her own way in the world."

Her mother folded her arms across her chest and delivered her final, clinching argument. "What kind of family would we be if we didn't care enough about each other to check up on one another occasionally? If Weezy needs rescuing, then we'll rescue her. She'll thank us in the long run."

"What makes you think she needs rescuing?"

"We've heard so little from her. If everything were fine, she'd be writing long letters about her adventures in the big city. In fact, you've had only postcards from her, and I've received one letter in which she obviously struggled to fill up space without saying anything. I've had those letters before—oh, how I've had them!" Persis threw her hands to her head.

Grace knew where the conversation was heading. Soon they would review her own misconduct during her months in Michigan. Her fingers itched to clench themselves around the matriarchal crepey neck.

She stood and reached for her hat, gloves and purse. "I really must get back to my painting, Mother. I have a deadline."

Even walking fast to dispel her anger, she was shaking when she reached her house a few blocks away. She removed her hat and gloves but knew she couldn't settle enough to concentrate on her work. She made coffee and sat fuming. Her gaze focused on the telephone. It wasn't true that Weezy had no father. She did have one. Dared Grace call him after all these years?"

After lengthy debate and with trembling fingers, she picked up the phone and requested from the operator the number for Menno Langston in Grand Rapids. She jotted it, and asked the long-distance operator to connect her. A voice vaguely familiar, a voice she hadn't heard in twenty-one years, answered. "Alana Langston speaking."

It struck her she was unlikely to be popular with the Langstons. They might even refuse to talk to her. It would be best not to identify herself. She spoke formally, like someone's secretary. "Can you tell me where I can reach Edgar McCurdle?"

"He's in Battle Creek," Alana said. "Give me a minute, I'll find the number." She went away, came back, read off a number. "It's the sanatorium, but they'll call him to the phone."

Grace made a note of it, offered a formal thanks, hung up, and sighed deeply. It was as easy as that, after all these years. If she called, would Edgar be willing to speak to her? Or would he slam down the receiver on hearing her voice?

She probed back in her mind to that day of painful memory when the men with the summons confronted her and informed her that Patience also carried a child of Edgar's. The stab of betrayal had overwhelmed her. She'd acted without thinking, grabbing Weezy and rushing off to her mother.

Now she wished she hadn't. Her mother had taken over, contacted Jonathan, filed for the annulment, and arranged a new marriage. Grace's life had been snatched from her hands and never returned to her.

It won't happen that way to Weezy, she vowed. Not if I can help it. If Weezy is involved with someone, I'll offer support and backing while letting her work things out for herself.

Of course, she wouldn't be allowed to do that. Persis would swoop down on Weezy in her usual disruptive way. Edgar's help was needed in this.

She picked up the phone and, struggling to keep her voice from shaking, gave the operator the number for the Battle Creek sanatorium. When a woman answered, the call was switched to Edgar's floor. She waited, trembling, while he was summoned to the phone.

His still-familiar voice in a casual, "Hello?" brought a welter of emotions, joy, hope, anger and just plain panic. She heard the operator say, "Person-to-person call from Mrs. Grace Ward in Boston."

"Grace, is that you? Hello?" He actually sounded excited and pleased. She couldn't repress a sigh of relief. He added, "Grace? How are you?"

How was she?—almost speechless with trepidation, actually. With a sense that some voice not her own was speaking, she managed to say, "I'm fine. How are you, Edgar? I was concerned to learn you were in the sanatorium."

"I'm recovering. I admit I drank too much—but I'm a reformed character. God, it's good to be in touch, Grace. I hear you're a famous painter these days."

"I'm a painter, yes, but hardly famous. Edgar, have you heard from Weezy lately?"

"Sure. She writes regularly."

Again she felt that stabbing sense of betrayal. Weezy didn't write regularly to her mother. Just those two short notes on postcards: I met my dad; he's in a sanatorium; we got along great. And: I'm living in the Village with Del, working for a literary agency.

"Edgar, would it be possible for you to go to New York and look in on her? Just to be sure she isn't in need of parental advice?"

"Sure, in fact I've been thinking of going to see her. I'll be discharged tomorrow and I've never been east. Wouldn't want to interfere in Weezy's life, but just a visit, to make sure she's okay—I'd do that."

"That's exactly what I mean. Are you well enough to travel?"

"You bet. Give me your address and I'll send you a report. I'm sure Weezy's fine. A great kid, good head on her shoulders. You did a swell job of raising her, Grace."

When she hung up, still trembling, she yet felt a vague longing to go on talking to Edgar, just to hear the sound of his voice. She wished she'd suggested he call her after he talked to Weezy.

CHAPTER 23

Del

Bradley had written that since the new choirmaster seemed eager to try out the job, he himself could leave earlier than he'd planned. "I hope to see you at the end of the week, dear."

Del quit her job ahead of time and took the night train to Grand Rapids for a farewell party and a renewal of old acquaintances. After much waving and well-wishing from family and old friends, the couple boarded the train back to New York and set out to "do" the town like tourists. They visited places Del had never yet gone, the top of the Empire State Building, Staten Island, Palisades Park. They explored the museums and art galleries, and ate at the Russian Tea Room, a musicians' hangout where a famous symphony conductor at a nearby table was pointed out to them by a seat-mate. Though Hilario still invaded Del's thoughts, and occasionally she felt a stab of excitement when she fancied she caught a glimpse of him rounding a corner or heard his voice in a crowded room, she consoled herself she wasn't encountering him on purpose so she couldn't be accused of unfaithfulness.

In early September, when Bradley went off to a three-day denominational conference, Del found herself, for the first time, with nothing to occupy her, no job—and her classes at Columbia hadn't yet started. It seemed a good time to catch up on her reading but she couldn't settle. She wandered from bedroom to living room to window thinking of things to do. Clean out cupboards and closets? But why bother, when she'd so soon be packing to move.

When the phone rang, she tried to pull herself out of a blue funk. A male voice said, "This is your new super, Jerry, uptown. The Abramson's van has went; they're cleaning the apartment now. I wanted to let you know."

"But it's—"

"—more than a week early. They got into their new place sooner than expected."

Del felt an unpleasant sinking sensation. The time was here, the moment to abandon her Village flat. She'd been pushing this ahead of her, trying not to think of it.

She sighed. "I'll come up there. Thanks." She felt bereft. She looked around at familiar, friendly furnishings while an inner voice protested. *Can't do this. Can't give up this place.*

No more baths in her crazy living room sarcophagus. No more bumping elbows with guests in her tiny kitchen. Never again to squeeze into a bathroom that had once been a closet. So why didn't she feel celebratory?

She lectured herself. True, she'd been happy here. But surely she'd be happier in a roomy uptown apartment. Life moves on. Why balk at something that promised to be better?

A tap at the door sent her across the room to open. In the hall stood Weezy, well dressed, looking surprised. "Aren't you ready? We're supposed to go shopping."

Del confessed she'd forgotten. She let her cousin in, then went to the couch and sprawled on it, wiping away tears.

Weezy stood over her with a puzzled expression. In her form-fitting navy skirt and sky-blue blouse, she'd become the chic New Yorker. She'd even cut her hair shorter. Hands on hips, she demanded, "You miss Bradley that much?"

"Our new apartment." Del choked out the words. "It's ready early."

"That's to weep over?"

"Weezy, this has been my home for six years. I've shared this place with people I care about: my childhood friend, Jan; my boyfriend, Hal Fletcher, before he went to Alaska; even Danny when he first came to New York. The place is a part of me."

"So, why not stay put? It wouldn't cost much to remodel. Think about it. A partition around the bathtub would give you a U-shaped living room, seating area by the window, dining area near the kitchen." Weezy cupped her hands as if enclosing spaces.

Del frowned. "Bradley wants a family. This place isn't practical."

"It has two bedrooms, one for the kid."

"A cold water flat, fourth floor walkup?—for the Minister of Music of a big church? Come on!"

Weezy tossed her head. "Talented people don't have to put on the dog. The church should count itself lucky to have him."

Del sighed. "It's too late for cold feet. He paid almost a thousand dollars for the lease uptown." She made the effort to ease herself from the couch. "Let's go have a look."

"So get dressed." Weezy picked up a magazine, flipped through, and as Del walked away, changed the subject to confess that she hadn't managed to sell her story about Robbi. "It was rejected twice. Too downbeat, I guess."

From her bedroom Del commented that Robbi was dedicated to music, and dedication wouldn't do at all for the current women's market. These days the magazines preached that women shouldn't even want jobs. "Our role is to offer backing and support to the man in his work. You need to change the ending—create a male rescuer, let Robbi joyfully abandon her career to become a housewife. I read that garbage all the time." Ignoring Weezy's groan of distaste, Del pulled on her black skirt, buttoned up her white blouse, looked at herself in the mirror and decided that now *she'd* become the staid Bostonian. She ran a comb through her coppery hair. "I hope you don't mind giving up the shopping trip?"

"I look forward to seeing your apartment."

When Del stepped into her bedroom to get a tape-measure from her desk, she noticed there two letters for Weezy. She brought them to her cousin, explaining that they'd arrived several days ago. "I haven't seen you to give them to you. I hope they're not urgent."

Weezy opened and read her mother's letter. "Lord!" Her face settled again into a grimace. "Mom's coming to town! There's to be an exhibit of her paintings. Gran's coming with her." She looked up. "You're moving out; I can't bring them here. What'll I do?"

"I'll sublet this place to you."

"Oh, good idea." Weezy fanned her face with the letter. "I'll invite Mom to stay here with me. I'll warn Danny, if he drops by, not to mention the Belle Turrets." She opened the letter from Edgar. "My God, Dad's coming, too!" She looked at the date on the envelope and added, "He's arriving tomorrow morning, early, and hopes I can meet him at the railroad station."

"You don't have to worry about Edgar," Del assured her. "He's not judgmental. I doubt he'd turn a hair if you introduced him to Yuri and told him the truth. In fact, I suspect that the two men would hit it off just great."

"Really? You think so?"

"If he criticizes, I'll remind him of his own escapades." Actually, Del was relieved that Weezy's parents were taking over and she would no longer need to feel responsible for her younger cousin.

Weezy giggled. "Maybe you're right. At least Dad won't tell Gran. Mother tells Gran everything." She glanced again at her mother's letter. "Some guy named Reggie is threatening to get in touch with me. Mom says I don't have to see him unless I want to. Well, I don't want to. When he calls, tell him I'm at a week-long writer's conference out in Yosemite or somewhere."

"Okay, will do." Del put on her hat, located her purse, and stepped to the door. "Let's go."

Weezy hastily bent to reclaim the shoes she'd shed, stepped into them, and followed her cousin to the door.

On the subway ride uptown, Weezy chatted about the visits. "It'll be fun showing Dad around town, introducing him to Yuri. But Mother—I wouldn't dare. Someone could spill the beans."

"We'll all be very careful what we say—and you'll live in my apartment, all proper." Del suppressed a smile. "Assuming you can survive for two weeks without Yuri, that is."

"It won't be easy, but I'll play dutiful daughter and mend some family fences. Mom's a good artist—I can't think why."

"Why wouldn't she be?"

"Artists are—you know—wild creatures. They throw off the shackles, live with their true love and what the hell. When you slink home to a proper, pre-arranged marriage, you say goodbye to the artist's life."

"Surely some artists live conventional lives." Del couldn't offhand think of any.

"Nah, they keep the dark stuff hidden. At the Belle, you see the other side."

Del had heard tales of the Belle, and how Weezy had become the star of her creative writing class by recording what the women told her of their lives. Of one story, her professor raved that it was the best ever submitted to him by a student. When, flying high, Weezy met Del at the downstairs restaurant for dinner afterward, she waved the paper with its A plus grade and forced Del to admit that maybe the Belle Turrets was indeed the right place for a budding writer.

"Wouldn't it be funny if your mother had a secret lover hidden away?" she speculated.

"Couldn't happen. Mom's too scared of Gran."

Grace had sent Weezy a brochure about her upcoming show. When Weezy handed it over, Del struggled, on the jerking train, to read its contents.

> Grace Ward is fast becoming famous for her seascapes, those stormy waters with jagged waves wilder than any the ocean can produce. Often criticized for lack of realism in her New England coastal scenes, the artist does for the sea what Georgia O'Keefe does for flowers: she heightens awareness through exaggeration to the point of evoking a sensual response, compelling the viewer to share her vision of sexual excitement and raging fury in the angry, choppy waves.

"Angry, choppy waves," Del repeated. "That's the Great Lakes. The ocean doesn't chop, it rolls. I believe Grace is painting the Michigan shoreline."

Weezy turned to stare at her. "What an incredible thought!" She frowned, chewed her lip, considered. "You may have unveiled an artistic secret." Her brown-eyed gaze sought Del's blue one in a wondering look. "Tells you something, doesn't it?"

"It tells me Grace has been carrying the torch for Edgar."

"God, Del, I wonder if I can contrive to bring them together?"

"I wouldn't rush it. You might upset the applecart. Sounds like there's great fury in those raging seas."

Weezy chuckled. "Now that you're a sedate married woman, perhaps I should give *you* a try at reuniting them."

The subway came out into sunlight. Del pointed to their stop, Columbia station.

At the apartment, they found the short, matronly, salt-and-pepper-haired former tenant, Mrs. Abramson, running a buffer on hardwood floors already highly polished. The door stood open. Del stepped in ahead of Weezy and made the introductions above the electrical hum. "Remember me? Delia Boynton? This is my cousin, Weezy."

Mrs. Abramson nodded, switched off the buffer, and murmured a polite, "Nice to meet you." She reached up to smooth her hair.

"Place looks great," Del said. Actually, to her, it merely looked empty.

The two young women wandered across a long living room painted a buff color, sporting flowered drapes at the large front windows. The older woman followed and told them she was leaving the drapes. "I hope that's okay."

"They'll tide us over until we get new ones." Del spoke politely. She hated flowered draperies.

Weezy stepped to the bay window and looked out onto the Hudson River below Riverside Park. Obviously trying to cheer her cousin, she said, "Aren't you lucky, Del. No more windows opening onto walls."

Del followed her gaze. Clouds had blown in and the view had become sunless and gray. She shrugged. Nice view, but she didn't want to look at it forever.

They walked through empty rooms. Weezy valiantly pointed out possibilities. "This will make a darling child's room. Can't you just see it with candy striped curtain and bedspread?"

"Brad wants this for his music room." Del wished her cousin wouldn't try so hard to be cheery. She had to do what she had to do but no one could require her to be happy about it. She wandered to the kitchen and peered into empty cupboards, well scrubbed. She remarked, "Brad wants to paint the living room a basic gray with one wall charcoal."

Weezy urged, "Let's go see what furniture's available. I've never shopped for furniture."

When they returned to the foyer, Mrs. Abramson handed over the keys. "Give me ten or fifteen minutes to finish up here, and then the place is yours."

"No hurry," Del said. "We're going shopping."

"I hope you'll be as happy here as we've been." The older woman added that she'd posted schedules for garbage pickup. "You'll need to be prompt in putting it on the lift." She added a reminder to call the gas and electric company and Ma Bell.

Del nodded, thanked her, and wished her happiness in her new location.

Riding down in the elevator, Weezy commented, "You should be excited. That's your first home as a bride."

Del's shoulders slumped. How could she get excited about apartments when she'd hoped to be off on another archeological dig by now? She wouldn't have minded living in a tent, just so she could explore ancient cultures. With a sigh, she confessed that in the kitchen she'd thought only of the dreary procession of meals she'd have to cook. "In the bathroom, I saw myself scrubbing up after others." She leaned against the wall as the car creaked downward. Then, fearing to crush her hat, she straightened. "Mother would say I'm selfish." She managed a wavering smile. "A spoiled only child."

Weezy seemed puzzled. "If you love Bradley, this should be fun and thrilling."

Del remembered Brad's departure, hours earlier. "I guess I want things the way they are now, Bradley sharing my old apartment."

"Well, then, if Bradley loves you, he'll brave the wrath of his church members." Weezy stepped off the elevator ahead of Del. "Too bad if they don't approve of Greenwich Village."

Del shoved the door open and led the way out into the windy street. She suggested they go somewhere for coffee. "There's a Dutch Kitchen on Broadway."

They turned their backs on the sweeping river view and headed east, holding their hats against the wind. When they slid into chairs in the restaurant, Del remarked, "I'm being silly. I need to grow up. It's wife-and-mother time."

"I'm wondering about your feelings for Bradley." Weezy inspected her cousin across the table as if hoping to find the answer on her face. "There should be joy in the prospect of sharing an apartment with him." Del felt her face flame as she recalled her fantasies of Hilario. She could hardly confess them even to herself, let alone to a companion.

A waitress hurried toward them with a coffee pot in hand. Del sipped the coffee served to her, burned her tongue, made a face. "Watch it, stuff's hot." Since Weezy still seemed to await an answer, she forced out words. "Bradley's good to me. He let me give him a tour of the museum yesterday."

Weezy commented dryly, "I expect he'll also agree to let you cook his meals and clean his apartment."

"Isn't that what women are supposed to do? Or should I be an old maid with hair in a bun, trotting off to glue potsherds?" When Weezy shrugged without comment, Del explained, "I come from a long line of women who didn't want to be housewives. Mother played in an orchestra; Grandma Kingsley ran the County Poor Farm."

"Then you need to speak up to Bradley. Tell him you want to keep your flat and he can join you there."

But there was no room in her tiny kitchen for extensive cooking, no walk-in closet for storage of Bradley's music and their winter clothing. As for baby equipment—there wasn't space for so much as a crib, let alone buggy, stroller, change-table.

"What do you *really* want to do?" Weezy demanded.

"Go on a dig."

"I mean, realistically?"

The thought popped into Del's head: Share my village flat with Hilario. Appalled that the image of the handsome folk dancer kept intruding, she didn't speak but shook her head.

CHAPTER 24

Del

Though Del wandered with Weezy through the showrooms of a large furniture store, she found nothing she wanted to buy. At each display, she paused, debated, shook her head, moved on.

Weezy complained. "You have the enthusiasm of the Dormouse in *Alice*. I fear you'll sleep through the Mad Hatter's tea party."

In truth, Del couldn't focus her mind on furniture. She was feeling trapped—to the point of panic.

Over lunch in a department store tea room, Weezy suggested that Del might simply request from Bradley more time to prepare herself psychologically for the move. "You could stay on in the Village until there's actually a child to worry about. You needn't anticipate future needs that may not materialize."

Del explained that it was becoming increasingly difficult to locate a rent-controlled apartment in Manhattan. Bradley was lucky; the minister of his church got them the Abramsons' place.

"I hope you don't mind my saying this—" Weezy put down her fork, which dripped cheese sauce onto the plate from its impaled cube of Welsh rarebit. "—I have to admit I agree with Danny. You rushed into this marriage too quickly. I don't get the feeling you're ready."

"I'd jolly well better get ready." Del rubbed her hands together in a washing motion. "I dragged my feet through four years of college, and then broke up with Brad after 'keeping him on the string' as Mother puts it. The wedding announcements were ready to mail; the non-refundable deposit had been paid on the house. Mom was so angry she hardly spoke to me for a year. I can't do that again; I can't keep playing games that way. I have to move forward with the life I've been given."

Weezy shrugged. "I've had similar conflicts with my mother, only over a career, not a man. She and Jonathan had their hearts set on my being a social worker. Granny, too. Even now I don't dare tell mom I'm working for twenty-six dollars a week. She'd scream bloody murder. 'For this we sent you to college?' If she didn't, Gran would."

Del sank her head in her hands and tried to shut out the clattering tea room so she might focus on the reasons she rushed into marriage. "Meeting Bradley again after all those years—it seemed so *destined*."

Weezy was blunt. "You mean he seemed sexy?"

Del reminded her she'd need to watch her language; her mother was coming. "But to put it crudely, that night on the dunes I actually, for the first time, felt I wanted to have sex with Bradley. After all those years of knowing the guy, finally I experienced desire. You can't imagine my relief. This was the man everyone saw as the perfect mate for me. Now at last the idea became plausible. He'd learned things about women. He knew—well, since we're being candid, he knew how to ensure a great physical experience. That night he seemed almost a substitute for my sexy, non-marrying folk dancer."

"Almost—but not quite?"

"Well, you know—my moments with Hilario were experiences out of time. Dream moments, too good to be true."

"If you lusted for Brad, it strikes me you should merely have had a one-night stand, not a marriage."

Del sighed, remembering. It had seemed so good to be the fair-haired princess again instead of the rebel. Her Hollywood-style honeymoon proved to be all glamour and hand-holding beside the Falls. "I thought I was handling things well. This morning I still felt I wanted all of it—big apartment, kids." She put herself back into that mood, trying to be the woman Bradley wanted.

"It can't hurt to tell Bradley you need more time."

"Weezy, the deposit! And his plans. In his mind he's already painting and decorating those rooms. Not to mention the convenience, close to his work."

"He'll learn to compromise." Weezy gestured toward Del's abandoned fork. "Hurry, eat your lunch. I'm meeting Yuri at three."

Del pushed her plate aside, stirred her soup, and then pushed that too aside. She dutifully returned the fork to her plate. "I'll eat later. Just now I can't swallow." She forced a smile. "You and I will both have to mend our ways before

Grace gets here. I waste food and dither over decisions. You've forgotten how to be ladylike."

Weezy shook her head so hard it seemed her pageboy would be messed, but her hair fell back into place. "That's something I'll never forget. 'Keep your clothing neat, keep your skirts down, keep your legs together, keep your voice low, keep your hands quiet, never call attention to yourself.' To all of which I say, 'Fuck it.'"

Del laughed. "Weezy, you're incorrigible."

"Just like dear old dad." Weezy grinned.

Back on the subway, Weezy confessed, "I have to admit I'm annoyed with your Bradley. He's out to change your life. He wants you living elsewhere, he wants you doing different work. He wants, he wants."

"Men are like that. They have a picture in their minds of what a wife should be. Meeting their expectations is what marriage is about."

"If that's true, I'm glad I'm a mistress."

Del frowned and glanced to right and left. "If you don't stop using off-color words, you'll blurt them when your mom's here. Lust, mistress, fuck it—your vocabulary is getting—it's that awful Belle Turrets place. You're letting those women—"

"So? Mom can't throw me out of the house, I'm already out." Weezy stood. "Here's my stop. I'll come by your place tomorrow with dad."

"Thanks for shopping. Say hi to Yuri and Edgar for me."

Weezy waved and stepped onto the platform. The door closed; the train moved on. Left alone, Del tried again to recall why all those years with Bradley had seemed so important, why marriage had presented itself as the next step in an inevitable progression.

How in the world did I arrive at that conclusion? she wondered.

She left the subway at her stop and hurried to her building. She faced Saturday night alone. Perhaps Danny might be free. They might take in a foreign film. Danny loved filmmaker Jean Cocteau and didn't care how often he saw *The Blood of a Poet*. At last count, it was nineteen times. Del, too, longed to see the film again. Though she hadn't understood it, she loved its poetry in motion and the beauty of the French language.

In the lobby of her building, she unlocked her mailbox and found a telegram from California. She tore it open.

ARRIVING TUESDAY SANTA FE CHIEF TO HELP FURNISH NEW APARTMENT MOTHER

Frozen, Del stared at the paper. This was all she needed, her mother mixing into this devil's brew of husband, apartment, furniture. Bradley alone she might handle. Bradley and her powerful mother together represented a team she'd never be able to cope with.

She couldn't face the prospect. The sole reason she'd felt this marriage might work was the fact her mother was far away. Climbing the stairs, she tried to believe the visit wouldn't happen. Something would intervene to prevent her mother from getting on that train—an earthquake, a tornado, a tidal wave. World War III.

Bright with afternoon sun, her apartment awaited her like a refuge. She dialed Danny's number. No answer. She started to call her old friend and roommate, Jan, but replaced the phone. How could Jan, happy with her home and husband, thrilled over her child, understand her friend's failure to want what she herself already had? Del knew what her long-time confidante would say, could hear it as clearly as if the words had actually come over the wires. "Don't worry, Del, you'll love the new place once you're settled. It will develop its own cherished memories. You're just suffering last-minute willies."

Del's head throbbed. She swallowed aspirin and lay down with a cold compress. After hours-long thrashing and more aspirin, she fell asleep, to wake at five-thirty, that hour her Midwestern friends still called dinner time. No New Yorker would dream of eating so early. But the Chinese restaurant up the street was open all day, and with luck she'd find Danny there on a Saturday. Feeling the need to talk to someone, she flung the compress aside, heaved herself out of bed, re-did her makeup, combed her hair, smoothed her clothing, and went out.

On spotting Danny among the few early patrons in the restaurant, she hesitated. He was with someone. Early for that. Danny usually sought his sex-partners late at night on Riverside Drive. Hesitating to intrude, she started to turn away, but suddenly recognized his companion. She gasped; she froze. Her heart stopped and then started again, pounding hard. Sitting next to Danny was the man she'd both longed and dreaded to see—Hilario!

She planned a hasty retreat but was too late. Danny had seen her; he waved. She moved slowly toward the table, feeling conspicuous and foolish, wishing herself elsewhere. The moment seemed to stretch to eternity. Breathless, embarrassed, choked with emotion, she faced the fact she should have sent Hilario notice of her marriage. As a former lover, he'd deserved that much.

Danny smiled but Hilario only stared. He shifted his chair to stand as she approached. He held out a hand. His hair fell into curls on his forehead; his brown-eyed gaze burned so intently into hers that she felt inflamed by it. She felt her legs tremble. She wished to be elsewhere.

"Good evening, Mrs.—uh—" He bit his lip. "Don't tell me, I'll remember. Baxter? No, Boynton."

"Del will do." She struggled to regain her poise. Uncertainly, she held out her hand. She forced herself to move forward and clasp his. "I often don't remember my new name myself." She feared her voice sounded tremulous and her hand felt shaky.

His expression softened into a look of regret. "We've missed you at folk dancing. You were getting good at it."

"Thank you, I miss dancing." Del drew a deep breath and steadied herself. The worst was over. A picture of the dance group flitted across her mind and with it a pang of regret that Bradley had shown no interest in sharing or even investigating her new hobby.

Hilario released her hand and held her chair for her. He didn't loom over her as Bradley and Danny did; he was less than two inches taller than her own five-seven. In high heels, she matched his height. But he knew all the right moves; he knew how to charm women. Even after he shoved it back, a lock of his brown hair curled over his forehead, tempting her to reach out and smooth it. She'd once laughingly warned him that if he really wanted his hair to remain in place, he'd need to give up dancing. Though he kept whipping out his comb between dances, those fast-moving polkas and schottisches defeated, within minutes, his efforts at control.

His complexion was very fair, and he looked to her more Irish than Spanish. He'd explained that he was born in Barcelona, a part of Catalonia. Catalans, he said, had a Keltic strain in their background. Smiling a bit grimly, he'd added, "It puts me in a peculiar position. I don't fit into the local Hispanic community, not even when I give my name as *Elario*. They seem to resent the fact I speak Spanish but look Anglo."

Maybe that was why he so often imitated Bogart, she reflected. Maybe he was unsure who Hilario Soler might be. Like Danny, he felt he didn't belong anywhere.

"Well! Talk about a surprise!" He reseated himself, put his elbows on the table, and leaned close to her. "None of us dancers had the least idea you were engaged. You never mentioned it to a soul." Including me, the words suggested. She heard the implication: I wasn't that important to you.

She flushed in embarrassment. Danny intervened, trying to inject a casual note. "We're having almond chicken. Shall I order for three?"

Del nodded and forced her breathing to normalize while she sought a way to explain herself to Hilario. "I wasn't engaged. The decision was sudden. I'd broken up with Bradley four years ago, never expected to see him again, and when we met, I just—"

She couldn't continue. She felt surprised to find herself so flustered in this man's company, to still feel so strong an attraction and an overwhelming urge to move closer to him, to reach for his hand. She hoped she hid it successfully.

While she hesitated, Danny studied her in bafflement. "Del, surely you haven't tanked up so early? You seem remote, out of it."

She forced her gaze to turn to her old friend. She explained she'd swallowed a lot of aspirin. "I had a splitting headache earlier. I must have over-medicated."

"Doesn't sound good. Is something wrong?"

"Something's very wrong." She focused on her newest worry. "My mother's on her way here. She wants to help me decorate my new apartment. Only problem: I don't want the place." Embarrassingly, tears flooded her eyes. She fought them; she hadn't meant to weep. She swallowed hard, twisted her fingers together and confessed, "I don't know what to do. I'd planned to confront Bradley and refuse to move from Greenwich Village, but I can't take on two of them."

Both men eyed her in bafflement. Hilario frowned. Danny, still looking puzzled, said, "Riverside Drive's a lovely spot."

"Maybe it's too nice. I'll feel like the princess locked in the palace."

While Danny rubbed his chin and pondered, Hilario spoke up. "What you need is an evening of dancing to take your mind off your troubles. And I'm just the man to be your partner."

She bit her lip, fought a rising joy, and stifled her conscience. She dabbed at her eyes and gazed at him. "Is there a dance tonight?"

"There's always folk dancing somewhere in town." He reached across the table to let his fingers touch hers. An electric charge shot through her. She barely heard his words. "Didn't I tell you to stick with me, kid? I have the answers—really."

Her heart pounded at his touch. She couldn't speak. She knew she shouldn't do this but she nodded and whispered, "Let's go."

CHAPTER 25

Del

That evening, Danny too joined the dancing. After about an hour, Del excused herself to Hilario and sat down to wait out a Swedish hambo, a difficult dance which she, in common with others, hadn't yet mastered. She looked around for Danny, didn't see him, but shrugged off his absence. She'd grown used to these sudden disappearances.

Never having been in the Y before, she'd expected to know no one, but in fact she saw familiar faces. Two women came over to her, asking, "Where've you been? We missed you."

To avoid announcing her marriage, complete with explanations as to why she'd come here with Hilario, she countered with a question. "How come you're dancing here tonight?" One of the women told her that folk dancers traveled all over the area to go dancing.

The hambo, a fast dance with complicated footwork, was done to cheery music which seemed to brighten the room. Del envied Hilario's partner. The woman didn't even need to grasp Hilario's shoulders; she simply linked her hands behind her head and let him fling her about. It looked like fun; Del had hoped to learn. It'll never happen with non-dancing Bradley, she warned herself.

She watched closely as each couple skipped, side by side, and then turned to face each other. There was a beat in which every woman's right toe touched down behind her left foot. Then they whirled. Del knew that missing that beat could mean disaster. She feared to attempt the dance lest her feet become entangled with her partner's as she circled.

With her mind still nagging about her mother's impending visit, she flashed on a recent letter from her father. *So you finally brought Bradley into the family! Your mother's insane with joy. I'm lucky to get my meals cooked, the way she dances around the kitchen.*

He'd gone on to warn Del to brace for a visit. *I know your mother will want to help decorate your new apartment.* The letter had arrived a week previously. She'd tossed it aside, never dreaming her mother might come all the way from California for just the one purpose. She should have known better. Given the right circumstances, Millie Kingsley could move mountains. Moving herself was a minor undertaking. She would come, she would select furniture for her princess, she would discuss with Bradley the decorating of the place, just as she'd done when Del was engaged previously. Del well recalled feeling she'd lost control of her life. Now it was *déjà vu* time.

"I hate being a princess." The thought struck her with such fervent intensity she wondered if she'd spoken aloud. She glanced uneasily at the women flanking her on either side. Both seemed intent on watching the dancers. She decided the music must have drowned her mutterings.

The hambo ended. Hilario came back, smiling, holding out his hand. "Next comes a schottische, an easy dance."

She jumped up to the electric charge of his touch. Counting to herself, she concentrated on the pattern. One-two-three, hop; one-two-three, hop—

The schottische was followed by a Viennese waltz, her favorite. She loved being swung around the room in Hilario's arms, and the waltz seemed graceful compared to the galloping polkas and hambo. She relaxed and circled with Hilario to the rhythms of Strauss, pretending they were together in another time and place, long ago Vienna.

Later she joined a Yugoslav line dance. Now Hilario was at the head of the line, his hair falling into his eyes, his red bandanna waving. He dipped, bounced, turned, weaving, leading the dancers around the floor to the exotic strum of the tamburitsa.

More dances followed. She sat out some she didn't know. Before long she heard with regret the music of the last waltz. By now she felt ready to dance all night, and admitted to Hilario that she longed for a commercial dancehall that stayed open late.

"Some of the gang are off to Coney Island," he said. "Why not go along? No dancing—but fun." At her hesitation, he added, "It's just nine-thirty."

Three couples were going. They urged her and Hilario to join them. She decided it would be all right. Coney was brightly lit and she was in a group.

On the subway, not knowing what to talk about with Hilario, with whom she could hardly discuss Bradley, she listened as the other dancers spoke of things they'd done together. It seemed they'd all, some months previously, attended a folkdance festival in Massachusetts, afterward bicycling around the state together to visit famous sites like Old Ironsides and the House of Seven Gables. Del gathered that the couples were of varying backgrounds, Polish, Swedish, Russian Jewish—and of course, Hilario, the Catalan. Though none was married, they showed no embarrassment about traveling together. Del envied their sense of freedom and wondered why, in her single days, she'd never achieved it. They talked of Franz Kafka, and discussed and raved over a new Swedish filmmaker named Ingmar Bergman.

Coney Island proved noisy and glittery, food smells combining with the fishy, salt-air breeze from the beach. The group rode the Steeplechase, the roller coaster. To Del, motion became hypnotic. After the rides, she walked with the others along the Boardwalk, watching people shoot at wooden ducks and occasionally win gaudily dressed kewpie dolls. The foot long hotdogs smelled good, and she ordered one, slathered with mustard and catsup. She tasted Hilario's knish, shared her hotdog with him, and drank strawberry fla-vored seltzer water.

One by one, the other couples drifted away. After midnight Del found her-self alone with Hilario, walking on the sand at the water's edge, watching white breakers roll in out of the darkness. Barefoot, shoes in hand, they splashed through cold waves that nipped at their legs. Hilario rolled his pant-legs and Del held up her skirts. She wished there were a way to make this night last throughout eternity.

To force the thought out of her mind, she talked of the difference between great lakes and ocean. "Even my feet can tell them apart." Here, the waves sucked outward with force. She couldn't remember ever feeling such suction in Lake Michigan.

Hilario glanced at her, and in the light from the midway she saw his baffled expression. He admitted he'd never been to the Great Lakes. "Are they so dif-ferent?"

"Very. The air lacks this salt tang. There aren't such long stretches between waves." She enlightened him about her reason for comparing. "My cousin's mother, who's a painter, paints Lake Michigan beaches and calls them New England Seascapes."

Why, she wondered, was she telling Hilario about Grace? She changed the subject to ask about his classes at the technical school where he studied to be a television cameraman.

"I graduate in January," he said.

"And then?"

It seemed he planned to apply to the California television stations. "They're less well established than those in the east. I have hopes of doing something creative in camera work out there."

She recalled how, when they'd gone out together, he'd asked questions about California, seeming to see it as a magical place. She'd hesitated to disillusion him by confessing she didn't find it so. Los Angeles was overcrowded, and San Diego was all dreary Navy installations combined with rows of Spanish-style bungalows, each with its palm tree out front. Ridiculous things, palm trees, mere feather-dusters on long poles. When her mother boasted of the palm tree beside her house, Del argued that she favored a good, sturdy oak any day. To Michigan eyes, palms were not trees and shouldn't be so called.

Hilario asked why she'd never joined her parents.

She hesitated over the answer. "There was my job. I loved it until I encountered the recent problems." She splashed through an oncoming wave and ran up the sand as it rolled in.

Hilario remarked that to him the west sounded fresh and exciting. "When you told me about that avocado ranch, I hoped I'd see it someday."

She hastened to explain that it was only a ranchette, a couple of acres in the foothills. "Nice view if you like a barren landscape, sagebrush and chaparral."

They crossed the beach to the boardwalk and sat on the sand to put on their shoes. Time to go home, yet Del wished never to part with Hilario, never to face the empty apartment, the letter from her mother, the grim reality of the days ahead with her mother and Bradley.

Hilario glanced at his watch. "One a.m.—late for a long subway trip. Why not stay here? We can rent bicycles in the morning and ride on the Boardwalk."

Del's mind formed an instant answer: I can't do that, I'm married. She surprised herself by saying instead: "Where would we find a room so late on a Saturday night?"

"Taxi drivers know." Before she could protest, he stood up and flagged a taxi at the curb. He offered her a hand up. In a daze of indecision, she followed him across the sand to the street and slid into the cab.

They soon pulled up before a motor court with a vacancy sign. Del waited while Hilario paid the driver, and then accompanied him into the small lobby.

While he stood at the desk signing for the room, she fingered her wedding ring and told herself she shouldn't be doing this. She'd forfeited the right to this kind of adventure.

"How about having a nightcap?" Hilario pointed toward the nearby bar. She nodded and they went across the parking lot and into the dark and quiet room. Later, walking along the path to their cabin at the rear of the court which now sported a *no vacancy* sign, she forced out words of protest. "I'm the wife of the Minister of Music at a big church. This isn't right."

"We're only here to sleep—and not for long at that. It'll be dawn in about four hours."

While he unlocked the door, she urged, "No hanky-panky."

He flung the door open, reached in to flip on the light, and turned back to her. A Bogart smile played on his lips. "Would I be guilty of such a thing?"

"Yes." She entered the room ahead of him.

"Sweetheart, you wrong me." He smiled more broadly while holding the door.

She switched on the light. The cabin had a double bed. She gasped. "You asked for twin beds. I heard you."

"None left. This was the last vacancy in the area."

He stepped in behind her, closed the door, grasped her shoulders, and turned her toward him. His arms slid around her. She knew they weren't going to just sleep. This was all too easy. They'd done it before. It had become instinctive for her to move into his arms, to slide close to him.

He kissed her. He unbuttoned her blouse, grasped her breast, and slid a warm hand inside her bra. She couldn't make the effort to stop him. She had to admit to herself she'd often longed for this. In her mind she heard the song: *My heart, at thy dear voice—*

Within minutes their outer clothes were off and they were in bed. He'd released her breasts from the bra and was holding and kissing them. She sighed, realizing he'd always been exciting in bed; he'd known how to sweep her away. The times she'd been with him had all been memorable.

She forced out a protest. "We have to stop this. Moral questions aside, I didn't bring equipment." She envisioned herself sharing Grace's predicament, pregnant by the wrong man. How would she explain *that* to Bradley and her mother?

"I brought mine." He fished in his pocket.

"Did you plan this ahead?" she queried. "Did you and Danny set me up?"

He laughed. "I doubt if even Danny has that kind of influence over our resident Californian. I know for sure I haven't." When she pointed out that he'd come prepared, he admitted that he lived in hope where she was concerned. "It's so great with you, Del."

This was the first time he'd called her by name. He'd always stuck to those Bogart words, kid, baby, toots, sweetheart. She melted. When his hand moved downward, she felt her legs turn to jelly. She stopped telling herself to end this. Why keep insisting when she knew she wouldn't? She reached up to adjust the errant lock over his forehead. Then she sighed, relaxed, settled down to enjoy. Hilario's kisses traveled down her body. She grew excited in a way she never had with Bradley. She flung her arms across Hilario's shoulders, wanting to pull him closer. As he moved on top of her she urged him to hurry. He met her eagerness with his own, and they were soon moving together toward a grand crescendo. It seemed so right; she stopped thinking of consequences.

When she awoke next morning, the other side of the bed was empty. Sunlight leaked in around closed curtains. She raised her head and looked toward the bathroom. The door was open, the room deserted. She heard no sound of running water.

"Hilario?"

No answer. She was alone. Puzzled, she hopped out of bed, glanced out the window, saw only an empty courtyard. She hurried to take a shower. When she'd dressed and opened the bathroom door, she still saw no one around. She went to the cabin door, peered outside, and saw Hilario coming along the walk with a carton containing steaming cups. He smiled and, as he approached, held it toward her.

"Continental breakfast," he said on entering. "Coffee, bagels and cream cheese, courtesy of the management. Room service courtesy of H. Soler. Aren't I good to you?"

While she held the door open, he carried the steaming carton inside and set out the mugs of coffee on the small table by the window. Del opened the curtains and sat down. He offered her a bagel on a napkin along with a small package of cream cheese. "For the Californian with the wet hair." He grinned and sat down opposite her.

"I'm not a Californian. And yes, you're good to me. Too good." She fingered her damp locks.

"How can anyone be too good?" He creamed his bagel.

"You know what I mean. Last night shouldn't have happened."

"Why not? Once more for old times' sake? You jumped the gun on me when you sneaked off to Michigan to get married."

"New Jersey, actually."

"Anyway, you gave me no time to throw a party. I'd have invited all the folk dancers."

She frowned. "Hilario, or Bogey or whoever you are, I'm serious. I must *not* see you again."

"What, no bicycling on this beautiful morning? I've already checked out the rental places down the street."

"Okay, bicycling." There would be time before Weezy would show up with Edgar. Weezy would surely want her father to herself for a while. "But no more—you know—last night's stuff."

He paused, a chunk of bagel halfway to his mouth, and asked, "Del, are you really in love with that guy? Danny thinks you're not. If he's right, you've made a whopper of a mistake. You and I were a great team."

"Of course I'm in love with Bradley." Del forced out the words. "I wouldn't have married him otherwise."

"Wouldn't you? I can think of half a dozen reasons, all bad, for marrying someone you don't love. Money, status, security, family pressure, unplanned pregnancy, the convenience of the familiar—"

Del was silent. She couldn't seem to find the right words to explain. Finally she managed to say, "You're off to California. You have a new life ahead of you."

"You could go, too." He wasn't about to let her off the hook.

She managed a small laugh. "Come on, Lari, be honest. You know you're not the marrying kind. Nearly thirty, wildly popular with the folkdance women, enjoying bachelor life—what possible reason would you have for marrying?"

"Same as any man's. Being in love, wanting a home and family."

"You didn't exactly try to sweep me off my feet. I never heard the word marriage from you, nor even words like commitment and permanence."

He sipped his coffee and studied her. His eyes shadowed. He set the mug down. "I couldn't, Del. I had to support my mother. My father left the country when I was ten, to return to Spain and fight to save the new Republic. He left us a bank account to tide us over for a year or two until he returned, but he never did return. He died there. My mother couldn't find a job because she spoke little English. I wasn't quite thirteen. Our money was gone and I had to lie about my age and take a job to support the two of us." He set the cup down and rubbed his chin. "I've been doing that ever since—until now. Last month, at last, she landed a good position as housekeeper to a Spanish nobleman. She can manage on her own now, and I'm free."

He stated all of this matter-of-factly, without an appeal for sympathy, yet it sounded like a story straight out of Charles Dickens. Del could hardly credit it—a thirteen-year-old boy supporting his mother? Once again she was at a loss what to say. She hadn't suspected Hilario might face family problems. She'd taken him for the man he presented to her: a confirmed bachelor enjoying his life as it was, moving lightly from one amorous adventure to another, reveling in each as it came along.

"Why didn't you tell me?"

He gave her a wry smile. "No man ever won fair maid by spilling out his frustrations and grousing about his fate. Anyway, I doubt I have a right to complain. My father felt passionate about democracy and went to Spain to fight for it. I'm sure I'd have done the same under similar circumstances."

"But I thought—good lord, I thought you weren't the marrying kind."

"Del, you didn't know me." His hand touched hers.

"You made sure of that. You played Bogart."

He sighed. "That wasn't such a great idea, I guess. Looks like we both made some mistakes, huh?" He hooked his fingers with hers.

CHAPTER 26

Del

At home in late afternoon, Del couldn't believe what she'd done. Not quite four months married. Could she, Del Kingsley Boynton, the spinster archeologist, have proved unfaithful already?

Those hours with Hilario had been beautiful and memorable. Strange to think such ugly words should apply. Infidelity. Adultery.

She tried to convince herself it couldn't have happened. She warned herself it must never occur again. She must wipe out the memory. Bradley must never know.

She thought of Bradley, who claimed to have shelved his first marriage out of love for her. He deserved better. His presence was everywhere in this apartment. His clothes hung beside hers in the closet; his photo of his deceased mother nudged her Petoskey stone collection. His biography of Bach lay open, face down on the coffee table; his sheet music was stacked on the bottom shelf of her bookcase. His radio, with its channels for the new f.m. stations, stood in the corner. She switched it on and heard chamber music. Haydn?

Weezy called to say Edgar was with her and they'd been seeing the town. "You were so right about him, Del. When I confessed about Yuri, he didn't raise an eyebrow. How did I get so lucky as to have him for a father?"

Del reminded her Edgar was raised by Gramps who was like that. "Gramps would have asked if you were happy in the relationship. If you were, it would have been fine with him." Del hoped Edgar wasn't being over-nice. She felt Weezy's situation—and hers—could portend disaster.

"That's exactly what Dad said. 'If you care for the guy and enjoy being with him, why not?'"

Del still pictured them both on the road to ruin. She tried to switch her mind away from Hilario, tried not to see herself as Hester Prynne complete with a giant A.

"We hoped you'd have dinner with us," Weezy added.

Del spoke up. "Why don't the two of you come here for dinner?" It was just what she needed, a project, a meal to prepare to take her mind off last night. "It's my final chance to entertain before I move."

"*If* you move."

"Oh, I'll move." Del felt she'd now hopelessly compromised her right to stand up to Bradley. If he couldn't have a faithful wife, at least he must have the apartment of his choice. Besides, her mother would soon add her insistence. "Come at six."

Weezy agreed and hung up. Del took from the refrigerator the pot roast she'd meant to serve for Bradley's homecoming. Though her modern pots couldn't compare to Gram's wonderful old Dutch oven, she felt she could offer her cousins a fair imitation of Gram's cooking. She'd helped out often in the Stormland kitchen.

When Weezy and Edgar arrived, the apartment looked festive, the table appealing with a blue checked tablecloth and Del's best Village stoneware and hand-blown glass. The air was fragrant with the combined odors of roast and gingerbread.

"Smells like home," Edgar remarked on entering. "I can close my eyes and believe I'm at Stormland."

Edgar, in tan slacks, blue shirt and new tan loafers, looked natty enough to rival his father, Natty Nat. His hair was slicked back, his face had rounded out, his healthy color had returned. Torn-shirt days behind him, he seemed a different person from the man Del had seen as the family's black sheep.

"I hadn't realized your apartment was so perfect for entertaining," Weezy said. "It looks inviting. If you move, I may take it over permanently."

"Oh, do! Keep it in the family; I'd love that." Del waved Edgar to the over-stuffed chair. "Take a load off, Cousin." When Weezy asked what she could do to help, Del suggested she pour the cherry cider. "Precious stuff. Took a lot of shopping to locate it in New York." She'd bought wine but, remembering Edgar's problems with alcohol, put it away. "I'll bring the roast." She lit the candles, and then carried in the platter of roast flanked with little new potatoes, carrots, and chunks of cabbage, just as Gram had always served it. A New England boiled dinner, she called it.

When they sat down to eat, Del asked how Edgar was enjoying New York. He answered with enthusiasm. "I feel like a kid again. We rode the double-decker bus, crossed the harbor on the ferry, stood at the top of the Empire State Building. We've ogled sky-scrapers and lunched on foot-long hotdogs."

Weezy told Del her dad wanted to visit the Natural History Museum. "I volunteered you to take him there. I have to work tomorrow; a writer's coming to town for a conference and I'm running the office while Mr. Lauritz wines and dines him. But I hope to get off early and meet you. Can you do it, Del? In the evening, we'll try for tickets to *Streetcar*."

"I'm told the young actor, Brando, looks like me." Edgar grinned. "I *was* a bit of a swell, if I do say so myself."

"You're as handsome as he is right now, Dad," Weezy assured him.

Edgar winked at Del. "How in the world did I survive without my daughter?"

Since Bradley was due home the following evening, Del begged off, next day, from attending *Streetcar*. She took Edgar through the museum, and then joined Weezy's farewell dinner for her dad at an Italian restaurant and wished him happy traveling. Weezy had tried to talk him into staying a few days longer, but he insisted New York was too expensive for a man of leisure like himself. "I just came to check that you're okay. Grace worries, you know."

"If you stay, you can see Mom's art show," Weezy reminded him. "It starts Friday."

"And *my* mom arrives Wednesday," Del added. "You could visit with her, too."

Edgar demurred, saying he'd heard those art shows were like cocktail parties. "I'm not yet up to that." Del suspected that what he really wasn't up to was an encounter with an old love, Grace, and an old adversary, Millie.

Alone, later, in her apartment, Del reverted to worries about the other forthcoming encounter: hers with Bradley. She wondered if she could face Bradley without letting her features reveal her guilt. She planned different greetings, discarded each, and decided to retire and pretend to sleep. It would be nearly midnight by the time he arrived. Pretense should be easy.

At eleven, she climbed into bed, read for a while, then switched off the light. On hearing Bradley come in, she pulled the covers over her head. He clattered around the apartment, opened and closed the refrigerator, ran water in the bathtub, splashed.

When he stepped into the bedroom, she stirred, faked a yawn. She flopped over just as he planted a bare knee on the bed and leaned to kiss her. His kiss landed on her cheek.

"Good trip?" she mumbled.

"Great. Tell you about it in the morning, dear." He slid under the covers. She felt his nude body, still damp from his bath, against her back. When she asked if he'd seen the telegram, he professed to be delighted to learn that her mother was coming. "She and I were pals. I can't wait to see her again."

He slid an arm across Del's waist. She pretended to drift off. To her relief, he took the hint, settled down and turned away. She had a reprieve.

Since she hadn't fallen asleep until almost dawn, her mind alternately remembering Hilario and scolding over doing so, Bradley was up before her in the morning. She awoke to the smell of coffee, and when she entered the living room, tying her robe, found him sitting at the table, also in a bathrobe, with his steaming mug. He looked cheerful, the same old Bradley. Nothing had happened, she assured herself. She'd need to keep that fact in mind. She'd gone to Coney with friends, not an event to be embarrassed about—just something to mention casually.

He smiled. "You didn't need to get up, dear. I was coming back to bed."

The phone rang. Bradley set down his mug and reached for it. "Hello? Yes—sure, we can move in at once. I didn't know the apartment was vacant. I got home late, haven't talked to my wife yet."

He hung up, beaming. "The Abramsons are out. The super says he checked and the place is ready for us."

Del nodded. "Weezy and I went up there on Saturday. I have the key."

"Wonderful! We can start painting this very morning!" Bradley swallowed the last of his coffee and stood up, adding that hopefully the job would be finished by the time Millie arrived. With a wink, he suggested a quick one, and then remembered. "You don't like quick ones. We'll postpone the great moment. It'll be all the better for the anticipation." He began putting on clothes laid out on the bathtub-cover. Del told him she appreciated his sensitivity to her feelings.

"Selecting and purchasing paint will take all day," she remarked.

"Nah, I've done that—last week while you were at the museum cleaning out your desk, I had the paint set aside. We can pick up the cans on our way."

She bit her lip. The calm discussion she'd hoped for, explaining her reluctance to abandon this apartment, receded. He'd been thoughtful of her and now she must be thoughtful of him. Bradley inspected his arms as if he'd already splashed paint on them. "Hope I remembered to order paint thinner."

"Bradley, I haven't even had my first cup of—"

"I know. Here, grab some cups, we'll take the coffee and the pot with us. We can pick up a couple of Danish at a grocery store near the new place."

Dressed only in slacks, Bradley went, bare-chested, to peer in the closet. "I'm in trouble. We'll need old clothes, and I discarded mine when I moved. Hey, here's a thought: how about buying used stuff at Goodwill?"

"You're bursting with good ideas." Del couldn't keep the caustic tone from her voice. As so often with Bradley, she felt railroaded and lacking options. She'd hoped for a quiet moment to sort out her tumultuous emotions.

Failing to read between the lines, he rubbed his hands together eagerly. "Get dressed, will you, dear? I'll wash out the pot and get it ready to go. I can't wait to see our apartment. Oh, and I'll want my piano there as soon as possible. Remind me to call the movers."

Del went into the bedroom and dressed. Her hands shook. A stifling panic stopped her breath. Yet she knew she had no right to be angry with him. *He was the wronged one.* Whatever would he say about her night with Hilario?

She was in the path of a runaway train.

Without furniture, untouched by morning light, the new apartment looked worn and drab, the tired walls and ceilings that had enclosed someone else's life. Bradley didn't seem to notice. He set the paint cans and spackle on a spread newspaper on the living room floor, then followed Del to the kitchen where she set down the bag containing coffee pot, Danish, and sandwich-makings for their lunch. From there he toured each room. She heard him exclaiming, "So spacious! So much bigger than I remembered!" He returned and stood beside her to survey the kitchen. "Perhaps we should hire professionals in here. All those cabinets—enamel is miserable to work with."

"Fine, let's do that."

"You and I can get right to work on the living room and bedroom." He went on to mention that it had occurred to him they could buy box springs and mattress and sleep on the floor until they obtained a bed. "That way, we can move in tomorrow."

Panic overwhelmed her. "What's the rush?"

"There's your mother, for one thing. We'll want to be living here when she arrives."

"Bradley, we don't even have a chair for her to sit on."

"I've already picked out a table and chairs. They're on layaway."

"Without consulting me?"

He grinned. "You'll love them."

Her panic turned to fury. She clenched her fists and fought it. Again, he didn't notice. He was busy tugging on the used trousers he'd bought. He explained that it was only a kitchen set. "You and your mom can pick out the dining room stuff. Your mom grew up in the furniture capitol of the world."

It was déjà vu time. She'd been through this long ago in Michigan. "Brad, this is *our* apartment."

"Sure it is, honey. But we want Millie to feel needed, don't we?" He slipped on white overalls and added a painter's cap. "Okay, let's get to it. Spackle first. Where's that mixing pan?"

Driven by his eagerness to have the apartment ready when Millie arrived, Bradley worked feverishly. Del poured and mixed paints and did woodwork and touch-ups.

That night Del professed exhaustion. She fixed drinks for both of them, putting very little liquor in her glass but doubling the alcohol in Bradley's. In bed, Bradley leaned over to kiss her, then fitted himself in beside her, spoon-fashion. He worked his hands inside her pajama pants. She cringed at his touch; she tried to think of an excuse to stop him. Luckily, he grew drowsy from his labors and the drinks, and in time, after repeated pleas from her to slow down and give her a chance to rest, dropped off to sleep. She disengaged and rolled over. Sooner or later, of course, she'd have to face the event, but vowed to postpone it by pretending to have period-cramps.

By Wednesday, the apartment looked different, though to Del's eyes it appeared little brighter. She'd have chosen a warm desert-rose shade, and she found the gray and charcoal gloomy.

Bradley insisted the two styles were compatible. "The right furniture will fix it. If not, we'll find a painting with bright color."

He slapped enamel onto the door of the hall linen closet. Del went to clean up for her trip to the station. She was to go alone while Bradley awaited delivery of the mattress and springs. That very evening they were to begin carrying boxes of their stuff from the Village, giving Weezy their old place. Weezy planned to cook dinner for Yuri. It was her first opportunity to do so in a proper kitchen and she'd given careful thought to the menu.

Del rode the subway to Grand Central. The rush and noise of a train station never failed to set off her hunger for travel. "Starting condition," her father called it. He always claimed that when he got into starting condition, he had to pack up and go somewhere, if only to the mountains or the desert. She wished she could pack up and go somewhere—Michigan, maybe. She dreamed of getting on a train and vanishing from sight, just going off by herself to gather Petoskey stones on her favorite beach.

Or better, with Hilario. There were shops in Petoskey where one could use a wheel to polish stones gathered from the shore. The two of them could work together, side by side.

The train was thirty minutes late. Nervously checking and re-checking her hairdo, Del sat in the waiting room trying to think what to say to her mother. She planned to talk about Grace and the upcoming show, about Edgar's visit, about the hotel room she'd reserved, about anything to forestall questions regarding her life and marriage.

When the train was announced, she watched the line of people coming off, and soon spotted her mother. Though a small woman, conservatively dressed in a maroon linen suit and unobtrusive black hat, Millie dominated her surroundings. She wore her clothes with flair. People turned, eyed her. Once, when Alana had complained that the Langston girls had all been beauties, that she didn't know how she'd ended up in a family where she had to compete with potential movie stars, Del had seen the point, though she'd politely denied the fact to her aunt.

Millie knew how to preserve her good looks even in the hot California sun of her home. She never stepped out of the house without a large-brimmed hat, never failed to use moisturizing cream several times daily. Her dark hair, cut short, curled naturally around her still-unlined face.

She waved to Del, retrieved her luggage from a young sailor in uniform beside her, and thanked him with a smile. How typical of my mother to recruit the U.S. Navy to assist her, Del thought.

The sailor wandered off. Del hugged her mother, kissed her cheek and took the luggage. "You're looking well, Mother. How was your trip?"

"Tedious. I missed your dad but he couldn't get leave. I did see a couple of celebrities in the L.A, station; they were off to make a movie somewhere: Dorothy Lamour and what's-his-name, the handsome one."

"They're all handsome, Mother. Hollywood doesn't hire homely actors."

Millie looked around. "Speaking of handsome, where's my new son-in-law? I've been dying to see him again after all these years."

The word *handsome* brought Hilario to mind, but Del squelched his image. "Bradley's painting the apartment," she explained. "We got in ahead of time. We have no furniture yet, but—"

"So we'll all sleep on mattresses on the floor! What fun! I love camping out like that." When Del confessed she'd reserved a hotel room, Millie nixed the idea. "You think I never slept on a mattress on the floor? Dear, your father and I did it for months when we bought our house in California. It was war time; you couldn't buy furniture."

Del had feared this, her mother choosing to stay in the apartment with them. She protested that they'd bought only one mattress.

"No problem, we'll get another. We'll stop at a furniture store and have one delivered." She laughed at Del's look of distress. "It'll be cheaper than a New York hotel, and you'll have it later for guests. Anyway, I'm buying your furniture as a wedding gift."

There was no arguing. Millie always knew exactly what she wanted to do. Del managed a dutiful, "Thanks, Mother."

"I'll leave my luggage checked until Bradley can come for it." She took Del's arm. "I can manage with my overnight things. Let's find a furniture store."

Del told her there was one a few blocks from the new apartment. "We'll have to take the subway."

"Fine, where do we board?" She looked around. "Lordy, I hate these crowds. Every time I come to the city, I wonder how you stand the confusion."

On the ride home, Millie asked questions about the new apartment. What size were the rooms? Had Del measured them? And what about the windows? Would they all need drapes or might some do with curtains? She said, "We must be careful not to over-furnish. It's such a temptation; we'll want to buy every nice piece we see. It's easy to get carried away." When Del quoted Weezy's suggestion about white birch, she added, "White birch would be lovely against the charcoal."

At the furniture store, Millie spotted a sofa-bed for half price and proclaimed it just the thing. "It'll let Bradley's music room double as a guest room. Don't look so alarmed, dear, I'm paying."

"It's flowered," Del protested.

"Tiny lavender flowers, lovely against gray walls."

"But the drapes are flowered too, orange."

"Those will have to go. Flowered draperies are out. So forties. We're almost into the fifties."

"Mother, we can't afford—"

"Not to worry, I'll make the draperies. We'll rent a sewing machine."

She wrote a check. Over the salesman's protests of the California bank, she insisted her money was good even if distant. He told her the couch could not be delivered until morning. The truck had gone already.

"I knew we shouldn't have rushed to cancel that hotel room," Del said. "Where will you sleep?"

Millie suggested her old apartment. Del squirmed. "Weezy's there now."

"There's a second bedroom."

Del wondered how she was to sneak off by herself long enough to call Weezy and warn her not to let Yuri drop by. And how in the world would Weezy get in touch with Yuri to notify him of the change of plans? She couldn't call him at home and risk speaking to Deborah. There seemed no means of contact.

CHAPTER 27

❀

Weezy

Leaning back to talk to Del on the phone, Weezy kicked off her scuffs and put her feet up on the coffee table. "Don't worry, Cuz. When Yuri comes, I'll introduce him as a client and suggest we dine out."

"Didn't he plan to spend the night?"

"Sure, but we still have the suite at the B.T." She chuckled over the anxiety in Del's voice. "Relax, it'll work out."

"Unless he says the wrong thing and spills the beans."

"Yuri's no dummy. When I introduce my Aunt Millie, he'll get the message. I'll be proper and formal."

Del told her they were leaving at once for the Village, where her mother wanted to hit the sack early. "See you shortly."

Weezy hung up and glanced around. The apartment seemed bare, shelves and bookcases empty, Bradley's radio gone from the corner. Packed boxes waited by the door. Feeling a let-down at the loss of her intimate evening with Yuri in her new place, she wandered barefoot and wiggled her toes as she scuffed the loose-weave piling of the carpet, far less soft and luxurious than that at the Belle Turrets. She'd looked forward to cooking dinner for Yuri. She consoled herself that there'd be time for that in the future.

She opened the cupboard and peered at empty shelves. All that remained were three non-matching plates and four cups, one with a broken handle. Everything else had been packed except for two fry pans, three sauce pans and a casserole dish. Yuri had assured her it would be fun to eat here. Village pinch-hitting was an adventure, he said, *La Boheme* right out of the Met.

Still, relatives must be accommodated. How often during her lonely childhood Weezy had wished for aunts, uncles and cousins! Now that at last she had them, she could scarcely complain of the inconvenience.

She put away the wine she'd bought, along with candles and holders, and made herself a cup of tea. In her scuffs again, seated at the table overlooking the street, she debated about painting, making this apartment her own with her choice of colors. Perhaps on a Saturday, Yuri could come and help.

Wednesdays and Saturdays Yuri saved for Weezy. Thursdays he worked late so he could take off early on Friday. He had a lengthy commute to Long Island, and the Sabbath dinner, he'd told her, was prompt even though, with his only child away at college, there remained just him and Deborah. Jealous of those intimate candlelit meals, Weezy had hoped to share a similar one with Yuri here.

She decided dubonnet would be an interesting color for these walls, with white enamel woodwork and a white throw over the sarcophagus. Better wait, though. Del had been reluctant to move, and might yet flee Bradley's companionship and return here to her old stamping grounds. Weezy sensed that the marriage was not going well.

When the tap at the door came, Weezy had finished dressing and was in the bedroom smoothing fresh sheets. She dropped everything, opened up, and saw between Del and Bradley a small but handsome woman in a maroon suit and black hat.

"So this is Aunt Millie!" She held out her hand. The woman grasped both her hands and drew her into a formal embrace, no pressed-to-the-bosom hug such as Aunt Alana had offered at first meeting.

Yet her words were warm. "Just imagine finding you, after all these years! Your mom snatched you right out of my arms and took you away." She rose on tiptoe to peck at Weezy's cheek. "I never dreamed I'd see you again."

"I've heard you were the first besides Mom to hold me when I was a newborn." Weezy freed her hands and drew the door wide. The trio entered. Behind them hovered a young man, no doubt someone Bradley had brought along to help with moving. When he trailed uncertainly into the room, Bradley introduced him, but with Aunt Millie raving on about the miracle of reunion, Weezy didn't catch his name. She heard only, "—friend from the church." She shook his hand and offered a welcome. Then, pointing, she told Bradley that everything was packed. "I finished up for you."

"That was a big job." Del stood with arms akimbo. "We appreciate it."

"Least I could do, getting this lovely apartment without even having to pay for the lease."

Bradley studied the pile of boxes, rearranged them, and passed a large one along to his friend. "We need to get going. It'll take a while to load the stuff into the truck." He took a box under each arm.

"Be careful, that one has my Petoskey stones," Del cautioned. "They scratch easily." While Bradley and his friend departed with their first loads, she carried her mother's suitcase toward the small bedroom. Weezy told her she was giving her aunt the larger one. "I've just put on fresh sheets."

"That's kind of you," Millie said.

Weezy offered her aunt a seat on the couch and asked if she'd like a cup of tea. Millie said she'd eaten at the Dutch Kitchen. "But thanks." She patted her stomach.

"I'll have to leave you alone for a while," Weezy confessed. "I've a dinner engagement with a client. I hope you won't mind."

"Not at all. I look forward to an early bedtime in a bed that isn't rolling across the country." Even when she smiled, Millie seemed formal and reserved compared to the exuberant Alana and Vi, more like Bea, the suburban socialite matron. The two younger members of that big family must have grown up socially conscious, determined to make a proper impression, Weezy reflected.

Sitting beside her on the couch, Weezy told her she'd missed her at the family gathering in Michigan. "Sorry you couldn't be there. I loved getting to know everyone—Dad, my grandmother, Aunt Alana—and of course, Del, whom I met on the train."

Millie nodded. "How's your mother, dear? It's been so long since I had news of her, I thought she'd dropped off the planet."

"She's fine." Weezy's gaze focused through the open door onto the bedroom clock, and she peered to see if it was time yet for Yuri. She didn't want to be so obvious as to consult her wrist watch. "She's busy arranging for an upcoming art exhibit. In fact, you've arrived just in time for it. I'll ask Mother for an extra invitation for you."

"I'm sure her memories are painful. You mustn't insist." Millie leaned back and closed her eyes, admitting she'd love to see Grace again. "It's been—what? Twenty-one years?" She straightened. "Mind if I take off my shoes? They're pinchy."

Weezy urged her to make herself comfortable. "I only wish I had amenities to offer. At the moment, I'm short of towels, glassware—"

Millie explained that she'd bathed at Del's place after she got off the train. "You needn't fuss over me; I'm used to making do. You go ahead with whatever you'd planned."

Working with their assistant, Del and Bradley already had most of the boxes removed. Grasping the last of them, they started for the door. Del paused to announce that she'd ride along in the truck to help unpack. "Will you be all right, Mother?"

"Goodness, Del, I stayed alone in this apartment last time I visited. Don't you remember? You were called back to the museum."

"Oh, yes, art thieves. What a headache!" Del pecked her mother's cheek. "See you in the morning, then. Sleep well."

They left. Weezy closed and automatically locked the door. Millie patted the seat beside her. "Sit down and tell me all about you. Del says you're a Smith College graduate working for a literary agent. It sounds fascinating." She leaned back, wiggling her toes inside her stocking feet, removing and replacing a bobby pin in her hair, and confessed that she'd done some writing in her younger years.

Weezy asked about Millie's past career. "You were a librarian, I hear."

"Yes, I'd hoped to be a musician, but that was no career for women back then." She folded hands on knee. "I'd like to hear about your work as a literary agent."

Listening for Yuri's step on the stair, Weezy explained about the form-critiques she sent out. "The author imagines he's receiving a personal commentary but actually it's an assembly-line product. For instance: 'Your hero, Blank, needs to encounter more difficulties in his attempts to solve his problems, relying less on the help of his partner/lover/friend.'"

Millie wrinkled her nose in distaste. "Everyone knows that!"

"You'd be surprised how many don't. Half the stories we receive show the hero rescued by friends or Fate."

"For this stuff the writers pay you money?" Millie marveled.

"Sure. We help them." Weezy straightened. Were those footsteps out there? Uneasily, she ran her forefinger along her chin and wished Aunt Millie would go off to bed. She went on, "It's my job to fill in the names of the characters so the critiques sound personal."

"By the way, Weezy, you must tell me about Del's wedding."

"Oh, it was an adventure, rushing off to New Jersey like that. Excuse me, Aunt Millie, I think I hear my client coming. Is there anything I can do for you before I leave? You'll want to sleep in Del's room—it's the most comfortable bed, I believe."

A tap at the door confirmed her guess. She stood up, touching her hair to check on it, wishing for the many mirrors at the Belle. She reached for her sweater. She opened the door wide so Yuri could see her aunt, who was getting up from the couch. Yuri stood there with a grin which softened to a reserved smile when he noticed the older woman.

"Mr. Yurovski, my Aunt Millie from California. She's staying with me overnight because my cousin has no extra bed in her new apartment." Weezy managed to sound cool and formal.

As she'd known he would, Yuri played along. He stepped in and held out his hand. "Nice to meet you, Mrs. um—" He nodded at Weezy's hasty hint. "Of course, you're the mother of the former occupant of this apartment. So you've come all the way from California?"

"Arrived this afternoon," Millie confirmed.

"A good trip, I hope?"

"Lovely. I did enjoy the fall colors. So beautiful."

"Fall colors? In September?"

"Yes, in the mountains. Utah, Colorado."

"I hope you'll excuse us." Weezy slung her sweater around her shoulders and moved closer to Yuri. "We haven't eaten."

"Of course. You run along. It's nice to meet you, Mr. Yurovski."

As she clattered down the stairs beside Yuri, Weezy apologized. "Del reserved a hotel room for her mother but the woman prefers to stay with relatives. I'm sorry, Yuri, I'd looked forward to cooking a meal for us."

"It's not a problem." Yuri impulsively reached for her hand, hesitated, drew his own hand back "That's the trouble with an apartment. Relatives expect to be invited. Lucky I haven't yet canceled at the Belle." Holding the outer door for her, he consulted his watch. "Almost eight. How about we pick up Chinese takeout and eat in the suite?"

"Good idea. I'm disappointed, though, I'd planned quite an elaborate—"

Yuri suggested they wait on the meal-cooking until all the relatives had gone home, meanwhile continuing to meet at the Belle Turrets. "That will forestall these embarrassing encounters." He smiled and, once they'd turned the corner, took her hand.

At a nearby Chinese restaurant, they ordered a variety of dishes. Carrying the packages, Yuri signaled a taxi. Within minutes they were back at the residence hotel which only that morning Weezy had thought she'd moved from. The lobby was now festive with Halloween decorations, black and orange streamers, grinning artificial pumpkins, papier-mâché black cats following papier-mâché witches. Weezy gasped. "Jumping the gun a bit, aren't they?"

Yuri told her they made a big thing of holidays so the women wouldn't feel abandoned. The men would have less free time now that summer was over. Many wives and children spent the summers in Newport or Cape Cod, leaving the men free to be with their mistresses. In the fall, they reverted to sneak-encounters.

Yuri touched her shoulder with his free hand to guide her to the elevator. He added, "Neither Thanksgiving nor Hanukah are a big deal to my wife. I won't be forced to leave you alone. As for Christmas—well, for Deborah it doesn't exist, so you and I can celebrate together. It'll be my first experience of decorating a tree. I always wanted to do that."

They passed Betty Ann, who lifted her brows in surprise. "Back so soon?"

Weezy offered a casual wave and claimed that since she had no furnishings in her new apartment, they were keeping the suite for now.

"That's good. We'd miss y'all." Betty Ann smiled and hurried on toward the coffee shop.

The suite seemed bare, the closet door open to reveal emptiness. Weezy closed the door and drew the draperies against the coming twilight. Yuri put down the packages and switched on a light. When they'd set the table, the place grew more cheery and inviting.

Yuri reached for Weezy and drew her into his arms. He shed her sweater and laid it aside. His lips pressed against hers. His hands moved along her shoulders, found her blouse-buttons, undid them, slid inside, touched her bare shoulders, and moved downward. Her breasts seemed to reach toward his fingers. She always felt surprised all over again at finding herself so wildly attracted to this man. He wasn't at all what she'd planned for herself. Too old, not tall nor even wondrously handsome—yet he was a bundle of lovable energy. He seemed so warm, so caring.

"Aren't you hungry?" She gasped out the words, shivering while her nipples reveled in the touch of his fingers.

"Starved. Saturday to Wednesday is an interminable length of time. We need to sneak an extra day in there."

She laughed. "I meant for food."

"Um hum. In twenty or thirty minutes from now." He nuzzled her neck, cupped a breast, and drew her toward the bedroom.

She managed a breathless reminder. "The stuff'll get cold."

"I love cold Chinese, don't you?" In the bedroom, he shut the door with his foot, then picked her up and put her on the bed. "It's lucky we kept this suite. Good old Aunt Millie, may she be comfortable in her temporary digs."

"She should be. I gave her the best bed." Weezy kicked off her shoes, and held her arms out to him. "God, Yuri, I missed you, too. I may get home late. Let's hope Aunt Millie doesn't wait up."

"You've certainly managed to surround yourself with family. First your father, now—"

"Dad's a good sport; we had fun together. He wanted to meet you but I didn't know how to arrange it."

"I want to hear all about his visit—later." Yuri rolled on top of her. She enjoyed his lengthy kiss. Then she squirmed out from under him to shed her blouse. She reached up to unbutton his shirt. When he'd removed the shirt, she let her arms encircle his bare shoulders to draw him down again. She loved the feel of him against her. She put her hands on his face and leaned her head back for another kiss. His mouth came down onto hers; their tongues touched.

Suddenly it struck her Millie now knew what this man looked like. Panic stabbed at her; she felt a sense of exposure and vulnerability.

She reassured herself. No reason their paths should ever cross again. She relaxed, put the thought out of her mind and focused on Yuri. His hands unfastened her skirt and slid along her body. She unzipped his fly, sensing the growing hardness within.

"You feel so good," she said. "I love touching you."

"I love it, too," he told her.

"I don't have my robe here," she warned. "If you take off all my clothes I'll be—"

"Nude. I think I can handle that." He kissed her breast lightly.

CHAPTER 28

Grace

In Boston, Grace Ward had planned to give full attention to her career for this one day, to concentrate on how to deal with the critics at her art exhibit. Instead, she kept thinking about the Langstons and Millie Kingsley.

Weezy's mention of Millie had opened the flood gates of memory. It all came back. Grace saw herself young again, sitting next to a youthful Millie in the large dining room at Stormland, at the massive walnut table looking out at oak trees and robins. She smelled strawberry preserves cooking, and saw, opposite her, Edgar, the handsome, the desirable, bent over his plate, his brown hair falling across his forehead to give him a boyish look. She stole glances, hungering for his closeness, his smile, the male smell of him—and longing for freedom from those stupid parental questions: Can he support me? Is he a good catch?—a suitable mate for a Hannaford?

Right now she didn't want to recall that dilemma, nor think of Edgar, whom she'd loved as passionately and hopelessly as ever the ill-fated Lucia di Lammermoor of opera fame had loved her Edgardo. Those handsome Edgars she and Lucy had gone mad over, and had believed themselves betrayed by—oh, melodrama! Lucy died of love while Grace had longed for a similar fate. But for having to care for baby Weezy, Grace might well have played Lucia and killed Jonathan. When he heaved himself on top of her in the night, the thought had more than once crossed her mind: stab him and then rush downstairs with blood on her nightgown to sing of Edgardo. She knew by heart the mad scene from *Lucia*.

But she'd restrained herself and, convinced her own life was over, had lived only for Weezy. She'd tried to lose herself in painting. She'd allowed no mention of McCurdles or Langstons.

Yet equally strong, now, was her desire to mend fences with her daughter, who seemed to have become pals with Millie's Del. Thus, when Weezy asked her for invitations for Millie and Del and Bradley to attend her opening, Grace felt obliged to extend them, though Millie was the last person she'd have chosen to include.

Now the meeting would happen. She'd best brace for it.

The phone rang and she answered. Her mother's voice, lowered from contralto to baritone through the years, asked, "Are you ready?"

"Getting dressed now, Mother." Concentrate, she commanded herself. Think. This is about clothes for New York. Grace had planned to go to town early, have lunch and then shop for something special for the show, an outfit more flamboyant than her usual restrained style, an outfit to impress Weezy.

Weezy isn't the one I need to impress, she reminded herself. It's the critics. Especially the *Times* man, and that formidable Tolliver Petrie, the freelancer whose critiques appear not only in the newspaper but in places like V*ogue* and *Harper's Bazaar*, even *Esquire*, shafting the unwary from every direction.

"I'll pick you up in half an hour," Persis Hannaford said. "Don't keep the taxi waiting."

"Yes, Mother." To communicate her annoyance, she made her tone of voice sound painfully proper. Unfortunately, her mother hung up too soon to notice. Grace hurried to the bedroom and opened a drawer.

"I wish to God mother weren't going," she confessed aloud as she gazed at her reflection in the bureau mirror. She piled clothes onto her bed and slammed the drawer shut. By herself, she thought she might get along with Weezy. Her mother always threw a monkey wrench in the works.

She drew on her hose so hastily she snagged a thread and watched a ladder develop. With an unladylike, "Damn and shit," she pulled the hose off, tossed the pair aside, and fumbled for another. The second pair had a snag but no ladder. She applied colorless nail polish to the thread. Forcing herself to be calm and careful, she slid her legs into the hose, straightened the seams, and fastened the tops to her girdle garter.

"I'm tired to death of trying to please people," she grumbled as she yanked at the straps of her slippers. "Who the hell cares what Tolliver Petrie thinks? So he claims I don't paint what I see. How does he know what I see? Does he follow me to the beach?"

She stood up, reached for her slip, pulled it over her head. She flipped through the dresses in her closet and talked to herself. "I don't need critics, I just need paint and canvas—and some great views. Everything else is irrelevant." She rampaged through her clothes. "Except Weezy, that is." Once they'd been so close. But now Weezy, the loving, laughing child, had been transformed into a young woman who seemed to feel only resentment toward her mother. And all because of something that happened more than twenty years ago.

Grace decided it didn't matter what she wore. She would purchase a new gown in New York. She meant to head for Lord and Taylor as soon as she got her mother settled in a hotel room. She grabbed a dress and slid into it, feeling tempted to do what Weezy had done months ago, discard old clothes and start over with the new look. Show her daughter that she too knew how to dress with big-city sophistication.

When Persis called to her from the front hall, she had only to touch up her lipstick and put on hat and gloves. She tried for a rakish angle, but on studying herself in the mirror, felt silly. She wasn't the type.

In the living room, her mother eyed her. "You're sharp today."

"Do you think so? I'm tired of my old clothes."

"Try varying them with different accessories. Scarves can do wonders." Persis opened the door and held it. "Dear me, the sun's going under. I pray it won't rain."

Grace felt a shaft of hope. Maybe her opening would be rained out. The fearsome Millie Kingsley and the unspeakable Tolliver Petrie wouldn't brave the downpour. Maybe, maybe.

She couldn't be so lucky, she decided. She grabbed her purse and overnight case and followed her mother out. The taxi waited at the curb. They climbed in. Persis told the driver to go to the train station.

"At least, I remembered the umbrella." She kicked the item in question against the overnight case at her feet.

Weezy had invited both women to stay in the Village apartment, but Persis said she couldn't manage the four flights. Instead, they'd made a reservation at their usual hotel, where Weezy was to join them for dinner before the opening.

"We'll finally have a chance to find out what Weezy's been up to," Persis remarked. "I worry about that girl. She's too young to be on her own in the big city."

"She's an adult. Leave her alone." Grace couldn't bring herself to confess that she'd sent Edgar to check.

"Adult! She's a naïve, inexperienced adult who's ripe for trouble. I find it suspicious that she didn't find a place of her own when the Kingsley woman's new husband moved in. What kind of *ménage a trois* is that? You don't share quarters with a newly married couple."

"She rented a room in the next door apartment and kept only her mailing address at Del's place."

"Oh, I know that's what she told us—a likely story." She eyed her daughter. "You don't seem concerned. She's *your* child, after all."

The cab jolted and Grace shifted uneasily. "Mother, I wish you wouldn't meddle. You make things worse."

"Checking isn't meddling." Persis bent to pick up her umbrella and used it like a cane to lean on while she watched to make sure the taxi took the short route.

Before long the car screeched to a halt. "Train station," the driver said.

Grace knew all about her mother's snooping talents. She worried throughout the train ride, throughout lunch and her solitary shopping trip. Having tried hard to keep her distance, to give Weezy space, to restore good relations by demonstrating trust, she didn't need for her mother to ruin everything.

When she returned to the hotel with the new gown she'd purchased, her mother, who'd stayed behind, ostensibly to rest up for the evening, glowed with that triumphant look Grace knew and dreaded. Persis burst out with her news as soon as Grace stepped into the room. "Weezy's up to something! You'll never guess where she's been living!"

"Mother, I have no idea. I don't even want to—"

"The Belle Turrets!"

Though the name was unfamiliar to Grace, her mother proved all too willing to enlighten her. "It's an unsavory residence hotel for women where men are allowed upstairs in the rooms."

Grace stared. "However did you discover that?"

"Simple. I called Weezy's boss. He wasn't hard to find. The Lauritz Literary Agency is in the directory. I asked for Della Eloise Ward, and he told me they had no such person working there, but did have an Eloise McCurdle. I said, 'That's the one.' He said she was on lunch hour. When I identified myself as the grandmother, he gave me her address. I called the hotel and asked about their rules."

"Mother, are you trying to drive the kid away altogether?"

"I am trying, God help me, to avoid watching another member of my family go through what you went through. You were lucky, Jonathan proved patient and understanding, but—"

"Call that luck?" If so, it was luck that had made her life a desert of loveless marriage. Grace sighed and flopped into a chair. Her head ached again. This would be the third time in one day that she'd taken aspirin, which always made her feel disengaged.

"You bet I call it luck. If he hadn't been so caring, you'd have wound up a single mother trying to raise a bas—"

Grace flung up a hand. "Don't say it, Mother. Weezy was born in wedlock."

"Just barely, with only hours to spare." Persis drew herself up. Though lacking great height, she could make herself seem tall. Her dewlaps flapped. "I will not go through that with another generation. Whatever Weezy's up to, it will be stopped."

Grace sighed. That terrifying finality. In a previous lifetime, she thought, her mother must have been a priestess of Amon-Re. Only an attendant of the sun god would dare be so imperious.

"Leave it alone until after tonight, will you?" She slipped her shoes off and wiggled aching toes. "I've invited half the art critics on the east coast to my opening, not to mention Millie Kingsley. It's not the moment to fight with Weezy."

Persis frowned. "I don't intend to fight, just to take charge."

By evening, the multiple doses of aspirin had put Grace in a state of semi-awareness. Her headache had receded but she felt it somewhere in the distance waiting to return. At the reception, she stood beside her mother in a receiving line of two. In her new formal gown of kelly green, she reached a hand to other hands, heard praises of her work, smiled back at smiling faces, and repeated, "I'm so glad you came." She tried not to worry about Weezy, who was resplendent tonight in a peach-colored Grecian gown Grace had not bought for her, a gown that looked far too expensive for the salary of an apprentice literary agent.

The meeting with Millie hadn't produced the shock she'd anticipated. No longer the intimidating young heiress of Stormland, Millie had become a California matron of fifty-something. Still petite, still a beauty—but age had left its mark. Grace couldn't decide exactly how. Complexion flawless, hair free of gray, chin showing no sag, figure slim—it was simply a kind of settled quality about her, an absence of youth rather than a hint of age.

"Twenty years is too long," Millie said. "We must get together, Grace. Will you be staying on in New York?"

"Mother and I go home tomorrow, but I'll be back periodically to check on things. The show lasts three weeks."

"Give me a call," Millie said. "Maybe we can have lunch. I'll write down Del's phone number. By the way, have you spoken to Del? She's here somewhere with her husband, Bradley."

Grace assured her Weezy had introduced them. "Her husband seems charming. Del claims she remembers being flower girl at my wedding. I'm amazed. All that time ago, and she was such a little thing!"

Millie looked around for her daughter and called her over. "Del, dear, come talk to Grace." Her gaze moved on, and she gasped. "Why, there's Mr. Yurovski! Yoo hoo! Mr. Yurovski, hello there!"

"Mr. who?" Blinking, Grace followed Millie's gaze. She sensed her mother moving closer. Del hurried over, almost too quickly, as if trying to cover a gaffe.

"Mr. Yurovski is a client of Weezy's," Millie explained. "They had dinner together the other night." She gestured toward a slim, wiry man with curly brown hair, who'd acknowledged her greeting with a barely perceptible nod. He was holding two drinks, moving away from the punch bowl in the company of a blonde woman Grace recognized as his wife, a well-groomed person in a powder-blue suit and salon-perfect coiffure. He handed one drink to his companion.

"I've met Deborah Yurovski," she said. "She's a patron of the arts. But why would Weezy dine with them?"

"Just with him, unless his wife joined them later. I gather he needed a literary agent for his book."

Stepping close to her mother, Del spoke up quickly. "I understand Mr. Yurovski is writing a novel. It's Weezy's job to dine with prospective clients and provide guidance in their work."

"Even married men?" Persis Hannaford snapped. "Alone?"

"Literary agents don't ask if clients are married. It's business."

"I suppose." Despite sounding dubious, Persis was the first to hold out her hand to the approaching couple. "Mr. and Mrs. Yurovski, I believe. I'm Persis Hannaford, mother of the artist. I understand you know my granddaughter, Eloise—uh, McCurdle." She spoke the name with an expression of distaste.

Again Del seemed to speak up quickly. "I've been telling them about your novel, Mr. Yurovsky, and Weezy's hope of marketing it for you." Was she offering the man a hint? Grace wondered.

If so, Mr. Yurovsky picked up on it. He managed a self-deprecating smile. "I have to confess the novel isn't written yet. I've an idea and an outline. I wanted to consult an agent before proceeding, so as—you know—not to waste time on something unsalable. Miss McCurdle was kind enough to dine with me and offer pointers."

Mrs. Hannaford reached a hand to Deborah, who juggled the drink her husband had just handed her in order to free up her right hand. She draped her fingers into the older woman's firm handclasp. Her thin lips contrived a smile.

Mr. Yurovsky turned to Grace. "So Miss McCurdle is your daughter, Mrs. Ward? I had no idea. She did mention that her mother was an artist, but the name McCurdle—it threw me off."

Feeling uneasy, Grace tried to fight her way past the aspirin fog. She sensed something important occurring through all this fake over-politeness, but she wasn't getting it. She commented, "I hadn't realized Weezy had progressed to the point of wining and dining clients. I assumed she was little more than an office girl."

"Fact is, I sought her help. She seems so knowledgeable, a very talented young woman. Published in a national magazine—at her young age! I read her article, and the bio mentioned that she worked for a literary agent. I got in touch. Of course, since she's your daughter, I'm not surprised at her abilities. You're such an accomplished family!"

Having freed her hand from Persis Hannaford's grip, Deborah took her husband's arm. "Darling, I had no idea you planned to write a novel." She added, to Grace, "He's so modest. He'd have sprung it on me after it's published."

"*If* it's published," he said. "Long road ahead yet."

Grace remarked to Deborah, "I met you once at a fund-raising banquet for student artists. You wouldn't remember me, you were at the speaker's table. You gave a talk on Impressionism."

"I often do," the blue-clad woman admitted. "It's my field of expertise."

"I've heard good things about the help you've given young artists." Grace knew all too well that Deborah was a close friend of her nemesis, Tolliver Petrie, the critic who complained she failed to paint what she saw.

"I like your work very much." Deborah spoke politely now and Grace couldn't tell if she was sincere or not.

"It has a stark quality," her husband added. "One can feel the wind blowing across the water. We hope to own a painting."

"Please feel free to look around," Grace said.

Persis added, "I wish you luck with that novel, Mr. Yurovsky."

He thanked her and turned away, his wife holding his arm. Grace noticed that Del had slipped off and gone to speak to Weezy, who stood with Bradley before one of the paintings. She saw Weezy glance around, spot the Yurovskys, and flinch, going pale. Grace felt threatened by Weezy's uneasiness and feared her mother, beside her, had noticed. She squelched an urge to turn to her mother and check her expression.

Flanked by Del and Bradley, Weezy moved quickly into another room. Grace suffered an uneasy suspicion that there must be more than agent/client relations between Weezy and Mr. Yurovsky, and had no doubt her mother had reached the same conclusion.

When Tolliver Petrie hurried over, Millie excused herself and wandered off to look at paintings. Grace longed to delve into her purse for another aspirin but knew she'd had more than her limit. She forced a smile for Tollie and wished the day would end. Though this was her show, she lacked control over whatever was happening.

CHAPTER 29

Weezy

Spending the night alone in Del's old apartment, now vacated by Aunt Millie who'd gone uptown, Weezy tossed, turned and worried. Her eyes refused to stay shut; her midriff churned. For what seemed hours, she stared at the dim square of window. Finally she got up, made herself a cup of cocoa, and sat in a chair thumbing through a magazine on which she couldn't concentrate. She kept remembering that awful moment at the exhibit when Del had grabbed her arm and offered a hasty warning: "Yuri's here; the cat's out of the bag. Mother let slip that you dined with him." Though she'd hastened to add her invented excuse, "I claimed he wanted to discuss his novel with you," Weezy panicked. Del commanded, "Don't look, your gran's watching."

Too late. Weezy had glanced and grimaced. She sighed. "Gran's always watching. She has no conscience about invading my privacy."

Del nodded. "I remember from way back. Battleaxe Hannaford, Gramps used to call her."

Bradley came around to flank Weezy on the other side and touch her arm. "Try not to look guilty; it's no one's business what you do."

"If you bump into Yuri, say something about his book outline," Del urged. "Offer advice, act professional."

The two of them propelled her into the smaller room. Bent on coping, she turned back, shaking her head. "I'll seem conspicuous if I hide. It's best I face them."

She disengaged her arm and, braced and rigid, walked back into the main room. She sought out Yuri where he stood with his wife. Suppressing a pang of jealousy over the powder-blue arm nestled in his, she strode up to the couple.

"Mr. Yurovsky, what luck to meet you here." She offered a formal smile along with her best professional manner. "I have good news. My boss likes your synopsis and agreed to handle your novel."

He matched her formality; he freed his arm to extend his hand. "Miss McCurdle, how gratifying. I truly appreciate your efforts on my behalf. Uh—may I present my wife, Deborah?—Miss McCurdle, dear, my literary agent."

Deborah extended a limp hand. "This is quite a surprise! I had no idea my husband contemplated doing a novel."

Yuri said, "The world is full of people planning books. It's the result that counts."

"I suppose the proof is in the pudding," Deborah agreed.

Maintaining formality, Yuri added, to Weezy, "I hadn't realized Grace Ward was your mother. What an artistic family!" Weezy wondered why the floor didn't open and swallow her. Surely this was the end of the world—her world, anyway.

"We're trying to decide on a canvas to buy," his wife said. "I hope you'll excuse us, Miss Ward—um—McCurdle. I want to consult the critic, Tolliver Petrie." She waved vaguely toward the receiving line where Petrie stood talking to Grace.

"Of course. It's nice to meet you. Our agency will be in touch, Mr. Yurovsky." Weezy felt surprised to find she could still speak. Trying not to tremble, she wandered back to Del and Bradley, and grasped Del's arm, more for support than companionship.

Aunt Millie spotted them and at once moved toward them. She was resplendent in a slinky black outfit, Japanese, with gold embroidery of a flowering tree stretching down the front. Weezy stifled the urge to glance toward her mom and Gran to see if they'd noticed her embarrassment. When Millie requested a glass of punch, she went to scoop some from the large crystal bowl. She struggled to keep her hand steady.

"Quite a coincidence, having your client turn up here," Millie remarked to her.

Del spoke up. "Not really, Mother. He's married to a well-known art patron." She added casually, to Weezy, "Your mom knows his wife. She mentioned they met at a fundraiser."

Weezy's panic deepened. She forced a pretense of indifference. "Small world, isn't it?"

"We have a painting we want to show you." Del again urged Weezy toward the other room. "It's proof of my theory that your mom paints Lake Michigan. November storm, Christmas trees on the horizon."

"Christmas trees? An island?" Weezy tried to pay attention.

"No, huge waves shaped like evergreens."

They moved closer to the painting. It was indeed a storm scene, with gray sky, gray water, enormous waves. On the horizon, rough water stabbed the sky in shapes reminiscent of jagged pine trees.

"Sailors on the Great Lakes try to remain ashore when they see those Christmas tree waves," Del said. "Those things can snap an oreboat in two by lifting each end out of the water and leaving the middle unsupported. That's how the Edmund Fitzgerald sank."

"Better not break the news to Mother that she's painting the Great Lakes. She'll be upset." The words came from somewhere, so Weezy assumed she spoke them. She fought to hide her own inner turmoil and give her attention to her mother's problems.

Shaking her head reflectively, Millie declared, "It's as if Grace's life began and ended with Edgar."

Weezy feared Persis might maneuver her own life so it would begin and end with Yuri. Granny could cause disaster if she chose.

She'd worried throughout the interminable evening. Now the night was becoming even more interminable. Back under the quilts, she again lay sleepless, thrashing, reviewing events. At 4:30 she gave up and heaved herself out of bed.

She decided to dress and go to the Belle. It was Yuri's day. Though usually he worked mornings and showed up only at lunch-time, she hoped that under the circumstances he might alter his schedule. He, too, had to be concerned—though perhaps not so much as she, since he didn't know her formidable grandmother.

At five in the morning, the streets of the silent city were dark and deserted. She summoned a taxi. At least there'd be people to talk to later at the Belle. She felt she'd go crazy sitting alone, sleepless, in the Village apartment.

She was surprised by the wave of nostalgia that hit her when she wandered into the deserted but festive lobby. She'd loved it here. She'd met interesting people, learned of lives very different from her own, written her best stories—and enjoyed every moment of Yuri's attentiveness. In this "unsavory" hotel she'd felt protected and—happy.

Odd, she thought. Four months ago I was dubious about moving in. Now I hate to move out.

Hoping to find Yuri waiting, she rode up in the elevator. The suite was empty. Why had she expected him so early? What excuse would he offer to his wife if he dashed downtown at daybreak? She shed her sweater, stretched out on the bed to wait, listened for footsteps in the hall, and in time dozed off.

On waking, she checked her watch and found she'd slept for almost three hours. It was after eight now. She felt disoriented. She'd dreamed Grannie Hannaford was sweeping, eliminating treasures along with dust, smashing her granddaughter's treasured collection of ceramic animals, one by one, as she pushed her broom ahead of her.

Weezy got up, dug in her purse for comb and lipstick, and tried to hide with powder the dark patches under her eyes. She went down to breakfast, and in the coffee shop, waved to familiar women at their usual tables.

She seated herself and looked around. Definitely, she'd miss all this. The dancer's table, over-full now, held six women crowded into a four-person seating area. As always, the ballerinas sat erect and held their heads high, stretching their necks. Slim and willowy, they all dressed the same, in what seemed almost a uniform—narrow skirt worn ankle-length to hide stretch tights, ballet slippers, long hair done in a roll or bun at the back of the head. The only variation was in the hair color. Uninterested in conversations not pertaining to dance, they were seldom disturbed since no one else had reason to invade their circle. After breakfast, she knew, they would all go to the gym for their limbering exercises, then on to the pool for a swim.

In a far corner she saw the actress table, recognizable even though actresses didn't go in for uniform clothing. On the contrary, each woman tried to be distinctive in her own way, to exaggerate her unique qualities. Weezy saw an abundance of colorful imported cloth and hand-made jewelry, copper or cloisonné, from Village shops, especially bracelets and earrings. That circle too was one few others cared to join, since the women usually carried with them pages of script, and cast about for someone to read lines and prompt them while they memorized their parts. There always seemed to be a reading in progress, either in the coffee shop or the lobby.

Often recruited, Weezy had enjoyed snapping out lines from plays. Today, however, she'd given that table a wide berth. Her mind wouldn't focus. She'd have avoided even a writers' table, had there been one, but she had yet to discover a fellow writer at the Belle. Oddly, there was no musicians' table either. The musicians seemed to be individualists who didn't group together with colleagues. The opera divas generally sent down for meals and ate in their rooms. There were many women who rarely entered the coffee shop, who seemed to do nothing but walk their clipped, jeweled, beribboned poodles. They, too, hovered together, and none had so far deigned to make eye contact with Weezy, let alone talk to her. They were said to be gangsters' molls. To Weezy their lives seemed pathetic.

She'd just been served hotcakes when Betty Ann came in and asked to join her. Weezy gestured toward the empty chair. In her full-skirted neon-blue dress, Betty Ann sat. Weezy noticed she'd switched to a more sophisticated hairdo, short and gently waved around her face.

"You look great," she said.

"I can't say the same for you. You look like you lost your last fray-und." It was her relaxing day; she wasn't even trying to hide her southern accent.

"To tell the truth, I'm feeling that way."

"Why? What happened? Y'all break up?"

Weezy tried to think how to explain. Around here, mothers weren't considered a problem. Most of these women had cut the ties and seemed to give family little thought. She just stated facts. "My mom's a painter, and my guy showed up at her exhibit last night with his wife."

"Oh, God." Betty Ann's features immediately reflected sympathy. "I know how you feel. Awful, ain't—isn't it? It happened to me a couple of times. Watching a wife simper over your guy could drive a person to drink."

"That, too," Weezy agreed.

"Too? There's more? The wife caught on and there was a scene?"

"No, but I'm sure my mom and gran suspect something. Mom knows his wife, and Gran's a snoop."

Betty Ann shrugged. "What can they discover? Believe me, management won't give out names of guests. They wouldn't stay in this business long if they did."

"A private investigator will ask the other women."

"We won't rat. We're all in the same boat. If he shows a picture, we'll deny knowing you." She tilted her nose up, waved her fingers and mimicked, "Never saw the woman before. Sorry."

"He'll park outside and watch for me."

Betty Ann smiled, put a hand on Weezy's arm, and assumed her more proper voice. "Relax, girl. Stakeouts don't work around here. No one even learns the names of the ball team's mistresses or the gangsters' molls. Columnists are dying to know."

Feeling exposed and vulnerable, Weezy wished Yuri would come. Going on nine. She'd been so sure he'd show up early.

Betty remarked that the hotcakes looked good. Weezy eyed her plate, and then shoved it toward her companion. "Take them, I haven't touched them. I'm so nervous I can't eat." Betty thanked her in formal tones, poured syrup, and dug in.

On leaving the coffee shop, Weezy stopped in the lobby to buy the morning papers. Returning to the suite, she tried to concentrate on the reviews. Most of the critics were kind, even the *Times* man. Tolliver Petrie still harped on Grace's weird-looking ocean. Weezy knew her mother would be upset over this, but she couldn't risk phoning the hotel to talk to her. Gran would ask questions she wasn't ready to answer. She needed to talk to Yuri first. She longed for him to walk in, take her in his arms and assure her everything was all right, that whatever happened, he would visit her as always.

Still, he didn't come. She pushed her way through the rest of the papers, trying to concentrate on the day's news. She sent down for a Danish and coffee. She paced; she stood looking out the window, drummed her fingers on the sill, and watched a barge on the East River. She listened for footsteps in the hall, but they all passed her door. She worried that Yuri'd been scared off and she'd never see him again.

After eleven, the knock finally came, and she flung open the door. He stood there, obviously distraught. His hair was uncombed, his tie askew. He inched inside the door, and breathing hard, rasped, "I was followed! Some guy tailed me all morning. I went to my office, trying to shake him." After a pause for breath, he added, "He hung around in a doorway across the street. I finally went out and boarded an express subway train, and when I saw him come aboard, I jumped off as the doors were closing and dumped him. But someone else may be watching this place." He kept his distance; he didn't come close nor give her the longed-for hug and kiss. "I'll need to—"

"That's my gran," she said. "She has no scruples about invading her family's privacy. But what can she do to us? I'm twenty-one and have the right to—"

"I'd no idea you were related to Grace Ward." He sounded downright accusatory. "She's well known in art circles." He frowned, nervously adjusted his tie and smoothed his hair. "Weezy, what have I done? You're not the type of girl a man takes as his mistress. I never should have—My God! A famous artist's daughter! And I'm twice your age! And now the whole world will know."

She found this conversation unsettling. Why didn't he move closer and embrace her? "What's my age got to do with it? I'm old enough to make my own decisions."

"Weezy, Weezy, think about it: a Beacon Hill girl—living in the Belle Turrets? Unthinkable! It shouldn't have happened. And I—I'm responsible."

Suddenly Weezy saw the light. It was Deborah he worried about. Deborah who, prepared to overlook a call girl, would see the daughter of a well-known artist as a threat.

Yuri kept shaking his head. "This is all wrong, Weezy. I feel like a dog for the way I've demeaned you. My conscience battered me all night."

Her temper rose; her voice tightened to a higher pitch. "Demeaned me? You can't demean me; I'd never let you do such a thing. I make my own decisions."

He kept shaking his head. "You're not the type for a Bohemian world. Old Boston family, D.A.R. grandmother—I read your mother's bio. You don't belong in this hotel or this—this mess."

"I'll decide where I belong." Weezy snapped out the words in fury. "And since *when* is this a mess? Yesterday it was a lovely arrangement."

He put his head in his hands. "We can't do this any more. I can't live with myself. I'll be your patron in a proper sort of way, supplementing your income, but—no more hanky panky."

"Hanky panky?" Her throat tightened to a near screech. "Is that what our relationship has been to you?"

"Darling, of course not. You know I've lived for our times together. My world was black and white before I met you. I've told you, you brought color. But I—I feel so ashamed. I got carried away; I didn't stop to think what I was doing to you." He again smoothed his hair. "We can't even discuss this now. I need to leave at once, in case they've picked up my trail. Whoever followed me may come here, and I don't want to cause you more scandal."

Meaning he didn't want to cause himself scandal that might reach Deborah's ears. She forced herself not to scream. "If that's the way you feel, you're free to go." She imitated her grandmother's technique of drawing herself up to appear taller. "I can handle my life; I don't need you. And if you think I would accept your money without having a—"

An expression of desperation crossed his face. He took a step closer. "Weezy, please, *please* let me explain. This is awful. I'm old enough to be your father; I should have known better."

Weezy felt sure the truth was, he wanted to rush back to dear Deborah and reassure her, restore his marriage, promise to behave.

"It was such a cynical thing to do, to use you like that so I could be part of some stupid club," he added. "I can't believe it of myself. It's not me."

"Just go if you're going." She spoke angrily.

"Oh, God, I've made you mad. I didn't mean it that way, I—"

"Go, will you?" She pushed at him. When he breathed a desperate, "Please, Weezy," she pushed harder.

His face so white it looked green-tinged, he stepped out. She closed the door quietly, resisting the urge to slam, and stood clenching her fists, feeling her body shaking. For a while she just lingered there struggling for control.

She had no idea what to do next. If she rushed out behind him, it would give Gran's Private Eye a golden opportunity. There might be a camera in her face. Then would come family confrontations throwing more dirt on something that had been beautiful.

No, she couldn't leave, not even by the fire escape. She would have to hang around here with nothing to do, books and typewriter gone. Just sit steaming over Yuri's defection, which was designed, she felt sure, to salvage his marriage.

She paced furiously, then threw herself on the bed and sobbed.

PART III

SAUGATUCK AND PETOSKEY

CHAPTER 30

Weezy

Weezy escaped the Belle Turrets by borrowing a blonde wig from one of the actor-residents and wearing dark glasses. She altered her normally-erect posture to play the role of a timid, uncertain young woman who'd wandered into the Belle by accident. On leaving, she stood looking around as if she didn't know her way, and finally drifted toward the subway. She boarded, transferred to the shuttle train across town, and then, on the IRT, departed the station at the stop after her own. She walked the extra blocks glancing behind her to see if she were being followed. Though she saw no one, she stopped at a grocery store for fruit and milk, and before leaving, peered outside to check for loiterers.

Still shaky, she kept telling herself the argument didn't happen. She couldn't fight with Yuri; she couldn't even really feel angry with him, just disappointed because it seemed so apparent he was trying to protect his marriage. Even there, she knew she wasn't justified. He'd told her in the beginning he loved his wife and had no intention of risking a break-up. She should have known that after last night's fiasco he would rush back to Deborah.

While climbing the four flights to the apartment, she pulled off the itchy wig and fluffed her hair. She felt weepy and longed to flop on the bed to shed threatening tears. Later, perhaps, she'd call Danny or Del. It would console her to talk to friends.

At the top of the stairs she encountered her mother, sitting, chin in hand, with a glum expression. Grace looked as rumpled and distraught as had Yuri earlier. Her hair was mussed by much finger-combing, her blouse unbuttoned at the top. She sat hugging her knees.

Weezy panicked and stood still, holding her wig and bag of groceries. Her mother was not one of the people she'd longed to talk to. In no mood for dissembling, she forced herself to pretend surprise. "Mother! What brings you here?"

"I'm waiting for you." Surprisingly, the words were matter-of-fact, not angry or accusatory. No frown accompanied them.

Weezy swallowed hard and tried to stop shaking. She braced for probing questions about Yuri. Grace released her knees and stood up. "Where've you been? What's the wig for?"

Weezy glanced down at the object in question. "This? It belongs to a friend. At a play-reading, it was part of the costume." She marveled at her new-found ability to invent lies. "I've also been grocery shopping." She tried to sound welcoming. "Come in. If you'd let me know, I'd have left the key in the mailbox for you."

She unlocked the door. Her mother followed her into the apartment, looked around, and commented that it was bright and cheerful. "I'm surprised Del gave it up. A Village flat is a treasure hard to come by." She dropped into the overstuffed chair. "It's nice and sunny, unusual for New York." She pointed to the sarcophagus. "What's that?"

"The bathtub. Part of why Del moved. The tub in the living room wouldn't do for Bradley's lifestyle." Weezy awaited accusations. To forestall the inevitable deluge, she took the groceries to the kitchen. "I'll make coffee and hunt up some Danish."

"I'm not hungry," Grace said. "Too upset. I had a phone call from Millie."

Here it came. Surely, they'd talked of the Yuri situation. Grace would demand full disclosure. Weezy felt naked and exposed. She clenched her fists until her fingernails dug into her palms.

But Grace went off on a different subject. "Millie claims I paint Lake Michigan." She sounded appalled, as if she'd been accused of something sinful.

Relieved that her own chastisement was not yet at hand, Weezy moved around making coffee. She pretended not to understand her mother's concern. "Big deal. Great lakes—ocean—a beach is a beach. You paint shorelines."

Her mother persisted, raising her voice to be heard above the sound of running water. "Don't you realize what this means? Now that Millie has planted the idea, others will pick up on it. Nosy Parkers will wonder why I'm fixated on the Great Lakes. Won't take them long to dig out the sordid truth. The tabloids will print every detail of my past with Edgar. Grace Ward's hidden affair and her child will be the gossip of the art world. You and I will have paparazzi pursuing us."

Calmer now that she knew the question of the moment was not Yuri, Weezy spooned coffee into the top section of the percolator, turned on the gas, and returned to the living room. She assured herself nothing had been discovered; Yuri had shaken his pursuer and she'd escaped the Belle Turrets in disguise. It was just her guilty conscience tricking her. Hands on hips, she eyed her mother, noticing the rumpled pageboy hairdo, and came up with a consoling thought. "What can they say? The story isn't scandalous. You didn't have a child out of wedlock nor even a shotgun wedding. Dad was a willing groom. The fact the wedding occurred just before I was born—that was Gran's fault."

Grace fingered the buttons on her blouse, buttoning and unbuttoning the top one. She managed a faint chuckle. "Don't let Gran hear you say that." Lowering her hands, she added, "I couldn't bear to have those events hashed over by reporters. Gossip always comes back to you sounding so much worse than what really happened."

"So, why not upstage the dummies? Tell the story yourself."

"Oh, lord, I couldn't. What good would that do?"

"For one thing, you can tell it your way. For another—" For another, it might lead to a reunion with Edgar. Weezy liked that idea; she'd have a real family. If everyone knew Grace carried a torch for Edgar, that she still painted scenes from her sojourn with him, why not display the man himself? Contrive a romantic tale rather than a skeleton in the closet.

"I don't even want to think about those days." Grace put her hands to her forehead.

"Seems you're destined to think of them, whether or no. Question is, will they be a deep dark secret or simply a part of your life?"

"I'm for keeping them hidden. Blessed be privacy."

"Can't be done. Too many people know. Millie wasn't exactly reticent about her theory last night, and it fits with what that critic's been saying about your non-ocean."

"I can't bear to—"

"Yes, you can, Mother." The percolator began popping. Weezy smelled the coffee, started off, then paused in the kitchen doorway and turned back. "A person strong enough to cope with a New York exhibit and all those critics is strong enough to handle her own past. We'll go to Michigan, you and I, and you'll discover that the Stormland folks are ordinary people. Dad's not the

Ogre of the Midwest. He was just a guy trying to secure his future against the time when his rich mistress would leave him."

"I can't face those people."

"Mom, we're not talking American Tragedy here," Weezy reminded. "Edgar didn't murder Patience, he dutifully married her. He would have raised the kid if it had lived."

Grace gasped. "The child died?"

"They're both long dead—Mother and child."

"I had no idea. I assumed that Edgar was still—" Her voice trailed off. Her fingers paused in kneading her forehead. Her hands dropped. She got up, paced with hands clasped behind her, and finally stepped to the window. "Did he remarry?"

Weezy shook her head. "Maybe he should have. When he's alone, he drinks too much."

"That's Edgar. No common sense. A charming rogue. He used to take me riding around the dunes on his motorcycle. In my craziest moments, I sensed he wouldn't do for a lifetime."

"Then why did you insist on going back there to marry him?"

Grace shrugged. "Why do young people do what they do?—mad impulse, I guess."

The smell of coffee filled the apartment. Weezy moved into the kitchen, turned off the gas and poured. When she returned carrying a tray, her mother was seated again. Weezy set the steaming cup beside her while pointing out that the impulse hadn't been mad at all. "Fathers have rights." If Persis had had her way, she reflected, no one in the Michigan family would have known of her—Weezy's—existence, not even her father or her other grandmother. Her mother would have married Jonathan in the early days of pregnancy, and she'd have been adopted by him without further contact with her genetic family. Not even the Boston folks would have known she wasn't Jonathan's. She shuddered over her grandmother's audacity, her assumption of the right to decide for other people whether or not they'd know of their descendants.

"We'll go to Michigan and everyone will be happy to see you," she assured Grace. "You'll find that the ogres exist only in your mind." She set down her own cup and offered cream and sugar. She handed her mother a spoon.

While Grace creamed and stirred her coffee, she gazed into it as if she might find answers there. "Tell you what. We'll go—but not to meet people. I want to walk on the beach at Saugatuck. I want to see if it's true I've been painting the lake all these years. If it is, I'll come to terms with it. You're right, it's better to speak up than to let the critics ferret out the secret and make a thing of it."

Saugatuck was close to Grand Rapids. Edgar was staying with Grandmother Vi. Weezy could see him, talk to him about Yuri. He would understand, as her mother would not. He'd offer comments and consolation. Best of all, Weezy liked the idea of not being available when—if—Yuri tried to get in touch again. Let him worry for a while. Let him know she wasn't always available. Let him learn not to take her for granted. "We can go right now if we fly out," she said. "I have only the weekend off; I'm due at work on Monday."

"Now?" Grace stared at her. "You mean, just get on a plane and go?"

"Why not? It beats going back with Gran to Boston, or staying here for a polite visit with Millie."

"You have a point: why not?" Grace looked around for the phone. When Weezy brought it to her on its long cord, she made a call to an airline, asked for schedules, and reserved a flight. She hung up to announce that a plane left at three-ten. She consulted her watch. "Almost noon—I've just time to go back to the hotel and grab my overnight bag."

"What about Gran? Don't you have to take her home?"

"I put her on the 9:40 for Boston. Told her I still had things to do for the exhibit."

"Gran's gone?" So maybe Yuri hadn't been followed after all. But no, Gran had had plenty of time in the last two days to hire a P.I. Her departure from New York wouldn't change anything.

Weezy pinpointed her problems as stemming from Grace's and Edgar's separation. Because of that, she'd been a lonely child with a rejecting stepfather. Denied the extended family she'd have had at Stormland, she'd grown up needy of masculine attention and over-ready to become involved with a man. She ought now to cement those Michigan relationships which would add stability to her life and make her feel less devastated by Yuri's preference for his wife.

"Shall I make sandwiches for a quick lunch?" she asked.

"No, pack your bags, we need to get going immediately. We'll eat at the airport."

They had closed the apartment door and were about to leave when Weezy heard footsteps and turned to see Del coming up the stairs. Del looked even worse than Grace or Yuri. Her face was paper-white, her eyes bloodshot and teary. Another distraught person! It must be in the stars, Weezy thought. Was

Mercury in retrograde or what? She set down her overnight bag and asked, "My God, Del, what happened?"

Del looked startled. She eyed the suitcase. "Weezy! Grace! Going somewhere?"

"We're off to Michigan. Mom wants to see for herself if she paints the lakes. What's up with you?"

Del flung hand to head, leaned against the wall, and took a moment to catch her breath. "I just—I had a weird attack. We were shopping for furniture—that is, Mom and Brad were. I tagged along. They'd found a bedroom set they liked, and when Mother brought out her checkbook—" She paused, took a deep breath. "Well, suddenly I felt this awful tightness in my chest. I literally couldn't breathe. I had to rush out into the air. I told them I had cramps and was going home. I hurried away and—and I can't go back. That breathlessness recurs every time I even think of it."

"You didn't go home?"

"No, I came here instead."

"Belated anxiety attack," Grace diagnosed. "Brides are supposed to have them before the wedding."

"Del should get far away from that family menagerie," Weezy theorized. "You must come with us to Michigan, Del." Energized on finding that two relatives needed her help, she set down her suitcase and put a hand on Del's arm. "You can't think straight when you're under pressure. You need to relax and get your life together."

"Yes, come," Grace said. "Weezy's right, you need distance from family pressures. I'll call and make another reservation."

"Michigan?" Del stared. "Now?"

"Plane leaves at three-ten," Grace told her. "You've just time to go home and throw a few things in a suitcase."

Weezy protested. "She shouldn't go near that apartment. Brad and Millie may be there by now. I'll loan you whatever you need, Del. It'll only be for a day or two."

"What on earth will I say to Mother and Bradley?"

"Say my mom wants to check out her painting models, and you decided to go along. Write a note and ask Danny to deliver it—after our plane has taken off and it's too late for them to stop you."

"They'll think I'm crazy."

"Face it, you are crazy: crazy in need of space and a chance to think, crazy for breathing room." Still grasping her cousin's arm, Weezy guided her back to the apartment door and fumbled for her key. "My wardrobe is at your disposal. I used your clothes when I came here, and I'm glad to return the favor."

Del called Danny, who, on learning of the situation, agreed to deliver the note and brave the wrath of the recipients. "I just hope they don't kill the messenger," he said.

The women took a taxi to Grace's hotel, stopping at Danny's to leave off the sealed envelope. They ate soup and salad at a La Guardia cafe, and soon were on their way to Detroit. An hour later, they boarded a small plane for Grand Rapids. From there, a short bus trip took them to the lakeshore. En route, they chatted about everything but their immediate problems. By unspoken agreement they put those on hold until they could give them their full attention.

The early-October days still offered lengthy twilights. Shortly before six, they reached the art-colony town of Saugatuck, where the sun still hovered above the pine trees. Weezy stood admiring a charming main street designed to tempt artists. An enormous sand dune, wooded except on top, loomed over the area.

"Old Baldy," Grace said. "I've painted it several times."

Weezy nodded. Often in her childhood she'd studied her mother's paintings and tried to imagine herself walking around this place.

A river separated dune from town. She looked around for a ferry boat. There it was, down near the bend, just as she'd known it would be.

"The Kalamazoo River," Del said, pointing. "There's a buried city at the mouth of it." She seemed calmer now; apparently she'd stopped worrying what Millie and Brad were thinking, stopped agonizing that she shouldn't have walked out on them like this.

Grace nodded. "So I've heard, though Edgar and I searched for the city and found no trace except an old Boardwalk." She added, pointing, "The hotel is across the river."

Weezy would have suggested calling for reservations, but her mother seemed eager to see the spot she remembered so fondly. They caught a taxi, crossed a bridge, and moved past tawny dunes and woodlands of pine, aspen, beech and maple trees. At the lakeshore, a two-story wooden hotel faced the road. Grace whooped with joy at finding it still there.

"There are rustic cottages behind it, overlooking the lake," she added. "Keep your fingers crossed for a vacancy. I didn't have time to call from New York."

In the lobby, the clerk nodded in response to Grace's hopeful question, and shoved a registration slip across the counter. When she'd signed it, he slapped keys onto the counter and explained how to reach the cottages. She assured him she knew the way.

The three women walked along a shaded path thick with pine needles. The air was spicy with woodland fragrances. Dark-shingled, their cottage stood hidden among the trees. On entering, they found the rooms lined with knotty pine. A large, rustic fireplace was laid with logs. Weezy admitted she loved the place already.

Tears sprang to Grace's eyes. In a shaky voice, she commented, "It's just as I remembered it. The furniture might be new, but otherwise—" She wandered to the bedroom and peered into the bathroom. "Plumbing's modernized, I think."

"Is this where you and Dad came?" Weezy hardly needed to ask. Grace's teary nostalgia spoke for itself. She watched her mother touch a finger to her eye.

Weezy tried to imagine her mother as a young woman madly in love. She'd never thought of her mother as madly anything. Cool, controlled, distant—that was the mother she'd known. Once, when Weezy was still a toddler, Grace had left Jonathan for a few months and taken the child to live in a tiny Greenwich Village flat. She must have thought then, Weezy speculated, of separating, perhaps divorcing. Weezy retained vague memories of being in a playpen while her mother, beside her, painted pictures and hung them. Unlike at home where she rarely hung her work, the walls of that tiny apartment had been covered with paintings. Weezy didn't recall how the adventure ended but she supposed Gran must have found them and taken them home. One morning she'd awakened in her old bed.

"Come see the lake." Grace sounded excited. She kicked off her shoes, peeled off her hose, and hurried out, her bare feet a contrast to her severe dark blue travel outfit.

Del and Weezy followed her example and hastily shed shoes and hose. Barefoot, they ran across the bluff. Sparkling blue water shone between the trees ahead. Soon the woodland opened to reveal the vast expanse of the lake. A stairway led down to a wide beach below.

"It's so different from the ocean," Weezy marveled. "No surf. No salty, fishy smells."

Grace ran down the steps and across the beach, the younger women following. Small waves lapped the shore, and a sandy, washboard bottom was visible through the clear water. Sandpipers with long beaks explored the wet sand of the shingle. Weezy felt stabbed by a sudden longing to have Yuri here to share this, followed by a letdown as she realized that couldn't happen. She'd sent Yuri away. They would no longer walk on the beach hand in hand as they'd done so often at Far Rockaway.

She shivered. Her mother asked, "Cold?" She shook her head and wondered how long she'd keep thinking of Yuri, missing him. Right now she believed it would be forever. A wave of depression washed over her.

Grace held up her skirts, put her feet in the water, and breathed deeply of the fresh air. "This used to be my favorite spot on earth. I can't think why I stayed away so long."

Weezy stepped into the water. It felt icy. She retreated. Del lifted her skirt and waded out beside Grace.

"We should have brought a camera." Weezy shook off her depression and concentrated on her companions. "What a picture, you two standing knee deep in that vast blueness."

"I used to think of this as my very own lake," Del said. "Our apartment building in Chicago was so close the waves washed against the bricks. Oh, I'm so glad I came! It's wonderful to be here—to be away from that chaos. They'll think I'm crazy, but—but I don't care." She breathed deeply of the fresh lake air. "Let them think what they like."

"Good for you." Weezy nodded. She reflected that this should have been her lake, too. If her mother had remained married to Edgar, the couple might have owned a cottage on these bluffs. She'd have spent her childhood exploring the dunes. She could even have brought Yuri here.

Wading back to shore, Grace ran along the beach. The younger women followed. Soon all three were splashing and cavorting. An oreboat steamed on the horizon, trailing smoke. The sun had sunk low over the lake. After it set, the water turned from blue to silver and calmed to a vast mirror.

"It's true, I *have* been painting the lake all these years," Grace dropped onto the sand, stretched her legs, leaned back on her elbows, and gazed outward. "Millie was clever to realize it. I must thank her; she brought me back to this place where years ago I left a part of myself."

"Yes, a marvelous idea." Del flopped down beside Grace. "I escaped a trap."

Lucky women, Weezy thought. For her, there was no such moment of celebration. She feared she did something foolish, sending Yuri away. She wondered if she'd over-reacted. He had, after all, warned her he loved his wife. What did she have to get angry about? He hadn't deceived her.

So why was she so upset and teary? Why was she missing Yuri so desperately? And feeling so lost and forlorn?

CHAPTER 31

Weezy

The three women sat at the small table beside the fireplace, a meal in front of them ordered from the dining hall, which, though the food was good, none of them had yet attacked with enthusiasm. A cheery fire crackled beside them. Weezy merely toyed with the trout, while Del abandoned the effort altogether and put her fork aside.

"It's decision time," Del confided. "I have to leave Brad, and I don't know how I'll tell my mother, let alone Bradley."

Grace asked, "Did you have a fight?"

Del confessed she'd never worked up the courage to fight. "I don't seem to know *how* to fight with Brad. He just pushes ahead with his life and expects me to trail along—and I can't find the brakes. I keep wanting to say, 'Hold here, let me think about this.'"

"Doesn't sound like a great relationship." In the firelight, Grace studied Del's face as if she might find answers there, and asked why Del had married the man. Weezy's gaze flipped back and forth between Grace of the puzzled expression and Del of the worried one. She awaited the answer Del seemed to struggle for.

Del confessed she hardly knew any longer. She gazed into the flames as if seeking reasons there. "Fear of getting too old to have children? The conviction I needed to make a change in my life?" Her coppery hair fell across her face and partly hid her eyes, which now, in the firelight, looked greenish, reflecting the green of her form-fitting, princess style dress.

She picked up her fork and speared peas. Grace asked bluntly if there was someone else. Del admitted, "Sort of."

"It hardly seems compelling: a sort of love?"

Del smiled. "He's a real love, a mad, passionate love. I'm not sure he's the right man. I have a habit of falling for unsuitable guys."

"What, you, too?" Weezy burst out. "It must run in the family." When her mother flicked a questioning glance in her direction, she knew she'd said too much. She bit her lip, feeling her face flame.

Still pondering her own problems, Del appeared not to notice Weezy's discomfiture. Interlocking her fingers, she went on. "All through high school, I had a crush on a Polish boy, nothing in common between us. I was at the head of the class; he was at the bottom and proud of it. Stanley Kowalski and then some. I knew if I married him, it wouldn't last a month. Yet I couldn't get him out of my mind. Dreamed of him for years; still do. By comparison, Bradley seemed so *suitable*. I try hard to love him but no feelings come through. I hate to tell you the shenanigans I've invented since my marriage to avoid sex. I fix him dynamo drinks loaded with alcohol, hoping to make him sleepy. Yet in theory it seems so simple: fall in love with someone suitable rather than someone with whom you're sure to have problems."

A smile played on Grace's lips. "I suspect your mother told you to let your head rule your heart. I remember how Millie loved that saying."

Del nodded. "You're so right. Now I'm in a predicament. Can't face living out the future I've forged for myself."

"There's always the Reno solution—or Vegas. If you can't afford it, I'll loan you the money."

"Thanks. Luckily, I still have my bank account in my own name." Del put the peas into her mouth and chewed abstractedly, seeming not in the least aware that she was eating. Then she laid her fork down as if that one bite were all she meant to have. "My problem is: what will I say? What reason can I give? Bradley has done nothing wrong. Mother will never forgive me."

Grace speared a small pickle, waved it on her fork, and announced that she was about to impart a bit of wisdom she'd taken forty years to learn. She intoned it solemnly. "We don't owe our mothers an explanation. You're an adult; you have the right to your own life." Weezy wondered when her mom had achieved this insight. Recently, she thought.

"I've quit my job and I have no source of income," Del confessed.

Grace assured her she'd find another job. "You might need to leave New York, but after all, your future is on the line here. Once you have children, it's darn near impossible to get away. Now is the time to go."

During this exchange, Weezy had watched the play of firelight on her mother's and cousin's faces. She wished she could talk so freely. She'd have loved to discuss Yuri, the happy times, her feelings of loss and desolation. How, all unplanned, she'd fallen for him, a man with a wife he was attached to. She groped for words: I forgot to factor in emotions. I meant to be a modern woman focused on my career. Now I can't figure out how to disengage my feelings. I need Yuri; I want him.

Talk about unsuitable men! Del at least confined herself to men who were free and available. Involvement with a married man was the worst problem of all. Weezy could still see in her mind's eye Deborah's small but possessive hand on Yuri's sleeve.

How she'd scorned the women at the Belle Turrets who fell in love with their guy and moped! How easily she'd convinced herself it couldn't happen to her! Her, Weezy, the free spirit, the recorder of life, who'd come to the Belle merely for financial aid toward a promising career!

"Bradley probably suspects how I feel," Del went on. Flushing, she added, "He found the diaphragm I keep handy. He was obviously disappointed; he'd assumed I was trying for a baby. I had to talk fast, pretending I wanted to wait until after Christmas to get pregnant. I doubt he believed my silly excuse about being too busy right now to risk being in a delicate condition."

"Then you've only Millie left to cope with," Grace said. "I suggest you go on to Reno and write to her—write to both of them—from there. Just facts—things weren't working out. Best to end it before children arrive. Sorry, Mom and Bradley."

"Bad time, when she's our guest in New York."

Grace assured her there was no good time. She speared two ripe olives and chewed thoughtfully. "I guarantee that each day you remain makes the going harder. Finally, you're buried to your eyeballs and it becomes impossible to leave."

Story of Grace's life, Weezy wondered? Had she dreamed of leaving Jonathan and returning to Edgar but kept postponing the moment of confrontation?

Weezy wished that something so simple as a trip to Reno might solve her own problems. Even a divorce seemed effortless compared to luring a married man back into her life. She had no way to contact Yuri, didn't know his home phone number. At best, she might hope to encounter him someday—with his wife—at another art show.

She forced her mind back to her cousin's problem and confessed that personally, she'd found Bradley stuffy. "He never seemed right for you."

Del picked up her fork and attacked her trout. She admitted that she felt she'd foreclosed on adventure in her life. With a sigh, she added, "Truth is, the guy I care for grew up in Spanish Harlem. His background is very different from mine. I've always heard that sort of thing causes problems."

"Catholic?" Grace asked.

"His parents were—but his father became an agnostic. He fought and died for the Loyalists in the Spanish Civil War. Hilario never talks to me of his personal beliefs. He likes to play Bogart and kid around."

"But what a fascinating background! I was twenty in 1931 when Spain was declared a Republic, and I remember the celebrations—how we all believed that feudalism was ended forever. And then came Franco and the horrors of war—Have you seen Picasso's painting of Guernica?"

"Of course. I was eleven and I remember, too—Gramps celebrated by putting a single candle on a cake in honor of the new Republic. He taught me a Spanish song for Democracy, *Los Quartros Generales*. Still, Hilario's not someone I feel secure with."

Grace nodded. "I know what you mean. A battle rages in your mind. This man is so suitable, that one so-o-o attractive. Believe me, there's no right answer. You have to take risks—or face boredom."

Weezy broke in. "Hold that thought, Mother. You need to risk seeing Edgar the Ogre again."

Once more a faint smile crossed Grace's lips. "I laid myself open for that one."

"Well, Dad *is* involved. He could be questioned about the past, too."

"Oh, Lord, what price fame! Why did I seek it?" Grace put her head in her hands. "It never ends, does it? One youthful indiscretion and—"

Del put down her fork, shoved her chair back, and stood. Leaning on the mantle, she commented that when one person links genes with another, it's forever. "Families joined can't be unjoined. Your descendants are his descendants. Your grandchildren will be his grandchildren. A hundred years from now the genealogy charts will show the linkage."

"You make it sound like an everlasting prison sentence."

"No, it's a fact of life. You're forever linked to Edgar. I keep asking myself: Can I link myself that way to Brad? And the answer keeps coming back, no. Loud and clear: no. I can't do this."

"Brava. It was a short marriage; it should be easily undone." Weezy, too, shoved her chair back and rose. "This talk of eternal linkage is too much for me. I need to call Dad."

"Whoa, not so fast," Grace protested. "I'm still debating about seeing Edgar. Give me time."

"Will five minutes suffice?" Weezy stood waiting, gazing at her watch and listening to the crackle of the fire.

Grace studied her skeptically. "Who let *you* off the hook? Del and I have man problems, but you don't?"

"Oh, I—at the moment, I—" Weezy tried to claim to be free of problems, but found she couldn't speak the words. She desperately longed to talk about Yuri, to shout his name to the universe, to ask, did I do wrong in sending him away?

Alas, Gran would be privy to the information. Some risks were not worth taking.

Grace studied her. Suddenly, as if in blinding insight, she zeroed in on the cause of the uneasiness. "What's with you and Aaron Yurovsky? There were such sparks flying last night, it's a wonder no one got electrocuted. This morning your gran hired a guy to investigate the man."

Weezy gasped. "He really *was* being followed!"

Grace lifted an eyebrow. "How did you know that?"

Weezy hastily invented another lie. "I ran into him at the subway station. He *said* he was being followed. I couldn't believe it, even with Gran in town. Never thought she'd go that far." She took a deep breath and confessed, "I do care for Mr. Yurovsky, but there's no future in it. He's married."

"Not happily," Grace said.

"What?" Startled, Weezy couldn't conceal her surprise.

Grace smiled knowingly. "His wife is having an affair with Tolliver Petrie. The whole art world is talking."

Weezy felt she'd been blasted by an explosion. She tried to settle back to earth. She focused on controlling the thumping in her midriff. "Mother, are you sure?"

Grace shrugged. "No one can be sure about gossip, but those two have stopped being circumspect."

Weezy felt a new burst of hope. But second thoughts soon came. Was Yuri devastated and intent on getting his wife back? Had he used their affair as a way to scare his wife into behaving herself?

It didn't seem possible. All those times he'd rushed in and grabbed Weezy so eagerly, was it a fake, a pretense? She couldn't believe it. She could still hear him calling her Eloise. She could recall his interest in her life, her writing, her classes, her job. He'd read and commented on her stories.

"No wonder?" Grace probed.

"I—I'm surprised. Yur—Mr. Yurovsky seems attached to Deborah." Weezy longed to spill out the whole story, but too often she'd trusted her mother only to have Gran wind up privy to her confidences.

"At the moment, I'm only his literary agent," she said.

Then Gran's Eye won't find out anything?"

"There's nothing to find."

"Glad to hear it. Aaron Yurovsky is too old for you."

"Mother! Didn't you just say we all have to take risks?"

Grace laughed. "I didn't mean you. All mothers want to protect their children."

"Not funny." Weezy spoke angrily. "I reserve the right to live my life, free and unprotected."

Still chuckling, Grace shrugged. "Go and call. We'll never finish our meal until these matters are settled. You girls have hardly touched this delicious lake trout."

"Are you serious about Edgar?"

"I am. I'll try not to be swept away this time by his notorious charms."

There was no phone in the rustic cabin. Weezy searched her purse and found her address book. "I'll go to the lobby,"

"Wait for me," Del said. "I want to call Danny and find out how my mom reacted to my absence. Not that I can't guess about her fury, but still—"

"You have to face the confrontation eventually." Grace added, to Weezy, "Keep in mind that Edgar may refuse to come near me. He probably thinks I kidnapped his kid."

"You did. But I believe he's forgiven you."

Del declared that Edgar didn't hold grudges. "That is not one of his failings."

Together, Weezy and Del stepped out into the darkness. As they walked from light to light along the pine-needle strewn path, Weezy planned what to say to her father.

Del said she envied Weezy, having a mother so easy to talk to.

"Are you kidding?" Weezy asked. "That's deceptive. She's a snitch, she reports to Gran."

Through the trees, they could see the main building, brightly lit. They hurried toward it, and at the bank of phones in the lobby, each entered a separate booth. When Weezy called the long-distance operator and gave her Michigan grandmother's number, Vi answered.

"Grandma, this is Weezy."

Vi let out an audible sigh of relief. "Weezy! At last you called! Where are you?"

"We're in Saugatuck." Weezy puzzled. "Why 'at last?' Has it been so long since I—?"

"Our Saugatuck? At Lake Michigan?"

"The one and only. We arrived a few hours ago. Mother wanted to check out the place where—"

"When we heard you were in Michigan, we expected you in Grand Rapids."

"How'd you hear that?"

"Fact is, there's someone here who knows you—a visitor from New York. He flew in hoping to find you. His name is—uh—I'm not sure I can pronounce it. He told us to call him Yuri."

Too astonished to speak, Weezy stood holding the receiver, staring across the lobby. Her grandmother asked, "Hello? Are you still there?"

"I'm here, just speechless. I can't believe Yuri is in Michigan."

"He claims you two had a fight, and afterward he couldn't find you to straighten things out. Seems he checked everywhere. He waited hours at your apartment. Finally called Del hoping to learn where you were. Instead he reached Bradley, who told him he understood you'd gone to Michigan with your mother. Then he called Edgar and decided to fly out here. We've been expecting to hear from you. Maybe he and Eddie can drive down to Saugatuck and get you."

"Oh, no!" The words exploded out of Weezy before she thought. "I mean, I'd love to see Dad; in fact I was calling to invite him. But I can't have Yuri here."

"You're that mad at him?"

"No, it's just—my mother's with me, and she knows nothing about him."

Vi chuckled. "It's a bad idea to practice to deceive. I learned the truth of that the night I tried to elope with Nat McCurdle, when Dad intercepted us at the hotel and sent me home. I don't advise it, Weezy, it leads to embarrassing situations."

"You're right, deception is silly." Weezy gathered her courage. "Put Yuri on the phone, Grandma. I'll talk to him."

In a moment she heard the familiar New York accent. At the sound of his voice, she felt her spirits soar. She moved out of darkness into daylight. He seemed to feel the same. He said, "Weezy, darling, what a relief to hear from you! I've been worried to death; I got a friend to fly me out here. I'm so terribly sorry for the misunderstanding. Please forgive me."

All the pain flooded back. She couldn't stop her anger from surging again. "Misunderstanding? I didn't misunderstand. You called our relationship hanky panky."

"No, I called the circumstances hanky panky: hiding out in the Belle Turrets, keeping things secret."

Relieved to be in touch with him, Weezy backed down. "Perhaps I did misunderstand. But I hated the way you seemed to play daddy and take charge of my life. I make my own decisions. So please—no more of that."

"I promise never to do it again." Yuri spoke humbly. "Say we can meet and you'll let me try to repair the damage."

"Of course, we'll meet—but back in New York tomorrow night. My mother's here in Saugatuck."

"It's okay to tell your mother about us, Weezy—darling. I've left Deborah. I moved to a residence hotel for men early this morning. I didn't get a chance to say so, in all the worry about being followed—and our fight."

CHAPTER 32

Weezy

Weezy stared at the bright crystal chandelier, so out of place in this otherwise rustic lobby. She tried to take in what she'd heard over the phone. After a silence, she finally managed to say, "I had no idea you contemplated anything of the sort. You told me you had a solid marriage." Suddenly she panicked again. Could this have happened because of her? Much as she loved Yuri, loved being with him, even loved hearing his voice on the phone, she shared her mother's reluctance to be a co-respondent in a divorce case. She ran her free hand through her hair.

"I hope this isn't because of me," she added.

"No, I didn't plan this. Matters came to a head with Tolliver Petrie last night. I learned Deb's been—uh—seeing him and uh—they've decided they want to be together permanently. I guess I precipitated the decision. I felt pretty angry, but if that's the way it is, it's best I know."

Weezy held the phone away from her and let out a sigh of relief. Petrie was to be co-respondent, not herself—and Yuri would be free. Following on this thought came a sense of guilt. She should console, not celebrate. The man's marriage was breaking up. It had to be painful for him. She made herself say, "Yuri, I'm so sorry. This must be awful for you." But not quite as awful, she hoped, as it would have been before he met her.

"I knew about Deborah and Tollie," he admitted, "but Deb claimed it was over." He explained. It had started as a tea and sympathy thing when, in art school, Tollie lost a contest big time, landing at the bottom, being forced to recognize he wasn't destined to find fame and fortune as a painter. "That's always hard on eager young people. In every music and art school there have to be a tragic few who lack the talent to compete. I, too," he confessed, "felt sorry for Petrie; he'd been so dedicated. I applauded Deb's efforts to console him. I didn't realize I was destined to find myself playing the accommodating husband out of a Thomas Wolfe novel while my wife comforted the struggling *artiste*." She heard him draw a deep breath. "I insisted she break it off. When she claimed she'd done so, I tried hard to renew our relationship. That's why I hesitated to get involved in—well, you remember." He sighed. "I discovered last night that Deborah and Tollie had merely learned to be more circumspect."

Astonished, she stared unseeingly at a chandelier. "You never hinted at any of this."

"I didn't want you brushed with that sordidness. I placed you in a better world."

Weezy idly let her gaze follow an older couple entering the lobby and heading for the desk, a woman with blue hair, a tall, bent gentleman who hastily removed his fedora. She tried to pull her thoughts together. "Yuri, you really need to come down here so we can talk. I'm only thirty or forty miles from you. Maybe Dad will loan you his car for the evening."

"I could ask. What about your mother?"

She made a quick resolve. "I'll tell her. Your news puts a different spin on things."

"Just a minute." After a silence on the phone, he returned to say Edgar was willing to loan his car. Weezy gave the name of the hotel and explained how to reach it. Yuri told her Edgar looked forward to seeing her in the morning, and that he himself would arrive shortly. She promised to await him in the lobby.

"I can't believe all this is happening," he said. "I'll wake up and none of it will be real. Not last night, not this morning, not now."

"Unless we're both dreaming the same dream, it's happening."

"I feel like a character in grand opera. I just want to go on saying, 'Addio, addio.' But I guess I should hang up and get started for Saugatuck. Good luck with your mom."

She asked to talk to Edgar again, and when he came on, she repeated the information about the hotel. Edgar promised to drive down in the morning. "Love ya, Weezy. Glad you and Yuri are back on speaking terms. He seems a nice guy. I could see he meant a lot to you, the way you spoke of him in New York."

"I tempered my comments, Dad. I had no idea he meant to leave his wife. That makes a difference."

"You said it!"

"Dad, I can't wait to have you here. Come early so we can breakfast in the hotel dining room and climb Old Baldy. It'll be great, seeing my birth parents together."

"I'll keep that in mind and try not to fight with Grace."

"Give Grandma a hug for me. I love you, too."

When Weezy left the phone booth, she sought Del to announce her big news, but saw that Del was still on the line. She crossed to the other booth and watched as her cousin jotted something in a notepad, hung up, opened the booth door, and held out the pad.

"Train schedules to Petoskey," she said. "I've decided I need to go walk on the beach in the city of my childhood. I'll gather fossils, drink sulphur water from deep in the earth—and gather my courage for the coming confrontation. It's going to be a rough one. Danny says Bradley's heartbroken and my mother is furious."

Weezy blinked. "Petoskey? You're full of surprises."

"I made a reservation on the night train. It leaves here in less than an hour. I've called a cab—I need to hurry."

"You're going *now*? By *yourself*?" Weezy wanted to nix the plan. The woman was distraught and shouldn't be alone.

Del shrugged. "It was helpful talking to you guys, and I've made my decision, but the announcement has to be mine." Del slung her purse over her shoulder. "I need to be alone in a place Bradley never shared and brace myself for it."

"I didn't know you shared Saugatuck with him."

"I waited tables at a summer resort at Ottawa Beach, just north of here. Bradley used to visit me there. This is Bradley country; we drove to these dunes many times. Up north in Petoskey I'll reclaim my own self."

"Did Danny suggest this when you phoned him?" Weezy asked.

"No, but he reminded me I needn't go to Reno. Bradley can get an annulment in New York on the basis of my refusal to have children."

"But will he do that?"

"He will if I give him a choice of that or Reno. He hates scandal. I have to confront him and my mother and start the proceedings. It'll be the hardest thing I ever did, which is why I need to be alone to rally my courage."

"Shall I come and see you off on the train?"

"We can say goodbye as well here. What's with Edgar?"

"He's coming tomorrow. But guess what? Surprise! Yuri was with him."

"*Yuri*? Does he know Edgar? I didn't know they'd met."

"Seems he got the information from Bradley about our trip, and on learning we were in Michigan, he called Edgar who invited him to come."

"He must really want you back."

"Del, he's on his way here. He left his wife."

Del didn't even blink. She flipped back her long, coppery hair, and admitted, "I'm not surprised. I knew something had to be going on in his marriage. Deborah was too nice to be real. Women don't give their husbands leave to roam—not if they care about them."

Weezy confessed, "I wondered about that, but I thought I was being naïve. I understand that in Europe mistresses are taken for granted, and I supposed New Yorkers had achieved a similar level of sophistication."

"Well, this'll make things easier for you two." She pointed toward the door. "My taxi is here." She commented that since she had no clothing of her own in the cabin, she needn't go back there. "I have my purse, money, and my return ticket. I'll stroll on the beach and find a Petoskey stone. That'll give me courage to go home for the Great Confrontation. Tell your mother I said thanks for providing this trip. I feel so much better after talking to you both."

"You're sure you'll be all right? I hate to let you go off alone."

"I'll be fine. I love Petoskey; it's full of good memories from my childhood." Del gave her cousin a quick hug. "I'll meet you tomorrow night at the Detroit airport for our flight home." She headed for the door and the waiting taxi, then turned back to add, "And Weezy—I'll have to move in with you in the Village. I hope you're willing to share the flat?"

"You needn't even ask. See you there."

Del waved and hurried out, her purse swinging, her long hair bobbing against her shoulders. With a new bounce to her step, she climbed into the cab. Weezy watched it drive away.

Suddenly alone, Weezy became aware of the churning in her midriff, and knew she had to cope with the next step in her own life—telling her mother about Yuri. There must be no more secrets for Gran to ferret out. Those secrets gave Gran power.

She walked back slowly along the dimly-lit path, scuffling fallen leaves, stepping on and crunching seed pods. She tried to think what to say. She could find no right way of telling any mother, especially her own, that her daughter had been a kept woman.

Don't talk about the past, she counseled herself. Focus on the future. Yuri will be free.

The words sounded wonderful. She said them over in her mind until they made a song and she walked to them: Yuri will be free.

When she entered the cabin, Grace had finished her meal and pushed her plate aside. She glanced up. "Well? Did you reach Edgar? Is he coming?"

"Yes to both questions." Weezy closed the door, crossed the room, and sat again at the table by the fire. "And Del has gone to Petoskey. Says she needs to be by herself, to work up her courage and figure out how to cope with her mother and Bradley."

"Should she be alone?" Grace asked. "Are you sure she's not depressed?"

"She didn't seem to be. I felt she was looking forward to the moment when all this would be behind her."

Grace nodded, and then frowned. "Edgar's coming here?"

"He promised to drive down early in the morning, to have breakfast with us." Weezy took a deep breath and plunged in. "Mother, you'll never guess what happened."

Grace was biting her lip. She studied her daughter's face in bafflement. "Well, then, you'd better tell me."

"When I called Dad, Yuri was there."

"Yuri?"

"Aaron Yurovsky."

Grace reacted with predictable astonishment. "What? Do they know each other?" Then, quirking an eyebrow, "So he's Yuri to you, is he?"

"Yes, he is, Mother. The truth is, I've been seeing him. I broke it off and sent him packing. What I didn't know was that he'd left his wife—because of Petrie, it seems."

"He's left Deborah? I *am* surprised; I thought he never would. He seemed so complacent." Grace went on to talk about the affair. "I heard that Petrie was having a hard time facing his own lack of talent, and Deborah sympathized. It soon developed into—well, you know. But how in the world did you get involved?"

"I was trying not to, which is why I broke off with Yuri yesterday. Seems he became so upset he got in touch with Dad, who urged him to come to Michigan."

A smile touched Grace's lips. "My goodness, what passion!"

"Mother, don't be snide. We've agreed that people have to take risks. I took a risk and told Yuri I'll be waiting for him if he drives down here. He's going through a bad patch in his life right now and I want to help if I can."

"Oh, Weezy! I admit the worm seems to have turned but—"

"Yuri's not a worm. He's a sensitive guy who tried hard to keep his marriage together for his mother's and daughter's sakes."

"That's great, I applaud it. But I don't like to see my daughter involved in a sordid partner-exchange."

"Well, I am involved. I really care for him."

In the flickering firelight, Grace studied her for a moment in silence. She bit her lip again and frowned. "Care? As in wanting to be the second Mrs. Yurovsky?"

"Mother! I'm busy developing a career in writing and publishing. I have an interesting job as a literary agent and I love it. I wined and dined an author just last week. Right now I don't want to be anyone's wife. But when Yuri comes, I won't send him away—nor I wouldn't if Gran were here."

Grace frowned, started to protest, and altered her statement. "I suppose you're entitled. I wish it weren't so. He's too old for you. But I'll stand up to Gran for you."

Tempted to say, "It's about time," Weezy swallowed the words. Maybe her mother was learning to cope at last. She'd taken the news about Yuri with surprising calm. Weezy reached out to hug her mother. "Be nice to him for my sake."

Grace sighed. "You're asking a lot of me—meet Edgar, meet Yuri—but I'll try."

CHAPTER 33

Weezy

Weezy paced the lobby. People came and went. It seemed to take Yuri a long time. She worried that he'd got lost in the dark on strange roads. She stepped outside and was just in time to see a car pull into the parking lot and slot itself near an overhead light. Not being familiar with Edgar's car, she walked toward it to check—and saw Yuri emerge from the driver's seat, dressed in slacks and open-collared sport shirt. She started running and came up to him just as he turned toward her. He flung out his arms for an embrace which she warmly returned. They hugged each other tightly.

"Oh, Eloise," he breathed. "Oh, darling. You scared me to death! Don't ever disappear like that again."

"I guess I was wrong to be angry," she confessed. "I felt sure you'd got involved with me only to get back at Deborah."

"I would never do that. How could you think such a thing?" He held her off. "All our wonderful times together—you imagined they didn't mean anything to me?"

"It didn't seem possible, but—oh, dear, I don't know what I thought. I'm just *so* glad I was wrong. Let's forget about it." She gave him another hug. She just wanted to be close to him, to have his hair tickling her cheek, to smell his aftershave, to feel his arms around her, to know she'd found him again.

"Yes, let's." He broke away to lock the car and then turned and walked with her toward the hotel. Clasping her hand, he speculated, "I probably set you up for that idea by saying I wanted to preserve my marriage. I *did* want to at one time, but the situation has become increasingly hopeless—or maybe it was hopeless all along and I just didn't realize it."

"You were trying not to notice. I can understand that."

"It seemed so harsh, accusing one's wife to the whole world including the family. I felt like a cad." He gave her his arm as they stepped out onto the woodland path, adding, "I guess I was foolish. Before I left Vi's house, I called my daughter, Leah, and learned she'd heard rumors about her mother and Tollie, had wanted to talk to me about it, but feared upsetting me. Seems we were all keeping still lest we upset each other. It would have been so much better if we'd confronted the situation honestly from the beginning."

"Hard to do," Weezy conceded. "I've just finally worked up the courage to tell my mother about us."

"What did she say? Was she angry?"

"Not as much so as I feared. She did say she thought you were too old for me."

"And what do you think?" He laid a hand over hers.

"Darling, you know what I think; I've told you. You're exactly the right age. I never did cotton onto *boys*." She squeezed his fingers.

They bypassed the hotel and took the walkway to the cabins. Still holding Yuri's arm, Weezy, eager to pull him along toward her mother, yet felt uneasy about the meeting. He remarked that he hoped Grace and Edgar would hit it off better this time. "Without Edgar, I fear your mother may face a lonely old age. She's getting famous, and men are notoriously wary of famous women. No man wants to be Mr. Bette Davis. But Edgar still seems to see her as the nineteen-year-old he fell in love with; he doesn't care about her fame."

"It'll be wonderful for them to get together," she confessed. "We'll be a real family at last."

They reached the lighted cabin. On throwing the door open, she saw her mother still sitting at the table before the fire. Grace shoved back her chair and stood. Weezy stepped in ahead of Yuri and, excited yet apprehensive, presented him. "Here's Yuri, Mother. Of course, you two know each other."

Grace came forward, her hand extended. "Not all that well, dear. Hello, Yuri. It's good to see you again."

Yuri took her hand. "Mrs. Ward—Grace—I do owe you an apology for not having approached you properly about your daughter. I fear Weezy and I have both been wrong in trying to conceal our great friendship. I realized last night that it couldn't be done."

"It certainly did create complications," Grace said. "My mother even hired a private investigator to look into the matter."

"Yes, I saw him waiting outside my office this morning." He smiled ruefully. "I understand Mrs. Hannaford is likely to cause difficulties."

"Causing difficulties is Mother's life work." Grace sighed. "We'll all have to learn to overlook it, I guess. Do sit down, Mr. Yurov—uh, Yuri. Have you eaten?"

"Yes, Weezy's grandmother—other grandmother—kindly offered me dinner. She's an outstanding cook." He moved to the chair she indicated, where he waited, standing, for her to return to her own seat.

"So Edgar is staying with her now?"

"Just until he's fully back on his feet, I understand. He has a place of his own which is rented out. Vi's is a small house but I was offered a room at Stormland."

"Oh—Stormland." Grace sank into her chair. "The very name gives me shivers. There never was another house like Stormland. My life began there—and sometimes I feel it also ended there." Rubbing her chin, she changed the subject. "If it wouldn't seem like prying, I'd love to know what's up with you and Deborah."

"You mean you hadn't heard the rumors?" Yuri asked. "I thought everyone knew but me."

"I heard rumors. I'm not prone to listen to gossip."

"Nor am I, but I'm afraid in this case the gossip was accurate. I suspect the Tollie-Deborah thing has been going on for a long time." A pained expression crossed his face. "I feel pretty foolish for overlooking it. I've just learned that even my daughter was onto them."

"The spouse is always the last to know." Since Grace hated clichés like this, Weezy knew she was struggling hard to come up with the proper words for the occasion.

In the flickering firelight, they talked about Yuri's daughter in college and his concerns about her in this situation. "It's devastating for young people when their parents divorce." When Grace offered words of consolation, Yuri, seeming embarrassed, changed the subject and mentioned the success of the art show. He congratulated Grace on getting good reviews from several top critics. He asked if the women would like to go out for a drink somewhere. Grace begged off saying she was tired from two very trying days. "Why don't you two go? It's out of season here but there must be someplace for drinks and dancing. Probably the desk clerk can tell you."

Yuri turned questioningly to Weezy, who rose and suggested they make inquiries. Yuri nodded, and after a few words to Grace about appreciating the chance to get to know her better, to which Grace responded in kind, he followed Weezy to the door.

When they were alone, Weezy confessed, "We don't have to go dancing; I'd be happy to just stroll on the beach with you. Do you suppose we can do that in the dark?"

"There's bright moonlight." Yuri squinted upward at the moon between the trees. "Let's try it."

They walked on along the path. At the bluff's edge, they looked down and saw two bonfires near the water. Clearly, others too found the shore appealing. They returned to inform Grace. "We're going down on the beach, Mother. People are having bonfires down there. We won't be out late."

Grace suggested that Yuri might sleep over on the couch in the cabin, and in the morning pick up Edgar before catching his train. Yuri thanked her but said the folks at Stormland were expecting him. "Mrs. Langston promised to leave the door unlocked for me."

"We could call her," Weezy said. "It'd be fun for you to sleep here." She was reluctant to let Yuri leave. "Besides, it's hard to find your way in the dark. In daylight, I believe I can direct you to Stormland."

"Well, if you're sure it's no trouble."

"No trouble at all," Grace said.

Weezy spoke up. "I could share your bed, Mother, and let Yuri have the other room."

Grace brightened. "Good idea." Weezy appreciated her mother's acceptance of Yuri without the anticipated battle. She repeated that she and Yuri would return soon. Then she led the way back along the woodland path to the main building, where they phoned Edgar and promised to show up early to get him for breakfast. Edgar offered to make the call to Stormland himself. "I'm a real father now, loaning my daughter my car," he joked.

The three-quarter moon was still in the East, above the jabbing pine trees on the bluff. It lit the beach but left the lake in a vast darkness out of which white wavelets rolled ashore. Yuri and Weezy went down the steps, and in a shadowed area Yuri sat and stretched out on the sand between the two bonfires. "Let's relax a few minutes," he said. "This has been the worst twenty-four hours of my life." He reached for her hand. "Promise me we'll never fight again."

With a chuckle, Weezy flopped down beside him and stretched out on the still-warm sand, hands behind her head. "It wasn't exactly fun for me either."

"From the moment I spotted you at the art show in your Grecian gown, and realized that Grace Ward was your mother, I sensed disaster."

"Darling, I thought I told you—"

"You did say she was an artist, but you never mentioned the name Ward. Since I knew no artist named McCurdle, I didn't make the connection."

"Oh, dear, I guess we were both keeping secrets. I didn't want Mother to know about us because then Gran would know—and, well, I guess you've seen what Gran is like."

"Just call her Hepzibah Pyncheon, eh?"

"Oh, she's worse than Hepzibah. Hepzibah had a permanent frown but wasn't mean. Persis arranges people's lives. Dad calls her the Battleaxe."

"Yes, I believe I heard him say something of the sort. Your dad and I really hit it off, by the way. I like him. Your mother was being so polite I couldn't tell—"

"Poor dear, she's probably scared to death of making me mad again. I was pretty rough on her; I practically went off speaking terms. I was furious with her for not standing up to Gran and Jonathan so I could know my birth father. I guess I can understand her fears…But tell me, what's to happen now? How do things stand between you and Deborah?"

"Deborah says she plans to go to Vegas. I expect she means it. She sounded pretty determined."

Her fingers grasped his and forced out words she hated to speak. "I hope this is not in any way because of me, Yuri. You must know I care for you very much—but right now I have no desire to be a housewife. I'm just beginning to develop a career as a writer, and it takes time. I want to stay on in my literary-agent job until I've learned all aspects of the business, and then I might quit and write for a while, do a novel about the Belle Turrets—and anyhow, I don't want you to think—I mean, we can go as we were, but—Oh, I'm not saying this very well."

His hand massaged hers. "Weezy, darling, I wouldn't think of snatching you from your career after such a great start, a story in a national magazine. I was so proud of you for that. All I ask is that we be together."

"Yes, I want that, too," she admitted. "But no more 'patron' stuff. I don't want you supporting me, Yuri. I feel indebted when you do that; it fouls up our relationship."

"Darling, at the moment there's no danger of that. I'll have to split my assets with Deborah, you know. I'll wipe out my bank account just buying her half of the business—I owe her that since she ran it while I was in the Army—and I still have to support my daughter, not to mention the expense of the divorce."

"Wow! Welcome to the world of the hard up! Maybe you and I could share a Village apartment and each pay half."

"Great. I've always wanted to live in the Village."

"But we do need time to settle these things. The divorce may be rough on you. You tried so hard to keep the family together and—"

Yuri suddenly heaved himself up on an elbow, leaned over, and looked down at her. He reached out to touch her hair. He confessed, "Four months ago, I'd have been devastated—but right now I hardly care. It's Leah I worry about. It'll be hard on her, but luckily she's grown up; we'll be spared the night-mare of a custody battle." He put both hands on Weezy's cheeks and leaned down to kiss her. "Now that I have my Eloise back, all's right with the world. My world, anyway. How about your world?"

"My world is fine," she said. "I like my job and I'll be living with Del so I'll have few expenses. I understand her rent is about twenty-five dollars a month. I'll survive until you come back. Once you're free, we'll decide about sharing a Village flat."

He repeated, "Just so we're together." He kissed her again, more firmly. His hand stroked her hair. She heard the sound of waves lapping the shore, along with the distant laughter of people toasting marshmallows around bonfires, and thought she could stay right here with him forever, seeing the moon peek through pine boughs.

Then his hand moved down to her thigh and alarm sounded in her brain. She whispered, "Yuri, I didn't bring equipment on a trip with my *mother!*"

"I think I have some in the back pocket of my jeans." He reached around and patted his pocket. "I planned to wear these pants on that trip to Lake George you and I never took—the time Deborah was supposed to give a talk in Chapel Hill and it was canceled."

"I remember. She got sick or something."

"All those trips Deborah was taking—all those lectures. I wonder now how many of them were for real?"

"At least they gave us weekends at Far Rockaway." Weezy sat up and looked toward the nearer bonfire. "I think we should take our stroll along the beach and find a more private spot."

"Good plan." He stood and held out his hand to help her up. They scuffed through loose sand to the water's edge, where they removed their shoes and walked hand-in-hand along the cold, hard-packed shingle. The beach was lit by moonlight. They soon left the bonfires behind them and trudged toward a deserted area. When Yuri asked what had become of Weezy's cousin, Weezy explained that Del had gone to Petoskey hoping to work up her courage to leave Bradley. Yuri nodded his approval of the move. "She'll do much better with Hilario."

Weezy looked at him in surprise. "You know Hilario?"

"All folk dancers in town know Hilario. They're all talking about how he fell in love at last, only to have his girl marry someone else."

"You folkdance? I didn't know."

He smiled. "There's a lot about me that you don't know—and lots about you that I don't know. We'll have a chance soon to find out." He squeezed her hand. "Just think, we can be together openly. We can dance at the Hebrew Y. You'll love Israeli circle dances; they're fun. And I'll love taking you. We'll double-date with Del and Hilario."

"Did you know Del, too?"

"No, but I saw her with Hilario. I thought they made a great couple."

"Yet you congratulated her on her marriage."

"It seemed the proper thing to do. Doesn't mean I approved. I also knew her roommate, Jan, and Jan's husband, Irv. It's a small world, you know."

Having rounded a point and left the bonfires behind, they turned toward the dark shadow of the bluffs and scuffed again through deep sand, up and over a dune, down into a small private hollow where no lights from cottages showed through the trees. Lying on the sand, they moved into a tight embrace. Yuri nuzzled his face against Weezy's neck.

"I meant every word I said when I told you that you'd brought color and dimension to my life," he said. "Don't ever, ever think I didn't mean it. My life was black and white before I met you."

He raised his head, kissed her, and then held her tighter and yet tighter until flesh melted into flesh. The sand still felt warm from the heat of the day as he pressed her down into it. She hugged so hard her arms ached. Then she relaxed as his hands moved over her body. She wanted to savor to the fullest this moment she'd so recently feared would never come again. She wanted to experience everything she'd almost lost. She raised her head to bring her lips to his.

CHAPTER 34

Grace

Alone in the cabin after Weezy and Yuri left, Grace paced. She felt she ought to worry about Weezy, and about the coming confrontation with Persis who would soon learn that Weezy had been seeing a married man. She couldn't focus her mind on these matters. All she could think of, had thought of since the moment she looked up at the familiar landmark of Old Baldy dune, was Edgar. It had all come flooding back—the meeting with him, his bloody head when she ran to rescue him after he'd fallen off his motorcycle, her hasty search for her handkerchief to serve as a makeshift bandage, her alarm at realizing no one was around to help—and then his chuckle as he opened his eyes and said, while she held his head in her lap, "This is the best excuse I've ever found for meeting a girl."

She couldn't resist a responding laugh. "You're not dying, I guess."

"Not yet for a while," he'd said. "But I had quite a blow, and this is very comfortable." And he'd closed his eyes and relaxed in her lap again. He'd asked her name. "I like to know the person whose lap I'm using."

She gave only her first name. "I'm Grace. Who are you?"

"Edgar McCurdle." With his eyes still closed, he reached up a hand to her. "Nice to meet you, Grace. Give me a minute, and I'll return your lap to you."

Dabbing with her handkerchief, she told him, "Don't hurry. You have a cut on your forehead and it's bleeding."

"Use my handkerchief; it's bigger than yours." He fumbled in his breast pocket for a handkerchief and handed it to her. It was big enough to go around

- 259 -

his head, and she managed to make him a bandage which, with his brown hair tumbling over it, made him look natty and swashbuckling.

It was weird having a stranger lying with his head in her lap—and she wasn't at all sure if he was really shaken by his fall or was taking advantage of the situation. She didn't want to push him off until she made sure he was all right. Meanwhile, to make conversation, she said, "You must be Scottish."

"Three quarters of me is," he admitted. "The other quarter is Pennsylvania Dutch. I have a Swiss Mennonite grandmother. I live with her because I don't get along with my stepfather, and I work in the family construction firm—up in Grand Rapids. I'm here because I like the dunes." He opened his eyes. "That's all about me. Now tell me about you."

"I'm studying painting at the Chicago Art Institute," she said. "I came to Saugatuck for summer term, and I've been painting the dunes and the town."

"Did you know there's a buried city under us?" he asked.

Startled, she grasped a handful of the tawny sand she sat on, with its sparkling quartz granules, and let it run off between her fingers. "Underneath us? Right here?"

"Yup—the town of Singapore, covered by blow-sand in the nineteenth century, after the lumbermen clear-cut the dunes." He sat up slowly, and for a moment held his head in his hands. Then he lowered them and added, "If you want to walk around a bit, I can show you the town's old boardwalk. It's still there, part of it anyway."

"Don't you think you should see a doctor?" she asked. "You could have a concussion."

"Nah, it's just a little bump. It doesn't amount to anything. Sand's easy to fall in."

He checked out his motorcycle and declared it okay. He leaned it against an elderberry, and they walked together through loose sand to the far side of a dune, where indeed they found a long row of huge boards, inches thick, whitened by age and the scrapings of sand. Edgar explained that at one time the river had run right along here, with the boardwalk lining it, and with bars along the boardwalk where lumbermen and mill workers relaxed in the evenings. "It was quite a town in its heyday. The founders hoped to rival Chicago. They weren't aware of the destructiveness of blow-sand. It didn't take long for the 'walking dunes' to silt up the harbor and cover the buildings."

She marveled that Michigan could already have its history and its ruins. She confessed she'd thought of it as the West, the newly settled area. Edgar assured her it was already historic. "My people have been Michiganians for generations."

Edgar offered to run her into town on his motorcycle and take her to lunch. "It's the least I can do after you rescued me and bandaged my head so expertly."

When she hesitated, he promised to stick to the road. Not that it was much of a road, more of a wagon track, but at least, he assured her, the sand was hard-packed and if he was careful, the bike would not tip over. She gave in, packed up her easel, and went with him.

During lunch—vegetable soup and Welsh rarebit on toast—Edgar probed, trying to learn more of her background. She didn't want to admit to her proper Bostonian upbringing. She was having fun just being a girl he met on the dunes, no longer Miss Hannaford of Beacon Hill. She'd grown tired of Miss Hannaford of Beacon Hill, the girl properly reared to do the proper thing. Before leaving home, Miss Hannaford had become engaged to an older, suitable gentleman already wealthy after having inherited a downtown Boston department store. Hoping Edgar hadn't noticed, she slipped off her diamond engagement ring, tied it into her bloody handkerchief, and put it in her pocket. Engagements could be broken; they weren't like marriages. Though her mother might have a fit, she suspected she might soon get around to breaking hers. She found Edgar far more attractive than Jonathan Ward had ever been.

Edgar suggested that after lunch they climb Old Baldy dune. She asked if he really felt up to it, after the blow to his head. He assured her he never felt better. They climbed the dune, giggling as the hot, loose sand slid from under their feet. Edgar held out a hand to her, and she experienced an electric charge when she clasped it. It was like nothing she'd ever felt in the company of her fiancé.

All of that month, whenever Edgar had free time from his construction job, they rode around the dunes together. Edgar usually had with him a picnic lunch made by his grandmother, who was clearly a marvelous cook. They would cuddle, lying on the sand, and Edgar's hand would come closer and closer to the spot known as "her privates." She didn't stop him. She liked being just a girl named Grace. It gave her such a wonderful sense of freedom. Even when he reached for her hand and drew it to his own crotch, she didn't protest. It was exciting; it felt good. Her mother was far away and needn't know.

After a month, Grace's art instructor took a job in Grand Rapids, painting murals for a new bank, and urged her to come with him and continue her studies. She happily did so; it allowed her to be closer to Edgar. She arranged to board with his family, so that they were able to see each other daily. They spent a lot of time at the amusement park on Reeds Lake, and often rode out to the Lake Michigan dunes on his motorcycle.

Both Edgar and his grandparents probed, wanting to know more about her, and little by little it slipped out that before leaving Boston, she'd been affianced to a man who owned a department store. She underplayed it; she made it sound like a very small, unimportant store. She didn't confess to his wealth. Anyway, she didn't need Jonathan's money; she'd inherit plenty from her mother, who'd been left a near-millionaire when Colonel John Hannaford, Grace's father, died in World War I. She'd already written to Jonathan confessing that she was having serious doubts about marrying him and thought she should break the engagement. He wrote back asking her not to do anything in a hurry. "We'll talk about it when you come back to Boston," he'd said.

Pacing now around the familiar cabin where she and Edgar had stayed many times, she remembered those days vividly—so vividly that the memory almost wiped out that awful moment when she'd confronted the men with the summons and fled with Weezy back to her mother. She thought now that it wasn't so much anger toward Edgar as guilt toward her mother that had driven her to flight. The summons, and the discovery that Edgar had another girlfriend, had confirmed for her what her mother had always claimed, that Edgar was not a steady, reliable man who could support her and help raise a child. She suddenly felt that she'd been very foolish to insist on coming back here and marrying him. Her mother was right; she was lucky to have a loyal fiancé willing to take on a ready-made family. Jonathan had repeated his offer to marry her, and she ought to have taken him up on it. No one need ever have known Weezy was not his child.

No, I couldn't have done that, she acknowledged to herself now. I had to give Edgar a chance.

Still, she hadn't given him much of one. She hadn't even listened to his explanation about Patience. She should have done that—and should have stood by him. She'd had half a lifetime to regret her actions.

Even yet, she didn't know the right thing to do in the situation. She sat down by the dwindling fire, clutched her head, then got up and paced again. She poured herself the last of the bottle of wine she'd ordered with dinner, and sat by the fire sipping it. In time she decided to go to bed, not that she could sleep, but she didn't want to be up when Weezy and Yuri returned. She didn't feel ready to cope with that situation. Right now she could think only of Edgar and the meeting in the morning.

True to their word, Weezy and Yuri came in early and said goodnight to each other. Weezy showered and climbed into the other side of Grace's bed. Though she found it hard to lie still, Grace tried not to thrash.

In the morning, the pair took off shortly after dawn, as Yuri needed to catch the early train for Chicago, where he would transfer to the West Coast express for Nevada. Again alone in the cabin, Grace showered, dressed carefully, then decided the dress made her look old, and changed into something lighter, turquoise and summery. She spent a lot of time on her makeup while trying to think how she'd talk to Edgar. She couldn't imagine making conversation; she was all a-twitter. Yet she knew she had to act calm and matter-of-fact for Weezy's sake. Weezy looked forward to her parents' reunion.

The pair arrived about nine o'clock. Edgar stood in the doorway, looking very much as he had twenty-two years before, still slim and with an abundance of hair. He gazed at her; he, too, seemed at a loss for words. Then suddenly he came over and embraced her. He said, "I guess it's proper to kiss a former wife," and kissed her. She could only manage to gasp out a breathless, "How are you, Edgar?"

"I'm recovered now," he said. "I was in the sanatorium for a while—I guess you heard. I had a bout with liver trouble. Stupid of me, I drank too much."

"I hope you'll remember to knock that off in the future."

"Oh, I'm a reformed character. Now that I'm a dad, I have to behave myself." He grinned. "How have you been, Grace?"

"I'm fine." She didn't want to admit to being rattled, or to fearing she'd aged more than he had.

"You're looking good. I've been hearing all about your great art show," he said. "I'd like to have been there."

Weezy was beaming at the sight of her parents reunited. Grace held the door wider and invited the pair of them to come in and have a seat. Weezy urged that they go to the dining hall and eat breakfast. "I'm starved." Grace nodded, closed up the cabin, and walked between the other two along the path to the hotel lobby.

Edgar breathed deeply of the pine scented air and remarked that, though it had been many years, it all seemed very familiar. "I never came back here alone," he confessed. "I couldn't bring myself to do it."

So—their brief encounter had meant something to him after all. It hadn't been just a casual affair, with her as just one of the harem. Maybe she'd been too cynical.

Birdsongs accompanied them along the path. On arrival, they were guided to a table in the hotel dining room, and to cover an awkward moment, all three devoted themselves to studying the menu. Grace wondered what on earth they were to talk about. But once their orders were given, Edgar and Weezy began discussing Yuri, and Grace reminded herself that the point of this meeting was to provide their daughter with two parents, not to reunite her with Edgar. She relaxed and tried to think how to participate in the discussion. Weezy remarked that Yuri had caught his train and gone, and that she looked forward to his being free of Deborah. "I'm not the type to be with someone else's husband."

"I should hope not," Grace said. "I can't imagine you involved in that situation."

"It was kind of fun for a while," Weezy said. "But it soon became unfun."

"Unfun—what a handy word," Edgar said. "So much of my life up to now has been unfun. I think I'd like to fix that, starting now."

Grace blushed, wondering if he referred to her flight from Michigan and from him.

Edgar and Weezy talked about Yuri, about how he would suffer money shortages after the divorce, at least until he'd paid Deborah off and had the business in his own name—and about how, after that, he hoped to start a literary branch of his publishing firm which Weezy might run. While they chatted, Grace eyed Edgar and tried to see him realistically, as the man he really was and not as the man she'd loved wildly, hated wildly, and dreamed about. But memories flooded back. She recalled so well the way his hair always fell over his eyes—it still did—and how the color of his hair matched the color of his always-laughing brown eyes. It was that hint of perpetual laughter that made her distrust him, and made her feel like such a fool for having insisted that her mother bring her back to Michigan to marry him.

Pull yourself together; you're Weezy's mother and you're supposed to be concerned about her, not Edgar, she cautioned herself. But her emotions swung wildly and she couldn't think of anything to say. Yuri did seem to care for Weezy and be good to her. Once he was free, she couldn't object to him. Her mother would object, of course; she'd see his divorce as scandalous and Weezy's involvement as a repeat of a former disaster.

Before she'd formed a comment on this, Weezy finished the last of her toast, pushed her plate aside, and announced to her mother, "Dad's car had a funny ping in it, and I promised him I'd take it to a mechanic in Saugatuck for a check. I guess I'd better go do that now."

"I'll give you a blank check," Edgar said, reaching in his pocket for his check book.

Grace panicked. She felt sure there was no ping. They'd cooked up this excuse between them, so she and Edgar might have time alone. She protested, "But it's only thirty miles back to Grand Rapids; surely the car will go—"

They weren't listening. Edgar signed a check and handed it over. "You can just fill in the name of the mechanic and the amount. We'll see you later." As Weezy hurried off, Edgar turned to Grace and smiled. "Isn't it great to have a daughter? She and Yuri were both so concerned about that ping—didn't want me driving an unsafe car. I feel so cared about."

She swallowed her words and managed a faint, "Yes, it's very nice."

Edgar wiped his lips with his napkin and urged Grace to finish her breakfast. "We can take a short walk on the beach while we wait. It's been twenty-one years since we walked on that beach together."

Grace looked down and realized that she'd been pushing her eggs around her plate until they'd become congealed in a yellow, streaky pattern. They looked inedible. She put jelly on her toast and made herself take a bite. She announced that she wasn't very hungry this morning. She spoke quickly to cover her embarrassment, remarking, "It's funny, I rushed down here wanting to see if I really painted Lake Michigan instead of the ocean—and now I realize how foolish I was to worry. The art critic wasn't thinking about me or my work at all—he was thinking about running off with Yuri's wife. It just shows you, doesn't it, how self-centered we artists can be, fancying the whole world is focused on us."

Edgar reached out and gently squeezed her hand. "Whatever the motivation, I'm glad you rushed down here, Grace. It's so great to see you again—and to spend the day on the dunes with you and Weezy. The dunes have always been memorable to me."

"Yes, to me, too." Grace forced herself to admit the fact. She nibbled at her toast, and managed to give Edgar a small smile. "I remember you with a bloody head, ever so dashing in the bandage I put on."

He smiled, too. "I remember having my head in your lap. It was very comfortable. I pretended to be concussed so I could stay there a while."

His casual reminiscing took some of the embarrassment out of the situation. She relaxed, nibbled another bite of her toast, then put the last of it on her plate and drank her coffee. When the waitress came with the pot, she waved her away. "I've had enough." And to Edgar: "If we're to walk on the beach, we'd better go now. I don't suppose that 'ping' will take long to fix."

"I hope not," Edgar solemnly agreed. He laid his napkin aside and got up to hold her chair for her.

They stepped out into a crisp autumn day with a gentle lake breeze. Edgar remarked that he well remembered the place. "It hasn't changed at all, except that they've fixed a loose board at the top of the steps. You once stumbled over it and I caught you."

"I don't recall that," she said. "You do have a good memory!"

The lake glittered in the morning sun. They went down the steps together to the beach, and strolled across the sand to the hard-packed shingle where the waves lapped up. To the right, they could see the pier and lighthouse. To the left, the shoreline circled around to a point. They started walking in that direction, and soon decided they needed to shed their shoes and stockings. For Grace, this meant lifting her skirt to unfasten her hose. She turned away from Edgar in order to do so. He laughed and promised not to look.

Being barefoot on cold sand seemed to add up to more intimacy than she was ready for with Edgar. Grace felt embarrassed again. Again Edgar managed a casual manner that put her at ease. He remarked that he'd always felt he made a mistake in not going to Boston after her. "I often thought of doing so," he confessed, "but I was afraid of your mother. She's an intimidating person."

"Yes, she even intimidated me," Grace told him. "It took me years to learn to handle her."

She feared he would ask whether she'd have gone with him if he'd come to Boston looking for her. She couldn't answer that question. She only remembered the terrible conviction that she'd been a fool; she'd fallen for an unfaithful man; she'd justified her mother's criticisms.

As if thinking along similar lines, he said, "It was folly for me to get involved with Patience, but I honestly never dreamed you might come back. Of course, I didn't know you were pregnant."

"I did write to you—several times," Grace said. "The management at the home where I was staying must have intercepted the letters. I suppose Mother told them to do that; it's so like her." The memory of that place, long screened from her mind, came back to her. Terrified on learning there was a baby growing inside her, she'd seemed to walk around in a perpetual state of fright, hardly aware of her surroundings. The other girls had tried to be friendly but she couldn't warm up to them. They were different; they knew all about babies and had taken this risk out of sheer love for their boyfriends. She hadn't even known she was taking a risk. She shared with them, however, the hope of keeping the baby and returning to the boyfriend. Eventually she'd thawed and grown chummy with two or three of them. Determined to see Edgar again, and reinforced by the other girls, she held out against her mother's urging that the baby be adopted out.

Lucky I did, she thought now. Jonathan had had mumps in his adult years and had been left sterile. It was probably the reason he'd accepted Weezy. For herself, she couldn't imagine life without Weezy.

"I was so naïve in those days," she added, "such a well-brought-up young lady. My mother had never talked to me about sex at all; she didn't even tell me why I started bleeding each month. An older girl at school explained and told me what to do about it. It wasn't until I went to that home for unwed mothers that I finally learned the facts of life, and knew for sure where babies came from and what you and I had done to produce one."

"I'm afraid I wasn't any help to you." Edgar reached for her hand and squeezed it. "I had a vague idea about baby-making, but the guys always claimed it was safe as long as the moon wasn't horned. When it got to the half, and had no more horns, I thought we could relax. I never dreamed I was putting you at risk." He ran his finger along the back of the hand he held. "I was a wild kid but I wasn't heartless, honest. I wouldn't have chosen to put you in such a situation."

"Those were horrible times," she said. "I always felt I had no control over my life. I'm just so glad things are better for girls now. Not that I did a good job of enlightening Weezy. I guess you know she only recently learned she had another family."

Edgar chuckled. "Yes, we heard all about it. At Stormland, she told us of her discovery."

"She was furious with me for keeping it from her. In the future I'll try to do better. I'll be truthful about my feelings and about whatever is going on."

"Good plan," Edgar said. And with a hesitant smile he added, "You can start by telling me if you think there's any possibility you and I might get together again—permanently, I mean."

She gasped. "Ooh, that's a big question, Edgar." She flung her hand to her chest. "I mean, I have my painting—I have a life in Boston—and you have a life here."

"But you can paint here, right?" Edgar smiled and gestured toward a hillock of sand. "Let's sit a while, shall we?" Still holding her hand, he guided her to the hillock, where they stretched out together on sand newly warmed by the sun.

They were still there, talking about past disasters and future possibilities, an hour later when they saw Weezy running toward them, waving.

"I knew I'd find you here," she said. "I'm glad you waited for our dune-hike until I came. I've looked forward to going with you."

Edgar said. "Old Baldy, here we come." He got up, brushed sand off himself, and offered a hand to Grace. He asked Weezy, "Is the car fixed?"

"They said it had a build-up of carbon. You need to take it on a long trip to blow the carbon out. You could do that by driving out East, Dad."

"Sounds like a plan." Edgar nodded. He didn't relinquish Grace's hand as they walked through the sand to reclaim their shoes and then climbed the bluff to find the car for the drive to Old Baldy dune.

CHAPTER 35

Del

At dawn, Del awoke in the train-seat and shifted her cramped position. She'd had to go coach as the train offered no Pullman cars, but, lulled by the rocking movement, she'd slept well, curled up on the seat. Now she looked out at rolling hills where every hollow was filled with morning mist. Bright fall colors poked out of the swirling white fog. Red and yellow woodlands flashed past, with occasional glimpses of silver water between the trees where the train skirted Lake Michigan. In the pre-dawn darkness she'd awakened briefly to the glare of station lights at Traverse City.

A passing conductor told her, "Petoskey in twenty minutes." She nodded, got up, stretched, and reached to the overhead rack for her package. She'd managed to buy a thick hand-knit sweater at the gift shop near the Saugatuck station. Though the shop had closed, the proprietor lived above it and had come downstairs to open up on seeing a customer. Lucky, Del thought. The weather was noticeably cooler this far north. She put on the sweater, tied the belt, and hugged her arms, enjoying the warmth of wool.

There were few passengers on the train; a large group had left at Traverse City. Those who remained were asleep, stretched out or curled up on the seats.

On his return, the conductor paused beside her. "This your first trip to Northern Michigan?"

"I lived here as a child," Del told him. "I went to school in Petoskey."

"You came to see the fall colors, I expect? We get a lot of tourists this time of year. Train was full going up Friday night."

Del nodded. She hadn't even thought about fall colors when she'd rushed to board the previous night, but found them an added bonus.

She still hadn't figured out what to say to her mother and Bradley. She decided not to think about it. She would allow herself a half-day vacation, and then go back and find a way to cope.

Other people stirred and sat up. She heard comments: "Look at the colors!" "The maples are beautiful!" A man in a seat ahead informed his companion he'd once made maple syrup from the sap of the trees. "Michigan maple syrup is every bit as good as the Vermont brand."

It was after seven, and still sunless, when the train pulled into Petoskey. She inquired of a young man getting off with her if he knew of a good café. He pointed across the street. "Rena's over there is great for breakfast. Good pancakes, good coffee."

She thanked him, drew her sweater tighter against a cool lake breeze, and hurried, along with other passengers, across to the brightly lit café. Snug in a warm booth, she ordered pancakes and coffee. This was fun, doing something by herself. She wondered why she'd always before waited to find a companion to travel with her.

"Where's the best place to find Petoskey stones?" she asked the waitress.

The woman told her she needed to get away from the center of town. "The nearby sand is picked over. Go north along the beach."

After a hurried breakfast—she had only about five hours to be here—Del followed directions and walked to the lakeshore. She felt a wave of nostalgia when she came upon the old artesian fountain with perpetually running sulphur water. She remembered how she and her mother used to come each day for a healthy drink, and felt homesick for the mother of those days who was a friend and companion. She recalled how she'd at first been turned off by the water's rotten-egg smell, but persisting, had learned to like it. Now, as she drank, memories of her childhood flooded back. She vividly recalled being lifted up to the spurting fountain; she almost felt her mother's hands at her waist. Tears started to her eyes. She and her mother had been such pals then, had spent hours together exploring the town and hunting fossil coral on the beach. They'd seemed to share so many interests; they'd listened to records together, sewn doll clothes together, and wandered along the beach. Since their small apartment called for little housework, Millie had always been ready to go out with Del after school to stroll about seeking adventure.

When had all that changed? When had her mother begun pressuring her to do things she didn't want to do? Was it because of Bradley?—or simply because

Del had grown up and chosen to go her own way? There came a time when they'd fought over everything, from Del's choice of clothing and friends to her chosen profession. Millie claimed archeology was impractical for a woman, and she didn't want to see Del suffer the heartbreak she'd experienced in trying for the impossible career of musician.

Well, mom may have been right about that, she thought.

At the rocky beach, she had the place to herself; there was no one else around at this early hour. Seagulls wheeled and screamed overhead while she scuffed among the rocks in search of stones with the telltale spots to label them fossils of ancient coral. On finding one, she knelt down and dipped it in the gently lapping water. When wet, the stone clearly revealed the hexagonal design of the ancient coral. Yes—a Petoskey stone, the first addition to her collection in more than twenty years. A beauty, too. She would need to polish it.

She walked on toward the more private beach beside the big hotel. She tried to imagine her mother here, sharing this adventure, but now it was Hilario who occupied her thoughts. She would love, she thought, to bring him here, to share this fossil-hunt with him.

As if on cue, the sun came out. The fog lifted, the air warmed; the lake rippled and sparkled. Del shed shoes, sweater and hose, and laid them on the sand near the trees. Then she made her way gingerly back across the stony area, studying every rock. She soon had a second Petoskey stone, and a third. She waded out to dip them. Other fossils with stringy fibers were called Charlevoix stones, and did not, she knew, polish up so beautifully.

"Everything petrifies here in Little Traverse Bay," someone had once told her. "They even found the head of an early day explorer."

I don't need anyone's head, she thought, remembering. Those can stay in the bay.

After a half-hour of hunting, she ended up with five stones, two of which were large enough to fill her palm. She decided she would take only the large ones, one to add to her collection, one to pass along to Weezy. She put on her shoes, carried her hose and sweater, and returned with the two large stones to the main street, where she looked for a polishing shop. Strolling along, she soon found one, luckily open on Sunday. "Fall colors weekend," the elderly proprietor told her when she commented on this. "Big tourist time."

There were three wheels to be coped with, a grinding wheel to remove the surface detritus, a shaping wheel, and a polishing wheel. He showed her how to use them. "Hold the stone lightly against the wheel; don't press." He gave her a rubber apron to wear and set a spray of water dripping onto the wheel. She quickly ground off the outer accumulation of lime to reveal the design in the stone. When she moved on to the second wheel, the bearded proprietor offered to help her shape the stone into a cat, a lighthouse or any form of her choosing. Thanking him, she shook her head and said she preferred nature's choice of shape.

More than an hour later, she had two beautiful stones, polished to a jewel-like glitter. The proprietor showed her how to wax and buff them. She paid him for the use of his wheels, and stepped out again into the sunshine, holding the two stones. With time left for a quick walk around the town before catching her train to Detroit, she climbed the hill to the old section, where the enormous summer homes or "cottages" of wealthy Chicagoans sat on the bluff overlooking the lake. It was another place where she and her mother had walked together, admiring the towers, turrets and cupolas of the Victorian era on tree-lined avenues of beautiful old houses. Her stroll brought nostalgia as she recalled her companion of those days, the mother she'd adored. She wondered if she'd ever find that mother again—or had Millie changed inalterably through the years?

Back on the main street, she found a produce shop and bought a bag of fruit to take with her on the train. She also stopped at Rena's café for a take-out ham sandwich. She wanted to be equipped in case the Detroit train lacked a Pullman.

At one o'clock she boarded the train, feeling refreshed in body and renewed in spirit. The two polished stones had cost her nearly forty dollars, counting the trip up here and back, the meals, the sweater, and could probably be bought in a tourist gift shop for four or five dollars. Folly, her mother would say. But for her the trip had been worth the money, and the old Millie of her childhood would have understood.

As the train pulled out, she looked out the window at the shining big sea waters of Gitchi Gumi and promised herself she would remember Petoskey. And she would reminisce with her mother, and find a way, in time, to bring the older woman around to her own way of seeing things.

It was seven o'clock when she took a bus from the Detroit train station to the airport. Grace and Weezy were there already, and after commenting on her lovely hand-knit sweater, steered her to a café for a quick dinner. While they awaited their meal, Del presented Weezy with one of the Petoskey stones. Weezy raved over it. "It's beautiful! Shiny—like a gemstone. But—do you really want to part with it? Shouldn't it be in your collection?"

"I have another for my collection. This one's for you, to remind you of your Michigan roots."

"Thanks, Cousin, I'll treasure it." Weezy put it carefully in her overnight bag, wrapped in a sweater. "It will be my special memory stone. I'll have the two small ones made into jewelry—pendants, maybe, one for each of us."

"Great idea. I'd love a Petoskey stone pendant." Del moved her arm as the waitress placed before her a plate with a hot roast beef sandwich, which was really no sandwich at all but two slices of roast beef on bread, slathered with gravy. But it looked good. Since it offered a quick meal and time was short, the others had ordered the same.

While they ate, Weezy mentioned that her mother had arranged to have an art exhibit in Saugatuck in the spring. Del congratulated Grace. She inquired if all went well in the meeting with Yuri. Weezy nodded, looked dreamy, and declared it was wonderful. When Del asked what had happened with Edgar, Grace blushed and said nothing. Weezy confessed that things had seemed a bit formal at first, over breakfast, but everyone had loosened up later as they climbed the dune together. Grace admitted that Edgar was still the same attractive devil he'd always been, and she could easily fall in love again, though she didn't guarantee she'd trust him.

"You don't have to trust him, Mother," Weezy said. "You're not a vulnerable teenager any more. You're a successful artist with a great career. Whatever he does, Dad no longer has the power to devastate you."

"I wouldn't bet on that," Grace said with a laugh. "Right now, as a brand new widow, I shouldn't even be thinking about him. But we'll see what happens. I'll be back in Saugatuck in the spring to prepare for the show, and Edgar promised to come and help out."

"I suspect he'll travel to Boston long before that," Del ventured. "Knowing Edgar—he doesn't let grass grow under his feet once he's made up his mind."

Grace blushed again, bit her lip, and changed the subject. "What about you? How was Petoskey?"

"Oh, Petoskey is my favorite place on this planet. I feel so—renewed, so ready at last to take my life in my own hands, to deal with people and problems."

"Congratulations. That's a hard place to get to. Would you like to call Bradley and your mother from here? I'll pay; I know long distance is expensive and you didn't have a chance to buy traveler's checks."

"Thank you, I appreciate the offer, but the phone in our Riverside Drive apartment isn't hooked up yet. However, if you're eager to spend money, I'd love to make a quick call to let my true love know I'll soon be free."

"Meaning Hilario, of course," Weezy said.

Grace nodded. "All right, my offer holds. Finish your dinner and we'll find a public phone. I just thought we should let Millie know you're safe. She must be worried."

"I sent a telegram. I'll go up to Riverside Drive first thing in the morning. I know she's furious and will scream that I'm crazy, out of my mind, off the deep end; but I'll hold tight to my new stone until I feel like a rock myself and can let the words bounce off. Eventually, she'll calm down. Meanwhile, I'll keep remembering it's her own pain she's really screaming about—her loss of her musician brother, of whom this situation brings back memories."

"It's all in being sure of yourself," Grace said. "You can withstand any barrage if you're clear in your own mind about what you want to do. I knew that once, but I forgot it."

"I'll stay at the Belle Turrets and let you entertain Millie in your apartment," Weezy said. She glanced uneasily at her mother, but when Grace offered no protest, she went on, "Yuri paid for the whole month; I may as well use the place and let you and your mom have the Village flat to yourselves. It'll give you a chance to mend fences."

"Thanks, Cuz—but Mom may insist on going home early. She hates New York and will be in no mood to let me wine and dine her. However, I can but try, and I appreciate your offer."

"I'd think you'd want to talk her into staying a while and meeting Hilario."

Del shuddered. "I don't plan to mention Hilario to her until my annulment is final. She has never taken kindly to the men who upstaged Bradley in my life. A Hispanic—I'll need the utmost diplomacy in telling her."

"That's crazy. Yuri says Lari's a nice guy. Yuri met him at the Hebrew Y where they do Israeli circle dances. Hilario goes there often."

"What a small world!" She shook her head. "Fancy those two knowing each other! I don't see my mother accepting him, though. At least not until Bradley is long forgotten."

"What will you do about Bradley?" Grace asked.

Del shrugged. "Actually, Bradley and I were finished with each other years ago. You can't manufacture a relationship and then breathe life into it, like Pinocchio trying to become a real boy. There has to be a spark that can grow. I didn't realize that because of my guilt-feelings toward my mother. As I men-

tioned, Mother adores Bradley, who replaced her musician-brother." She
sighed. "It was a terrible trauma for her, losing her brother and her position in
his orchestra when Aunt Laddie and Uncle Rob married. I felt it was up to me
to mend things, to bring a musician into the family. But I found I can't relive
her life and fix her problems."

"It's sad for creative people to lose their art," Grace said. "Poor Millie, it
must have been devastating. If I hadn't had my painting, my life would have
been insupportable. But you're right; you can't fix it. She has to do that herself."

When they finished eating, Grace got from the cashier a fistful of change
and handed it over to Del. "There's a public phone right outside the restaurant."

Del called Hilario, who answered at once. At his "hello?" she felt a familiar
thrill. *My heart, at thy dear voice...* This is true love; this is the person I belong
with. She knew it now; she felt sure of it.

"I'm glad I caught you at home." She spoke warmly.

"I study on Sunday nights." The responding warmth in his voice belied the
mundane words. "Where are you? Danny said you'd left town."

"Only temporarily—but I've left Bradley for good."

"Yes, Danny told me that, too. We had dinner together to celebrate. We're
both happy about it. Or I should say, he's happy, I'm ecstatic."

"How could Danny have known? I wasn't sure about it myself when I talked
to him."

"Maybe you communicated subconsciously. When are you coming back?"

"Right now. My flight goes in fifteen minutes. Weezy and I should be home
by eleven. Want to drop by our Village flat? I think I have a bottle of wine."

"Wine isn't good enough for this occasion. I'll buy champagne."

"Wonderful. I'll see you soon."

Del hung up feeling an uplift of joy. As she rejoined her aunt and cousin,
Grace remarked that she was positively glowing.

"I just love the sound of that man's voice," she admitted.

"I know what you mean," Grace agreed. "I had goose bumps when I heard
Edgar's voice on the phone a month or so ago. They were just a hint of the
goose bumps I felt when we met last night."

"I'd love it if you and Edgar would get together again," Del said.

"Me, too," Weezy said.

"I wouldn't rule it out," Grace confessed. She grasped Del's arm, and then Weezy's. "Come on, they've called our flight."

She hurried them out onto the tarmac. Weezy clutched her overnight bag. Purse slung over her shoulder, Del wore her new sweater and carried the bag containing fruit and her Petoskey stone. She touched her hair to check on it, just in case Hilario should choose to meet her at La Guardia.

The three women boarded the plane just minutes before it took off.

978-0-595-34858-9
0-595-34858-0

Printed in the United States
30446LVS00003B/45